PASSIONATE WARRIOR

MARY ELLEN GRONAU

THEIR CLASH OF WILLS EXPLODED
INTO FIERY LOVE

MAN AND WARRIOR WIFE

A slow smile parted Neil's lips. "As my wife you will not dare to disobey me. There will be no more delays. The wedding will take place immediately."

Dorcas drew a sharp breath. "Nay," she whispered.

Neil whirled around to where his father and Duncan stood. "I demand the hand of your daughter in marriage, Lord Duncan. Now! If it is not done, there will be no wedding, and no peace."

Dorcas rushed forward. "Nay, father, you cannot do this!" She turned to Neil, her face a mask of fury. "You promised to wait until Angus returned. You promised!"

"I am just a warrior whose promise means nothing, remember?" he taunted.

Dorcas snatched an eating knife in desperation and lunged toward Neil. He grabbed her arm in his viselike grip and easily disarmed her. "You are mine and what is mine, I keep," he said in a voice so only she could hear. Suddenly his mouth claimed hers in a savage kiss. Dorcas fought fiercely to escape but found herself helpless under his passionate onslaught. She was unaware of the ribald comments surrounding them, or of the laughter. There were just the two of them as her knees grew weak. . . .

PASSIONATE
WARRIORS

Mary Ellen Gronau

BANTAM BOOKS

NEW YORK · TORONTO · LONDON · SYDNEY · AUCKLAND

PASSIONATE WARRIORS
A Bantam Book / September 1989

ISBN 0-553-28055-4

Published simultaneously in the United States and Canada

Bantam Books are published by Bantam Books, a division of
Bantam Doubleday Dell Publishing Group, Inc. Its trademark,
consisting of the words "Bantam Books" and the portrayal of
a rooster, is Registered in U.S. Patent and Trademark Office
and in other countries. Marca Registrada. Bantam Books,
666 Fifth Avenue, New York, New York 10103.

For Stephanie

PROLOGUE

The clang of steel against steel shattered the peace of the meadow, rousting birds from their nesting places and sending small animals scuttling for safety. The metallic clashes of weapons grew louder as fierce-looking men shouted and groaned from the heat and pain of battle. The blood of both sides flowed freely, and the combatants scarcely seemed to be the same men who had laughed and joked hours earlier. What had started as a mere raid on the McMahons' cattle had developed into a fight to the death between the McNeil and the McMahon clans.

Kevin Kirkpatrick had left his new bride's bed to join the raiding party, unhappy to have to deny himself her soft and yielding body. He had turned beet-red at the good-natured ribbing that had come his way when his wife, wrapped in a blanket, had run out of their hut for one more farewell kiss. Now his sightless eyes stared up at the heavens, blind to the white clouds floating aimlessly in the blue sky. His skull was a pulpy mass, smashed by an enemy's mace.

Guy Murdock swung his sword to the right, decapitating his adversary. Blood spewed in a great arc as the man's head tumbled to the ground, the lifeless body crumpling a moment later. Glimpsing a movement on his left, Guy turned, but not quickly enough. His last thoughts were of his fine son, and what a strong warrior the boy would make someday.

Neil McNeil fought like a demon against two men. His sword flashed left and right while blood dripped down his bare arm and fell onto his bearskin vest, but, wildly exhilarated, he was only vaguely aware of his wounds.

Neil neither hated nor loved the McMahons, though he knew that the full-blooded Irish clan hated him and his people and that he could expect no quarter from them. They called his father, Cedric, traitor to his people for marrying a Viking chieftain's daughter. Little did the McMahons know of survival among the enemy.

Neil had been weaned on stories of his father's past—how he had been stolen away by a band of raiding Vikings when he was a young man and had become a slave in the household of Gunnar Nordstrom. Cedric often had said he learned everything there was to know about treachery, deceit, and cruelty from his captors.

Honing his own wits to knife-edge sharpness, Cedric had watched for a chance to free himself from slavery and return to Erin. When he learned of a treacherous plot to murder Gunnar Nordstrom, he warned the chieftain and earned the man's respect.

Through wile and quick thinking, he made certain Gunnar never forgot him, and soon became his arms bearer in battle. After again saving the chieftain's life during a raid on Britain, Cedric was rewarded with his freedom . . . and Gunnar's only daughter. Gunnar encouraged Cedric to return to Erin with Astrid, his new wife, to gain control of more land for the Vikings.

Cedric settled in the south of Erin, where the McNeil clan held extensive lands. He built a stronghold near the Slaney River and promised the peasants protection from other clans and Viking raids. His prosperous fields grew wheat, barley, and hay. Thousands of head of cattle and flocks of sheep roamed the lush green hills, and the wool from the sheep was dyed and woven by the peasants before being transported for sale in Dublin or Wexford.

Many members of his clan celebrated Cedric's return, but others turned their backs on him, declaring him an outlaw. And most other clans fought him as only bitter enemies could. The most fierce was the McMahon clan.

The two settlements were close by each other, and it was easy to raid, and to plunder, and to kill. There wasn't a time Neil had known when the McNeils hadn't been fighting the McMahons. Just as now.

A cow tasted better when it was known to have come from the McMahon herd. If some of the McMahon clan died during the raid, so much the better. It would mean fewer to battle in the future.

Out of the corner of his eye Neil saw Uland fall, and he grimaced. Elbert and Rufus were holding their own, but he'd lost sight of his close companion, Selwyn. It appeared they were getting the worst of it, for today they were outnumbered. He knew that three of the six men with him were dead, whereas only two of the enemy lay dead. His own arm was weary from wielding the sword. He tried to concentrate on breathing evenly as he slashed out again and again. Finally, he grew tired of playing with his opponents and struck out with all his strength at one, cutting the man in half.

Suddenly a piercing war cry rent the air, making more than one man's hair stand on end.

Neil feared no man, but even he shuddered at the sound, for it could not be human. It came again and he faltered. He felt a stabbing pain in his side and could hear the scraping sound of sword against his ribs as it was pulled back. His eyes glazed over as he fell, but he did not cry out.

He hit the ground hard, knocking off the horned Viking helmet he wore in defiance of the Irish who mocked his mixed blood. The early morning grass was cool against his cheek, and it smelled of the sweet freshness of the coming spring. Neil lifted his head, then blinked to clear his vision of the apparition that greeted him.

On a knoll overlooking the meadow stood a sight that took his breath away—a tall, sleek woman in battle dress, her slender, bare legs spread wide. An abundance of gleaming red hair fell to her waist in soft, curly waves. A helmet was tucked into the crook of one arm; in her other hand was a sword, red with blood.

The beauty suddenly threw back her head, and he could see the white column of her lovely neck. She let loose another cry, as though in victory, and he thought that it must be a Valkyrie calling him home to Valhalla. He laid his head down wearily and let the darkness wash over him.

Far-off voices broke into Neil's senses as he weaved in and out of awareness. He tried to silence the voices. He'd been traveling down a labyrinth, chasing after the red-haired sorceress who remained always just out of his reach. He cried out, "Wait! Take me with you! Do not leave me!"

She was so close. All he had to do was reach out and touch her. If he could only seize her hand, then she could lead him. But she remained silent and elusive, beckoning him onward, but not allowing him near enough to touch her. Was she a witch sent by Loki to lure him to that dark place without light? Or was she indeed, Valkyrie, testing his prowess to see if he was worthy of entering that great hall beyond, Valhalla?

He frowned in frustration. He was lost. Ahead of him loomed a gray wall. He heard her laughter in the distance, and his frown deepened. Was it laughter, or was she crying? He was hot, so hot. The voices spoke more urgently. He tried to understand their words, but could not, and so he drifted off into the dark caverns of his mind.

Tears streamed down Astrid's face as she gazed down at

her one remaining son. She'd borne seven children in her lifetime, but only two still lived: Her daughter, Nissa, and Neil, her beloved son. She wiped the tears away angrily and looked up at her husband with burning eyes.

Cedric stood by her side, his face an expressionless mask, but Astrid knew he was being torn apart inside. She placed her small hand on his arm, as much to receive his strength as to give comfort to his aching heart.

"Never," she said softly, "have I asked you for anything in all the time we have been together, but I ask you now. I beg you, if our son lives, please send him to my father." She saw the imperceptible tightening of Cedric's jaw and rushed on. "If you do not, our son will seek revenge and mayhaps die upon the battlefield. Is that what you want? Do you want to see Neil die as Kirk and Olaf did? I can no longer give you sons. You could beget sons elsewhere, but will you take away Neil's right to rule after you? Will you deny me the right to take comfort in him?"

Cedric looked intently at her. Panic shone clear in her eyes. She had spoken the truth. She'd never asked him for anything since he had taken her as his wife, nor had she ever questioned his authority. He knew she grieved for the children lost to her, though she did so quietly, and it tore at his heart to realize how she suffered. He had suffered also, but never more than now. She was right. If their son lived he would be filled with such rage, he would return to the McMahons, mayhaps to challenge them even more recklessly than he had today.

Astrid mouthed the word "please" and Cedric nodded.

1

<hr>

A.D. 987

The dragon-headed prow of the Viking ship arched majestically over the gray waves of the Irish sea. Arms akimbo, Neil stood on deck, staring at the waters stretching before him, the vessel beneath his wide-spread legs slipping easily along. A breeze ruffled his dark hair and made the full sleeves of his tunic ripple gently over the powerful muscles of his arms. He was going home. Erin. A lump formed in his throat and he swallowed it back, taking a deep breath of the sweet summer air. He smiled as he remembered the summer five years before when he had been sent out of harm's way, as his mother saw it, to his grandfather in Norway. He'd been furiously angry at his father's adamant refusal to allow him to stay at home.

His smile widened at the thought of how grateful he was to his mother now, and how dismayed she would have been during the past five years at the countless bloody battles he had engaged in with his grandfather. Surely she should have known, though, for her father was notorious for the pleasure he took from fighting. Still, Neil was reasonably certain his mother had no idea of the frequent and grave dangers he had faced. But he had not been reckless, a trait his grandfather would not countenance on the field of battle or off. Neil could admit now that he had been extraordinarily foolish five years before—even though at seventeen he'd been old enough to know better.

Suddenly he threw back his head and laughed, the deep, rich sound filling the air for long moments. If there was one thing his grandfather had taught him, it was that he had to be more cautious. His eyes warmed at thoughts of Gunnar's home, and of Anika, the woman who gave him a special reason to be more careful. It was past time that he settled down, and Anika, sweet and gentle Anika, was just what he needed; he would tell his father about his intention to wed as soon as possible after reaching home.

"Are you trying to scare the sea monsters from our path to insure our safe journey?"

Neil turned to look at Selwyn, the man who had been his companion for as long as he could remember. The bastard son of his mother's maid, Hilda, Selwyn had been raised with Neil. As boys they had discovered all there was to discover, and though Selwyn served Neil with as great devotion as any servant might, he was not afraid of his friend, or of speaking his mind to him.

"The men think you've gone mad, laughing at the wind," Selwyn said teasingly.

Neil chuckled. "You know what it is that makes me laugh."

"Aye, I know," said Selwyn, smiling back. "Actually, I am surprised that you agreed to return so quickly. I would have expected you to present your chosen woman to your parents."

His grin faded and Neil made a face. "The message from my father made it seem as though there was not a moment to waste in returning."

"You still believe something is wrong?"

"Aye," Neil said slowly. His father had left the reason for the summons home out of the message he had sent.

Whether his father or mother was ill, Neil did not know, only that he was urgently needed by his kin.

Selwyn clapped his friend on the back. "Well, let us hope that in the last few years you've learned something of importance under Gunnar's shrewd eye. In all the time spent in Norway, the Valkyrie did not once appear. I hope that it is past, and she will not stretch out her hand to beckon you again in Erin."

Startled, Neil watched Selwyn saunter away. He'd not thought of that vision in years. When his wound had mended enough that he regained his wits and it had become clear he would live, the apparition he had seen on the battlefield haunted him. But gradually, the vision had winnowed into the recesses of his brain. Interesting, if a bit odd, he thought, that Selwyn remembered the incident confided so long ago. Now a picture formed in Neil's mind of long legs and thick red hair, but the face was blurred. He shook his head to clear it and vowed to resolutely face whatever might come his way. If it was a fight to the death with the McMahons, then he was ready. The Valkyrie had spared him once, mayhaps she would again.

Neil surveyed the settlement built high on a hill looking down upon a green valley. Smoke curled up into the air from the wattle cottages. Cattle grazed on a nearby knoll and sheep dotted the hill beyond the settlement. He knew children would be running and playing within the walled village as the adults went about their tasks. It would be a comforting sight. He hadn't realized until this moment how much he had missed his home and family.

He spurred his horse forward, and Selwyn followed. They rode through the gate to the frenzied barking of the dogs. The children continued their play, ignoring the strangers, but the adults stopped in their work and stared suspiciously, ready to spring should the two men prove to be enemies. When recognition dawned, they called out greetings and ran toward them, welcoming their chieftain's son and his servant.

Neil and Selwyn exchanged greetings with their old friends, and marveled at the changes that had taken place in their absence. The settlement had grown, with more thatched houses and a mill built against the far wall. Their progress to the wood keep where the McNeil and his wife lived was impeded by the eager questions hurled at them by their curious friends and relatives. Neil patiently answered them, all the while making toward his home that stood safe with a steep hill at its back.

Near the front gate of the keep Selwyn spotted his mother and dashed to her side while Neil answered yet another query on how those who'd remained in Norway fared. Then he stopped in his tracks. His father stood in the entrance. Cedric was smiling, his eyes clouded with unshed tears. Though his body was still trim and firm, his face had a haggard look about it, and his hair was heavily streaked with gray. Neil was taken aback both by how weary his father looked—and how relieved.

Wordlessly, he stepped forward to greet his father, whose arms quickly closed in a hearty embrace.

"Welcome home, my son," Cedric murmured. He moved back and held Neil at arm's length, eyeing him critically. His son had matured from a handsome boy into an impressive man. Lean and hard-muscled, Neil stood a head taller than his father. His dark hair was as Cedric's had once been, and his deep blue eyes stared back with keen interest and warm affection.

"If you are through with our son, let me welcome him home also, my husband."

Cedric moved aside and Astrid came forward to be encircled in Neil's arms. He smiled down at his mother and kissed her forehead. Except for a slight graying at the temples, Astrid's blond beauty was as Neil remembered. She even smelled of the same sweet lavender, her special scent that he remembered so well. Neil placed an arm around each of his parents, and together they strolled into the keep.

Neil surveyed all the old, familiar furnishings of the great hall, the enormous oak banquet table, the tapestries depicting valiant battles, the harp hanging on the wall. A pig was roasting over the fire in the enormous hearth, scenting the air with delectable aromas. He sighed in contentment. It felt so good to be back. He looked at each of his parents, hardly believing that he was at last home, and smiled. "You both look fit enough, and for that I am grateful. From the urgency of your message I was afraid that something had happened to one of you."

Cedric broke away from his son, frowned, and sat heavily in a chair before the fire. "Nay, we are well enough. But there is serious trouble brewing, and before it gets completely out of hand, I want to stop it. I need your help, Neil."

The smile left Neil's face as he stared at his father. It was hard to imagine that Cedric wanted to stop a fight before it even got started. His father was one to meet trouble head on and Neil could not imagine any difficulty that Cedric would run away from.

"Where does the trouble lie, father?" he asked softly.

"The McMahons," Cedric replied with a sigh.

The frown on Neil's forehead deepened. He might have known that accursed family was the cause of his father's concern.

"They grow bolder with each passing year," Cedric went on, "raiding our livestock, in broad daylight no less, raping our women, ravaging our fields."

"You do not let them get away with it, do you?"

"Nay, we retaliate, then they pay us back in kind." Cedric passed a tired hand across his brow. "I am getting too old for this business."

Neil, startled by his father's statement, glanced quickly at Astrid, but his mother stood with hands clasped in front of her, staring at Cedric, her face an unreadable mask. He looked at his father once more and was suddenly jolted by the truth of Cedric's words. He did look old. Old, as well as weary.

"You need have no fear, father. I am here now and will fight by your side," he declared earnestly.

Cedric looked up into his son's deep blue eyes that mirrored his own and shook his head. "Nay. I did not call you back to fight, but to make peace. Duncan McMahon feels as I do. We are both too old, too tired, to continue our fruitless warring. We want peace now, and as long as we still rule our people, we will work to that end."

Neil frowned. "But I do not understand. You just said that things have not changed since I left. The feud is still very much alive."

"Aye, that it is. But only because of the young, hot-blooded ones. It is no secret that Duncan's eldest son, Hugh, holds no love for us. He viciously and unceasingly yaps at our heels. His chief ally is his sister, who is as fierce a warrior as any man I have ever seen." Cedric chuckled. "We've been bested by that pair too many a time."

"A woman!" Neil said incredulously.

"Aye. A firebrand, too, who is a beautiful creature but has no womanly virtues to my knowledge."

Neil was appalled by his father's lack of concern that he'd been beaten by a mere woman.

"Her twin, Angus, left Erin some time ago to plunder in his uncle's country, Brittany, or so I've been informed. It is said that one of the other boys is better suited for the life of a monk. The rest of the children are either too young to fight or girls."

"You seem very knowledgeable about your enemies," Neil commented dryly.

"Aye, I have had to learn much about the McMahons to insure our success over the years. I am certain Duncan knows a great deal about us as well, or he would not have come to me with his proposition."

"What proposition?" Neil asked warily.

"Sometime back, and in the company of Cousin Egan, the McMahon came riding in here on my word that no harm would come to him. He knows about you. He has three daughters of marriageable age. He proposes a union between our two families."

"That's out of the question!"

Cedric eyed his son, unperturbed by his outburst. "Nay," he said calmly, "it makes sense. The power to bring peace to our clans lies with you. I have told you of the one girl, the eldest who is Angus's twin and a hellcat. It is said that the other two daughters are as lovely as she, but have sweet and gentle natures. You can have your pick."

Cedric looked at his wife and smiled. "Your mother has put up with a good deal from me. All with the patience of a saint."

Astrid moved forward to place a hand gently on her husband's shoulder. "I have done what I have because I wanted to. I've had no regrets," she said softly.

Neil was struck by the love that shone in her eyes as she gazed upon her husband. Cedric lifted her hand and placed it to his lips. Neil had never before seen such a display of affection between them and felt it was too intimate a scene for him to witness, but he could not draw his eyes away. It seemed that his parents were lost in their own world and had forgotten all about him. If he'd ever had any doubts as to their feelings for each other, they were at last put to rest.

Cedric pulled his gaze away from Astrid to look at his son. "Would you deny your mother the privilege of spoiling her son's son?" he asked quietly.

"What you ask is impossible!" Neil blurted out.

Cedric sighed. His son was twenty-two years old, past the age when he should have been married and had a family of his own. He said simply, "I am old, Neil. I will fight if I have to, but my heart is no longer in it. You have the power to relieve our people from further sorrow and destruction." He raised his hand. "Do not give me your answer now. Think about it. We will discuss it at length later."

He pushed himself up with difficulty. "There are things I must attend to," he said, and left his son.

As Neil stood in his chamber, a glass of mead in his hand and a frown upon his forehead, the door opened and Astrid stepped into the room.

"Your father's words disturb you," she said knowingly, placing a hand on his arm.

Neil looked at her hand without really seeing it, and nodded.

"There is more to his request than an old man's whim, my son. He is ill."

Neil jerked his head up to stare in puzzlement at his mother.

"He is afraid he will not live to see a grandchild. Your sister's sharp tongue prevents any would-be suitor from asking for her hand, and you have not yet shown an inclination for marriage. Cedric fears he will die before knowing there will be a future for the McNeil line."

"How sick—"

"More than he allows to show. I prayed to his God, and to Odin, that you would arrive in time." She squeezed Neil's arm pleadingly. "Please, comfort your father in the time he has left."

Neil's mind spun with what his mother said. He turned to seek more information, but she slipped quickly from the room.

The girl sat before the polished brass oval, twisting her dark auburn hair into several braids, then intertwining them into a crown on the top of her head. Her father had said she must dress in her finest for the visitors. She'd donned her best gown, but had decided at the last moment that something more had to be done with her hair.

She eyed her reflection critically, turning her head from

side to side. With her hair up she looked older than her seventeen years. She made a moue at the image staring back at her and reached for one of the copper combs on the dresser.

"Thaaalliaa!"

The girl jumped as her name rang through the hallway. The comb clattered to the dresser and her hair fell in loose braids about her shoulders.

The door to her chamber flew open, crashing against the inner wall as a wild apparition stalked into the room. Dressed in the garb of a warrior, she stood with her feet spread wide, her hands on her hips, and glared at Thalia. Chain mail covered the upper part of her body. Beneath her tunic her long legs were bare, except for the leather lacings of her sandals that crisscrossed up the calves and tied just below the knees. Her flaming red hair tumbled down her back to her knees. Like lightning bolts, sparks of anger shot from her green eyes.

Thalia's hand fluttered to her throat. "Gracious, Dorcas," she exclaimed, laughing nervously, "you scared the life out of me."

Dorcas moved forward slowly. "You deserve it," she growled. "Where are they?"

"Who?" asked Thalia innocently.

"Not who, what!" spat Dorcas. "My hair ornaments. The copper combs that Angus gifted me with. Where are they?"

As her sister grabbed her roughly by the arm and shook her, Thalia cried out in pain. "Oh, Dorcas, you are so mean! You seldom wear them. I just wanted to borrow them for today."

"Borrowing implies that the lender knows the whereabouts of her property. To take things without one's knowledge is stealing. You stole them!"

"I did not!" Thalia cried, outraged.

"Girls, that is enough," came an authoritative voice from the doorway. An older woman, whose dark hair bore no relation to either the copper tresses of the infuriated Dorcas or to Thalia's darker auburn strode into the room. She gazed disapprovingly at her two daughters, whose only resemblance as sisters was their emerald eyes, which matched her own.

"Mother, Dorcas is being mean and selfish again," complained Thalia.

"I am not, you little thief!"

"Well, you won't wear the silly combs anyway."

"Whether I wear them or not has nothing to do with it. They belong to me."

"Girls, stop it!" Heloise shouted to be heard over the uproar. She sighed in exasperation as she looked from Dorcas to Thalia, while the two glared at each other. "Thalia, you know that you should not take things without first asking permission," she said quietly, "and why are you not dressed, Dorcas?"

Dorcas blinked and looked down at her attire. She saw nothing unusual about her armor. Raising her head, she looked bewilderedly at her mother. "I am dressed."

Heloise threw up her hands in frustration. "*Presentably* dressed."

Dorcas snorted. "I do not see why I should have to attend our 'guests' anyhow. I am not going to marry any low Viking. Let him choose between Thalia and Gwendolyn if he desires a McMahon bride."

"Dorcas!"

Heloise's eyes darkened in warning, and Dorcas quickly shut her mouth.

"You have to make an appearance because your father promised the McNeil three daughters to look at. Would you have it said that Duncan is not a man of his word?"

"Nay, mother," Dorcas replied, her meek tone belied by the stubborn glint of steel in her eyes.

"Good. Now, Thalia, give your sister her combs. You have your ivories. They will look lovely against your dark hair."

Dorcas held out her hand and grinned smugly as Thalia slapped the combs into it. Then she glanced at Thalia's dressing table and her eyes grew wide at the sight of a gold filigree arm band inset with enamels. "My bracelet! You little pirate! I've been looking for this for a fortnight!" She snatched it up and stalked across the room, then whirled to face her sister. "If I catch you in my things one more time, I am going to chop off those light fingers of yours!"

"Dorcas! Go get dressed," Heloise ordered.

"I am dressed," Dorcas muttered mutinously, but only when she was in the hallway, out of her mother's earshot.

She slammed the door to her chamber and marched over to the dressing table. Throwing down the jewelry in a fit of anger she swore aloud. This whole situation was intolerable. To think that her father would parade his daughters before those Vikings so that he could marry one of them off! Outrageous. She would never marry a pig of a Viking, never! She would never marry, period.

She looked into the polished glass in front of her and barely recognized the image that stared back at her. The wide, frightened eyes gave the lie to her stormy protests. She struggled with herself, trying to find the courage to bar the chamber door, but knew that she would not disobey her father.

She had no doubt that she would be passed over for one of her kinder, gentler sisters. Thalia and Gwendolyn were both endowed with sweet natures—*when Thalia wasn't thieving,* she added silently. A half sob, half laugh escaped her at the thought, and she wiped at the tears she hadn't realized were slipping down her cheeks.

Oh, dear God in heaven, what had Duncan been thinking of when he agreed to such a plan? In spite of their differences, she loved her sisters dearly and did not wish to see either one of them thrust into a hellish life. If only Hugh and Angus had been there when that snake Egan

McNeil had come to her father with his pleas for peace. Mayhaps they could have prevented all of this.

At the thought of Angus, Dorcas was filled with a deep sense of loss. Angus was her twin, her other self. *Damn him for running off to fight in that accursed foreign place with that accursed uncle they'd never before seen!*

"Nay, God, I did not mean that," she murmured aloud. "I do not damn my brother. Stay by his side. Keep him safe so that he may return to me whole and well," she prayed.

She had begged her father, and Angus, and her uncle to let her go along, but they had all forbidden it. She hated the idea that Angus was able to embark upon such an exciting adventure without her, and grudgingly admitted that she was jealous of her brother's freedom. But her feelings about his leaving went deeper than that. She and Angus had never been separated for more than a few days at a time, and she felt as though half her life were over when he left. With the loneliness, and the dreams . . . She shuddered.

Since Angus had gone, she had been haunted by strange dreams. She'd awakened from them gripped by a cold hand of fear and had intuitively known that Angus was in trouble or had been hurt. The feeling would pass, and she knew also that he lived, because there were other, happier dreams. But those confused her just as much as her nightmares, and though she begged her father to let her go to Angus, he stood firm in his refusal to allow her to do so. So she had only Kevin and Hugh now.

Kevin was no help at all. He believed that whatever their father did was right. How could Duncan possibly think that by uniting with the Vikings, there would be peace? There would never be peace. She knew that as well as Hugh did.

Oh, if only Hugh had been at home instead of off in the north seeking the hand of that mealymouthed little Deirdre. Dorcas snorted in derision, thinking of the timid child that Hugh courted. That one had been rightly named—little sorrow. Deirdre was the most sorrowful excuse for a woman that Dorcas had ever known. Why, she was probably afraid of her own shadow! Dorcas simply could not understand what her eldest brother saw in the girl. She knew that he sought to marry again after losing both Moira and his son in childbirth three years before. He had been lonely since his wife's passing, and the grief he felt was painfully real. He had loved Moira deeply, as they all had, but Dorcas simply could not fathom his reasons for chasing after that scared, spineless creature, Deirdre.

Hugh would be enraged upon his return to discover what Egan McNeil had done. Dorcas's eyes narrowed to cat slits. It was all that interloper's fault. If he had not come to her father to propose such a union in the first place, Duncan would never have thought of it. She wondered what McNeil's motive was. After all, he was cousin to Cedric the Traitor.

Dorcas did not trust the man. Egan was greedy and sly. She shuddered as his dark image came to her. She would just as soon cut out his heart if that one touched her. And he did try to lay his hands on her whenever he could. The last time he visited her father, she had passed him in the hall, and he'd placed his hand upon her arm. The memory of how her skin had crawled beneath his clammy touch remained vivid. She had warned him then that if he ever touched her again, she would lop off his hand. After that he'd left her alone, but she had been aware of his eyes always on her. She had been relieved upon his departure.

Dorcas's keen hearing caught the sound of her door opening quietly. She turned and smiled as her young sister glided toward her. There was something ethereal about Gwendolyn. Hers was a true beauty that came from within, and Dorcas envied her sister's serenity. She was such a sweet and gentle child. Almost sixteen, Gwendolyn was more than willing to wed and bed a man.

Dorcas shuddered. The long-ago scene she'd witnessed

as a child still haunted her. She would never let any man touch her.

"Fagan came running to tell Father that someone is on the rise and will be here shortly," Gwendolyn said in her soft voice.

"The Viking pigs, no doubt," Dorcas said.

"I hope that you are not going to call them that to their faces," Gwendolyn said. "It is not even true. Only the woman is of full Viking blood. The children are half Irish."

"But their ways are Viking ways," Dorcas snarled. "They raid and plunder and steal our land. I will always call them Viking pigs."

"Dorcas," Thalia said from the doorway, "you are not yet ready, and they will be here any minute."

"I am as ready as I will ever be."

Thalia stared in openmouthed amazement at her sister's foolish courage. "Father will be furious. You will get a beating."

Dorcas shrugged. "I would rather take a beating than prance around like a dolt in front of a *Viking*. I will not be the chosen one."

"I have heard that they are bigger than giants," said Thalia, her face flushed.

"They would eat you up and spit you back out without a moment's hesitation," Dorcas snapped.

Thalia stuck her tongue out in answer, but Gwendolyn's eyes grew wide. "Are they really so horrible?"

Dorcas ignored Thalia and turned to her younger sister. Seeing the frightened look on Gwen's face, she put an arm around her. "Oh, sweeting, I did not mean to alarm you. They are men. Like any other men, they bleed and die, and if I were the chosen one, my 'husband' would not live to see the light of day after the marriage feast."

Gwendolyn looked searchingly at Dorcas. "Why do you fear marriage so?"

Dorcas was startled for a moment, then shrugged. "I do not fear it. I merely want no part of it. I have my reasons."

"Well, I do not think you have reason to fear that you will be chosen," Thalia said. She wrinkled her nose. "Who would want a warrior for a wife?"

Dorcas smiled slyly. "Precisely my thoughts."

"Well, we had better hurry before Father gets too angry," Gwendolyn said.

"You two go ahead. I will be along in a minute."

Gwendolyn turned questioningly at her sister's words, but Dorcas waved her out of the room. She did not want to have to face her reckoning until absolutely necessary.

She'd lied to Gwen about not fearing the marriage bed. In truth, she was terrified of the idea. She shut her eyes to block out the image that always came to her when she thought about it. She would never be able to allow any man to touch her in an intimate way. The scene she had witnessed had been revolting and disgusting, and it still terrified her. It was the reason she had become a warrior against all that was law. After what she had seen, she had sworn vengeance on all her family's enemies, but especially on the half Vikings, the heathen McNeils. To that end she'd devoted her energies. Too ashamed to tell anyone what she had seen, she kept her secret, and it left her with a deep-seated fear, along with her silent vow never to marry.

2

Cedric glanced apprehensively at Neil, riding beside him in silence. His son's face was set in grim resolution, and Cedric swore silently. How could things have become any more complicated? If he weren't so desperate for peace, he would have let Neil go his own way, but as it was, he had his people to look after, and Neil after him. It was a great responsibility. More often than not, his own desires came second to those of the clan. It was just as well his son faced that realization now as later.

Neil stared blankly straight ahead, his mouth a tight, firm line as their horses plodded along. He was aware that his father was eager to reach their destination and had tried several times to speed up the little procession, but Neil, unwilling to meet his destiny, held his destrier in check, forcing the others to slow their pace.

He'd gone over and over in his mind his conversation with Cedric the night he'd returned to Erin. After his father had been sated with food and drink, Neil had broached the subject that had been troubling him all day. He'd informed his father of the happenings in Norway and of his activities. Cedric had laughed heartily at some of Neil's escapades, clearly proud of his son's skill as a warrior.

Neil then smoothly introduced Anika into the discussion, telling his father of her beauty and virtue.

"If you want grandchildren, father, let me return to Norway. I will bring Anika home as my wife. She will ease the burdens of my mother and comfort you both."

Cedric frowned, and his words cut into Neil like a knife as he answered slowly. "If it were only that simple. Your marriage to a Viking maiden, no matter how sweet and kind, would not be countenanced here. There is a great move in Erin to rid the land of all Vikings. This is my home, Neil. The land of my father, and my grandfather, and my grandfather's father. I wish to be buried here when my time comes, not to be pushed back into the sea. I want to know that what I have built will be here after I am gone.

"You will one day lead our people. You are young and strong and can fight our enemies. But someday you will be old like me and will grow tired of the battles. Peace between the other Irish clans and ourselves is necessary now. I want to see our cattle grow fat off the land so that there is enough to feed all of our people the winter through without slaughtering half the herd. I want to see the fields yield a full harvest without being burned. Only with a union between the McNeils and the McMahons can this be accomplished."

"Then let Nissa marry one of the McMahon sons!" Neil said forcefully.

"Your sister has grown into a woman who does not know how to hold her tongue. I fear she would be murdered before the wedding night was out." Cedric sighed and shook his head wearily. "It is partly my fault that she is so wild. As my son and heir, you've received all my attention. No. I am afraid that only your marriage to one of the McMahon's daughters will give us the much-needed rest we seek from their assaults."

Cedric was struck by a fit of coughing that racked his body, and Astrid stepped forward to tend him. Concern for his father was equal to his concern for himself at that moment. By Odin, he was being asked to give up everything he wanted, needed, to take as wife some silly child he'd never before laid eyes on. He was twenty-two years old—a man in his own right. His father had no business asking this of him. He clamped his mouth in a tight line and asked, "What if I refused?"

Cedric looked up, surprised. He'd not considered for a moment that his son might balk at doing his bidding. He pushed away the cup of herbal tea that Astrid held out to him and replied in a deadly calm voice, "Then you would no longer be my son. You would be banished from the clan, and I would send a message to Gunnar of what I did and the reason for it. He would not give you refuge, for it would be against his law to do so."

Neil stared at him disbelievingly as Cedric was seized by another coughing spell. Deep down, he knew Cedric meant every word, more as leader of the clan than as his father. He took a tentative step forward, alarmed by the cough that shook Cedric, but was waved away. Not knowing what else to do, and afraid to say anything, he left the room. He rushed outside and saddled his destrier, then galloped through the gates furiously as though the hounds of hell were on his heels. He rode across the countryside aimlessly for an hour before finally returning home, still without having reached a decision. He strode into the hall and grimaced at finding his father's cousin Egan with Cedric. He greeted him curtly.

"I was just telling Cedric why Nissa did not return with me," Egan explained.

Neil slipped into a chair and signaled to a serving girl to bring him some mead.

"How is my sister?"

"She is well, but she and Cora are having too good a time for her to come home."

"I trust your own sister is in good health," Neil said politely, though he truly cared not one whit. He felt that

Cora was a silly chit and not a very good influence on Nissa.

Egan smiled lazily. "Cora is Cora, and Nissa is delightful, a most welcome diversion. But after two months with those two, I felt the need to retire from their presence."

The corners of Neil's mouth lifted as he nodded in understanding. He imagined that having two strong-willed women underfoot would be rather harrowing and could almost feel sorry for Egan. Almost, but not quite.

Though he made an effort to get along with Egan, Neil did not care for the man. There was an arrogance about him that made Neil want to keep his distance. Mayhaps it was because Egan had been left in charge of his estate at the tender age of thirteen, when his parents died. Even then he'd insisted upon running things without assistance.

Neil knew it had been hard on Egan. He had had to manage his lands and hold them against neighboring clans who looked to increase their own wealth, as well as be the leader of his people. It was hard to demand obedience from those older than he, but Neil felt Egan's brand of justice was unusually cruel and it had not changed over the years. Egan seemed to take sadistic pleasure in hurting others. Everyone but Cora. The one person he showed any love for was his only sister. He indulged her to the point where she was hopelessly spoiled.

He seldom smiled, and when he did Neil couldn't help thinking that it was with more of a contemptuous snarl than anything else. That, and cold eyes that missed nothing, made Neil avoid his father's cousin whenever possible.

"Actually," Egan said smoothly, "I came by to inform Cedric that the McMahon has agreed to a meeting." He turned to Cedric. "Have you told Neil of your plans?"

"Yea, but he has not reached a decision as yet," answered Cedric, eyeing his son.

Egan raised his eyebrows in surprise. "What's to decide?"

"Only my whole future," Neil drawled.

"You are planning to remain here, are you not?"

When Neil only shrugged without answering, Egan asked boldly, "Surely you will not desert your father in his time of need?"

"I do not need you to remind me of my duties," Neil said, bringing his mug of mead down on the table.

"My intent was not to anger you. I am merely surprised that you would not jump at the chance to seek peace where it is offered."

"What makes you so certain the McMahon wants peace?"

Egan smiled. "If I did not feel sure, I would not have proposed such a union."

Neil's eyes narrowed and his lips tightened as he sat back to contemplate Egan. So, this whole matter was not entirely Cedric's idea. "What do you get out of all this?" he asked slowly.

"Why, peace, of course, along with my lands free of being ravaged by the McMahons."

"But not free of other clans."

"True, but if I am attacked, I know I could count on both the McNeils and the McMahons for assistance."

Neil looked at his father. "You agreed to this?"

Cedric nodded. "It seems a small price to pay for all that we would gain." Cedric did not care much for Egan either. He'd tried to guide him as a boy, but had met with such stiff resistance, he'd finally given up. He'd sat by helplessly over the years as Egan ruled his lands harshly, demanding ever greater crop yields and wool production from his serfs and slaves as he meted out food and clothing with a miserly hand. More than likely Egan would try to use this new alliance to his own advantage by ravaging the lands and livestock of other clans. Cedric felt he could curb his cousin's desires for more power, but for how long? He needed his son beside him to see to it that Egan did not get out of control.

Egan quaffed his mead and smiled tauntingly at Neil. "Mayhaps Neil no longer remembers how to fight as the Irish do."

The smile that graced Neil's mouth did not reach his eyes. "You would be amazed at what I remember, cousin, and at what I have learned since."

Egan caught the warning light in the younger man's eyes and made no reply, and Cedric quickly changed the topic of conversation. If his son and Egan so blatantly showed their hostilities for each other before anything was settled, it would ruin everything he was trying to attain.

Neil was sitting before the fire in his room. It was deep night and he was surprised when an urgent knock sounded on his door. He opened it to find his mother's maid, Hilda, standing there with wide, frightened eyes. His father had had another attack and his mother wanted him to come at once.

Neil bolted from the room and ran to his father's chamber. Cedric lay on his bed, gasping frantically for breath. Neil flew to the bedside as his mother placed a hot cloth on Cedric's chest. The pungent odor of herbs filled the chamber. He felt so helpless as he stared at his father's ashen face. Cedric's eyes were closed against the pain. Soon his breathing became more even, and he opened his eyes to find two worried faces above him, staring down anxiously.

He smiled weakly. "I know that I do not have much longer," he said hoarsely, "but I am not dead yet."

"Nor will you be very soon, my husband. I will not let you go without a fight," said Astrid in her soft voice.

Cedric reached out and tucked her small hand into his. "It is so peaceful to lie here and let you tend me," he murmured. "If only the land could feel such peace."

His father's listlessness alarmed Neil. It was not at all like Cedric to give up without a fight, yet he seemed to be doing just that.

Neil studied his father's face as Cedric shut his eyes. He'd not noticed before how pale his father was. His skin was so white, almost translucent, and he looked as if he'd aged a lifetime since the afternoon. Neil's heart ached for him. Cedric was an old man, and Neil could not leave him to fight the McMahons alone. But how could he give up his Anika?

He groaned inwardly as the image of his sweet, beautiful Anika came to mind. She was so tiny, so delicate and fair. How could he give her up to face who knew what? Shy and pure, Anika would be his only through marriage. Now that dream was dead, for after seeing his father again, he could not leave. No matter what the cost, his father was right. The greater responsibility lay here, and he could not turn his back on it.

When morning dawned, he told Cedric of his decision. Before his eyes Neil could see the burden lifted from his father's shoulders. Now, two days later, they were on their way to the McMahon stronghold, invited as guests of Duncan McMahon. His mouth tightened as they approached the settlement. He'd made his decision.

Neil was uneasy about passing through the enemy's gate. So much could go wrong. But Cedric had insisted they agree to travel there. Duncan *was* a man of honor, but more, Cedric knew that trust had to begin somewhere. Within reason. His men would station themselves on the hill overlooking the McMahon stronghold.

Dorcas stood by the open window in her chamber, her arms wrapped about herself protectively. Soon it would be time to face the enemy. Her father had already sent an impatient message demanding her appearance in the hall. She'd instructed the serving girl to tell Duncan she would be down momentarily, but she found a dozen excuses to delay.

She was not worried that she would be the one chosen by the Viking pig, but she was concerned for her sisters. Thalia and Gwen were both endowed with sweet natures like their mother. They were kind and gentle, traits Dorcas had never developed. She'd had countless praises on her beauty, but she'd scoffed at them, and at any man who bestowed them. She knew she was much too tall. Instead of the delicate loveliness of her sisters, she stood only a couple of inches shorter than her twin, the tallest of the McMahon's sons. Because of her training as a warrior, her body was lithe, supple, and firm. She was unaware that her stance was so regal that a man was rendered speechless when setting eyes on her for the first time.

She sometimes wished she was more like her mother. Heloise exuded a serenity that awed Dorcas, a serenity she knew she could never attain. Her temper was much too quick and her tongue always got the better of her. Besides, she wanted nothing to do with men, except to meet them on the battlefield.

She shuddered. She knew that a man and woman came together, but she wanted no part of it. The horrible sight she'd witnessed so long ago haunted her, and she squeezed her eyes tightly shut now to block it out.

She'd been only twelve the night she had awakened to screams. Terror had gripped her like an iron fist as she'd bolted from her bed and run to the window. The night should have been shrouded in a peaceful darkness, but the sky was alight with red flames. She raced from her room to the great hall.

Torches blazed on the walls and a fire roared on the hearth. The room was crowded with the women of the village, all scurrying and carrying bandages and salves and pots filled with boiling hot water, tending to the wounds of the men who staggered into the keep. Dorcas stared in horror as one man, blood pouring from the wound that had nearly severed his arm, collapsed at her mother's feet, his death grown echoing in the girl's ears long after his last breath had left his body.

Her hand clamped over her mouth to stifle her sobs, Dorcas backed out of the room before anyone saw her. The Vikings had breeched the walls of the stronghold. If they reached the keep . . .

Frightened, she ran to Angus's chamber for comfort, but her twin was not there. The only place he could be was in the thick of the battle, and her heart turned over at the thought that her brother had disobeyed their father on such a serious matter. She had to find him!

She crept through the keep, sneaking past the hall and out a small back door. Tearing around to the front of the keep, she headed toward the village—and what she saw there made the bile rise in her throat.

Mangled bodies—arms, legs, and severed heads were strewn about. Red blood seeped into the thirsty ground. Fires raged through the cottages, flames leaping from one to the other to destroy the homes of her people. She made her way around the side of one cottage still untouched and halted in her tracks. Stepping back quickly, she peered around the corner, her heart pounding furiously.

Three Vikings had cornered a young maiden from the village. Dorcas watched, stunned and terrified, as they twirled the frightened, sobbing girl among them, ripping the clothes from her. One of the men lowered his breeches and threw her to the ground. He fell on top of the scream-ing, wriggling girl, plunging into her. She tried to twist her head from his grasp, but he pulled a knife and sliced her shoulder open. The girl screamed and her head rolled to one side. She lay so still, Dorcas's heart stopped.

The man laughed harshly and arose to let one of his companions take his place. Wide-eyed with fear, Dorcas stared at the blood covering the girl's thighs. They had killed her! She watched in horror as the second man, and then the third mounted the girl. When the last man was done, his white teeth flashed in a grin like the snarl of a mad dog, and he slit the girl's throat. Dorcas had to stuff her hands into her mouth to keep from screaming.

She did cry out when she was grabbed from behind. A hand clamped tightly over her mouth, and she looked up fearfully at the man who held her. She breathed an inward sigh of relief at seeing her father's trusted friend, Owen.

He thrust her behind him as her brother Hugh and another warrior reached them.

Hugh's eyes blazed with fury as his gaze whipped over his little sister. "You and Angus get back inside the keep now!" he whispered harshly, pushing her toward her twin, who was just as frightened as she.

Angus grabbed her hand and together they ran to the little door she'd escaped through earlier. Dorcas glanced back once and saw Hugh, Owen, and Guy engaged in a fight to the death, with the three Vikings meeting a swift end.

She and Angus had received a tongue-lashing and a beating from their father for leaving the safety of their home during the Viking raid. But what Dorcas had witnessed had been punishment enough. Shortly after, Angus began his training as a warrior, and everything he learned he passed on to his sister as she cajoled, pleaded with, and threatened him. Soon, she was as proficient a warrior as any of the men, and she vowed she would kill any Viking who dared to encroach upon their home. She was proud of her abilities as a warrior, and still remembered with keen pleasure the day five years ago, when she was fourteen and had at last been allowed to prove her capability. Since then, no one dared to question her desire to wield a sword.

Nay, she thought, she would not be the chosen one. But her heart ached for her sisters. One of them would have to be, and to Dorcas, that meant a life of hell. She silently promised that if this McNeil were unkind, if he did anything to harm whichever one he chose, she would kill him.

Her gaze wandered to the activity in the yard outside and her heart started racing. Through the gate rode six huge men. She recognized Egan McNeil and his boon companion, Quinn. She knew the McNeil, too, having met him in battle many times. But she did not know the other three men and she wondered which one was the son.

Her lips curled contemptuously, and her eyes narrowed as she watched them ride up to the keep and dismount. One of the men, the tall, dark stranger, looked about him warily, and she wondered disdainfully what he was so afraid of. Her father had given his word that no harm would befall them. Duncan was a man of honor, but honor must be something these foreigners knew little about. Her father had promised the McNeil three daughters for inspection. Well, three he would get. Dorcas whirled from the window and left the chamber.

Outside, Neil followed his father's lead and dismounted. The McMahon stood at the entrance to his home to greet them. He was a tall, broad man, his bright red hair tinged with gray but his body strong and fit from years of fighting. A younger man, the replica of his father except that his hair was a deep auburn, stood at his right. His expression was hard and unsmiling. Another man, different from his father with his dark hair and green eyes, stood on the McMahon's left, a welcoming smile on his face.

Neil eyed the three men, men he'd grown up considering his enemies, suspiciously. Then Duncan stepped forward and extended his hand to Cedric.

"Welcome to my home," he said in his deep voice.

"Thank you. Your generosity is most gratifying," Cedric replied politely. He turned, indicating Neil. "May I present my son, Neil."

Duncan turned his attention on the young man. His glance was sharp, and Neil felt as though he were on exhibition. Then Duncan grabbed him by the upper arms in greeting and smiled. "Aye," he murmured. "Young and strong. A fine match for one of my girls."

He gestured to his sons. "My own," he said. "Hugh." The auburn-haired man nodded abruptly. "And Kevin." The other young man's smile broadened as he nodded in greeting.

Cedric introduced the rest of his party, then Duncan swept his arm toward his keep. "Come, you will want to eat and drink. The ladies await us inside."

Neil entered the hall last and leaned casually against a wall as everyone else took seats.

"I must admit," Duncan said, "that I was wary of Egan's proposal to end our hostilities. But I came to realize that it is the only answer if we are ever to have peace."

Cedric nodded. "I, too, feel that this will end the hatred that has made us enemies and killed so many of our people." He smiled wryly. "I fear the young ones do not understand and would carry on the fight. But I long to see this land that I love grow green instead of running red with blood."

Duncan studied his longtime enemy, surprised at his words. He'd always considered Cedric McNeil a traitor for embracing the Viking cause. It never occurred to him that the McNeil's Irish blood would flow so strong. He nodded in understanding. "Aye, 'twould appear that our beliefs are very much alike. I, too, grow weary." He grinned suddenly. "It is fitting that our children put an end to the feud."

"My lord," Heloise said, entering the hall and approaching Duncan, "your daughters wish to know if they may serve you now." At Duncan's nod, she beckoned Thalia and Gwendolyn forward.

As the two girls poured mead for the guests, Neil surveyed them with disinterest. It wasn't that they were unattractive. They were both quite lovely, endowed with the delicate beauty of their mother. One was petite with dark hair, the image of Heloise, with the budding loveliness of the woman to come. The other was taller with hair that was a deep auburn, thick and luxurious. She approached Neil with a cup of mead, and he noticed how her hand trembled as she handed it to him. His mouth twisted wryly as he thanked her, and she hurried away.

He listened halfheartedly to the conversation between his father and the McMahon as he sipped his mead. Egan left the table and came over to him. "You could try to show a little enthusiasm," he whispered fiercely.

Neil stared at him without expression. "I am here."

Egan's eyes flashed angrily before he abruptly turned away. Neil ignored him and returned his attention to Cedric. His father was asking Duncan if he'd misunderstood Egan. Did not the McMahon have three daughters?

Duncan pursed his lips. "Aye, and Dorcas is supposed to be here," he replied tightly.

Just then the third daughter rushed into the room. She stood with her hands on her hips, her head held proudly, eyeing the McNeils with open contempt. Still in battle dress with her copper hair fanned out over her shoulders, she looked like some wild creature about to wreak vengeance on those in the room.

Neil's cup halted halfway to his lips. His breath caught as he stared at the virago before him. The vision that had haunted him since the last time he'd been home assailed him, making the blood rush to his head.

The Valkyrie!

But this was no illusion. What stood before him was flesh and blood. Through the fog in his brain he vaguely heard the McMahon introduce the apparition to Cedric as his daughter, Dorcas.

He watched as Egan stepped forward and placed his hand on the girl's arm to lead her to the table.

"I see that Lady Dorcas does not deign to serve us as her genteel sisters do," he said, his smile thin and goading.

Dorcas's eyes narrowed and her nostrils flared as she glanced at the offending hand. "Take your hand off me," she demanded in a low voice. Egan ignored her as he continued to urge her forward, murmuring, "Of course, your talents lie in another area altogether."

The next moments happened so fast, Neil wasn't at all sure that he was not dreaming.

Dorcas whirled away from Egan and drew her sword. Before anyone could act, she swung the weapon at Egan. The man screamed, and Neil watched in horror as Egan's right hand flew from his arm to the floor.

"I warned you, McNeil," the girl snarled, "never to touch me again. No man touches me."

Cedric was instantly on his feet. He and the McMahon wore no weapons, but Cedric's men, standing behind him, drew their swords, as did Duncan's. Dorcas backed away warily as Duncan shouted at his men to put their weapons away.

"Is this how you would show us a peaceful welcome?" Cedric bellowed, his face livid with rage. "If it is, it is an outrage that—" He was suddenly seized by a coughing spell that choked off his words.

Seeing the fury that glazed the eyes of Cedric's men, Neil knew he must act swiftly. If he did not, more blood would be spilled and all that his father dreamed of would vanish into thin air.

Dorcas's gaze was fixed on the group of armed men when she heard the crack of a bullwhip and her bloody sword was snatched from her fingers. She cried out in surprise and looked down at her empty hand. Before she could recover, the whip whistled through the air once again. She felt a stinging sensation at her waist and felt herself being imprisoned as the whip coiled around her middle like a slithering snake.

She yanked on it to free herself, but to no avail. She was helpless as she was yanked forward to land with a thud against the hard chest of her captor. Her heart pounded frantically as an arm held her in a viselike grip, pinning her to the tall, dark stranger. His other hand grabbed a handful of her thick red hair to jerk her head back.

Flashing green eyes stared unflinchingly at him. Neil saw her pulse jump nervously at the base of her white throat, the only evidence that she was frightened. Her nostrils flared with anger and her breasts heaved against him. He took in the fine planes of her face—her long, straight nose, the high cheekbones flushed with color, the dark brows arched above those fathomless emerald eyes, and long, curling lashes. He knew they would be as soft and fine as a babe's.

Dorcas studied the man as thoroughly as he did her. She was tall, but found herself having to look up to meet his gaze. He was the most handsome man she'd ever seen. His hair was thick and dark, and one unruly lock fell across his forehead to give him a rakish appearance. The darkest, coldest blue eyes she'd ever seen stared back at her, giving nothing away. His nose was long and narrow, and his full mouth was set in a straight line in his lean, tanned face. She fleetingly wondered what he would look like if he smiled, then chided herself for the thought.

She'd never before allowed any man to touch her in this manner, and her heart was beating with the fast cadence of a war drum at the feel of his hard body. An inner voice warned her that this was a man who took what he wanted.

Nervously, she licked her dry lips, and his gaze fastened on her mouth. A smile flickered across his lips, then as if he were bewitched, he slowly lowered his head. Closer and closer he came, and she stiffened when she realized what his intentions were. Her lips curled in a feral snarl and she spat in his face.

He jerked back in surprise, but his movement did not have the effect she had hoped for. He still held her in an unbreakable grip.

Neil's eyes narrowed dangerously. Nay, this was no illusion, he thought. This hellcat was real, and once she had been responsible for him almost losing his life. It was only fitting she now reap the rewards of justice. He grinned slowly, and Dorcas gasped. She was reminded of a wolf baring its teeth.

Without releasing her, Neil bent his head and rubbed his cheek against her shoulder, wiping her spittle off. Dorcas fought to free herself, then immediately ceased her struggles when he yanked her head farther back until she thought her neck would break.

Duncan was trying desperately to calm Cedric and keep the men at bay. Cedric was shouting for revenge against the insult shown them when Neil's voice rang clearly through the hall. "Nay, father. You heard Lady Dorcas say she'd warned Egan in the past. He should not have taken her words so lightly."

Cedric whirled on his son. "You cannot mean to countenance this action!"

"Nay, I do not. But we came here for the purpose of establishing peace between our clans. The foolishness of one man must be overlooked for the good of all."

Egan was groaning in pain as he rocked back and forth, holding a cloth to the bloody stub where his hand had been. Through eyes glazed with agony he watched Neil, still holding his prize, as he spoke to Cedric. All the hatred he felt for Neil flared within him, burning him. Neil had never liked him, he knew it. He'd always looked down on him. Well, he and that bitch who thought she was better than any man alive would pay. They would both pay, Egan vowed hatefully.

"You cannot mean you wish to go through with the bargain?" Cedric said unbelievingly.

"Aye, I do." Neil looked back at Dorcas. She was glaring up at him, gritting her teeth in frustration. "I choose the lady Dorcas," he said quietly.

"When hell freezes over, you will!" she declared.

He smiled lazily at her. "Your father gave me three maids from which to choose a wife. It will be you."

"Never! I will never consent to marry a filthy Viking. I will never marry."

"Dorcas!" Duncan shouted angrily. "You have caused enough trouble for one day. This will mean peace for our people. I agreed."

As Neil had spoken to his father, he'd loosened his hold on her. She struggled again to be free, at last breaking his grip when she sank her teeth into his upper arm. He jumped and swore under his breath as she whirled away from him. Her flaming tresses billowed out behind her as she put some distance between them.

She turned on her father like a wild beast that had been

cornered. "I never agreed to anything," she shouted, her eyes blazing furiously. "This was all your idea, yours and that interloper's." She glanced contemptuously at Egan. "I will fight the Vikings unto death. That is the only way we will be safe."

Cedric stared at the wild creature. If she were a man . . . All that fire wasted on a woman. What sons she would make! He took a deep breath and turned to face Duncan grimly. "I am an honorable man. I cannot allow the insult done to my family to pass. Since we have not reached an accord, there is only one alternative. We will meet on the field of battle. Prepare yourselves to face us in the glen between our homes in one week's time."

Duncan nodded wearily. Because of his daughter's foolish pride, they all faced death. "It is done. You and your party have my word that you may leave here unharmed." He turned to his eldest son. "Hugh, take your sister to her chamber and stay with her until I send for her. She will not dishonor our name again."

Dorcas was alarmed by the colorless tone in which her father addressed them. She had spoiled everything for him by her rash act and was sorry she'd shamed him. But it galled her to be put on display like an animal on the block. She knew she would get a beating for this. It did not matter. Just so long as she could fight the enemy. She followed Hugh unprotestingly from the hall.

3

Neil strode back and forth on the edge of the training field, absorbed in overseeing the men in combat practice. Cedric had ordered him to attend to preparations for battle with the McMahons. Neil's days were long and full of hard work. By the time the moon rose each evening, he was bone tired and ready for sweet sleep.

He felt no qualms about readying for a fight with the McMahons. He'd done his duty. It was not his fault things had worked out as they did. Mayhaps he should be glad that Egan was such a fool. Now he was free to follow his own path. Egan had even refused Cedric's offer of hospitality so that Astrid could see to his wound, preferring to travel on to his own estate where Cora would take care of him. In truth, the little ninny would probably faint dead away at the sight of her brother's wound.

If Neil felt any guilt, it was that his father was forced into doing something he deemed wrong. Egan had not even been properly grateful to Cedric for vowing to get revenge on his behalf. Instead, Egan had stared at Neil, his face a mask of naked hate, then turned his horse away without a word and left them.

Although Neil was sorry his father's dream of peace had

faded, he still felt a great sense of relief. The only things to mar his good feeling about the turn of events were the images of lustrous red hair and flashing green eyes that invaded his dreams. For a while now they'd even crept into his mind at the strangest times during the day, and he found himself having to push them aside forcefully, angry that he could not control his thoughts. Then he would concentrate with all his might on the vision of Anika and her soft blond beauty and her gentle blue eyes.

A sentry shouting from the wall that riders were approaching made Neil hurry up the stairs of the watchtower. He peered into the distance and saw a swarm of men both on horseback and on foot descending the far hill. He swore under his breath. Surely the McMahon was not attacking so soon.

As the troops came closer, Neil recognized the leader and grinned. Odin was indeed smiling on them, for it was Erik the Bold. Neil could not imagine what the man was doing this far north of his holding, but fortune was with them if his friend could be persuaded to remain for the coming battle. He flew down the steps and ran into the hall to inform Cedric of Erik's approach. Father and son stood in the yard as the body of men rode though the gate.

Their guest dismounted and greeted Cedric boisterously, grinning from ear to ear. His hard-muscled girth made up for his short stature, and he gave both Cedric and Neil bone-crushing hugs. He wore his blond hair long, and his full beard was neatly trimmed. His blue eyes sparkled merrily from under thick bushy eyebrows, and Neil recalled how more than one man had met a quick death because of underestimating Erik. Despite his size and his amiability, he could be a formidable enemy.

He turned his twinkling gaze upon Neil. "I'd heard that you'd returned. Welcome home," he said in a booming voice.

"Thank you," replied Neil, smiling. "But surely you did not come all the way from Wexford just to bid me welcome."

"Nay, though I was disappointed that you did not sail south to my home before journeying here so that we could raise a cup or two."

"Or three, or four, or a dozen," Neil added.

Erik threw back his head and laughed. "Aye, you know me well, my friend."

"Come," put in Cedric, "we will do so now."

Once they were settled, Neil asked his friend what had brought him inland.

"A long-overdue visit to my brother, Rupert," Erik answered.

"That's right, he married an Irish lass, didn't he?" Cedric asked.

Erik nodded. "Aye. With trouble coming from all sides, we felt it best if he gained a better foothold by intermarrying."

Neil glanced at his father and caught the imperceptible tightening of Cedric's jaw.

"It has worked out well," Erik continued, then added proudly, "I go to see my first nephew born two months ago."

Cedric's eyes glittered angrily and his mouth set in a tight line, but softened again when he spied Neil staring at him. After all, Neil bore no responsibility in this matter.

Erik stopped his cup of mead halfway to his lips when he saw father and son staring intently at each other. He could feel the tension crackling in the air as he asked, "You disapprove?"

Cedric turned his attention toward his guest. "Nay, I do not. In truth, it is what we'd intended, until our plans were spoiled."

Erik's eyebrows rose in query, and Cedric quickly supplied him with news of what had taken place within the last several days. He listened to the tale, the frown upon his forehead deepening, then asked, "Why would you want such a hellcat?"

"I have my reasons for wanting the red-haired witch," Neil answered in a deceptively calm voice.

Erik shook his head in wonder. "It sounds like you are well rid of such a vixen. If the man has two other daughters, surely you could have been a little more prudent in your choice."

At Neil's stubborn silence, Cedric sighed heavily. "You would have to see the wench in order to understand Neil's decision."

"Well, I cannot allow my close comrades to do battle on their own," Erik stated fervently. "If I and my men may join you, we would consider it an honor, and I know that Rupert will also come if I send a message. You have been gravely insulted. The deed must not go unpunished."

Dorcas wore a path in front of the hearth in the great hall as she brooded. She had indeed been punished for her actions by being confined to her room for two days on a diet of bread and water, but only after her father had given her a sound beating. She was not sorry for what she'd done to Egan McNeil. After all, she had made her warning clear and she was a woman of her word. She was concerned, however, by her father's lack of enthusiasm for the battle ahead. Duncan's attitude was one of utter defeatism before they'd even reached the battlefield and that frightened Dorcas. Though she was no longer banished from his presence, he'd ceased speaking to her. But every so often she would catch him eyeing her with a blank stare that sent a chill through her. She'd never known her father to be so without spirit. The rest of her family shunned her, too, and it made her both sad and angry.

Duncan looked up from where he and his sons were going over their battle plan and frowned at his eldest daughter. She was in deep thought, not seeming to realize that anyone else was about. He scowled and wondered if she was having second thoughts about her rash act. It would do no good if she was. The die had been cast. Now they must pay the consequences. He motioned to his sons to leave him and continued to watch his daughter.

Finally he spoke irritably. "Dorcas, stop your pacing."

Dorcas jumped and turned to face her father. She bit her lower lip in indecision, then walked toward him. When she reached him, she knelt down and placed her head in his lap as she'd done when she was a child.

Duncan had seen the pain, and anguish, and worry etching her face. He felt a pang of remorse at having treated her as though she had the plague. She was still his daughter, and very dear to him. Mayhaps he'd been wrong to include her in the bargain. She'd always declared that she would never marry, but he had thought that was her youth speaking. Once she found the man of her choice . . . He sighed. It was not to be, and now it was too late for all of them.

He lovingly ran his hand over her shining copper curls. "What troubles you, Dorcas?"

She raised her head, her iridescent green eyes clouded with bewilderment. "I have tried to do as you requested. I have looked into my heart and soul to ask forgiveness of God for my actions, but in good conscience, I cannot. Father, I am not sorry I did what I did. In truth, I'd warned Egan McNeil many times to leave me alone, but he persisted in laying his hands upon me whenever he could." She shuddered at the thought. "Egan McNeil is an odious man. Cruel and heartless. The last time he was here, I warned him what would happen if he ever touched me again. I am not sorry I did it. I am only sorry that you hate me for it," she cried, burying her face in his lap.

Duncan's heart grew heavy at his daughter's words. He had not known. He took her face in his hands, forcing her to look at him. "I do not hate you now," he said softly, "nor have I ever in the past, nor will I in the future. You are my eldest daughter and I love you. Your skill as a warrior, though it baffles me, makes me proud. Your beauty is comparable to none. You have a strength of body and spirit as well as a kind and gentle heart." He shrugged slightly. "I suppose I have always wished to see you happy, with a brood of children at your feet, for that is God's purpose in putting you on this earth. I merely wished to see those traits of strength, and beauty, and kindness passed on to your children."

Her fear showed in her eyes as she shuddered. "Not at the hands of a Viking," she whispered.

Duncan frowned at the fright on his daughter's face. For the first time in a long while he saw her not as the warrior who fought courageously at his side but as a vulnerable young woman. He suddenly remembered her earlier words and asked harshly, "Did McNeil take liberties with you?"

She blushed and stammered, "Nay, not . . . only in that he touched me."

"You say he did this often?"

"Yea, he did, and I warned him to stop. I told him that if he did not I would cut off his hand."

Duncan nodded in understanding. "If you gave McNeil warning, then you could do nothing else." A wry smile touched his lips. "However, that does not alleviate our present situation. There is no help for it but to defend your honor. If we die in the process, at least I will know that it has not all been for naught."

Panic showed on Dorcas's face as she grabbed his arms and cried, "Do not speak so, father. We will meet the Vikings and win."

Duncan smiled wistfully and brushed her soft cheek with the back of his hand. The confidence of youth always amazed him. He found he could not dampen her spirits by denying her her belief in him, so he kept silent.

Dorcas sat astride her gray horse proudly as she rode between Kevin and her father. Hugh was on Duncan's right. She should have felt drained from lack of sleep, but she did not. Never before a battle had she experienced a sleepless night as she had the night past. As she tossed and turned in her bed, she had felt as though she were no longer in control of the situation. She'd finally arisen to watch the dawn creep over the horizon, and had wondered fleetingly if it would be the last she would ever see. Then she had pushed the thought aside. She could not allow her father's defeatist attitude to rule her also. They would win. She glanced at Duncan but could see nothing written in his bland expression.

They reached the crest of the hill and Dorcas looked across the peaceful valley below. The far hill where the enemy should have been was empty. Her heartbeat quickened as she wondered if the Vikings had turned cowardly.

Even as she watched, though, dark figures appeared on the hill. Just a few at first, then more and more, until the entire hill was covered by the army of warriors. There were thousands of them. Where had the McNeil found all those men?

She glanced at Duncan, but her father sat looking straight ahead, his face unreadable. She looked at Hugh, then down the line of men on his right. There was Donald, and Fagan, and Brian, and Cameron. Dear Cameron, who was actually too old to fight but who would have chafed at the idea of remaining behind. Who had fixed her doll when she was a child, and kissed her knee when she scraped it. Who'd taught her the rudiments of war. Who should have been sitting before a quiet fire now, weaving his tales of old for the young ones. She turned to look at Kevin. He sat as their father, with unblinking eyes staring straight ahead. His mouth moved in a silent prayer. Her gaze shifted beyond him to Casey, and Balfour, and Travis, and to all the others on both sides of her who looked to her father for their sustenance.

They all trusted Duncan implicitly and would follow

him wherever he led, even unto death. But what they faced today was slaughter—outright murder at the hands of the Vikings. And it was all for her. Dorcas was overtaken by a wave of impotent fury as she stared at the motionless Vikings across the valley. She could not allow these men, these friends of hers, men she'd grown up with and who had looked after her, spoiled her, loved her, lose their lives because of her. She could not allow the destruction of her people.

With a sob of anger and frustration she spurred her horse forward. She was not afraid of being followed, for the men would follow only Duncan into battle unless he ordered otherwise. She was vaguely aware of someone's shout as she galloped down the hill onto the battlefield. Over her head she twirled 'round and 'round a spiked ball on a chain.

Neil watched in horror as Dorcas thundered down the hill alone. Had she gone mad? No one made a move from the other side to follow her. Cedric's destrier danced nervously, but he kept it in check for fear some fool would take his move forward to mean the attack was under way.

Dorcas galloped furiously into the valley, and her voice rang through the still air as she called, "Neeilll McNeeilll!" Her weapon flew from her hand and whirled in the air, then hit the ground to bounce harmlessly across the earth, scattering clods of grass and dirt in its wake before coming to a halt. Dorcas reined in sharply, making her horse rear. He pawed the air for a moment, then as his front legs hit the ground she stared up at the enemy and yelled in a clear voice, "I yield."

Neil stared in disbelief at the lone figure sitting regally astride her horse in the middle of the battlefield. The last thing he imagined was that Dorcas McMahon would say those words. Too stunned to do anything else, he merely gaped down at her.

Cedric eyed his son for a moment. When it appeared that Neil would not repudiate the girl's words, he turned

his horse about and left the hill. One by one his men
followed suit.

Dorcas seemed unaware of what was happening as she
continued to hold Neil's gaze. Tears streamed down her
face unheeded.

From the other hill, Duncan watched as Cedric McNeil
led his troops from the battlefield. He felt giddy with
excitement when he realized that no blood would be spilled
this day. His gaze shifted to his daughter as she sat staring
at the lone figure left on the far hill. Finally, Neil turned
his destrier and rode away, but Dorcas remained where
she was, as though turned to stone.

Sadness for his daughter suddenly washed over Duncan. She was willing to sacrifice herself for the good of her
people. He silently prayed for her safety, and hoped that
she would find some happiness in her decision.

Kevin turned to him. "Father?"

Duncan sighed. "Go get her," he replied, then wheeled
his horse around and left, his men following.

Kevin rode out onto the field, calling his sister's name.
She seemed not to hear as she continued to stare at the
now-empty rise. He sighed. Pride could be a terrible
thing, he thought. His heart ached for Dorcas, for he
knew what it had cost her to bend to McNeil's will. He
said a silent prayer for her as he reached for her reins to
lead her home.

Toward evening a messenger arrived from the McNeil
stating that the original bargain would be met. He wanted
to set up a time and place to sign the marriage contract.
Duncan sent the man back to his master telling him to
come in the morning if Cedric was agreeable and would
accept his hospitality once again.

After the man left, Duncan made his way to Dorcas's
chamber. He found her standing at the window, her arms
wrapped about her as if to ward off the cold, though it was

a warm summer night. She'd removed her chain mail, but still wore the linen tunic and short breeches of combat.

He walked over to her and touched her shoulder for she seemed not to know that he was in the room. She turned, and he noted the dullness of her eyes, as though she had given up and no longer held any hope.

He embraced her, and the tears behind Dorcas's burning eyes finally found release. "Are you ashamed that I am such a coward?" she asked brokenly.

"Oh, my sweet child," he murmured, "I am not ashamed of you. Never have I seen such a display of bold courage. To face an army of that magnitude all alone . . . I am proud to call you daughter."

She smiled shakily through her tears as she looked at her father. "And now I have committed myself. There is no turning back."

"Nay, you have the strength of the McMahons, and I place my confidence in you to honor our name."

She nodded resolutely.

"McNeil wants a signing of the marriage contract immediately," he continued. He caught the imperceptible tightening of her mouth and hurried on. "I told him it could be done on the morrow."

Defiance flashed in her eyes before being replaced by fear. McNeil was taking no chances. She was trapped, and knew that there was no escape.

After another sleepless night Dorcas arose with nerves stretched taut beyond endurance. She felt as though she were living in a bad dream, and she would eventually awaken to find herself safe and secure within the bosom of her family, and would laugh at her foolishness. But she knew this was real. Soon she would no longer be her own person. She would belong to someone else. A stranger.

Her lip curled in contempt at the thought of the Viking pig she was to marry. *Marry.* The word sounded so permanent, and her throat constricted as the image of the tall, dark stranger who was to become her husband filled her mind. Her heart beat faster as she imagined those cold blue eyes and stern mouth changing to the visage of a snarling wolf. She was not afraid of any man, yet that vision made her shiver. Instinctively, she knew Neil McNeil could be a dangerous man.

Her jittery nerves prevented her from doing anything right as she fumbled with her clothes and hair. Her maid, Enid, had long since scurried from the room after being thoroughly scolded by her mistress for her talkativeness. Dorcas dissolved into a fit of tears once more, both terrified of the unknown and angry at herself for succumbing to her feminine weakness. Only Heloise's timely arrival prevented further disaster as she took control of the situation to calm her daughter.

At last Dorcas entered the hall with dragging feet to face her retribution.

Neil was the first to spy her as, raising his goblet of mead to his lips, he happened to glance up. He put the goblet down slowly and stared at the beautiful woman standing nervously in the doorway.

Dorcas was dressed in a bright yellow kirtle. The edges of the sleeves and the hem were trimmed in gold bands. Gold braid highlighted the neckline and crisscrossed over her bosom to encircle her tiny waist. The hair at her temples was braided and intertwined with a fine gold chain from which two balls of gold hung. The rest of her hair fell in luxuriant red waves to her knees.

Neil arose as if hypnotized, and Cedric stopped talking as he eyed his son quizzically. All heads turned, then Duncan strode across the hall to take Dorcas's icy hand in his and lead her to the table.

Dorcas's heart pounded furiously. She was totally unnerved by the way Neil stared at her. She lowered her eyes and took the seat that her father pulled out for her, vexed because it was directly across from her future husband.

Neil continued to stare at Dorcas as he retook his seat. He found it inconceivable that only the day before she had been a wild creature ready to do battle. She looked the picture of lovely innocence as she sat with eyes downcast, a rosy blush creeping onto her face.

Too wrapped up in their own thoughts, neither one paid much attention as the terms of the contract were worked out—a contract that in essence would make them husband and wife as soon as it was signed. Only the formality of the ceremony itself remained to unite them forever.

Dorcas felt as though her privacy were being invaded and she fought down the urge to run from the room. She knew Neil was still staring at her, and tried desperately to keep from showing how terrified she really was. Why was he looking at her that way? She raised her eyes to glance at him and quickly lowered them again. His eyes were frighteningly cold, his mouth set in a hard line. He hated her. She could feel his animosity reach out to her, ready to crush her. Dear God, what was she getting into? She wanted to cry out that it was all a mistake. She did not mean it. She wanted to leave. But her feet wouldn't move and she didn't think she could find her voice even if she tried.

Neil wondered what game the witch was playing. So far he'd seen her spitting like a wildcat when cornered and brave enough to face an army all by herself. Somehow, he could not comprehend this new role of the sweet and demure maiden. Having witnessed her fiery temper and willful pride, he was sure of one thing. Dorcas McMahon was a woman who took what she wanted. She was far from innocent.

Dorcas's head jerked up as the conversation between Duncan and Cedric penetrated her senses. Cedric had just said he thought the marriage should take place immediately. Was her freedom to be snatched from her without delay? She had to stall, find more time to adjust to the situation.

She swallowed hard and said tentatively, "Nay."

Neil's mouth twisted in a grimace. Here it was, he thought, the time for her to go back on her word.

Duncan and Cedric turned to look at her in surprise, and Dorcas squirmed in her seat. "I—I mean, why so soon? Are we not allowed a period to become acquainted?"

Neil scowled at her and swore silently. Now the witch wanted him to court her! What was she up to?

Cedric raised his eyebrows. He should have remembered that women liked to-be wooed. Touched by the pleading look in her big green eyes, he grinned. "Of course, child. A fortnight . . ."

"Not longer?" asked Dorcas, panicking. "I know nothing of you, yet you would have me rush headlong into your lives. I need time to grow accustomed to my new life. Besides, I—I wish to have my twin here for the wedding."

Duncan frowned, realizing that his daughter was using every tactic she could to delay what lay ahead. "Dorcas, Angus may not be in a position to return," he said sternly.

She whirled on her father. "I could send a message to him. I could try. Please," she begged, looking from one man to the other.

Cedric coughed in embarrassment and reached out to pat the distraught girl's hand. "Of course you may send a message to your brother. All I ask is that you make haste in doing so."

Dorcas sighed in relief and nodded. She had a reprieve for a time.

She sent Harlan, one of her father's men, off to Brittany with her message for Angus's ears alone, knowing that the man was completely trustworthy and would follow her instructions to the letter. Then she sat back to wait.

In the days that followed, Heloise took command of her eldest daughter and insisted that Dorcas learn the rudiments of running a large household. Dorcas's mind reeled with all that her mother tried to teach her. It wasn't that she couldn't grasp it, she simply was not interested. More than once Heloise would be explaining something as they walked from building to building, only to turn around and find she was talking to thin air as her daughter stared off toward the training field. Then she would have to reprimand Dorcas sharply for not paying attention.

No matter how much encouragement she received, Dorcas felt incompetent. She studied her sisters while they worked without complaint and tried hard to copy them, but she felt so inferior. She was completely out of her element when it came to cleaning, or stitchery, or planning meals. She could feel comfortable only with a group of men to command or a weapon in her hands.

One afternoon she was relegated to the kitchen to learn the art of baking bread, after she'd spent a disastrous morning entangling the weaving loom. She knelt before a wooden trough on the floor, pounding and punching and slapping the dough in anger. The cook in charge shook her head and rolled her eyes heavenward as clouds of flour floated all around Dorcas. The girl was white from the top of her kerchiefed head to her knees.

Dorcas wiped the back of her hand across her cheek, worsening her already snowy appearance. She punched her fist into the dough furiously. Mayhaps McNeil should be told of her inabilities, she thought viciously. That way he would have the chance to escape from this farce that her father and his had planned for them.

Sitting back on her heels, she gazed at the lumpy blob with distaste. She wrinkled her nose and decided she would never make a good wife, for she could not get the hang of running a home. And she knew without a doubt that she would fail miserably in the role of a subservient mate. Thank goodness she'd not laid eyes on her intended these past two weeks since the contract had been signed. The last thing she needed was to contend with that loathsome creature.

A rich, deep chuckle filled the air, and she looked up

quickly. As though she'd conjured him up from her thoughts, Neil stood in the doorway. He bent his tall frame to pass under the lintel and walked toward her with a mocking smile curving his lips.

Her eyes shot sparks as she hurried to her feet. His grin deepened as his gaze slowly roamed the length of her, irritating her further. She gritted her teeth, and asked, "What do you find so funny?"

Neil shifted his gaze to her flashing eyes, the only evidence of color on her person. "Which are you planning to put in the oven, that mass you've been pounding so furiously for the last several minutes, or yourself?"

Dorcas glanced down at her apparel ruefully. For the first time she realized how she must look. Hot embarrassment flushed her as she snatched up an apron to wipe the flour off her face and hands. She glanced up to find Neil still grinning at her, which only infuriated her more.

With her nose in the air she marched past him and outside. She felt a swat on her backside and acted instinctively, whirling with an upraised fist. Neil quickly ducked as she swung at him, then grabbed her around the waist.

"Whoa, slow down," he said, laughing. "What did you do, sit in the flour?"

She gasped as he pulled her to him. "How dare you touch me!" she shrieked, struggling to break his hold.

He pinned her arms behind her. "It is my right to touch you, so you had best get used to it," he growled, scowling at her.

Fully aware of being pressed to the length of him, it was all Dorcas could do to keep from screaming as he held her locked to him. She trembled, out of fear of his strength, and out of rage at being unable to free herself. At last she stopped her struggles when she realized she was no match for him physically. Swallowing past the lump in her throat, she asked abruptly, "Why are you here?"

He grimaced and released her suddenly. "My father thought it was time I paid *court* to my intended."

Dorcas was quick to catch the reluctance in his voice. She snatched the kerchief from her head, and her hair tumbled down her back in disarray. Neil's eyes strayed to the mass of rich curls. The sun bounced off the glistening locks, making them shine like copper.

"Do not put yourself out on my account!" she snapped.

A small smile played at the corners of Neil's mouth. This was the woman he remembered—all fiery tempest. He shrugged. "I wouldn't want it said that I neglect my duties."

Dorcas's mouth compressed in a tight line. She turned and started to walk away, throwing over her shoulder, "I am sure you have other, more important duties to attend to. You may consider yourself released from this one."

Her arm was gripped from behind and Neil whirled her around to face him. "Are you saying that you are going back on your promise to my father?" he asked angrily.

She twisted her arm from his grasp and took a step back. "I said no such thing. I am a woman of honor and I will abide by my word. The bargain stands, though you are getting the worst of it, for I will not be a meek and obedient wife." She threw up her hands. "I will not even be able to run your home. Why you should want someone who does not want you, or why any other man should, for that matter, is beyond me."

"Believe me, it was not my idea," he retorted.

She stared at him in surprise. "Then why . . ."

"Because my father wishes it. Because our marriage will bring peace to our clans. Because," he added caustically, "you will bear my heir. I do not like this any better than you. You are hardly the woman I would have chosen to be my wife."

He did not want her either, Dorcas thought. Part of her was elated that he was as unhappy with the situation as she, while at the same time his words stung her.

"Well, at least we are of one accord," she shot back. "I

detest you as much as you seem to detest me." With that she ran back into the keep before he could stop her.

A scowl etched Neil's brow, and he swore under his breath as he watched her disappear through the door. What had he let himself in for? This whole mess could have been avoided if he'd only remained in Norway a little longer. He no longer had any control over his own life and he intended to make that little hellcat pay.

He swore again, realizing he'd not even had a chance to state the reason for his being here, and angrily went in search of Duncan.

4

Dorcas ran through the halls to her chamber. Tears fell unchecked down her face. She brushed them away angrily, muttering a few choice invectives under her breath. She had never cried so much in her life as she had these past weeks. It infuriated her that that man could reduce her to such impotent terror. If she weren't so afraid of the wrath of the entire Viking nation coming down upon their heads, she would stick a knife in his heart and be done with him. But she could not allow her family to suffer because of her.

She turned a corner and collided with something. Someone reached out to steady her, and through the blur of her tears she saw the smiling visage of her younger brother, Kevin.

"Where are you off to in such a hurry?" he asked, laughing. His smile faded as he saw her tear-stained face. "What is it, pet? What is wrong?" he asked with concern.

A fresh flood of tears overtook her, and Dorcas found it impossible to speak as Kevin guided her to his chamber. He kicked the door shut behind them, then he sat her down firmly in a chair and leaned over her.

"Dorcas, sweet, tell me what it is that troubles you so," he coaxed her.

She shook her head and between sobs tried to tell him. "You would not understand. No—no one understands!"

Kevin straightened and gazed at his sister. His lips curled in a wry smile. "What would I not understand? The helplessness you feel at being the chosen one? How you feel trapped by your situation, with no way out?"

Her tears stopped suddenly and she jerked her head up to stare at her brother, thinking he mocked her. But all she saw in his face was kindness . . . and sorrow.

"You do understand," she whispered.

"Aye, I do."

"Oh, Kevin, what a muddle! Why did that cur choose me? Why?"

Kevin shook his head. "I do not know. Mayhaps because you are not only beautiful, but proud as well. As proud as he." He shrugged and strolled over to the uncovered window. Staring out at nothing in particular, he murmured, "We all have our crosses to bear, pet."

Dorcas frowned, sensing he was thinking not only of her. "What cross do you bear, Kevin?"

He turned from the window and grinned engagingly at her. "We are not concerned with my problems, but with yours."

She arose and walked over to him. Touching his arm, she shook her head gravely. "Nay, Kevin. I am concerned for all those I love."

"How well I know," he said, covering her hand with his. "There is no one as fine or brave as you. When I think of the courage you showed, to put aside your own wants for the good of our people . . . It was a humbling lesson, Dorcas."

"But I do not understand. You are the one who has always given of yourself."

"Aye, me and my sanctimonious self-righteousness. But I chafe at the bit. Dreaming of the holy life and the good I can accomplish for others, and feeling sorry for myself because my dream of becoming a priest cannot be fulfilled."

A harsh laugh escaped Dorcas. "Oh, Kevin, I know that I have teased you unmercifully about your religious calling, but—" She stopped when she saw the pained expression on her brother's face. "You are serious." He made no reply, and she asked, "Does Father know?"

"I could not burden him. He has enough on his mind with worrying about you and Angus. Conan and Bevan are yet too young to show an inclination for war. That leaves only Hugh—and myself."

"It is just like you to put others first," she snapped. "You would make a fine priest. You must speak to Father."

"In time."

She shook her head in disgust. "Honestly, Kevin, sometimes you make me so angry."

He laughed and laid a gentle hand on her cheek. "At least I stopped you from worrying about your troubles for a little while."

"I am not really so worried as—as revolted and angry. I cannot change what must be for myself. Instead, I will handle it, somehow. But for you, your dream can be realized, Kevin. There is no reason why both of us have to suffer."

"As I said, mayhaps in time."

She kissed his cheek. "Thank you for confiding in me, dear brother," she said softly. Then she turned and left the room.

A frown etched her forehead as she made her way to the hall to seek out Duncan. She'd meant what she said about seeing her brother's dream come true. She had no idea if her father knew of Kevin's calling. If he did not, then it was time he learned of it.

She entered the hall but hesitated when she spied her father in the company of her betrothed. Her heart pounded a little harder as she gazed at his tall, muscular body. He was leaning casually against the fireplace, smiling at something Duncan said. The memory of being entrapped in those strong arms assailed her, and she suddenly felt hot. Her breathing came in short, uneven gasps as Neil looked up. Their eyes met and held, and without looking away from her, he murmured something to her father.

Duncan turned his head toward her and called out a greeting. "Come, daughter, join us."

She pulled her gaze away from Neil with difficulty, irritated that she was blushing so furiously. "I-I am sorry, father," she stammered. "I did not mean to intrude."

"Nonsense, child, 'tis no intrusion to greet your husband-to-be."

She pursed her lips and glanced at Neil. "I am not here to see *him*. It was you I wished to speak with . . . on a private matter."

"You can speak freely. After all, Neil will soon be a part of this family."

Neil pushed himself upright. "Mayhaps Lady Dorcas wishes to cancel our agreement. In which case, I will allow you to deal with her alone," he said smoothly, his eyes twinkling.

"This has nothing to do with you," she snapped angrily. "Stay then." She turned back to Duncan, dismissing her betrothed with a toss of her head. "Father, I wished to speak to you about Kevin." At Duncan's raised eyebrows, she plunged on. "He is most unhappy. He—he does not wish to pursue the life of a warrior, but rather that of a priest."

"What?" Duncan exclaimed, his face hardening.

"Please, Father, he has never said anything for fear that you would deny him. But I beg you, let Kevin go his own way. One of us should be allowed to try for happiness," she added. "You have Hugh and me. Soon Angus will return, and in a few more years Conan and Bevan will begin their training. What can one son matter? Please, father, let Kevin realize his ambitions. Let him know peace."

Duncan pondered his daughter's words. "Your mother mentioned . . ." he said. He suddenly looked up sharply and asked, "Why did Kevin not come to me himself?"

"With all you've had on your mind, he did not wish to burden you further. Don't you see, he is always placing others before himself. He is so kind and gentle. He would make a fine priest, father."

Duncan sighed, then said slowly, "I will speak to him."

Dorcas smiled, revealing the dimple in her left cheek, and bent to kiss him. "Thank you," she whispered.

He hugged her and chuckled. "That was not a yea, lass. I merely said I would speak to him."

Her eyes twinkled and her mouth was set in a smug line of satisfaction as she said, "I know."

Duncan laughed and shook his head, gazing at his daughter with resignation. "You always did know how to get around me. Now, show your intended out, my dear. And, Neil, tell your father we accept his most gracious invitation." He rose to clasp the young man's hand in farewell.

"We will look forward to your visit, Lord McMahon."

"Duncan. You must call me Duncan now."

"Duncan, we will see you in two days, then."

Dorcas was already walking from the hall, and Neil had to lengthen his strides to catch up. "What is happening in two days?" she asked as they stepped outside.

"My father wishes to have a feast honoring our betrothal. I came here to invite your family to the celebration."

"At McNeil Hall?" she asked, frowning.

"Aye."

"How can we be sure that we will not be set upon?"

His eyes narrowed with anger. "My father is not so dishonorable as that, and neither is yours. They want only peace, and will realize that goal once we are wed."

"There will never be peace between us, Viking!"

He shook his head, his anger fading. "You really are a termagant, you know. I wouldn't have thought you'd have any warmth for another in that cold heart of yours. I am surprised at what you did back there."

"Kevin is my brother," she said stiffly, "and I love him. I want to see him happy."

"You are modest. Not everyone would be so concerned for their sibling's welfare. You are very kind to think of him."

"And what of you, Viking," she sneered. "Do you not have love to show for your brothers and sisters?"

"Sister," he corrected her. "There are only two of us left. Two brothers and a sister died very young. Two others lived to manhood, but died on the battlefield. There is only Nissa and myself now. Aye, I suppose I love Nissa. I would not wish to see her unhappy. Her being a girl, I've never given it much thought."

Dorcas whirled on him. "In other words, women have no place in your heart. We are no more than slaves to bend to your will, unworthy of any regard."

"In certain areas," he drawled, grinning, "some women are highly regarded and are much in demand."

Her face reddened at the implication of his words. "You despicable pig. You slimy cur. You loathsome Viking."

"Someone should have taught you not to call people names," he said in an ominously low tone. "Didn't anyone ever tell you that it is impolite?"

She suddenly found herself crushed to the full male length of him. His mouth swept across hers roughly. When she started to protest, his tongue found its way past her teeth to invade the recesses of her mouth. She felt lightheaded and shockingly hot. She was aware of his arms, like iron bands, pinning her to him; of his chest, hard and unyielding, pressed against her breasts. Her heart pounded furiously, and she feared she would suffocate under the onslaught of his mouth and tongue. She was frightened. Frightened of what he would do to her, and frightened of her own reaction to him. His lips demanded everything from her, and she wondered what it would be like to give herself up to the delicious warmth flowing through her.

But she could not do it. She would not do it. He was her enemy. She would never submit willingly to this Viking pig. Never!

She made the growling sound of a provoked animal and went limp in his arms. His hold on her relaxed slightly, and she straightened suddenly, bringing her knee up between his legs. He grunted, releasing her so abruptly that she staggered backward.

She stood panting, her face suffused with color. "That should teach you, Viking, never to touch me again," she said shakily.

Neil stared at her through his pain, his cold blue eyes dark with anger. "Being touched is something you will have to get used to, bitch, for I will do more than *touch* you on our wedding night." His lips curled contemptuously. "So beware, wife. You will pay for this, I assure you."

Dorcas's eyes widened at his threat, then she whirled and ran inside the keep.

Neil watched her retreating back, then limped to his horse. A fleeting memory invaded his senses, of the sweet fragrance of wildflowers and of soft lips. He frowned, thinking of that mouth, so innocent, opening to him, beckoning him to taste of its honeyed sweetness. He swore under his breath as he turned his destrier for home. He was sure of one thing—Dorcas McMahon was no innocent maid. She could not have associated with warriors for so long and have remained pure.

"This is the most exciting thing that has happened in ever so long," Thalia said breathlessly. Her face flushed, she turned to her younger sister. Gwendolyn, too, was looking forward to the celebration at the McNeils. Both trepidation and excitement coursed through her veins as she asked enthusiastically, "Do you think there will be Vikings there?"

"Oh, aye," answered Thalia. "Father said that the McNeil is very eager to show his friends the prize his son will acquire to prove to them that peace can be obtained. There will be jongleurs, and acrobats, and all manner of entertainment. Why, there is even to be a contest of strength among the warriors."

Dorcas shifted to a more comfortable position upon her sidesaddle and glared at her sister. "Stop your prattle, Thalia," she said through gritted teeth.

"Hmph." Thalia tossed her head. "I should think you would be interested in seeing your new home."

Dorcas scowled. "I am not, so do not remind me again lest you find your saucy little derriere lying in the dirt."

Thalia stuck her nose in the air and replied airily, "Just because you are angry you have to ride like a lady for a change instead of charging into the McNeil stronghold in your silly warrior's garb is no reason to snap my head off."

"Why, you—"

"Girls," Heloise said sharply. "I would appreciate it if we could get through the next several days without hearing any squabbling between you." She glanced at Dorcas meaningfully. "I would like very much for our hosts to see that I have raised *ladies*, not savage beasts."

"Yea, mother," Thalia said meekly.

Heloise eyed her eldest daughter until Dorcas mumbled a reluctant reply, then she sighed. She would never understand her daughter's aversion to the idea of marriage, or her violent refusal to listen to an explanation of what happened between a man and a woman. She had been concerned about one of her daughters marrying the half Viking, yet she had never considered her eldest would be the one chosen as bride. After meeting her prospective son-by-marriage, though, she knew the choice was right. If only Dorcas would accept what must be.

Dorcas shifted again and grimaced. She chafed at wear-

ing a gown and having to ride sidesaddle. Thalia's pointing
that out so accurately did nothing to enhance her humor.
She had planned to ride as escort with the rest of her
father's warriors, but Duncan had forbidden her to don
her mail. Instead, he'd demanded that she dress in her
finery, stating that he expected her to conduct herself as a
maid should to make a good impression upon the McNeils
and their guests. She was not even allowed to participate
in the games of skill! Her lips tightened. She didn't care a
wit for what any of those Vikings thought. They could take
her as she was, or not at all. She wished fervently for the
latter.

The McNeil stronghold came into view, and Dorcas
surveyed it curiously in spite of herself. It was not unlike
her own home, with its high wooden wall enclosing thatched
cottages, pigsties, a mill, and the imposing keep. She was
surprised that it looked so well kept, then pursed her lips.
Of course, they were still at a distance. Mayhaps up close
it would prove filthy and unkempt.

As they passed through the gate, she looked about her.
She admitted grudgingly to herself that everything looked
in order. Well-fed, bright-eyed children watched them
pass from the doorways of the white cottages. The packed
earth around the homes was clean of refuse, and some
women sat in the sun in front of the cottages, spinning
wool. In the distance she could see men working in the
fields that stretched endlessly across the surrounding hills
and valleys. The McNeils were obviously prosperous.

She turned her attention to the wood keep, at least as
large as the McMahon's, and well built to withstand raids.
Surveying its facade, she noted the slits in the walls
where archers could hide. Were there any there today?
Her gaze fell to the main entrance, and she gasped. Neil
stood there with his arms crossed over his broad chest, his
eyes devoid of any emotion, watching her.

She halted her horse and stared back into those cold
sapphire eyes that gave nothing away. Her heart beat

faster as her gaze slowly raked over his powerful physique. She swallowed past the lump in her throat, and her tongue darted out to wet her dry lips as she raised her eyes to his once more.

Neil's mouth curved sardonically as he studied Dorcas in return. What was she thinking? She looked almost frightened of him. As well she should, he thought humorlessly. He had not been prepared for her faultless beauty and wondered irritably why it always surprised him so. Mayhaps because he knew her for the shrewish hellion she was.

Remembering his manners at last, he stepped forward, and Dorcas was struck by the pure animal strength of him. She could not tear her eyes from the muscles rippling beneath his tunic as he moved to her side, and she blushed, admiring his power.

Without a word he grasped her firmly about the waist and lifted her down, setting her on her feet. Her breath caught as he held her so naturally, as if this were an everyday occurrence.

"My lady, you surprise me yet again," he said mockingly.

She raised her finely arched eyebrows in question, and he continued. "I fully expected you to come riding in here in full battle dress."

One side of her mouth quirked upward. "I had every intention of doing so, but my plans were thwarted," she replied sweetly.

He chuckled, and placed her hand in the crook of his arm. "I believe you would have," he murmured. "Come, I will introduce you to my mother. She looks forward to meeting you." He shook his head in mock despair. "Though for the life of me, I cannot understand why."

She threw him a scathing look, ready to retort, when they stopped beside the four older people who were greeting one another. A petite blond woman who barely reached her husband's shoulder glanced at Neil, then turned her blue gaze on Dorcas, smiling slowly.

Dorcas regarded the woman just as intently as she was being studied. So this was the Viking chieftain's daughter. Dorcas didn't know what she'd expected, but it was not this friendly woman who smiled so pleasantly at her.

"May I present Lady Dorcas," Neil said. "My mother."

Dorcas inclined her head. "Lady McNeil."

The smile on Astrid's face widened, and she stepped forward to embrace her future daughter-by-marriage. Standing on tiptoe, she kissed Dorcas on both cheeks. Then she held her at arm's length to look at her. "Welcome to your new home, my dear," she said softly. "I hope that we will become great friends, and you must start by calling me Astrid."

Dorcas's mouth opened in surprise. She certainly had not expected to be greeted with such warmth. "Th-thank you," she stammered.

"Come," said Astrid, twining Dorcas's arm through her own. "Let me show you ladies to your quarters so that you may freshen up and rest." She turned to the two younger girls as they all strolled inside. "I hope that you and your sister will not mind sharing a room. I am afraid that with all the guests arriving, there simply was not space enough to put everyone in a single chamber."

Gwendolyn and Thalia assured their hostess that it was quite all right. Astrid led them up the staircase and along a winding corridor to Thalia and Gwendolyn's room. Then she, Dorcas, and Heloise continued farther until Astrid stopped at another door. She opened it and told Dorcas this was her room. At Dorcas's surprised look, Astrid smiled. "I thought you might like some privacy."

"Thank you," Dorcas said, amazed by the woman's consideration. Then she was left alone. Try as she might, she could find no fault with Neil's mother. She looked about the comfortable quarters, at the bed piled high with soft wool blankets, the beautifully carved chair, table, and cabinet, and knew at a glance all was in order. She wrinkled her nose and walked to the washbasin. Dipping a cloth into the cool water, she sponged her face and neck and resolved to make the best of her time here. Mayhaps it wouldn't be so bad after all, but then, she would have to reserve any definite opinion until later.

Dorcas sat at the banquet table looking about her curiously. They'd been at the McNeil's for two days, and in that time guests had poured endlessly into the stronghold, some staying in the keep but many pitching tents wherever they could find space, Viking and Irish alike. The festive atmosphere overrode any animosities between the clans, and everyone seemed content to put aside their differences in honor of the occasion.

The Vikings baffled Dorcas, for they were as ardent in their attentions to her as some of the Irish. She dismissed them all with a haughty air, but mused what would happen if she did flirt with some of them. Though she had no intention of doing so, she wondered peevishly if her betrothed would do anything. Neil seemed content to let her go her own way, as he did. This night was the first she'd seen of him since her arrival, except from a distance, and though he sat beside her, he treated her with an irritatingly polite indifference.

She picked at the food in her trencher, lost in her thoughts, when she was startled out of her reverie by a great crashing sound. She jerked her head up and her eyes grew wide at the sight of a brawny, barrel-chested Viking striding toward the head of the table. His face was marked with a scowl, and his lips were set in a tight line above the neatly trimmed blond beard.

"Is this how you treat your closest friend, Neil McNeil?" he asked with a sneer. The room became hushed as he stalked slowly around the table and stood over Neil. "I consider it an insult that the feast started without me."

"You were informed of the correct date," Neil said lazily. "I cannot be blamed if you couldn't sober up enough to be here on time."

Dorcas gasped and stared at Neil incredulously. Was he mad? He was deliberately baiting the fierce-looking man.

"Or, mayhaps," Neil went on, "you had trouble getting that old nag of yours up off the ground. You've spoiled unbearably that good piece of horseflesh I sold you."

Dorcas paled at the audacity of her intended. If the stranger felt insulted before, then he must feel twice so now.

A deep chuckle filled the air, and she turned to see the Viking wearing a grin. She blinked in disbelief. The whole scene had been an act, for she realized at last that the man wore no weapons.

He threw back his head and laughed as he pulled Neil from his chair, embracing him heartily. "Why is it that I can never rankle you?" he asked between chortles.

Neil grinned in return. "Because I have learned to take what comes out of that big mouth of yours with a grain of salt."

"You are indeed wise. Nor am I going to apologize for arriving late."

"At least tell me what delayed you."

"I have been enjoying the comforts of my brother's home these past weeks and have had much too much fun spoiling my new nephew."

Neil raised his eyebrows. His lips twitched as he struggled to keep a straight face. "I cannot picture you playing with a babe in arms."

His guest chuckled good-naturedly. "Nor could I until I met up with that little cherub. He is a fine, strapping fellow. Already as strong as an ox."

Neil laughed and shook his head. "If I did not know better, I would think you were the proud papa."

"Nay, I cannot claim that distinction, although I am beginning to wonder what I am missing. I see my brother's contentment, and you will soon know such happiness if you are lucky, and I have to wonder at my own luckless state. Wandering from wench to beautiful wench merely

to pass the time. Alas, that is a state I will have to carry on
alone, for soon you will be wed. Speaking of which, you
rogue, I have yet to meet your bride. Where is she?"

"Right behind you. May I present Lady Dorcas. This is
Erik the Bold of Wexford."

Erik turned and sucked in his breath. The last time he'd
seen her was on a battlefield and she'd been at a distance.
She was a fiery beauty, dressed in an emerald-green gown
that sparkled in the torchlight and set her eyes to gleaming. Her bright red hair was braided on either side and
pulled to the back of her head, intertwined with green
ribbon.

At last he found his voice. "By all the gods, I now see
that you could choose no other," he murmured. Taking
Dorcas's hand in his, he kissed it, his eyes never leaving
hers. She was the most luscious creature he had ever
seen.

Dorcas fidgeted uncomfortably under his scrutiny, noticing that her betrothed was frowning at his friend.

Neil knew Erik's reputation with the fairer sex and
made a mental note not to leave him alone with Dorcas.
As suddenly as the thought occurred, he chided himself.
What did he care for what his future wife did? The question nagged at him. He did care, but told himself it was
only because he did not wish her to dishonor him.

Erik continued to stare at Dorcas as he took his seat on
the other side of her, which served only to unnerve her
further. He leaned over and asked in a low voice, "Are
there any more like you at home?"

She laughed nervously, aware that Neil's eyes were on
them. "Yea, my lord," she answered clearly, "I have two
younger sisters. I will be happy to introduce them to
you."

"They could not be even half as lovely as you, for you
are beauty in its true form."

Her eyes narrowed at the implication that her sisters

were not pretty. "They are both quite beautiful, as well as kind and gentle," she said coolly.

Erik grinned. By Odin, the woman did have spirit. He wondered what she was like when really angry. He hoped that this wife of his friend would never have cause to turn her wrath on him, and sought to placate her by saying smoothly, "No doubt, with you for a sister."

He leaned across Dorcas to address his host jovially. "Neil, just for your lack of enthusiasm at my arrival, I expect to eat and drink heartily this night, and every night of my stay. And, I demand that you provide . . . ah, different amusement for me every evening."

"I am sure that that can be arranged," Neil said dryly. "Within reason, of course."

Erik chuckled as he raised his goblet in a salute to his friend. Was there a slight warning in Neil's words, he wondered. "Mayhaps you will join me."

Neil kept his face bland as he answered, "Mayhaps."

Dorcas eyed the two men in puzzlement, miffed that they seemed to share some private joke, then turned her attention to the acrobats performing for the guests.

5

Dorcas tossed and turned. She kicked the bedcovers away as if freeing herself of them would liberate her from the nightmare engulfing her, sucking her into the depths of terror. Whimpering with fear, she bolted upright. Her eyes stared wide and unseeing into the dusky gray light of the room. She shivered, recalling her vivid and horrible dream. What had it meant? Perplexed, she sat with her hands braced on the bed, taking deep breaths. She'd had some strange dreams in the past, but never one with the power of this one.

There had been Angus and the dark, swarthy visage of her cousin. Then Angus had been covered with blood. She frowned and shook her head as if to clear it. Nay. The man in the dream was Egan McNeil, and he was holding first Angus, then her. She shuddered, remembering how McNeil laughed demonically and thrust his severed hand into her face. Blood dripped in a steady stream from it and stained her gown. A faceless woman had appeared then in the dream and everything became drenched with blood.

Dorcas shuddered again. It had been hideous. Her heart constricted in fear. Was Angus lying dead even now? Nay, he could not be! What was she doing in the dream?

Always before, her dreams were of Angus alone. She'd never appeared in them. Was he coming home? Would he be in danger if he did come to Erin? With a tortured cry Dorcas leapt from the bed. Suddenly she felt as if she were suffocating. She couldn't stay inside. With shaking fingers she donned a russet gown and girdled it with a brass-festooned leather belt. She did not dress her hair, but merely ran her fingers through it to free it of tangles. Then she left the confining prison of her bedroom for the herb garden behind the main house.

She breathed deeply of the summer air in the quiet morning as she slipped silently down the path leading to the garden. The smell of mint and thyme and rosemary assailed her as she strolled past the neat little rows carefully tended by Astrid. The doubts and worries plaguing her seemed to subside with the clear morning air as she made her way to a bench at the far end of the garden. No one was going to bother her there. Mayhaps she could put things into perspective and make some sense of her nightmare now that she was once again calm.

Neil reached into the rosebushes and swore softly as thorns tore at his arm. At last his fingers found what they sought—a tiny, mewing kitten. It trembled with fright as he cupped his hands around it. Speaking in soothing tones and rubbing his thumb along the side of the kitten's head, Neil reassured the small animal.

He had been awakened from a sound sleep by a terrible crying, and had listened intently for the direction from which it came. He'd donned his breeches and left his room when he'd determined that the sound came from the rosebushes directly beneath his chamber window.

Neil smiled as the kitten purred and curled more comfortably into his hands. Chuckling softly, he said, "We'd best find a safe spot for you to rest from your ordeal and keep you out of mischief, little one. I do not intend to be your bed, for I plan to seek the comfort of my own once again."

Walking down the garden path while gently stroking the kitten, he glanced up and halted in his tracks. He was not alone. Someone was in the shadows. He moved forward quietly and discovered it was Dorcas sitting on a bench staring off into space.

She jolted out of her reverie when she realized she wasn't alone and gasped when she saw Neil.

"What are you doing here?" she whispered.

"I might ask the same of you," he retorted.

When she only shifted uneasily and clamped her mouth shut in mutinous silence, he added, "I was searching for a safe place out of mischief's way for this little one."

He held out his hands and Dorcas smiled at the surprising sight of the tiny white kitten. She reached out and Neil deposited it in her hands. It curled up in her lap and she grinned.

Neil watched her face, free of anger and distrust and hate, and was once again taken aback by her beauty. Dorcas caught him staring intently at her and fidgeted under his gaze.

He frowned, thinking that she looked guilty about something. Mayhaps he was thwarting her in an attempt at a rendezvous with a lover. The lines creasing his forehead deepened and his eyes narrowed in anger inspired by his supposition. "I did not mean to startle you."

Dorcas swallowed hard. Why was he looking at her that way? "I—I was not expecting to see anyone about this early," she stammered.

"Anyone? Or just me?"

She stared at him, puzzled. "What do you mean?"

"You've made a striking impression on every man here. Another woman might be carried away by all the attention and allow herself to agree to an assignation in, say, the garden."

Dorcas gasped and her eyes flashed angrily. "I am not *any* woman. I could not sleep, so I decided to come out here. If I am not allowed the freedom to roam where I will, then I shall leave." She scooped the kitten into her hands and stood up.

Neil grasped her arm as she made to walk past, but she shook his hand away and turned on him furiously. "I do not know why you should be so worried about what I do. You yourself told me that you were as unhappy with our situation as I. The only reason I will honor the bargain between our fathers is to protect my people. Hear me well, Viking, there will be no softening in my heart for you, just as I know you will have none for me. What I do is *my* business. You believe whatever you like. I do not care," she said contemptuously, then whirled and fled.

Neil swore softly as he watched her retreat. What had come over him? He hadn't meant to attack her, but it seemed that every time he was near the witch, he just couldn't help himself. She always managed to bring out the worst in him. He yearned to go back in time to the peaceful presence of his sweet, demure Anika. It appeared that he would never again enjoy her gentle ways.

Dorcas stood with her back pressed against the door of her chamber, her eyes squeezed tightly shut. She took a couple of deep breaths to still her pounding heart and raised the tiny kitten to her cheek to brush its soft fur over her skin. Oh, why was she singled out to be tormented so? Wasn't it bad enough that she had to suffer the cruelties of these Vikings without having to contend as well with the strange visions in her nightmare? The confrontation with Neil had made her forget for the moment what was plaguing her most. She had to see Duncan. Surely once she told her father of her nightmare, he could not deny her. She would go to Angus. Her face a study in determination, she resolutely left the bedchamber.

Dorcas sat in the box beside Astrid, watching the contests of arms waged by the warriors. Her mother sat on the other side of Astrid, and the two women conversed quietly and clapped politely at the skills displayed on the field. But Dorcas acknowledged nothing and no one. She was still fuming over the encounter with her father earlier that morning. When she'd presented her arguments to him, Duncan hadn't budged in his adamant refusal to allow her to go to her twin, stating that she could hardly run off to a foreign land in so short a time before her wedding. When Dorcas had exploded angrily, saying that the wedding could be postponed, Duncan had become furious. There would be no more delays. Whether Angus returned in time or not, the marriage would take place on schedule, in one month.

Now Dorcas sat, her mouth a tight line, her eyes a fathomless green as she stared sightlessly at the activities around her. She didn't even see Kevin approach until he spoke softly to her.

"Dorcas, Hugh and I need your help. We've no one to lay out our arms properly so that we will have easy access to them, and we were wondering if you would do it. I know it is a poor second to participating in the games, but we'd really appreciate your help."

"I thought Conan and Bevan were going to do it," she said.

Kevin grinned. "So did we, but the little mischief makers cannot be found."

"Oh, dear," exclaimed Heloise, "if those imps are making trouble again, I will make sure they can't sit for days."

Kevin laughed at the consternation on his mother's face. "No doubt they are, but we haven't time to find them. If misfortune greets them, then they probably will deserve it." He turned back to his sister and asked, "Will you?"

Dorcas's forehead puckered in a frown. "Father—" she began, but Kevin cut her off.

"Gave his permission."

Dorcas turned to Heloise and Astrid and asked, "Will you excuse me?"

Astrid smiled warmly. "You must not keep your brothers waiting. It would not do to hold up the games. Besides, you must do everything in your power to see that they win a prize."

Dorcas couldn't keep the smile from her lips as she thanked Neil's mother, and arose. Outside of her mother, Astrid was the kindest person she'd ever known. She wondered how the woman could have given birth to such a crude and surly brute as her son, Neil.

As she crossed the field to her brothers' tent, Hugh rushed forward to greet her. "Thank goodness you've come to help."

Of all her brothers, Hugh was the most like their father. Warm and generous when the mood struck him, which was most of the time, or blustering about the little things that did not go his way. But Hugh was also the only one of her siblings Dorcas would never cross in anger. No one equaled the fury that emanated from Hugh when he was aroused. But now there was only relief on his face at the sight of her, and she couldn't help smiling. "Where are our little brothers?" she asked teasingly.

"Who knows. Stirring up trouble, I imagine. Come. We have a mess inside and I am entered in the next event. I must find my battle-ax." He put an arm around his sister and led her into the tent.

Dorcas separated the weapons and stood ready with the arms needed for each event for her brothers. Being involved even in this small way made her come alive. She avidly watched the different contests, cheering her brothers on as they competed with the battle-ax—which they both lost to the Vikings, who were more expert in the sport—to spear throwing, and to sparring with swords. Hugh won that last event. Once, she turned her head and found Neil looking at her. The smile left her face as they

stared at each other for a moment, before Dorcas tossed
her head, shouting her brothers on to victory even harder.

When the judges made their final decision, declaring
Hugh the winner of the contest of swords against Erik the
Bold, she whooped with joy and threw herself into her
brother's arms, kissing him soundly. They strolled back to
the tent arm in arm. Neil stood in front of his own tent,
which was next to theirs, watching as they approached.
He sauntered over to them and held out his hand to
Hugh. "May I congratulate you on your victory."

Hugh looked down at the hand extended to him for a
moment before clasping it. "Thank you," he said coolly.

"I, too, offer my hand," came a booming voice from
behind him. Hugh turned to see Erik striding toward
them, grinning in a friendly fashion. The corners of his
mouth turned upward as he accepted Erik's hand, murmuring his thanks once again. His respect rose a notch for
the little man who had waged a hard-fought battle, and
who could so graciously accept defeat.

"I hope," Erik said, laughing, "that you and I will never
have cause to meet on a field of battle, Hugh McMahon,
for you are a worthy opponent." He turned to Dorcas.
"Did you have to show such an enthusiastic display at your
brother's victory?" he asked wryly, and was rewarded by
the stain of color in her cheeks as she lowered her eyes.

Hugh laughed and place an arm about Dorcas. "My
sister stands firm in her loyalties."

Erik glanced at Hugh, then back at the girl standing
shyly before him. "Indeed, it is rare when a woman shows
such devotion. I admire that. But then, the more I learn
of this particular young woman, the more I find to regard
highly."

Dorcas glanced nervously at Erik as he devoured her
with his eyes, aware that Neil watched with a disapprov-
ing frown. She thought irritably that he had no right to
look so fierce. After all, he did not want her. Looking

away, she gasped at the sight that greeted her on the field. Regan Fitzgerald, a distant cousin-by-marriage, was creating havoc among the horses and riders lining up for the race. His mount bucked and reared and pranced wildly about, jostling Regan's hefty posterior precariously in the saddle and stirring the other animals to frenzy. Dorcas wondered if the beast had suddenly gone mad. Poor Regan. As she watched his corpulent frame bounce about in uncontrolled abandon, she had to bite her lip to keep her laughter from erupting outright. Poor Regan? She felt more sympathy for his horse each time Regan landed with a thud on its back.

Her gaze strayed past the commotion on the field when she spied a movement behind one of the tents. "Oh, no," she murmured, drawing Kevin's attention. He looked questioningly at his sister, then in the direction she stared, and sucked in his breath. As one, brother and sister looked at each other and exclaimed, "Conan and Bevan!"

Neil had seen the havoc on the field and started running toward the madly plunging horse.

"Jump, man, jump," he shouted. Whether Fitzgerald heard him or not, Neil didn't know. Just as he reached the man, Regan went flying through the air, arms and legs flailing about. Before Neil could move out of the way, the man landed right on top of him, knocking the wind from him.

Neil tried desperately to get some much-needed air back into his lungs, and finally managed to utter through gritted teeth, "Get off me."

Laughter filled the air around them as Regan Fitzgerald was pulled off him and Neil was helped to his feet.

"Thank you, my boy," wheezed Regan. "I cannot imagine what happened."

He clapped Neil on the back, and Neil winced as pain shot through his shoulder. He took a step toward the now-quiet horse, feeling as though his whole left side was broken.

"It would appear that your beast ran amok and will have to be put out of his misery."

"I do not think that will be necessary," Dorcas interrupted grimly.

Neil turned and saw her with a hand clamped firmly upon the arm of each of her little brothers. She shoved them in front of her. "Well?" she demanded of the now-subdued boys, for when she'd snuck up on their hiding place, they were rolling on the ground, holding their aching sides from too much laughter.

Being the elder, Conan swallowed hard and stammered, "We—we did not mean for—for anyone to ge-get hurt."

"What do you mean?" Neil asked, frowning.

"I believe this is what they mean," Kevin said, holding out his hand to show the cockleburs he'd retrieved from underneath the saddle.

"This could have been serious," Neil said quietly.

"You are quite right," Regan blustered, turning purple with rage. "I could have been killed!"

Dorcas glanced at her cousin. That was something she doubted, for the man was endowed with enough natural padding to keep from being seriously harmed. As Regan berated the boys, his voice rising with fury, she grew apprehensive. Where was her father? Why didn't Neil put a stop to her cousin's ranting? Why didn't Hugh or Kevin step in? When Regan pulled out his whip she became alarmed and decided to take matters into her own hands.

Grabbing the whip from the man, she whirled to face her little brothers. Tears brimmed at the corners of their wide, frightened eyes.

"You've been taught never to mistreat an animal so," she said, cracking the whip on the ground. "Apparently the lessons have gone unheeded. Therefore, you will see what it is like to be abused at another's hands." She advanced on the frightened boys, then heard a gasp behind her. Someone grabbed her arm before she could bring the whip down.

"Cousin, wait!" cried Regan. "Surely you do not mean to beat them here and now?"

Dorcas turned to look at him with surprise. "Were you not going to carry out their punishment?"

"Nay. Th-that is, I only meant to scare them. I—I would never actually beat them."

"They deserve it," she snapped.

"Nay. It was merely a prank. All boys like to play tricks," Regan explained, laughing nervously at the murderous glare in Dorcas's eyes.

"Nevertheless, I shall teach—"

"Come, come, my dear," Regan interrupted. He placed his other arm about her shoulder and led her off the field, away from the crowd that had gathered. "You must not be so harsh. After all, I remember you as a child and some of the tricks you pulled. Now, come, we will let Duncan deal with your brothers. I am sure he will find a suitable punishment for them. You needn't worry, for I've not been hurt."

As the two boys sighed with relief, Neil stared in astonishment at the grins on Kevin's and Hugh's faces. "You may consider yourselves lucky that Dorcas stepped in to save you," Kevin said wryly to his young brothers, "but you still have to face Father. I would suggest that you try to stay out of trouble for the rest of the day. Now, off with you."

"But Dorcas was going to beat them," said Neil, perplexed.

"Nay," Hugh said. "She would never harm them. Cousin Regan's bluster is usually much worse than anything he might actually do. But when he's enraged he can lose control, even though he hates to see anyone suffer at another's hand. What she did was to play on his sympathies so he would not thoughtlessly beat them himself. We would not wish to go to war with a member of our own family over such a small incident, and that might have happened, for the right to punish one of our own belongs only to us."

Neil's gaze strayed to where Dorcas and her cousin stood talking. He saw Fitzgerald throw back his head and laugh at something she said. Would he ever understand these people who protected one another so fiercely from outsiders? As suddenly as the thought occurred, he chided himself for it. It did not matter. He had only to wed the witch. He did not have to understand her.

The race finally got under way after all the excitement. Dorcas stood on the sidelines, wishing she could have participated. When Kevin took the lead, she forgot all the lessons on ladylike demeanor that Heloise had tried to drum into her head, and yelled at the top of her lungs in her enthusiasm. But then she groaned with dismay as Neil pushed his mount forward the few remaining yards to the finish line. She held her breath as his horse drew abreast of Kevin's, and just as they reached the finish line, Neil surged ahead in victory.

Silent, Dorcas watched as Neil rode around the field waving in triumph to the cheering crowd. He looked like a strutting cock, she thought nastily. He stopped before his father and leaned down to receive the garland of flowers Cedric held out to him. The winner of the horse race was to bestow the garland on his favorite lady. Her heart beat a little faster as she wondered what Neil would do with it. Kevin had promised it to her if he won, in appreciation for all her help. She had caught the double meaning, for Kevin was not only grateful for her assistance at the games, but for her part in making his dream of the holy life come true.

True to his word, Duncan had spoken to his son shortly after Dorcas pleaded her brother's case to him. In another month, right after the wedding, Kevin would be leaving for the monastery and the life he wanted.

Her breath caught when Neil turned to stare at her. She returned his bold look steadily, though her heart hammered. He trotted over to the box where Astrid and Heloise sat. He handed the garland to his mother, and Dorcas could see him speak to her. Then she saw Neil scowl when Astrid answered him, and knew his mother was chastising him for not giving the garland to her instead.

Dorcas raised her head proudly and, ignoring the curious stares turned her way, whirled and walked away. She told herself it did not matter. Why should he bestow the prize on her? They meant nothing to each other. Nothing.

She stopped walking when she saw Erik ahead of her. He was practicing with a bow and arrow for the next competition. She studied his form for a moment. If he continued to hold the bow that way, he would never come close to the bull's-eye. She glanced at the target. As she'd thought, arrows dangled from its outer edge and lay on the ground. Worse, he could easily injure himself.

She approached him on silent feet and called out a greeting, making him jump. Her heart almost stopped when he whirled and pointed the arrow at her chest. She let out her breath in a sigh of relief when he lowered the weapon and smiled at her.

"I am sorry," he apologized when he saw the look in her eyes and her pale face. "I'm afraid you caught me unawares. I did not mean to frighten you."

She smiled. "It is obvious you know little of the art of the bow and arrow, sir, else you would know to point it at the ground when others are near." She laughed when he cast her a sheepish glance. "I forgive you, for I am partly to blame for sneaking up on you. Why should you wish to enter a competition for an activity about which you know so little?"

He grinned good-naturedly. "Foolish pride, I fear. Your Irish neighbors have participated in all of the games, showing their good sportsmanship, even at those not to their liking. I admire their spirit and I do not want it said that the Vikings are afraid to try something which they do not excel at. Alas, I much prefer my trusty sword to this particular weapon." He motioned toward the target. "Would you mind if I practiced?"

"Pray, continue."

She watched him struggle with the bow for a few moments, then said, "Keep your arm straight and level with your eyes."

He glanced at her in surprise before complying with her instructions. The arrow whistled through the air and hit its mark in an outer circle of the target.

"Aha!" he exclaimed excitedly. "I thank you for your advice."

She smiled and nodded at the target. "Now try again."

Erik readied the bow once more and let another arrow fly. It landed to the far left of the target. Two more arrows hit at the top and the bottom, and another strayed too far right and landed in the ground. He looked at her with exasperation. "Why can I not get a direct hit?"

"It takes practice. You are doing very well." She took the bow from him and readied an arrow.

"Why should you help me?" he asked curiously.

She shrugged. "I do not know. For a Viking, you seem exceptionally nice."

Erik studied the beautiful young woman. He'd watched the scene a little while earlier and had seen Dorcas leave the field when Neil flagrantly ignored her. He was baffled by his friend's apparent aversion to this lovely creature.

Dorcas let the arrow fly and it hit the line immediately to the left of the bull's-eye. His mouth dropped open in surprise as another arrow, and another, and another landed in a little circle around the small dot in the center of the target. Once again she readied the weapon, and this arrow struck the middle of the bull's-eye.

Erik gazed at her with amazement. Neil and Cedric had tried to tell him that this was no ordinary woman. She knew how to handle weapons expertly. His admiration for her grew. She knew how to handle herself, all right, and she was beautiful as well.

"Not all of us are fools," he said. "If you were mine—"

"But she is not," interrupted a cold voice.

Erik and Dorcas both jumped at the intrusion and whirled around. Neil sauntered toward them like a cat ready to spring, his eyes an icy blue.

"She is mine," he said with unquestionable certainty.

Erik's face suffused with color. "As what? Your slave? Your actions have proved that you do not care about her."

"It matters not *what*. She belongs to me."

Dorcas's temper rose quickly as she stepped forward to face Neil. "I *belong* to no one but myself, Viking," she said in a low, angry voice. "You will rue the day you chose me to wed, for I intend to make your life miserable. Do not ever make the mistake again of thinking that you own me. If you do, it may be your last thought."

Neil calmly took the bow from her and, without answering, shot an arrow at the target. It landed in the middle of the bull's-eye, shattering the arrow already there. Then he turned and looked her up and down disdainfully. "Do not ever underestimate me or try to play me for a fool, my dear, or you may regret it."

With high spots of color dotting her cheeks, Dorcas whirled and stalked away from the two men.

Erik turned on his friend. "You are the fool, Neil, for you have a treasure that should be cherished and all you want to do is break the girl's spirit."

"I do not want this!" Neil cried. "I do not want her!"

Erik shook his head in disbelief. "How could you not want such beauty, and virture, and courage? By all the gods, man, what do you want?"

"Anika."

"What?"

"I love another. Her name is Anika. Her grandfather, Siegfried, and mine were boyhood friends. She is the most beautiful, gentle lady I know," he said softly, lost in a sweet memory.

"She cannot hold a candle to Dorcas," scoffed Erik.

"You do not know her. She is pure and gentle, so small and delicate. Unlike that termagant I am forced to wed. Aye, Dorcas is a beautiful woman, but a hellion. I yearn for the softness of a woman's arms, and a peaceful existence. I cannot have that with that firebrand I am to marry, a woman with no womanly traits."

Erik shook his head. Neil was a bigger fool than he'd thought. "Dorcas is real. She is here and will soon be your wife. Anika is far away. You should forget her and try to make Dorcas happy."

"I seriously doubt that Dorcas will ever be happy," Neil muttered. "She lacks the temperament of a soothing and gentle nature. She is wild and untamable."

"You are blind, Neil. She is more precious than gold, and if she were mine I would treasure her all my days."

"Well, she is not yours," Neil said, his voice low with warning. "I am forced to do my father's bidding in order to attain peace. I do not like it, but I will stand by the bargain. So do not tell me how to treat my *wife* again, for it is none of your concern." He started to walk away, then turned back. "And keep away from her, 'friend.' I will not have my name dishonored because you are enamored of Dorcas. Mayhaps she has fooled you, but I know the cat has claws. I have a score to settle with that witch, and believe me, I will."

Frowning, Erik watched Neil walk away. If Dorcas meant nothing to Neil, then why did his warning sound like that of a jealous lover? He swore under his breath. Of all the women in the world that could have stolen Neil's heart, why did it have to be Anika Thornstein? He only hoped that his friend would come to his senses before it was too late. More important, he hoped Dorcas would not lose her beautiful spirit. Erik was worried, for Neil was strong and determined. Mayhaps he would break that girl in the end. She might be a match for Neil, but if she wasn't . . . He hated to think what would happen.

Dorcas watched Neil stalk past her where she stood behind a nearby tent. Dear God, what had her father's good intentions got her into? Neil truly hated her. He loved another. Anger flashed through her at the thought. Yes, he loved another, yet he was going to keep her tied to him as his prisoner. Her lips curled in a snarl. Neil McNeil was in for a rude awakening if he thought she would be cowed by his threats. She was her own woman, and it was time he learned that.

6

"I tell you, Fitzgerald, I've never before seen such handling of the reins. How you managed to remain atop your mount, I will never know. An excellent display. Excellent," Cedric declared.

Regan Fitzgerald preened at his host's words and at the murmured agreement of those gathered around them. "If it had not been for this young man's bravery, however, I might not be here now," he stated, heartily clapping Neil on the back.

Neil gave Regan a stiff smile before saying, "It was nothing, Lord Fitzgerald. I am glad that things turned out so well."

"So am I, my boy. So am I," replied Regan.

Neil's smile remained pasted on his face. Fitzgerald may have come out of the incident unscathed, but he was sore from crown to toe. He'd managed to finish the games, just. A soak in a tub of hot water had helped little to ease his aching muscles.

"I hate to think," said Regan, "what would have happened to those boys if I'd not stepped in when I did. Sometimes Lady Dorcas can be so intractable, it makes me shudder. I only hope that she will mellow when she has her own children." He winked, making the others laugh and Neil frown. "By the way, my boy, where is she?"

"I really do not know," Neil said coolly.

Erik eyed his friend, thinking that Neil not only did not know, but also did not care. It would serve him right if Dorcas were stolen from under his nose, for he did not deserve such a prize.

Dorcas sat before the polished brass brushing her long tresses to a brilliant sheen. Her bright eyes shone with determination as she carefully placed the copper combs in her hair. She arose and studied her wavery reflection. The dark green gown embroidered with gold thread in an intricate design of doves set off her emerald eyes to perfection. A thin smile touched her lips. Satisfied, she whirled and left her chamber.

The hall was filled with lights and laughter and music. Dorcas stood in the doorway surveying the room, when she was suddenly surrounded by men. She smiled at their efforts to attract and please her and laughed softly at their flattery. Aware of being watched, she looked around. Neil was scrutinizing her while frowning in disapproval. With a toss of her head she turned her attention to a calf-eyed youth on her right, making the young man blush. Her tinkling laughter filled the air when he paid her a compliment.

"My—my lady, there will be dancing this evening," stammered another of her swains. "Will you be so kind as to honor me when the time comes?"

"When the time comes, Lady Dorcas will be much occupied," a cold voice announced. Neil scowled down at the young man and reached for Dorcas's hand.

Her eyes snapped angrily as she forced a smile to her lips. Neil sucked in his breath when he felt her nails dig into his palm. She turned to face the young man, who wore a crestfallen look and said sweetly, "The first dance belongs to my betrothed, but after that . . ." She let the sentence trail off and lowered her eyes. When she looked up again her admirer was wearing a silly grin.

Without saying anything, Neil jerked on her arm, pulling her close to his side. "Come, my dear," he purred, "let us sup. You know that I cannot bear to have you away from me."

She glared at him as he led her away. "Everyone here knows that is a lie!"

"Do they?" he asked, cocking his brow. "Do not be so sure. As far as most are concerned, I am your loving and devoted servant."

"But you and I know differently. In truth, it is your Anika who holds your heart," she answered softly.

He stopped in his tracks. "How do you know of her?" He turned angry. "By what right do you speak her name?" he asked, gripping Dorcas's arms tightly. "Do not do so again, for she is purity and gentleness and I will not have you soil her name. Do you understand me?"

"And I am to be your wife!" she retorted hotly.

"Aye, you are, and I will not have you dishonor my name by your wanton conduct."

Her mouth dropped open at his remark. She broke free of his hold and laughed harshly. "I do not have to dishonor your name, sire. You do that yourself." Then she whirled and strode to the table, where she was helped into her chair by Erik.

"A lovers' quarrel?" he questioned.

"Hardly that, Viking," she replied tightlipped, to which Erik chuckled good-naturedly.

Neil seated himself on her right, but she ignored him, turning to Erik and flashing him a brilliant smile. She laughed and talked with a gaiety she did not feel, aware of the seething tension within the silent Neil. Erik soon became caught up in the heady experience of having the beautiful Dorcas's complete attention and forgot about his friend's earlier warning. The scowls thrown his way went unheeded as a charming Dorcas flirted outrageously with him.

Cedric watched the young people from his position at the head of the table. With growing amusement he observed Dorcas resting her hand on the little Viking's arm, actually bringing a blush to Erik's face. He noted his son's face was just as red, but from boiling anger at the inability to control his future wife without creating a scene.

"It would appear that I was wrong after all, McMahon," he said, leaning toward Duncan. "I once said that your daughter held no womanly traits to my knowledge. She is very much a woman, and I now have no doubt but what she could charm the very birds from the trees."

Duncan, too, had been watching the young people, but with growing trepidation. Eyes riveted to his daughter, he sighed deeply. "I fear Dorcas plays a dangerous game. Mayhaps one that could mean war."

The smile on Cedric's face widened. "She would love that, wouldn't she? But nay, my friend, you and I will not let that happen." He turned to look at a scowling Duncan. "We are too close to peace to let anything come in the way of it. I fear my son has a fierce pride in what he believes to be his 'possession,' and he will not tolerate the stain of dishonor on his name."

Duncan turned his head quickly to stare at Cedric. "Dorcas's actions are sometimes rash, but she would never dishonor herself or your son. Furthermore, I would never place her in a position where she might come to harm."

Cedric smiled reassuringly and shook his head. "Have no fear. She is safe enough. I will see to it. Besides, I think that my son's feelings run deeper for that girl than even he is willing to admit."

The dancing began and Dorcas watched other couples take the floor. She gritted her teeth when Neil made no move to rise and finally turned to him. "I promised you the first dance."

He studied her coolly before replying, "I fear that I am

unable to comply, madam. Fitzgerald did more damage to my person than I thought possible, therefore, we may only watch the dancing."

Dorcas smiled tightly and stood up. Staring haughtily down at Neil, she said, "That is just an excuse to keep me at your side. You were quite able to finish the games today after the accident, therefore, *you* will have to watch. I am going to dance. Erik, would you—"

Her words ceased as Neil sprang to his feet. "By all the gods, woman, you go too far!"

Dorcas felt a flicker of fear race through her. She shrank away from the thunderous expression on his face. The hall became hushed as heads turned in their direction. Dorcas found her courage and stared Neil in the eye as she said clearly, "I see no reason why I cannot enjoy myself. This is my feast also, and I wish to dance."

Neil's face darkened with rage, and he took a threatening step forward. "Even after I've stated my reasons for not doing so, you would throw convention aside and go your own way after I've asked you not to?" he asked in a menacing tone.

"You did not ask! You demanded!" she shouted.

A slow smile parted his lips. "Then we shall make my 'demands,' as you call them, permanent. As my wife you will not dare to disobey me. There will be no more delays. The wedding will take place immediately."

She gasped. Her face went white. "Nay," she whispered.

Neil spun around to where his father and Duncan stood. "The guests are all assembled. I demand the hand of your daughter in marriage, Lord Duncan. Now! If it is not done, there will be no wedding, and no peace."

"Neil!" Cedric shouted in order to be heard above the babble of the shocked guests.

"Those are my terms. Now, or not at all."

Dorcas rushed forward. "Nay, father, you cannot do this." She whirled on Neil, her face a mask of fury. "You promised to wait until Angus returned. You promised!"

"I am just a low Viking whose promise means nothing, remember?" he taunted her.

She snatched an eating knife from the table and lunged toward him. He grabbed her arm in a viselike grip and they grappled until he was able to disarm her. "You are mine, and what is mine, I keep," he said in a low voice so only she could hear. "Now every man here knows it." Suddenly his mouth swooped down to claim hers in a savage kiss. She fought fiercely to escape him, but was helpless in his fierce embrace.

She was unaware of the ribald comments and laughter from those in the hall. Just the two of them existed in their own world as her knees grew weak. The only thing that kept her upright was Neil's tight hold on her. Suddenly he released her and she staggered backward. His deep blue eyes stared into hers with a strangely mesmerizing effect. Slowly, she heard the laughter of the guests, then her father's voice.

" 'Twould appear we'd best get these youngsters wed on the instant."

Dorcas shook her head in numb disbelief. A sob escaped her as she ran from the hall.

Dorcas reached the safety of her chamber, bolted the door, and began to pace. How could this be happening? She had been so certain that if she showed Neil he meant as little to her as she did to him, he would let her go her own way. How could things have gone so wrong? A cry of anger escaped her as she picked up a pottery vase off the dresser and flung it across the room. It shattered into tiny fragments that slid down the wall, landing with a tinkling sound on the bare floor. Then she threw herself on the bed to cry out her rage and misery.

Neil lay fully clothed on his bed with his hands locked behind his head. He turned his face toward the wall at the sound of something breaking in the next chamber and heard muffled sobs. He looked back up at the ceiling and scowled.

Damnation, but he'd been angry! He kept telling himself over and over that he had done only what he had had to do. He had to teach that witch not to toy with him. She deserved to be as unhappy as he. How dare she threaten him! He would bring her to heel if it was the last thing he did. He would show her a sorry fate if she trifled with him again.

He would not tolerate other men laughing with her, touching her. He felt blind rage at the thought of another man embracing his woman. No, he thought, she was not an innocent. His first assessment had been correct: she was a wild temptress.

He remembered her lips yielding to his, her body molding to his. Mayhaps it was her plan to work her charms on him the way she had every other man who'd crossed her path.

Neil swore softly and vowed she would not shame him. Dorcas was his, and no one would ever take her away from him. Before he was through, she would know that and would never again question his rights over her. He fell into a restless sleep, dreaming of a long-legged, red-haired vixen who teased and tormented him, beckoning him onward but staying just out of his reach.

7

Dorcas stood next to Neil, numb with the shock of her wedding day. The ruby-red color of her gown only emphasized her chalky pallor, but Heloise had brought the dress to her chamber early that morning, saying Astrid requested that Dorcas wear it—for good luck. Dorcas had thrown the gown into a corner in a fit of anger, refusing to put it on. But when her mother had berated her harshly for her childish behavior, she'd meekly gotten dressed. She'd never before seen her mother so angry.

Now Neil led her through the pagan ceremony of the Vikings as one leads a sleepwalker. She wished she might cry out against the foreign ritual, but she could not find her voice. Besides, her father had warned her against doing such a thing, so she drank the contents of the chalace that Neil handed to her, knowing that it was the bridal mead, and watched as the sign of the cross was made over them with a replica of Thor's hammer. It was a sham. She was not married.

At last it was over and Neil led a pale, shaking Dorcas forward to greet their guests.

When her father leaned over to kiss her on both cheeks, Dorcas snapped out of her dreamlike state and pushed him aside. With eyes blazing, she pointed a finger at Duncan and said in an accusing voice, "This is a farce. I deny what has taken place here today as illegal."

"Our marriage is very much legal under Viking law," said Neil with a frown.

She turned on him. "But I am not a Viking. Under the laws of my people we are not man and wife."

"What matters how you are wed as long as a ceremony takes place and there are witnesses?" Cedric asked irritably.

"It matters greatly, for I am a Christian. By the laws of my church, I am not married."

Duncan motioned to Kevin, and when his son reached his side, whispered something to him. Kevin nodded and left the hall.

"We are married," Neil said fiercely.

Dorcas raised her head proudly and eyed him smugly as a murmur of doubt went through the crowd of Irish guests.

"Ahem. We can debate this in private, my child," Duncan interrupted, placing an arm around the newlyweds. Leading them away, he hissed, "Now, stop this nonsense, daughter."

A slight smile touched Dorcas's lips as she replied triumphantly, "It is not nonsense, father. I challenge you, or anyone else, for that matter, who has been brought up in the Christian faith to call this marriage legal."

"What is the meaning of this?" Cedric demanded. "What game are you playing?"

"I play no games. We are not married," she stated, then began to walk away rapidly.

Neil started after her, his face a mask of fury, but Duncan placed a restraining hand on his arm. "Have no fear, son, before the day is out, your marriage will be secure."

Dorcas approached her mother and Astrid. She'd been waiting for Neil to explode or to pursue her, and when he didn't, she felt giddy with victory.

Heloise pursed her lips as her daughter approached and eyed her disapprovingly. "Dorcas, how could you?"

"You know I am right, mother."

"Nay, you are not. You—"

"Heloise," Astrid interrupted. She turned twinkling eyes on her new daughter. "Dorcas must be admired for her strong beliefs."

"Beliefs, hah! She is just being stubborn."

Astrid's tinkling laugh filled the air. "That may be true, but she does have a point," she said, drawing startled looks from both women. "Our ways must seem very strange to you, my dear, and I can understand. However, I assure you the marriage ceremony that just took place is as binding as yours. You are one of us now, and I want you to know that I welcome you as my own daughter."

"Nay, I will never be a Viking."

"No one is asking you to become what you are not. I wish only for you to accept us as your family now."

"You do not understand. No one understands. Neil does not want me, nor do I want him. We have been forced against our wills into a situation that we both deplore. He—" Dorcas clamped her mouth shut hurriedly. She'd almost blurted out that he loved another. Instead, she said, "He hates me. He will try to harm me. I know he will."

"Oh, my sweet child," exclaimed Astrid, "he will not harm you. You are his wife now. He will seek only to protect you."

"I am not his wife. I am not!" Dorcas burst out. Then she wheeled and ran from the hall.

Heloise and Astrid exchanged puzzled looks. They'd both seen the terror in her eyes. With grim determination marking her features, Astrid strode toward her son. Taking Neil by the arm and turning him around to face her, she demanded, "What did you say to your bride?"

Neil stared uncomprehendingly at his mother. "What?"

"Have you threatened that child?"

"Have I . . . Where on earth did you get such a notion?" he asked in surprise.

"You must have said something to her to frighten her so."

Neil laughed derisively. "Dorcas? Frightened? That shewolf is not afraid of any . . ." The sentence trailed off when he saw the looks on the two women's faces. "What did she tell you?" he asked warily.

"She is under the impression that you will somehow harm her," Astrid said. "I warn you, Neil, if you hurt my new daughter in any way, I will have your father string you up." She turned on her heel and left him with his mouth agape.

Neil had never before seen his mother so angry, and was just as astounded as Duncan and Heloise by her outburst. He turned questioning eyes to his father and found Cedric staring at him narrowly.

"I did not threaten her!" he cried defensively, as though he were a boy being unjustly accused of some misdemeanor. He looked at Heloise, who stared back, her face unreadable, and swore soundly. Then he, too, left the hall.

Dorcas jumped at the insistent pounding on her door, and asked shakily, "Who is it?" She received no answer other than more loud banging. Irritated, she crossed the room and slid back the bolt. The door was pushed open, and she gasped when Neil forced his way into the room. He kicked the door shut behind him and stood glaring at her.

"What did you say to my mother?" he demanded, advancing on her.

"N-nothing."

He grabbed her by the shoulders and shook her. "You said something, for I've just received a tongue-lashing, for what I do not know. I am tired of your stirring up trouble."

Dorcas's eyes widened as she tried to picture Neil's tiny

mother giving him a setdown. She broke away and laughed harshly. "I merely told her what I told you. We are not married."

He stalked her slowly, growling, "We *are* married, and it is time that you learned to obey your husband."

"Ahem."

Neil stopped in his tracks and whirled at the intrusion. Duncan stood in the doorway, his hand covering his smile. Ah, the impetuosity of youth. They couldn't even wait until after the feast, he thought. He coughed again to keep from laughing, and said dryly, "You have guests that are awaiting your presence."

Neil's face darkened in fury. He'd be damned if he'd let anyone stand in the way of his meting out some much-needed punishment to his wife. "You interrupt me when I would chastise my wife?"

Duncan drew himself up to his full height. The smile left his face as he realized what Neil's true intentions were, and he retorted, "She is my daughter, and if I felt that she were being mistreated, I would not hesitate to see that the laws of my people protected her. Remember, she is allowed certain rights of her own under Irish law." When Duncan saw the look of amazement cross Neil's face, he said more softly, "At the moment she does not feel that she is married." He moved forward to place a gentle hand on his new son's shoulder. "Please, return to the hall and wait for us there."

With a scathing look thrown at his wife, Neil stalked from the chamber. Then Duncan turned to eye his daughter sternly. He sighed at the defiant glare she graced him with and shook his head. "Dorcas, why must you fight against what you cannot change? We struck a bargain that must be kept."

"*I* did not," she shot back, whirling away.

"Yea, you did!" shouted Duncan, losing his temper. "As much as I. You agreed. Will you dishonor our name by going back on your word? I cannot believe that of you.

You are made of sterner stuff than that," he ended more softly.

Dorcas flew to her father, seeking comfort in his strong arms. "I am so frightened."

He held her close and ran a hand lovingly down her red curls. "Oh, my child, there is nothing to fear. Neil is not a monster. He is your husband now, and will take care of you."

"It was all so strange."

Duncan smiled wryly and held Dorcas away from him. "That is what I came to tell you. I sent Kevin for Father Francis. He will marry you again to put your mind at ease."

Dorcas's heart constricted with fear at her father's words. She was thwarted once again.

"Come, show the Vikings your courage and make me proud to call you daughter," Duncan said, holding out his arm for her.

Once again Dorcas found herself beside Neil as they knelt in front of Father Francis to repeat the vows that would unite them forever. And once again she felt as though she were in a bad dream from which she would awaken soon to find herself safe and secure in her own bed.

Dorcas went through the rest of the day as one in a daze. She barely heard the felicitations of the many guests, and when Erik squeezed her hand reassuringly and murmured his best wishes, she turned to stare blankly at him.

Alarmed by her pallor, he said in a low voice, "Dorcas, you have nothing to fear. For all his fierceness, Neil will not harm you."

She made no reply, but turned to stare wide-eyed at the large man beside her who was in deep conversation with one of the guests. Her husband. She could no longer dispute that fact, for they'd not only been married once, but twice. They were now bound for all time. She shuddered as Neil took her arm and led her to the table.

Dorcas could only nibble at the food in her trencher. Her green eyes were bright with fear as they stared unseeingly out of her white face. She answered automatically any questions put to her, but otherwise remained silent. Neil watched her out of the corner of his eye. He could smell the fear within her. This was yet another side of Dorcas that confounded him, as her moods always did. He sat calmly listening to the ribald comments thrown at them from his friends, but was unable to find them amusing. The only one who did not join in the jesting was Erik, and Neil wondered at the quiet mood that had overtaken his friend.

As the hoot of laughter filled the air after one particularly coarse joke, Neil felt Dorcas stiffen and almost jump from her chair. Her face was bleached of all color and he knew instinctively that she couldn't take much more. He motioned to his mother, and when Astrid joined him, whispered something to her. She nodded, then led an unprotesting Dorcas from the hall.

Dorcas was limp as wet straw while Astrid, her mother, and her sisters readied her for bed. She accepted their ministrations uninterestedly as they undressed her and pulled back the covers. Heloise pushed her down on the bed and placed the covers over her, then bent to kiss her on the forehead.

"Everything will be fine, my sweet," she said reassuringly.

Her stomach tied in knots, Dorcas glanced around her strange surroundings. She closed her eyes to block out the nightmare that was happening to her, but quickly opened them when she was assailed by her long-ago vision. Her throat constricted in fear and her heart thudded painfully. Was she to have the same fate at the Viking's hands as the maid who'd been raped. Neil was her enemy—a Viking. He could use her as he saw fit, and there was no one to stop him.

As the women started to leave the room, Dorcas stared at her mother's back accusingly. The sound of male laughter could be heard coming nearer and nearer. The door opened and Neil was shoved into the chamber ahead of his friends.

One of the men looked expectantly toward the bed, only to find that Dorcas was already in it with the covers pulled up to her chin. He declared loudly that it wasn't fair for her to conceal herself from them.

Neil turned in time to see Dorcas wince. He'd forgotten all about the custom of the bride having to prove herself unblemished before witnesses. His mouth tightened in a grim line of displeasure at the thought of Dorcas baring herself before their guests. He took in her sickly pallor and her wide, frightened eyes, and quickly came to a decision. He muttered something to his guests, then firmly ushered them from the room.

Neil walked to the table to pour himself some mead. He took a sip, then set the cup down and shrugged out of the short mantle he wore over a voluminous linen tunic. He removed the tunic and tossed it over a chair before picking up the cup once more. What was wrong with him? He had had countless women; why was he acting like a lad about to take his first woman? Cursing silently at the case of nerves that had overtaken him, he eyed his wife speculatively.

Dorcas sat staring straight ahead, twisting the covers she held protectively about her. Neil was suddenly unsure of himself as he watched her, and decided that her behavior was what made him so uneasy. He could not understand her hatred of him, for he was sure that was what she displayed. She had no reason to fear him so. He'd been on the receiving end of the hellion's claws and could not believe she actually feared him. It mattered not. She was his wife and now belonged to him. It was time she learned that lesson. A slow smile played about his lips. He would show her.

He sat down on the edge of the bed to remove his boots and Dorcas was up in a trice. He turned and sucked in his breath at the sight of her naked splendor. Her red hair fell about her in luxurious waves, covering her breasts. He caught sight of a long, shapely leg and swallowed hard, eager to know her other charms intimately. His eyes traveled upward over her milky-white shoulders. He knew that her skin would be as soft as rose petals. His eyes met hers, staring back at him like two dark pools in her ashen face, and he frowned. "What are you doing?" he asked in a hoarse whisper.

Her voice shook as she answered, "Do not touch me."

Neil blinked in disbelief. "Do not be ridiculous. You are my wife. It is my right to touch you."

"If you touch me, I will kill you."

He turned his back on her and sighed. "When will you learn that you are mine to do with what I will?"

As he stood up to pour some more mead, Dorcas scurried to the dresser by the door and grabbed the sword that lay on top.

"Here, you need something to calm—" He stopped at the sight that greeted him as he turned and held out the cup to her.

Naked, she held the sword in both hands high above her head.

"I swear that I will kill you if you lay one finger on me," she warned him in a hoarse whisper.

He found her so funny that he burst out laughing. "Do you know how silly you look?" he asked, gasping for air.

An overpowering rage swept through Dorcas. Nothing could wound her pride more than being laughed at. She would lay odds that she'd killed as many men in battle as the pompous jackass in front of her! She lunged forward.

Neil neatly sidestepped, sticking out his foot as she came toward him. Dorcas felt herself falling, and landed with a thud on the bare floor, knocking the wind from her. The whole front of her smarted from the hard contact with the wood. Neil's foot slammed down on the sword that she refused to let out of her grasp. She felt herself being yanked up by her hair, and cried out in pain as she was flung on the bed.

Neil's chest heaved as he glared down at her in thunderous fury. Never taking his eyes off his frightened wife, he untied his breeches as he spoke. "It is time that you learned who is your master." He let the breeches drop to the floor. "There will be no pain, as you well know, so I do not see what it is that you fear. Nor do I care how much you hate me. Tonight you will be my true wife. Afterward I do not care what you do."

Dorcas's gaze flew downward. Dear God, the nightmare she'd witnessed so long ago was happening to her! Panicky, she tried to scramble to the other side of the bed, but found herself pulled back by Neil. He held her about the waist. She turned on him like a wild animal caught in a trap—biting, kicking, scratching. Her sharp nails dug into his shoulder, raking the skin away and drawing blood. He swore soundly as her teeth sank into his upper arm, making him jerk back.

With a low growl Neil pinned her arms above her head and fell on top of her. Dorcas arched upward, thinking to buck him off. Her eyes grew wide, and she cried out in pain as that alien part of him drove inside her. Neil groaned, and his mouth swooped down to cover hers in a brutal assault. She bit his lower lip, drawing blood. He jerked his head back, and drove into her again and again. She suddenly felt drained of all energy. She lay complacently beneath him, whimpering in shame and agony at each piercing thrust. Neil was beyond reason as he was overtaken with the need for release. Dorcas felt him stiffen and shudder, then he was still.

He rolled away and lay panting. With the slowing of his pulse, his anger subsided, and suddenly the horrible realization of what he'd just done hit him. He felt a movement beside him as a sob escaped Dorcas, and she curled up in a ball with her back to him. He leaned up on an elbow, ready to apologize for his actions, but stopped when he saw the bed. Struck dumb, he stared at the proof of his wife's virginity.

How could it be? She was a fiery, tempestuous savage, and far older than a woman should be for the marriage bed. He'd been sure that she had known men, for she was constantly in the company of warriors, and her flirtatiousness the past several days only gave credence to his belief that she was not chaste. Now he knew the reason for the fear he'd felt emanating from her. And truly, she had reason to hate him from this night on. . . .

He gingerly placed his hand on her shoulder, only to have her whimper like a wounded animal and shrink away. He pulled back as though he'd been burned. What was he to do now? Could he explain? Nay, he could not. He was sickened by what he had done. There was no excuse for it other than his accursed temper, and that was no excuse at all. Neil lay awake for most of the night wondering how to repair the damage that he'd done on this, his wedding night, and just as the gray light of dawn crept into the room, he arose and dressed. Then he left the chamber quietly so as not to awaken his bride, knowing he had to release the heavy burden of guilt shrouding him.

8

_____

Dorcas awoke a short time later and lay very still. She eyed her surroundings, the events of the previous night sharp in her mind. She turned her head slowly and breathed a great sigh of relief when she found she was alone.

She started to sit up, but winced as her body cried out in pain. Moaning at the effort it took to move, she finally pushed herself up and gasped when her eye caught the stained linens. Her heart beat faster at the sight of her own blood. She'd thought for certain that she was being torn asunder. It was just as she'd known it would be, with one exception. She still lived.

She closed her eyes, the vision of long ago coming to her. When she opened them again, she was frowning. She had been sure that she would die at Neil's hands and had never been so terrified. Another thought struck her. Mayhaps Neil would try to kill her yet. Her eyes darkened in fury. If he thought she would meekly allow it, he was sadly mistaken. He was her enemy, a hated Viking. She was a McMahon. Her father had instilled a deep sense of pride in her. She would never give in.

She'd been right in thinking that the experience between a man and a woman was a repulsive, disgusting, hurtful act. She would kill Neil McNeil before she let him touch her again.

Her thoughts were interrupted when someone rapped on the door. Dorcas hurriedly pulled the covers back over her and called, "Come in."

Heloise entered the room and regarded her daughter speculatively for a moment before sitting on the edge of the bed. "Are you all right, Dorcas?" she asked quietly.

Dorcas's eyes stared back like shards of dark green stone. She lifted her chin proudly and answered, "Yea, Mother."

Heloise sighed and grasped her daughter's hand. "I wish I could help you. If only you would have let me explain—"

"It would not have mattered," Dorcas interrupted, "for the deed was much worse than anything you might have told me. If I had truly known of the way of a man and woman, I would have let the Vikings kill me on the battlefield."

"Oh, Dorcas, it does not have to be so. Love can be—should be—a beautiful thing."

"Love! There is no love! He is an animal. It was ugly, so very painful. He tried to kill me!" At the shocked look on her mother's face, Dorcas rushed on. "Aye, he did. He drew blood."

"My sweet," she murmured soothingly, "a woman always bleeds the first time, and there is pain. It is the way of such things. Now you are truly a woman. The next time—"

"Nay!" cried Dorcas vehemently. "There will be no next time."

"Neil is not a monster! He is your husband and has the right to take you at will," Heloise said sharply. "He will not harm you, child, for he knows that he would have all of the McMahons to deal with if he did so. Your father has worked hard for this peace, no matter how tenuous. You must try to help him, and all of us, by being a good and obedient wife. It is for you to make your marriage what you will, Dorcas. You must find your own way. Now come, a nice warm wash will make you feel much better."

Long after her mother had gone, Dorcas sat in the great wooden tub mulling over Heloise's words. Aye, through luckless fate she'd become a part of the bargain between her father and Cedric, but she was still Dorcas. A warrior, a McMahon. Her father would not have to come to her aid. If Neil ever touched her again, she would deal with him herself. She wished fervently that she could go back in time, and that her "husband" would simply vanish into thin air. She felt no different now from the way she had two days before except that her body had been defiled by a stranger who'd put his claim on her, and she had not died as she surely thought she would. She vowed that she would not change. Not for McNeil. Not for anyone.

She sat before the polished metal, wrapped in a robe, brushing her long hair to a fiery sheen after she'd climbed from the tub, when there was a timid knock at the door. Dorcas smiled warmly as Gwendolyn entered the chamber, happy to see her favorite sister.

"Mother said that you were up and about. The ladies are gathering in the hall with their embroidery."

"And I suppose Mother expects me to join them," Dorcas retorted. "She knows how much I hate to sew. My stitches are never straight."

"That is only because you hurry so."

"Well, I cannot think of a less worthwhile occupation with which to pass my time," Dorcas grumbled.

Gwen turned away so that her sister could not see her smile. "Aye, I know that you have no patience for such things. The only thing that makes you comfortable is riding free as the wind across the land on that gray steed of yours, or wielding a weapon against your enemy."

Dorcas's scowl disappeared, and she smiled in spite of herself at Gwendolyn's teasing.

"That is why I felt you might have need of these," Gwen added, tossing a parcel on the bed.

Dorcas looked questioningly at her sister before unwrapping the package. She let out a squeal of delight upon discovering her linen tunic and breeches, and her sandals.

Gwen smiled at the happiness that shone on Dorcas's face. "I overheard Father telling Kevin to go home for Father Francis, and I asked him to bring these things also. I know how much you hate being penned in, how unhappy you've been. You can feel free only when you're able to ride with the wind at your back. I—I thought these clothes might help."

Dorcas stopped her loving inspection of her belongings and looked up. Gwen was smiling, and Dorcas thought that she'd never loved her sister more than at this moment. She threw her arms around Gwen and hugged her tightly.

"You are so thoughtful," she whispered. She held Gwendolyn at arm's length and smiled broadly. "And I shall use your gift immediately."

Gwendolyn frowned at Dorcas's enthusiasm. "Dearest, you have guests. Besides, the men are going hunting this morning."

"Aye, and so shall I," Dorcas answered, giggling as she donned her breeches and tunic. When Gwendolyn started to protest, she rushed on. "You know that I can hunt as well as any man here. Mayhaps, even better than some. I cannot conform to the ideas of most people about what I should be," she said, fastening the lacings of her sandals. "If I have to listen to one more word from Lady Maud on the *proper* behavior of young women, or of the *proper* ways to run a home, or of the *proper* ways to raise children, I shall go mad. I can no longer bear to sit about listening to silly gossip and idle chatter about mundane topics. I am a McMahon. A warrior. And I intend to remain as I am," she finished firmly, standing up.

"But—" Gwen never got a chance to complete the

thought as Dorcas headed for the door. Gwen rushed after her, ready to try to talk her out of rash action. Catching up with her, she said breathlessly, "Mother will be very distressed if you do not join the ladies, and Father—"

"Will have nothing to say in the matter," Dorcas finished. "I am now a married woman, remember?"

"But your husband . . ."

"Will have nothing to say either. After my introduction into 'marriage' last night, I've been thinking, and I have come to some very interesting conclusions. No one can change what I am, Gwen." Her eyes narrowed. "And no one had better try."

"Well, well. The last time I laid eyes upon the vision before me was on a battlefield, where I thought an alluring sorceress had come to tempt me."

Both women jumped and turned startled faces to Erik as he approached. His eyes traveled over Dorcas appreciatively and he grinned at her. "Are you ready to do battle again, my lady?" he asked.

"Only against a boar," Dorcas said, smiling.

"Indeed, and did you plan to instigate a little hunting party of your own with the other ladies?"

"Nay, Viking, I will be joining you."

"But, Dorcas, you cannot," broke in Gwendolyn. "It is one thing to go hunting with your family, but it is quite another when—when you are a—a guest of—the McNeil," she stammered, catching Erik's eyes on her. She had never spoken so boldly in the presence of a stranger. Gwen didn't know quite what to make of this Viking. He was fierce, as his behavior over the last days attested. Short and stocky, he was nevertheless powerfully built, and she had no doubt that he could take care of himself very well—and all those who crossed him. Yet he was also friendly, to Viking and Irishman alike, with a quick smile and an easy charm. His blond good looks stood out next to her own dark features, and she blushed furiously under his scrutiny.

Dorcas watched her sister, and caught Gwen's downcast gaze at the bold look Erik graced her with. Amusement shone in her eyes. "You've not yet met my sister. May I present Gwendolyn. Gwen, this is Erik of Wexford, better known as Erik the Bold."

Erik stepped hesitantly toward Gwendolyn, afraid to move too close for fear she would flee, yet wanting to be nearer to her. "You were right, Dorcas," he said, "your sister is very lovely. Mayhaps you would care to join Dorcas in her venture?" he asked hopefully.

Gwendolyn let out the breath she hadn't realized she'd been holding as she replied. "Oh, I dare not. I—I am not so brave."

Erik studied her for a moment. Her raven hair shone almost blue in the sunlight. Her hazel eyes held his for just a moment before glancing quickly away. "My disappointment is acute, my lady, but I will look forward to my return most eagerly."

"There will be time later for such honeyed words, Viking," Dorcas broke in irritably. "Right now there is the business of the hunt. Are you coming?"

Erik dropped the dainty hand he lingered over. He smiled ruefully at Gwendolyn and shrugged, then hurried to catch up with Dorcas.

Most of the men were already mounted when she and Erik approached them. He squeezed her arm reassuringly, and in a low voice informed her that he would saddle her horse. Duncan was aghast at the sight of his daughter. "Dorcas! Why are you dressed like that? Where did you get those clothes?"

Dorcas shrugged. "They are mine, father, and I am joining you on the hunt."

"You're what? You'll do no such thing, young lady. This is Cedric's party, and I do not remember his extending an invitation to you."

"May I remind you that you no longer have the right to

order me about, Father," she replied calmly. "As everyone is so eager to point out, *I* am now a McNeil."

"Cedric?" Duncan looked helplessly at his host.

Cedric eyed his new daughter-by-marriage, unable to conceal the twinkle in his eye or the twitching of his lips, and shrugged. "She is not my wife."

Duncan turned to Neil, who stood staring blankly at Dorcas. She turned her head slowly and saw him watching her. Her own eyes burned in anger and she lifted her chin defiantly, waiting for his reaction.

"Let her come," he said quietly, turning his attention toward his horse once again.

Dorcas hadn't expected him to capitulate so easily, and she felt a heady sense of satisfaction.

Her hair billowing out behind her like a fiery cape, Dorcas spurred her horse across the field. Her face was lit with the joy she felt at being able to ride freely across the land, as though she were part of the wind and sky that she rejoiced in. She laughed gaily as she urged her mount to greater speed, feeling more than seeing a presence close beside her. Out of the corner of her eye she could see Neil gaining on her, and she raced ahead. She laughed. Not even he would dampen her enthusiasm. She would not let him.

About the same time that Hugh spotted a movement in some brush ahead of them, Dorcas saw it too. She rode furiously onward, keeping an eye on the area where their prey was hidden, knowing that her brother would ferret out the quarry from behind. Suddenly a boar came tearing through the bushes just ahead of Dorcas. She raised her spear, ignoring the wild pounding of her heart and her parched throat, and threw her weapon with all her might, hitting the animal in its side. Hugh's spear found the boar's other side, and another spear from Neil, who was right behind Dorcas, found its neck, bringing the squealing boar down, just as Selwyn, riding beside, threw his spear into its hind quarters.

Dorcas was off her horse instantly, running to the wounded, angry animal as it tried to struggle to its feet. Neil's heart leapt with fear as he watched his wife running wildly to where the boar thrashed about, afraid that the animal would make rise and gore her. He soon found that his fears were unfounded. She swiftly raised her sword and pierced the boar's jugular as it snorted and tried once more to make its escape. A throaty laugh escaped her as she placed a foot on the animal and pulled her sword out of its hide. Then she threw back her head and let out a piercing yell that echoed through the quiet air.

A shiver of fear crept down Selwyn's spine. Once before he'd heard such a cry, at the moment an enemy's sword had found its way into Neil's side. He glanced nervously at Neil, but his friend had eyes for no one other than the red-haired witch. Selwyn looked away quickly, for Neil's face bore traces of naked lust. He surveyed the other men, and found that Neil was not the only one who stared at Dorcas that way, but mingling with the lust in their eyes was admiration and fear.

Neil's breathing was hard as he continued to stare at Dorcas. He was torn between wanting to beat her for her rash act and wanting to make love to her. She stood proud and defiant in her triumph, her hair streaming down her back in luxuriant disarray. Her head was tilted back, and she wore a smile of victory on her bewitching mouth. She'd never looked more beautiful to him than she did now—like some wild creature born of the earth. Free. Untamed. And his. Their eyes met and held, and she tilted her head back farther, as if defying him to deny her the kill. He wondered if he would ever truly possess her, and his hands clenched into fists. She belonged to him! He suddenly felt the urge to carry her off, away from everyone. He wanted her. On the instant.

As though he were in a trance, his eyes locked with

hers, Neil moved forward. Before Dorcas could react, she felt herself being lifted up onto his horse. He turned his mount and galloped off with her to the ribald laughter and catcalls behind them. Dorcas struggled against the arm pinning her to him, but he only tightened his grip, cutting off her air as he continued into the hills.

She tried desperately to twist her head to look behind them. Surely they were being followed—by her father, Hugh, someone? Yet she heard no hoofbeats behind them.

As though reading her thoughts, Neil said dryly, "No one will come to your aid. You belong to me."

She gave him a look of pure hatred. "I belong to no one."

Neil's only answer was a wicked chuckle, making her shiver with anxiety. He finally stopped when they reached a copse of trees. She felt his hold on her loosen, and she used this chance to jump off the horse. But as she slid to the ground, Neil held her fast, jerking her arm painfully. Without releasing his hold on her, he dismounted and found himself fighting a wildcat as Dorcas kicked out at him and twisted away, screeching, "You have no right to do this! How dare you! What do you want?"

He ignored the throbbing pain in his shin as he stared at her. Nothing was going as he'd planned. Somehow he had to reach her, for he did not relish a battle with his wife every time he went near her. He held out his hands imploringly. "I do not want to fight with you."

"What do you want?" she asked again, backing away warily.

"I want you."

Her eyes grew wide with incredulity. "Nay," she said hoarsely.

"Dorcas, I will not hurt you. I give you my word."

"Your word," she spat out. "The word of a Viking cannot be trusted. You showed me that last night."

"Last night was a mistake. I—it should not have happened. It does not have to be that way. Let me show you."

"Nay, you will show me nothing," she cried. She backed away from him, but he followed. Panicked, she found herself trapped when she felt a tree at her back and Neil swiftly closed the distance between them, grabbing her arms. He pulled her to him, whispering huskily, "I did not mean to hurt you. Let me prove it to you."

Her answer was cut off as his mouth covered hers. She was prepared to fight him, but instead of brutally subduing her, his mouth was gentle and persuasive. His lips brushed back and forth across hers, tantalizing her, his breath soft and warm against her cheek. His hands loosened their grip on her arms to stroke up to her shoulders. One cupped her neck, caressing her. An unexpected heat flooded through her, and she unwittingly moaned. At that pleading sound, he pressed his mouth hard against hers, his tongue urging her lips to part. All will to struggle against him vanished as her limbs grew weak from the strange new sensations coursing through her. Her hands lifted of their own accord to grasp his head, holding him to her as her fingers combed through his thick hair.

His mouth traced a feathery pattern down her neck, then covered hers once more. His hands kneaded her back gently and she found herself both excited and frightened. She tried to command some semblance of order to her thoughts. This was not the same torture she'd experienced the previous night—this sweet, heady rapture engulfing her. What was the Viking trying to do to her? She struggled to keep her guard up, but lost the battle as Neil's hands parted her tunic and with gentle fingers he caressed her breasts, exciting the peaks. He could feel her heart pounding under his touch. Very slowly he removed her top to bare her to his gaze. His eyes darkened as he bent his head to tease the already taut peaks with his tongue, making her cry out. Her legs were shaking so badly that he laid her gently on the ground. He crooned to her, allaying her fears, all the while caressing her tenderly.

He undid the lacings of her sandals and removed them. His gentle hands and mouth played with every inch of her feet, legs, and thighs, setting her on fire. He slowly removed her breeches, then sucked in his breath at the sight of his wife's perfect form. With her long red hair spread about her, she indeed looked like a Valkyrie, part of the earth, and sky, and sea. He felt a fierce pride. She was his. He would be the one to tame the shewolf . . . while he showed her the exquisite pleasures possible between a man and his woman.

His mouth swept across hers in an intense kiss, then moved lower, tasting the sweet nectar of her. Dorcas moaned, no longer in control of her body or her mind, and no longer caring. She closed her eyes as fiery sensations coursed through her. Suddenly her limbs trembled as though the earth quaked beneath her. She cried out in wonder and joy as a feeling of wild rapture embraced her. Neil was speaking softly to her, continuing to caress her with his hands and lips, working his way upward over her body.

"How can this be?" she asked breathlessly.

He kissed her forehead and eyelids, and nose before answering. "This is the way it should always be." He brushed his lips lightly across hers, sending shivers of delight through her, and she could feel his shaft probing that sensitive area where only seconds earlier she'd experienced such ecstasy. She panicked and squirmed beneath him, trying to free herself.

Neil sensed her fright immediately and sought to calm her. "Dorcas, I need you. I promise you that it will not hurt."

"Nay, you tricked me. Why did it hurt last night, then?"

"Because I was angry and I did not know you were innocent. What did you feel a moment ago?" he asked softly. As he spoke, he moved sensuously over her, and in spite of herself, Dorcas felt a growing warmth spreading through her. He watched the play of emotions on her face and demanded, "Truthfully."

"Pleasure," she admitted grudgingly.

"Aye, and you will know more now," he said, panting as he lifted her to him and entered her easily. He groaned softly, reveling in the warmth of her.

Dorcas tensed when Neil slid into her, but as he began to move, she realized he was right. There was no pain, and she relaxed. Tiny licks of flame ignited within her, soaring upward as Neil worked his magic. She was no longer frightened, but wanted release from the sweet torture that burned inside her. Helplessly, she clung to him, her body arching up against his. Hotter and hotter the flames grew inside her, and she cried out to him, wordlessly asking him to ease the fierce tightness deep within her. He murmured her name, then his mouth fastened on hers as he grabbed her hips and thrust powerfully into her. She lost all control, consumed by the raging fires of passion. Her world exploded into a million tiny fragments, and she cried out her joy.

Dorcas lay exhausted, too weak to move, savoring the delicious feelings that swept through her. Slowly, she became aware of Neil laying on top of her, of his breathing as it slackened. She could feel the mingling of still-pounding hearts. He lightly kissed her temple and nuzzled her neck, sending a thrill of excitment through her. Laying a possessive hand on her breast, he lazily circled the peak with his thumb, rekindling a tantalizing warmth within her. A wave of unease washed over her as she wondered what had happened. Instead of being angry with her, he'd pleaded with her. Instead of hurting her, he'd filled her with a great desire for him. What was this power Neil had over her, that he could either hurt her at his will or make her bend to it so easily? She'd sworn vengeance against the Vikings, and yet she'd given herself willingly to her enemy.

A spark of anger coursed through her and she pushed

against Neil's chest, disturbing him. He raised up to look at her, all traces of animosity and distrust gone from his features. Smiling, he placed a hand on each side of her head and bent to kiss her. She held him off, demanding, "What did you do to me?"

He jerked his head back to look at her quizzically, then he laughed softly. "I've made a woman of you, my sweetling."

She gasped and struggled to get free. "I was a 'woman' a long time before I met up with you, Viking." She ceased her efforts when she realized she was no match for him physically, and scowled at him. He lay unconcernedly on top of her, grinning hugely, which only served to increase her wrath. She slapped his shoulder peevishly, an action as effective as a horse swatting a fly with its tail.

Neil laughed again, then his expression grew serious. His eyes darkened and he lowered his head slowly, saying, "Aye, and what a woman," before capturing her mouth with his.

All thought lost, Dorcas was aware only of his lips touching hers, demanding a response she was powerless to deny him; of his powerful arms encircling her; of his soft and gentle caresses. An unstoppable force drove through her as she was caught up once more by passion. Nothing and no one else mattered as Neil tutored her well in the art of love.

9

_____

It was dark when Neil and Dorcas rode into the McNeil stronghold. Laughter and music floated from the keep to greet them. Neil pulled up on the reins and shifted his weight to ease the burden of his sleeping bride from his chest. In sleep, Dorcas looked the picture of innocence.

Neil smiled. He'd been consumed with the need to possess her time and again this day. He told himself that he was only trying to assuage his guilt for what happened on their wedding night, but he knew that he'd unleashed a passion within himself and his wife for each other that was unquenchable. He also knew that he had never before experienced such overwhelming pleasure with any other woman . . . never even imagined his body and soul could know such rapture.

Sadness filled Neil's eyes for a moment as he gazed at Dorcas. He'd been determined to teach this little firebrand a lesson, but he now wondered if he'd been honest with himself. He'd thought that once he'd had her, his need for her would dissipate. Instead, he craved her body more than ever. The picture of Anika came to him, and he sighed resignedly. It was Anika he loved, though it was a tame emotion compared to what he felt for the vixen in his arms.

He ran the back of his hand across Dorcas's cheek and kissed her forehead. She mumbled unintelligibly and snuggled against him. He sucked in his breath at her unconscious movement, tempted to turn his horse around and ride away with her, but instead sighed and whispered her name.

Without raising her head from where it rested on his chest, she opened her eyes to look sleepily at him.

"We are home," he told her.

Dorcas straightened to look around her, and Neil set her on the ground. Without his warmth next to her, she suddenly felt cold and wrapped his cloak more firmly about her. She blinked the sleep from her eyes and looked up at Neil questioningly. She was so lovely in the moonlight that his breath caught.

"Aren't you coming?" she asked softly.

He smiled. "I must see to the destrier's needs first. I will be along in a moment."

Without offering an argument, Dorcas walked toward the keep. Neil watched until she'd disappeared inside, then with a muttered oath he turned his horse for the stables.

Dorcas stopped uncertainly when she reached the noisy hall. Gazing at the revelry around her, her peaceful mood now broken, she wanted to slip to her chamber and the quiet it afforded. It was not to be, for Erik spied her and shouted a greeting. "Aha, the bride cometh!"

Heads turned, and other greetings followed. Dorcas felt trapped at the center of attention. Coarse comments and laughter reached her ears. She blushed at some of the lewd remarks, both embarrassed and angered by them.

Gwendolyn rushed over to her, frowning with concern. "Are you all right? We were so worried when you did not return with the hunting party."

Erik laughed loudly as he came up behind her and

threw an arm drunkenly around Gwen's shoulder. "I told you there was no need for worry. I knew that no harm would befall them." He turned to Dorcas. "Brother Hugh wanted to ride after you and Neil, but we, eh, talked him out of it." He smiled broadly.

"It was not for fear of my sister," Hugh said, sauntering up behind them, "for I know well that Dorcas can take very good care of herself. I was worried for the Viking." He burst into laughter, leaning heavily on a Viking maiden's shoulder. He was in no better shape than his inebriated friend, Erik. Now they both stood, guffawing in abandon.

Dorcas looked from one to the other of them as they doubled over in hilarity. She could not see what was so funny and eyed the two men coldly. "You are indeed right, brother, I can take care of myself, and so can the Viking," she stated icily.

Her assertation only set them off again. "I am sure that Neil can," Erik said.

"It would appear so," Hugh chimed in. He raised his cup in a salute to Dorcas. "To the conquered," he toasted. He started to drink but stopped the cup halfway to his lips when he looked past his sister. He held out the cup and shouted, "To the conquerer!"

Neil stood in the doorway, watching the scene, his expression unreadable.

Dorcas was furious at her brother's words. She knocked the cup from his hand and ran from the hall. Upon reaching her chamber, she slammed the door shut behind her, throwing the bolt into place, and leaned against it. She opened her eyes and stared at the image of herself in the polished metal across the room. Hugh's words spun through her head. Conquered, conquered, conquered! She cried out in anguish and clapped her hands over her ears to block out the mocking sound. It was not true. She was not conquered. She would never be conquered. Never!

She jumped at a pounding on the door and whirled away to stand in the center of the room.

"Dorcas, unbolt this door!" came Neil's angry voice from the other side of her haven.

"Go away!"

The incessant banging became louder and louder, until the bolt gave way with a splintering crash and the door flew open.

"How dare you!" she shrieked, backing away, frightened by the furious expression on her husband's face.

"I dare, my lady, because you are my wife, and this is *my* chamber also."

"Then I shall leave," she said haughtily, drawing herself up. She started to walk past him, but he caught her arm and spun her around.

"Not until you tell me why you are so angry. I saw you speaking to Hugh and to Erik. What was that all about?"

"Nothing," she answered shortly, and found herself being shaken until her teeth rattled.

"Do not ever lie to me, Dorcas, or I will make you sorry that you did. What was that business about the conquered and the conquerer?"

She broke away and glared at her husband, her eyes shooting sparks. "They know what we did," she shouted. "They know! And because of it they think that you have tamed me, that I will be a meek and docile wife to you. They *think* that you have conquered me."

Through great effort Neil held himself in check when he wanted with all his heart to laugh. He dared not. He knew his proud wife, this wild creature, for what she was: untameable and, ultimately, unattainable. Yet he found himself torn by his own emotions. He loved gentle Anika yet he wanted this firebrand. He wanted to show Dorcas time and again that he was master of her passionate body. She could fight him if she wanted to, but, aware now of the fiery ecstasy she could share with him, he wondered if he could ever get his fill of her. He'd had a mere taste. He was intoxicated. He wanted more.

He sighed and held his hands out in a gesture of helplessness. "In the act of love, the giving is more important than the taking. You did some conquering of your own."

Her puzzled frown told him a great deal. "You are tired, and so am I," he mumbled, sitting down on the bed to remove his boots.

"What are you doing?" she demanded.

"I am going to bed, to sleep, and I would suggest that you do the same. It has been a long day," he answered without so much as a glance in her direction.

Dorcas stood hesitantly in the middle of the room, struggling with herself. She was tired, but she didn't like the idea of lying beside her enemy. A little voice niggled at her. What did it matter? She'd already done so, and more than willingly. She was appalled by her wanton behavior. How had it come to pass? She was confused by Neil's tenderness and by her own reaction to him, and his words of only a moment before confused her more. What had he meant when he'd said that she'd done some conquering of her own? He'd set out to subjugate her, and she'd let him. Her eyes narrowed. He may have conquered her body for a time, and he might do it again, but she silently vowed that he would never conquer her spirit.

She undressed and climbed into bed beside her husband, keeping as far to her side as she could. She waited tensely for him to reach for her. Soon the sound of his rhythmic breathing filled the chamber. Only then did Dorcas relax and let sleep overtake her as well.

The knocking grew louder, interrupting the pleasant dream and making Dorcas burrow farther under the covers. But peace was short-lived as urgent whispering penetrated her senses. She raised her head sleepily to see Neil pulling on his breeches hurriedly. Her warrior instincts aroused, she bolted up, asking, "Are we under attack?"

Startled, Neil looked at Dorcas. Her tousled hair fell about her shoulders in soft waves. Her sleep-filled eyes were wide with concern as she gazed at him.

He smiled reassuringly and strode to the bed. "Nothing like that," he said. He bent and placed a light kiss on her forehead. "My father is having another attack. I must hurry to him. You go back to sleep."

He left a bewildered Dorcas staring after him. An attack? What was wrong with Cedric? He seemed fine earlier. Was he seriously ill? Would this mean that Neil would take over the leadership of the clan?

Suddenly she remembered the frightening coughing fit that had consumed Cedric that day in her father's hall, the day Neil had chosen her as his bride. She threw back the covers, slipped on a robe, and hurried from the chamber. She hesitated momentarily outside the door to Neil's parents chamber before rapping sharply on it. It was opened by Hilda. She quickly stepped back to allow Dorcas entrance.

Neil and Astrid stood on either side of the big bed where Cedric lay, their expressions revealing their fear and sorrow. Cedric's skin had the translucent quality of the very ill. His breathing was labored and his body was racked with the spasms of a hacking, dry cough as he fought to keep from choking.

To Dorcas, Cedric had always been a vital, fearless enemy. It was hard to imagine him any other way. But the man who lay gasping for breath was very ill indeed, and she felt a wave of compassion at the sight.

Sensing the presence of someone else in the room, Neil glanced up. When he saw Dorcas at the end of the bed, he demanded sharply, "What are you doing here?"

His question jolted her back to her senses. She turned wide, pitying eyes to him, but could not find her voice to reply.

When Neil saw the look on her face, his own features

softened and he walked over to her. Laying a gentle hand on her arm, he said softly, "You should not be here."

Dorcas's gaze traveled back to the lone figure in the bed. "What is wrong with him?" she asked quietly.

"I don't know. He just gets these attacks from time to time. Mother does the best she can to ease them. Please, go back—"

Ignoring Neil, Dorcas turned to Hilda. "Fetch Lady Heloise at once."

When the maid did not move, Dorcas took a step toward her and snapped out, "Unless you wish to see your master die, do it."

Hilda scurried from the room.

Still ignoring Neil, Dorcas moved to Astrid's side. "My mother is well versed in the art of healing. She will help him," she stated confidently.

Astrid pulled her frightened gaze away from her husband to stare helplessly at Dorcas. "I do not know what to do anymore," she whispered raggedly.

Neil was surprised to see his wife place a comforting arm around his mother. It seemed strange to him that this girl, who hated the Vikings with all her being, should look upon his father with much compassion, and should now be comforting his mother. His gaze strayed to Cedric once again. His father had always been such a vital man, quick of temper and ready to fight, but just as quick to laugh and love. He felt so helpless as he watched his father struggle to survive yet another night.

Hilda returned in minutes with Heloise, who rushed to Cedric's side. She examined him swiftly, and without looking up from her task, asked, "How long has he had these attacks?"

"Since the last of the winter snows," Astrid replied.

Neil stared at his mother's reply. So long. Why had they waited to call him home?

"What have you given him?" Heloise asked.

"Tea of coltsfoot. Sometimes of flaxseed. I've made packs for his chest of both, but it is not enough."

Heloise glanced at the maid standing just inside the door and rattled off a list of things she needed immediately, including hot vinegar and honey. Then she turned to Astrid and smiled reassuringly. "What you've done has helped, but I will try mullein. It is stronger, and more effective. Never fear, Cedric will be his old self again very soon," she added cheerfully.

Heloise stayed with Cedric for most of the night, and by dawn her ministrations had helped greatly to ease his suffering. Before leaving the chamber, she gave careful instructions on the use of the syrup she'd made for him. Dorcas listened to her mother, and, as always, was a little in awe of Heloise's knowledge as well as her gentleness. If only she'd listened more carefully to her mother in the past, then mayhaps she, too, would have had the healing powers—as well as knowledge of how to run a large household. But her destiny was not the same as her mother's. She'd discarded that notion years before, and now it was too late. She would never be able to give such comfort, for she had chosen a different path to follow.

She jumped when someone touched her arm, interrupting her thoughts, and looked up to find Neil gazing intently at her. Her heart lurched and her mouth suddenly went dry as she stared into his deep sapphire eyes. She would never be able to comfort this man as Astrid did Cedric, or as Heloise did Duncan. She did not want to. She couldn't afford to.

Neil continued to stare at his wife, wondering what thoughts ran through her head. He slowly became aware of the linen dressing gown that molded itself to every delicious curve of her body, and his hand tightened briefly on her arm. His eyes darkened as he thought of what lay beneath for him alone. He would never have with this woman the kind of relationship that his parents shared. Though she showed compassion and love for others, he knew that she would not for him. But she was his. She belonged to him now, and as long as he held her, she would do his bidding.

He uttered a one-word command, "Come," and Dorcas followed without protest.

Dorcas stirred and rolled over, tossing her arm across the bed. She opened her eyes slowly and gazed at the empty space where Neil should have been. She caressed the spot and pulled his pillow toward her, hugging it. She buried her face in it, and his special musky scent enveloped her. It was a pleasant smell. A little smile tugged at the corners of her mouth as she remembered the night.

They'd returned from Cedric's room, all traces of fatigue gone as Neil seized her upon entering their chamber, and kissed her with a hunger that stirred her own passions into a flaming desire. She was unable to resist the persuasive force of his kisses and caresses—bound powerlessly to him by the spell he wove around her, wrapping her in his cocoon of thrilling sensations. She marveled at the fiery passion that consumed her each time her husband touched her—so different from their wedding night.

She quickly pushed the memory of Neil's cruelty that night away, preferring instead to recall last night, and how, after he'd heartily satisfied her ravenous hunger for him, he'd held her protectively in the circle of his strong embrace. She stretched languidly, like a contented cat sure of its master's loving protection, and sighed. It suddenly dawned on her that the sun was already high. She wondered why Neil had let her sleep so late, and her heart lurched at the thought that he might have been called again to Cedric's bedside.

She dressed quickly and made her way to Cedric's chamber to see for herself how he was faring. When she found him sitting up in bed, she sighed with relief. He was still pale, but was laughing and joking with her father and Neil. She hesitated in the doorway until Cedric noticed her and bid her to enter.

"Is there anything that I can get for you?" she asked, coming forward shyly.

"Nay, daughter," Cedric replied. "So far a half score of people have asked me the same thing. I find that I am already tired of hearing that query, for I wish to be up and about."

Dorcas smiled and asked teasingly as she crossed to him. "How long has Mother decreed that you remain in bed?"

Cedric chuckled. "You know her well."

"Aye. I, too, have been where you are."

He nodded. "A day or two, and I already chafe at the bonds binding me to this bed."

Dorcas smiled knowingly as she straightened his covers. What Heloise told a patient and what she actually allowed were two different things. "Well, all you have to do is follow her orders to the letter and you will soon be out of that bed."

Neil watched his wife closely, touched by her concern for his father. It seemed that every hour he discovered some new side of her character that served only to baffle him further.

"Tell me, Cedric," Duncan asked, "how is it that you became so ill?"

Cedric squirmed as both Duncan and Dorcas looked at him expectantly. "I, ah . . . This was brought on when I fell into the river last winter."

At his father's answer, Neil jerked his gaze from his wife and stared incredulously at Cedric. "Fell into the river?" he repeated. At Cedric's silence he added, "Father, you know this country as well as you know yourself. How could you possibly have fallen?"

"It was an accident," Cedric answered shortly.

Neil held his father's gaze as he retorted. "You would not have such an accident."

"I tend to agree with Neil," Duncan said, frowning. "There is something that you are not telling us."

Cedric eyed Duncan steadily as he replied. "We have worked hard to establish peace between our clans. You cannot ask me to divulge something that could destroy all we've worked for. You do not want to know."

"I can, and I do," Neil said sharply.

"Son, let it lie."

"Nay!"

Dorcas was struck by a sense of unease at Cedric's refusal to tell them what had happened. She glanced at her father. Duncan was frowning off into space, and she knew he was thinking the same thing. Cedric's "accident" had something to do with the McMahons, but she was not at all sure she wanted to know about it.

"Cedric," Duncan said slowly, "if one of my people was responsible, then you deserve redress, and I must know who the culprit is in order to mete out his punishment."

"It is not important," Cedric insisted.

"Then you leave me no alternative." Duncan held his new friend's gaze. "I will question my people, and if no one comes forward to tell me what happened, I will have no choice but to punish them all."

Cedric's jaw tightened. "You need not do such a thing."

"I am an honorable man. Justice must be served."

"But we were enemies then."

"Do you forget that the agreement between us not only involved the union between Dorcas and Neil, but also restitution of properties and compensation for injuries on both sides for the last six months?"

Cedric sighed heavily and glanced away before once more looking at Duncan. "All right, I will tell you what I know, but I must first have your word that what I am about to say will go no farther than this room. Agreed?" At the nods of assent to his request, he added, looking meaningfully at Neil, "I must also ask that no repercussions be taken against the person involved. The tribunal must declare his punishment."

"I will wait to hear what you have to say," Neil said cautiously.

"I have a very good reason for making that request. You see, I am not sure what happened. All I remember is being hit on the back of the head as I knelt beside the river, and the next thing I knew, I was lying on the bank and Kevin was bending over me. He said that he'd fished me from the water."

Neil crossed his arms over his chest. "You think it was Kevin who knocked you from behind and pushed you into the river to drown, but then changed his mind?" He heard Dorcas gasp, but did not look at her. How convenient, he thought, that Kevin was no longer around. The young man had left the day after the wedding to join a monastery. Neil's first instinct was to ride to the monastery and throttle his new brother-by-marriage, but he knew that he could not. Not without having the McMahons ride down on them. But what could he trust Duncan to do about the matter?

"Kevin did not do it," Dorcas said firmly. "He rescued you because he is kind and good, but he did not attack you from behind."

"Dorcas, you must remember that there was no peace between us then," Duncan said, wondering why Kevin hadn't mentioned the incident.

Dorcas's eyes snapped in anger as she turned on her father. "Kevin did not do it! He is not so dishonorable as to attack a man's back."

"Your brother does not like war," Neil said guardedly. "Mayhaps—"

"My brother is not afraid to face his enemies," she broke in hotly. "None of the McMahons are. It is easy for you to condemn him when he is not here to defend himself, isn't it? Is that your 'Viking' honor?"

"Dorcas," Duncan warned, but he got no further.

"Kevin did not do it!" she cried. "He did not!" She ran from the room.

Neil started to follow her, but Duncan's quiet words stopped him. "Leave her, son. There will be no reasoning with her now, and in her blind fury she just might decide to run you through with her sword. Her temper will cool, but it must be done in her own time."

Cedric sighed wearily and laid back against the pillows. He was suddenly so very tired. "You know, of course, that she may be right," he said. "I did not see the culprit."

"Yet there were only the two of you," Neil pointed out.

"Aye, that is so. Now do you see why I wanted your assurance that no harm would befall Kevin? I know the extent of your anger when roused, and since I do not know the truth of what happened . . ." He let the rest of the thought trail off.

"And yet I would agree with Dorcas," Duncan stated thoughtfully. "My son has never before had reason to attack a man's back. True, he does not like fighting, but he is not a coward." Duncan looked up sharply and asked, "What did he have to say for himself?"

"I did not think to accuse him of it at the time," answered Cedric, startled. "My thoughts were muddled. He escorted me as far as the boundary of my land and left me to ride home alone. It was only later that I began to wonder about the incident."

"Then you do think he did it," Neil said.

"There is no proof."

Neil looked at his new father-by-marriage. A frown of concern marked Duncan's features, and Neil felt sorry for the man. In spite of their differences over the years, he'd come to respect Duncan. He was now responsible for the shewolf that was Duncan's daughter, and he'd come to know the fierce pride and loyalty the McMahon clan held for one another. Kevin was also his brother now, but he had to know the truth. He asked, "Lord Duncan, may I have your permission to speak with Kevin?"

Duncan smiled wryly. "Would it matter if I gave it or not?"

"Nay, it would not."

"Neil . . ." Cedric began.

"I wish only to speak to him, father," Neil assured him. "The truth must be known. If he is guilty, then he must be brought before the tribunal and judged."

Duncan nodded slowly. In the short time he'd known Neil, he'd learned to trust the young man's word. If he said that all he would do was talk, then Duncan believed him. "You have my permission."

Neil left his father's chamber shortly thereafter and went in search of his wife. She was not in their chamber, nor had any of the women in the hall seen her. He strode purposefully outside, muttering to himself about the hot-headed wench, and spied Gwendolyn and Erik coming from the garden. He called her name a little more sharply than he'd intended, making the girl jump and look up guiltily.

"Have you seen Dorcas?" he asked more gently.

"What's this? Married only three days and already you've lost your bride," Erik quipped. The smile quickly left his face, and he sighed heavily when he caught Neil's black scowl. It appeared that trouble was afoot. Would his friend and his wife never come to terms? He felt a burgeoning sadness creep over him at the thought, but it was quickly replaced by anger. Neil was a fool.

The scowl on Neil's face deepened. His lips formed a tight line, then softened when he saw Gwendolyn staring intently at him. The questioning light in her eyes made him squirm. "We had a slight altercation," he mumbled.

"Damnation!" Erik said irritably. "When are you going to learn to tread more softly with her?"

"It was not *I* who became so angry that I had to storm from the room, nor did Dorcas give me a chance to explain anything." Neil resented having all the blame for the trouble between them placed on his shoulders. "Besides, it is none of *your* concern what *I* do with *my* wife! I will find her with or without your help, even if I have to tear down this place board by board."

Gwendolyn became alarmed at the murderous expression on Neil's face. He was not a man to be trifled with in his present mood. She had no real fear for Dorcas's safety, for she'd witnessed the way Neil gazed upon her sister in the past days. Besides, Dorcas could hold her own against anyone. Afraid that Neil and Erik would come to blows that would serve no good purpose, she placed a restraining hand on Neil's and stated softly, "She is not here."

Some of the tension in Neil ebbed. He released his grip on Erik and turned to look questioningly at Gwendolyn.

"As Erik and I strolled in the garden, I saw Dorcas running to the stables. I called to her, but she did not answer. She rode through the gate a little while ago."

A muscle in Neil's jaw twitched and his eyes burned through Gwendolyn, making her flinch. "Did she have no one in attendance?"

"Nay."

He swore under his breath and hurried away from two pairs of bewildered eyes that stared after him. He almost ran to the stables, and quickly saddled his destrier. The little fool! What was she about? He had an idea where she might be headed, but he had no intention of letting her get there ahead of him. He rode furiously toward the village as Erik and Gwendolyn continued to watch in puzzlement.

Gwendolyn bit her lower lip. "Was I wrong to tell him?" she asked in a low voice.

"I do not know. I do know, however, that if any harm befalls Dorcas, Neil will have more than her father and brothers to answer to," Erik said.

Gwendolyn turned her head sharply to stare wide-eyed at him. She closed her parted lips and dropped her gaze when she saw him still looking in the direction that Neil had disappeared with a worried frown creasing his forehead. As usual, Dorcas had captured another heart. Gwendolyn was awed by her sister's ability to gain so much attention. It seemed that Dorcas didn't even have to do anything to have men fall over themselves to get close to her. A pang of jealousy stung her for a moment. Then she swallowed and murmured, "You admire Dorcas greatly, don't you?"

"Aye, I do," Erik replied softly. The silence around them slowly penetrated his senses, and he glanced quickly at Gwendolyn to find her head bowed. The implication of her words suddenly hit him like a bolt from the blue. He placed his hands on her shoulders and turned her to face him. Putting his thumb under her chin, he lifted her head, but Gwendolyn refused to look him in the eye. "I find Dorcas possessed with a fiery spirit that I can only marvel at." He sighed heavily. "However, it is one that matches Neil's own, and I cannot help but be worried for my friends. If I show my concern, it is because I am afraid for your sister. Neil is the most determined man I know when it comes to having his own way, and I fear that he and Dorcas are in for a very stormy time. I do not know which will come out the victor. I know only that I do not want to make a choice of giving my loyalties to one or the other." Erik ran a hand through his sun-bleached locks and added disgustedly, "If Neil would only wake up and realize that he and Dorcas belong together."

Gwendolyn raised her eyes to look at him searchingly. "You feel it too."

"Aye, they are as right for each other as . . ."

"As what?" prodded Gwendolyn, holding her breath.

"As we are for each other," he finished.

Gwendolyn let her breath out in a rush. "Oh, Erik."

He cut her off by holding a finger to her lips. "I have been through countless battles on the field and off, my sweet, and unlike Neil, who will enjoy the contest of struggles to the day he dies, I yearn for the peace and contentment of a settled life. I know that I am bold and brash, that I am sometimes too loud and abrasive, like a rough, unhewn block of wood before it is shaped and molded into a useful, worthy chair or table. I need your gentle hand to guide me, to smooth out my rough edges." He grinned lopsidedly and ran his thumb down her jaw-line, all the while holding her gaze with his own.

He felt he could lose himself in her deep hazel eyes. "It amazes me that you and Dorcas are sisters. She is like the thunder and lightning in a raging storm, while you are like the mist after a refreshing spring rain."

Gwendolyn searched Erik's face for the truth of his words. Since his arrival, she'd heard all the rumors concerning this bold Viking—not only those of his deeds in battle, but also of his love conquests. "Your smooth tongue speaks honeyed words," she said softly.

"But with sincerity. I—if you agree, I would like to ask your father for permission to court you."

"Most men would not ask me what I thought," she mused.

Erik smiled, sensing that she was referring to the situation between her sister and Neil, and answered, "I think that we can use Dorcas and Neil as a perfect example of how not to go about courting."

Gwendolyn frowned at his words. "Do you think they will be all right?"

"I can only hope so, but they must find their own way."

10

The horse's hooves pounded furiously over the turf as Dorcas pushed the animal to its limits. She silently cried out against Neil's accusations. A lonely tear trickled from the corner of her eye, but she dashed it away. She would not cry. Damnation, she was too mad to cry! She silently ran through her repertoire of curses, calling her husband every vile name she could think of. How dare he! Kevin was innocent. He could not possibly have tried to kill Cedric by attacking from the rear. She would prove it, and then she would gladly sit back and watch Neil eat his words. Dorcas spurred her mount onward. She must be far enough ahead of anyone before they missed her and came looking for her.

With her mind on reviling her husband, she paid no heed to the road, but gave the horse its head. She was concerned only with exonerating Kevin. Cedric had to be mistaken. Her brother could no more have attacked his back than she. Kevin could easily have ridden in the other direction instead of going to the rescue of that man and pulling him from the Slaney River. The Vikings would not get away with making such vile accusations against one of her own. She would not let them.

The farther north Dorcas traveled, the rougher the terrain became. She was almost within the magnificent sight of the mountainous region outside Wicklow. So intent was she upon her thoughts that she did not see the rut that she should have guided her mount around. The horse stumbled, almost unseating her. The gray stallion regained its footing, but Dorcas realized that the animal could no longer endure the pace. She slowed and was appalled when the animal started limping.

She was suddenly ashamed of driving her mount so hard, recalling the words she'd used to chastise her little brothers only a few days earlier about mistreating animals. She dismounted and patted the horse's muzzle, speaking to it soothingly. The animal neighed softly in response and stood quietly as she inspected its leg for damage.

Cursing her stupidity when she saw that she would have to go much slower in order to reach her destination, she sighed and, picking up the reins, started to lead the horse down the road. She hadn't gone very far when she heard a rumbling sound. She looked behind her to find a rider approaching on a black destrier. Neil was closing the distance between them. Damnation! If only she'd had more of a head start.

The rumbling became a roaring in her ears. She heard Neil shout her name above the din. Some instinct made her look up. She gasped in horror at the sight of rocks tumbling down the side of the mountain—headed straight for her. There was no way she could outrun the avalanche, but her mount needn't be crushed. She gave the animal a pat on the rump and it sped away at her command.

Dorcas spied an overhang in the solid mountain and ran for all her worth to the protection it afforded. Just as she dove for the shelter, a rock slammed down onto the side of her head. A small moan escaped her lips as she fell forward and blackness descended over her.

Neil saw his wife struck down and spurred his mount forward in wild abandon, not caring that he, too, might be crushed beneath the rock slide. His chest constricted in fear as he shouted Dorcas's name again and again, only to be answered by silence. He called on all the gods, both pagan and Christian. She had to be all right. She just had to be.

He leapt from the destrier's back a safe distance from the plummeting rocks and ran like a man possessed to where his wife lay so still and lifeless. He artfully dodged the huge rocks rumbling about him and at last made it to Dorcas's side. The rock had landed on her foot, pinning it to the earth after she'd been struck down. Thankful that it wasn't on her head, Neil lifted it away and threw it aside. Then he pulled Dorcas to safety under the overhang.

He saw her chest rise and fall in a steady rhythm and breathed a sigh of relief. He set about examining her and found that there were no broken bones, for which he was grateful. More than likely, she would be bruised and sore, but there should be no permanent damage. He leaned back against the rock wall, his eyes closed, and waited for his heart to slow.

Dorcas moaned and opened her eyes to find her head cradled on something soft. She tried to lift her head and moaned; it felt as if it might split in two.

"Easy," Neil said, helping her sit up. He slipped a supporting arm around her and drew her to him. "How near you came to death," he said gruffly. "You know you were very foolish." He felt Dorcas stiffen. She pushed herself away with difficulty.

"The only 'foolish' thing is your accusation concerning my brother," she replied coldly, holding a hand to her throbbing head.

Neil leaned back against the wall. He felt no desire to fight with his wife, but he would not be swayed from finding out what happened to his father. "I will soon know the truth," he said simply.

Her face flushed in anger as she cried, "What you really mean is that you will take your revenge against Kevin.

That is the only truth you know, Viking." She scrambled toward the entrance of the aperture, but found herself roughly pulled backward.

"You little fool! What are you trying to do, get yourself killed?"

In Dorcas's weakened state, she was no match for him as he easily subdued her. He pinned her to the ground with his body while she struggled and cursed him.

Only the night before, the vixen in his arms had been a warm and willing lover, giving of herself freely, without any inhibitions, Neil thought. He swore under his breath when he saw the unshed tears in her eyes. Her lips trembled and she let out a ragged sigh, finally giving up the fight, obviously angry at his strength and her weakness.

His gaze shifted to her trembling mouth. He wanted to drink in the sweet nectar from those ripe pink lips that could so easily revile him. He lowered his head slowly and kissed her with an ardor that drained her, making her yield completely to him. Slowly and methodically he slipped her gown off, placing kisses, light as butterfly wings, wherever he revealed her velvety skin.

Dorcas moaned at the blissful torture, delighting in the soul-stirring pleasure flooding through her. She arched upward as Neil's mouth found the rosy crest of her breast. His tongue swirled over the tip, sending shivers of thrilling sensations up and down her spine. She gasped aloud when his mouth closed over the peak, while the thumb and forefinger of one hand gently encircled the other. His other hand stroked slowly down the length of her until he found the hot, moist softness of her womanhood. As he once again wrapped her in his web of sensual pleasure, Dorcas gave herself to the flaming passion that blazed forth from her inner core.

Neil raised himself up to look at her, and she met his bold gaze. The smoldering intensity of her need was mirrored in his cobalt-blue eyes as he stared at her for a moment, before his mouth covered hers in a kiss that drew forth her very soul.

She whimpered and clutched him to her desperately. His mouth slid to the base of her throat, where her pulse throbbed, and she gasped for air like a drowning person who has at last made it to the surface.

"Now! Neil, now," she cried.

A low growl escaped him as he covered her with his body and entered her swiftly. He took her with a fierce possessiveness, reveling in the warmth that opened to him, welcoming him without reservation.

Dorcas felt a violent tremor rip through her and the world behind her closed eyes filled with a multitude of radiant colors.

Neil shuddered above her, lost in the rapturous ecstasy that swept through him. He marveled at the sensual ecstasy his wife awakened in him. Her passion was for him alone. The ardor with which she gave herself to him amazed him. But what amazed him even more was his desire to give of himself in turn.

He looked down at her as she sighed contentedly and slowly opened her eyes. He knew he could take her to the peak of rapture again and again, whenever he wanted, and knew that his own desire for her would burn hot for a long time. But would she ever come to him of her own free will, begging for his kisses, his caresses, his lovemaking? He gazed into her eyes, which were cloudy with the afterglow of their passion, and made a vow. Someday, someday soon, he would see her come to him, desperate for his love, willing to submit fully to him. As if to seal his silent vow, he captured her mouth in a savage kiss.

Dorcas offered no resistance as his lips parted hers. But as quickly as he'd claimed her, he moved away. She felt bereft when he pulled back to stare at her, a frown creasing his forehead. She winced at the accusation in his eyes, puzzled by the sudden change in him.

He rolled away from her abruptly, and without looking

at her began to don his clothes. "Get dressed," he said curtly.

When she reached out to touch him tentatively on the shoulder, Neil pulled back. He could not understand his craving for her, and it alarmed him, for even now he'd begun to feel the stirrings of desire once more. Her quick surrender baffled him. How could she yield to him so easily when she hated him? Unless she hoped to use her body to dissuade him from going after her brother.

He glanced at her, but she had her back turned as she dressed. He swore silently and looked away, wanting to explain, if not apologize, for his gruff manner, but he fought the impulse. She had to learn that he was her master. She would not change his mind.

He sat brooding in silence, staring at the rock-strewn ground outside the little haven, when something caught his eye, making him tense. The reflection of a shadow flickered across the bright sunlight on a patch of ground in front of the overhang. It lingered for a moment, then it was gone.

He crawled through the entrance and straightened to look up at the side of the mountain where the rocks had plummeted to the earth below. He was positive that the outline had been a human form, but now there was no trace of anyone.

Dorcas emerged from the overhang. He shook off his suspicions and said, "We'd best return home now. You will have to ride with me since your horse ran off."

Dorcas's mouth tightened with anger, but without saying anything she moved away.

Neil saw the difficulty she had in walking on her bad foot and reached for her so that she could lean on him, but she whirled away. "Do not touch me, Viking! Far be it from me to inconvenience you. I will make it on my own."

Neil swore soundly and followed her. Without any effort he picked her up and deposited her atop the destrier, then he climbed up behind her. "You would not make it ten feet down the road on that ankle." He snorted. "Now be still," he commanded, clamping an arm tightly around her as she squirmed to dismount. "You will find the ride less painful as well as swifter. Besides, I want your mother to look at that ankle as soon as possible. I do not want to be accused of abusing you when it was your own foolishness that brought this on."

"I do not find it foolish to protect one of my own, Viking."

Neil pulled up on the reins, and Dorcas turned questioningly toward him. He studied her face. Her mouth was set in a rigid line. In the depths of her fathomless green eyes—eyes that only a short time ago had mirrored desire, he saw the hate she held for him. His thought that she would use her body to dissuade him from his goal may not have been so far wrong after all. His own mouth thinned into a hard line, then he said, "Regardless of what you think, I will have the truth."

Dorcas looked away angrily. Her mind worked furiously, trying to find some way to stop Neil.

Upon returning to the stronghold, they were besieged with questions that Dorcas found hard to answer as Neil rushed into the keep with her in his arms. He blatantly ignored everyone, and refused to relinquish his hold on his wife until she was safely deposited in bed and Heloise had been summoned.

Only after Dorcas's mother confirmed Neil's belief that his wife had just a very bad bruise did he leave the chamber. Dorcas glared after him with such burning eyes that if Neil had chanced to look at her, he would have been reduced to cinders.

When she did try to get up, Heloise firmly pushed her back against the pillows. "Child, you must give that ankle some rest, at least for today."

Dorcas bolted upright to look anxiously at her mother. "I must stop him."

Heloise straightened, staring at her daughter in surprise. "He is just going to Cedric's room."

"Nay! You do not understand," cried Dorcas in frustration. "Neil must not be allowed to confront Kevin."

"And why not? Kevin is now his brother."

"He will harm Kevin. Mayhaps he will kill him!"

Heloise sighed and rolled her eyes heavenward. "Oh, Dorcas, don't be silly. Neil will do no such thing. Now—" Her words were cut off as someone knocked at the door and Thalia poked her head into the room. "May we come in?" she asked, smiling brightly.

"Yea," replied Heloise promptly. She picked up her tray of herbs and started to leave the chamber as Thalia and Gwendolyn entered. "Entertain your sister while I look in on Cedric," she threw over her shoulder on her way out. She turned as she reached the door. "And keep her in that bed." Ignoring the glare that her eldest daughter graced her with, she left the room.

The three girls were left alone in silence until Gwendolyn nudged Thalia sharply in the side, bringing her sister to her senses.

"Oh!" Thalia grinned as she held out a bouquet of tiny pink roses to Dorcas, "I thought you might like these to cheer you."

"I am not in the mood for flowers!" Dorcas snapped.

Thalia jerked her hand back as if she were afraid her sister might bite it off. She looked down at the roses, hurt because she could not please her older sister, whom she secretly idolized. Dorcas always seemed so sure of everything, so capable of taking care of herself. Aye, they squabbled as any sisters did, but Thalia truly admired Dorcas.

"Does your foot pain you a great deal?" Gwendolyn asked sweetly.

"It is not my *foot* that I am worried about. I am more concerned with what my 'husband' is going to do to our brother."

"Why should Neil want to do anything to Hugh?" asked Gwendolyn, thoroughly puzzled.

"Not Hugh! Kevin!" Dorcas cried.

"I do not understand . . ."

"Oh, never mind," Dorcas muttered, flinging herself back against the pillows. No one would believe her anyway. It seemed that her husband had won the respect of her whole family, for every time she tried to tell them the truth about him, they all scoffed at her. She turned her head and looked at her sisters disgustedly. The downcast look that Thalia wore suddenly penetrated her senses, and she apologized for her rudeness. "Thalia, I did not mean to be so unkind. The roses are very lovely."

"They are, aren't they?" Thalia said, placing them in Dorcas's hands.

Dorcas inhaled their sweet scent and ran a finger gently over a soft petal. Her eyes grew wide as a thought occurred to her and she jerked her head up to stare at Thalia. "Where did you get these?"

"From the garden, silly."

"You filched them from Astrid's rose garden?"

"I most certainly did not!" Thalia cried indignantly. "They—they were given to me."

"Who gave them to you?" Dorcas asked suspiciously.

A blush covered her sister's face as she answered. "Rory Fitzgerald."

"Cousin Regan's younger brother?"

"Aye, that he did. And Astrid knows about it," she added smugly.

"Well, well," Dorcas said. "Tell me more."

She was soon sorry that she'd asked, for Thalia went on and on about the fellow until she thought she would scream. Gwendolyn was no help in silencing Thalia's garrulous account of her time spent in Fitzgerald's company. For the most part, she stood with a madonna-like smile on her face as her sister described her swain's attributes in glowing terms. Occasionally, she would nod her head in agreement, adding an "Erik says this," or "Erik does that."

Dorcas was in no mood to listen to her sisters' gushing chatter. But she'd asked. So she sat there with a false smile, wishing they would leave.

Her wish came true sooner than she expected as the door opened and Neil stepped into the chamber.

Thalia's words died on her lips when she spied her brother-by-marriage. She shut her mouth quickly and swallowed hard, frightened by his fierce scowl.

Finally, Gwendolyn broke the uncomfortable silence. "Well, uh, we'd best leave you to rest, dearest." She bent to kiss Dorcas's cheek. "Here, I will put the roses in a vase for you," she added, taking the flowers from her. She then pushed Thalia ahead of her out the room. As she passed Neil, she stopped and murmured, "Thank you for bringing our sister safely back to us."

Neil's penetrating gaze left his wife and he stared at Gwendolyn. How could he have forgotten the fierce love and loyalty of the McMahons? It shone clearly in Gwendolyn's eyes as she looked steadily at him, and made him ashamed of his ill-conceived thoughts earlier of wishing he'd never rescued his wife. His face softened, and he nodded slightly in response.

The door closed quietly as Gwendolyn left, but he barely heard it. He was looking at Dorcas again. Yea, he was sorry for his thoughts. No matter how much she hated him, Dorcas was his, and what was his, he held. He remembered his blind panic and fury as he'd feared she would be crushed beneath those rocks, and it confused him. He should not care what happened to her. She was a shrew—hot-tempered and quarrelsome. But he did care. He told himself it was only because he was not finished with her yet. He had a vow to keep.

She was an exquisite creature. Fierce. Passionate. Beautiful. It made him a little uneasy. If his wife knew how to use the wiles that most women employed, would he be able to deny her anything? He grunted at his fanciful musings. The thought was absurd.

Without speaking, he stroke over to the chest that held his clothes and plucked out a fresh tunic and breeches. He threw them into a bag and slammed the chest shut.

Dorcas watched him in growing apprehension. At last she found her voice. "What are you doing?"

Neil had expected the question, but was surprised at the calmness in her voice. The tension left his body. He didn't look at her as he answered, "You know what it is that I do." Then he took a deep breath and faced her. Her eyes were wide with fright. His own eyes flickered when he recognized the accusation in hers. He opened his mouth to explain, but closed it abruptly. How could he make her understand? He tried again. "I must have some answers and only Kevin can supply them," he said gruffly. Unable to bear the look on her face, he turned away.

"Is that why you go heavily armed?" she asked caustically as he donned his sword.

"You know there are thieves upon the road, not to mention hostile clans whose land I will have to pass."

Dorcas's good sense told her that he spoke the truth, but she ignored it as her anxious gaze flicked over the knife and sword strapped to his waist. His whip hung from his belt. How could she trust her enemy? She just knew that the blood lust was too great for Neil not to harm her brother. "Then let me come with you," she cried. "I will be no problem for you, I swear it. My ankle is not so bad that I cannot sit a horse."

Neil's conscience nagged at him. He heard the panic in her voice. Why didn't he reassure her? He'd given his word to Duncan and Cedric that he would merely talk to Kevin. He wanted to explain that to Dorcas, but something told him she would not believe him, so what did it matter? "Nay, you cannot come. You would only slow me down. Besides, you must rest."

His voice brooked no argument, yet angered, she started to rise.

Neil heard a rustling sound behind him and turned to see her getting out of bed. Alarmed, he watched as she stood unsteadily and started to hobble toward him.

Her voice shook with barely suppressed rage. "How convenient for you to have no witnesses to your treachery, Viking."

Neil was across the room in two strides. He scooped her up and walked toward the bed. "You must rest after your ordeal," he said roughly.

She pushed against his chest, squirming for release, but he held her tightly, unconcerned by her frantic movements.

"You were not so worried about my 'resting' earlier," she snapped. "Let me go! You are a filthy pig and I do not want you to touch me. Put me down!"

Neil's mouth set in a tight line, and his eyes narrowed as he stared at his wife. She hadn't thought he was so filthy when they'd been trapped by the rock slide, he thought, his own anger surfacing. He released her abruptly, letting her drop to the bed, then was immediately sorry for his rough treatment when he saw pain flash across her face.

"I have business to attend to," he said more gently, "and you must rest that ankle." He caught the look of hatred she threw him and added, "Do not leave this bed for the rest of the day."

"Do you really expect me to lie here while you ride off to kill my brother?"

Neil's face looked as it if were carved from stone. "That all depends upon Kevin," he said shortly. He whirled and, picking up his belongings, started to leave the room.

"Neil!"

He stopped at the door.

"If you dare to harm a hair on Kevin's head, I will kill you."

He did not turn, nor even acknowledge that he'd heard her as he left the room.

It was four days before Neil returned, and in that time Dorcas fluctuated between furiously shouting at her father and refusing to speak to him. She'd gone to Duncan, tearfully expressing her concern for her gentle brother, and was shocked to learn that her father had sanctioned Neil's confrontation with Kevin. She'd ranted at him, accusing him of misplacing his loyalties, but succeeded only in bringing on Duncan's wrath. In turn he'd accused her of being a fool for continuing to look upon her husband as her enemy. If Kevin were guilty, then he would be brought before the tribunal to be judged according to the agreement of peace.

Frustrated and angry at her father's stubborn refusal to see the situation clearly, she had stormed from the room. Her father was the fool, she had thought bitterly, for putting his trust in the Viking. She'd seen a ruthless look in Neil's eyes more than once, and knew that he could easily cut down her brother if it suited him. All he had to do was tell them that Kevin attacked first. It would be so simple, and there would be no witnesses.

The day Neil returned, Dorcas could not still the trembling of her hands as she fumbled with the combs for her hair. She'd been out riding with Hugh and had just returned to the stables when shouts from the men reached her. Her husband was home. She had run into the keep, past a startled Heloise, not seeing the little smile that touched her mother's lips as she hurried to her chamber. She'd quickly changed clothes, cursing under her breath because she was all thumbs. As she stood in front of the polished brass, she muttered to herself because she could not manipulate her fingers the way she wanted to. Now was the time of reckoning. She prayed fervently that Kevin was well, for if he was not, then she would have to carry out her threat. That would mean war between the clans, but she did not care. Her family's honor was at stake.

She eyed herself critically and wrinkled her nose. At least Duncan could not call her to account for her mode of dress, she thought. She'd purposefully worn her linen tunic and breeches the last few days simply because she knew it rankled her father now that she was a married woman. During one of their heated exchanges, he'd stated that if she'd had any sense at all, she would use some charm on Neil instead of always baiting him. If she could only learn to make her husband content, rather than venting her hatred toward him, mayhaps he would forget they were ever enemies and be ready to accept her family as his. But that meant Dorcas would have to put aside her foolish pride and meet him halfway.

Dorcas pursed her lips, remembering her father's words. They had stung her to the core. Was she to forget all that she was, all that she'd been taught? Was she to embrace the Viking cause and destroy her people? Her eyes darkened as she stared at her reflection. Never! She could be as charming as any other woman, but she'd always felt it was a lie to say and do things that she did not mean. She had to be herself, didn't she?

Her forehead puckered in a thoughtful frown. Mayhaps there was something to Duncan's words after all. She would show him. She would show Neil too. Her husband's words the day she had found out about his Anika floated back to her. He'd told Erik that she, Dorcas, possessed no womanly traits. Well, she could when it suited her purpose . . . and now was the time to put some of them to use. It would throw him off balance and make it easier for her to strike when he least expected it. If he'd hurt Kevin, he would pay. With that thought secure in her mind, she left the chamber.

When she entered the hall, Neil was there with Duncan and Cedric. She stopped just inside the doorway and took in his powerful frame. Her heart pounded wildly and her throat went dry. Why did he have the power to disturb her so? He was clear across the room, yet she felt as though she were in his arms, and he was making her yield so readily to him.

She grew weak in the knees when he raised one booted foot to rest it on the bench in front of the fireplace, throwing an arm casually across his muscular leg. It irritated her that the sight of him could send her into such turmoil. He was too far away for her to hear what he said, but she noted his relaxed stance and quiet manner, and assumed all must not be as bad as she'd anticipated. She swallowed hard and walked across the hall, thankful her long blue gown covered her shaking knees.

The quiet conversation came to an abrupt halt and Neil straightened as his wife approached. He stared at her for a long moment without speaking. Could it be possible that she'd grown more beautiful since he'd left?

Dorcas took a deep breath and clasped her hands together to keep them from trembling. "I trust your journey went well?" she said at last, unable to wait any longer for him to speak.

"Aye," he replied.

She bit back a sharp retort, irritated by his short answer. It would not serve her purpose to start an argument now. "And how is my brother?" she asked as calmly as possible.

"He was well when I left him," Neil answered. He felt as if they were two polite strangers at their first meeting instead of husband and wife. He caught the flicker of relief that crossed Dorcas's face and his mouth twitched in amusement as she almost sighed aloud. He leaned forward, whispering for her ears alone, "Not one hair on his head is out of place."

She glared at him, but kept silent. Neil was laughing at her, but she did not care. She had the information she wanted. Kevin was safe.

"He could shed no light on what happened?" Duncan asked. "Did he not see anyone else?"

Neil reluctantly pulled his gaze from his wife's enticing mouth. He'd been thinking of what a pleasure it would be to soften those pink lips, to taste their sweetness. It was with difficulty that he looked at Duncan. "Nay, he could not. He said he thought there were other tracks besides Cedric's at the river's edge, but he could not be sure."

"Mayhaps he was lying," Cedric said quietly.

Out of the corner of his eye Neil could see Dorcas bristle. He suddenly felt the urge to reassure her, to make up for his lack of doing so upon his departure. "Nay, I do not think so. He swore upon the cross that he was not responsible. I believe him."

"Then who could have committed such an outrageous act?" Cedric demanded. He sighed heavily and ran a tired hand across his forehead. "I am sorry," he mumbled. "I do not believe Kevin would have done such a thing. It galls me to think that I have such a cowardly enemy, one who can attack me only from behind."

"Aye, I know what you mean," said Duncan. "I cannot imagine who could be so low."

Dorcas pondered her father's words. Her mouth curled with distaste, as she thought that any man who could not face his enemy squarely was indeed evil. The images of several repugnant characters flashed through her mind, including that of Egan McNeil. Now, there was a horrid, disgusting man, but for all his perfidy, she did not think even he would stoop so low as to attack a man from the rear.

She felt Neil's gaze on her, and turned to find him staring at her. She blushed under his intense look and stammered, "Y-you must be hungry after your trip."

His gaze lowered to her mouth. "I would prefer a bath before I eat."

She stared at the floor in confusion. Damnation! The way he looked at her, as if he could devour her, made her tongue-tied. She wanted to run from his penetrating gaze. Her heart was hammering so loudly, she was sure that he could hear it. She supposed she owed him something in return for her brother's life. Her eyes still downcast, she said, "I will see to it."

A frown etched Neil's brow as he watched her signal to a serving girl to follow her. As usual, Dorcas's moods baffled him. She'd appeared almost glad to see him, like a timid maiden greeting her long-lost lover. But that was ridiculous, he chided himself. She cared no more for him than he did for her. If anything, he should be suspicious of her soft and gentle nature. It could be the calm before the storm.

11

Dorcas bustled about the chamber, laying out clean clothes for Neil. She'd directed two hefty servants to place the wooden tub in the center of the room and fill it with hot water, and while they followed her orders, she gathered towels and soap. She dismissed them and told her maid to bring a tray of food so her husband might eat. When all was ready she wondered what was keeping Neil and bit her lower lip in indecision. She wasn't sure if she was supposed to inform him that his bath was prepared, and she fretted that she could not remember what Heloise had tried to teach her. The water was going to get cold and the food that Enid had brought some time ago would lose its freshness if he didn't hurry.

When the door opened, she jumped nervously and stared wide-eyed at her husband. Her heart fluttered as he gazed back at her from the doorway, and she wondered why his appearance always surprised her so.

Neil closed the door behind him quietly. Entering the chamber, he couldn't help thinking that his wife looked guilty about something, and he wondered what she was up to. A quick survey of the room showed him that all was as it should be. A steaming tub of water sat in the middle of the floor, while a tray of bread, cheese, and meat was on a table by the bed, with plenty of mead to wash it all down. He stretched his weary muscles and strolled to the bed, where he sat to remove his boots. For the first time in days he felt relaxed as he let the tension drain from his body.

Dorcas fiddled with the objects on top of the dressing table, arranging and rearranging them, all the while throwing anxious glances Neil's way. She was dying of curiosity, desperate to know what had transpired between her brother and her husband. As the minutes stretched out, she became more and more irritated at his silence. Why wouldn't he tell her anything? It was just his way of getting even for the threats she'd made, she thought. When she could stand it no longer, she ventured, "You said that you found my brother well. Is he happy?"

Out of the corner of his eye Neil had watched as Dorcas glanced at him again and again, and he'd found her anxious silence highly amusing, wondering when she would find her tongue and ask him about his meeting with Kevin. He felt a teasing mood come over him and answered lightly, "He seems so."

Dorcas waited for him to continue, and when he did not she turned, ready to bombard him with questions. The first query died on her lips when he arose and stripped off his tunic. Her mouth went dry as she took in the massive chest covered with a dark matting of hair. Powerful muscles rippled beneath his tan skin, leaving her feeling faint. She looked away quickly, disconcerted by the magnificent sight. It was the first time she had ever really *looked* at him, and the word that popped into her head to describe what she'd seen was beautiful.

She blushed, glad she wasn't facing him now so that he could ridicule her, and tried to push the thought of his body from her mind. Kevin. She was more concerned with how Kevin was. "What happened between you and

Kevin?" she asked bluntly, cursing herself for the tremor in her voice.

Neil's eyes twinkled. What fun it was to watch his wife's agitation grow. It was all he could do to keep a straight face. He shrugged and replied nonchalantly, "Nothing happened."

Dorcas whirled around, ready with a heated retort, and almost choked at the sight that greeted her. Neil was stepping out of his breeches. Her eyes grew wide at the strong hairy legs, the sinewy muscles that bulged with his movements. If his Viking god Thor came to life before her eyes, she knew he would be in the form of her husband.

She gasped as Neil straightened and faced her. He was powerfully, unashamedly aroused. Passionate heat scalded her as images of their wild couplings filled her mind. She whirled back around and clutched the table's edge.

Neil could no longer hold his laughter, having caught the fiery blush on her face before she turned away.

With her back safely to him, Dorcas fumed. He was laughing at her again. She jumped when he picked up her heavy hair and curled it around his arm. Shivers tickled down her spine when she felt his breath, soft and warm, against the back of her neck.

"Why do you turn away, Dorcas? I thought you wanted to hear about Kevin?" he whispered against her hair.

She swallowed hard. Her heart was pounding so furiously, she was sure it would fly from her chest. "I—I do. You—your bath will get cold," she said weakly. What power did this man have over her that she should react so violently to his nearness?

"You could join me," he said, running his hands down her arms.

She gasped and jerked away from him, scurrying to the window and out of his reach. "I have had my bath," she stated coolly.

Neil sighed and walked over to the tub. It seemed that his wife was willing to go just so far before she drew back.

As he climbed into the bath he thought again of his vow to break down her resistance until she came to him willingly, begging him to take her. The image aroused him even further.

Dorcas breathed a sigh of relief when she heard the splashing of water, and turned. Neil's face was a study in concentration as he soaped his arms and chest. She wondered if he was thinking of his confrontation with Kevin and felt that she would burst if she did not find out. "Are you going to tell me what happened between you and my brother?" she asked, exasperated.

Neil glanced up. Grinning lopsidedly, he shrugged. "I told you, nothing happened. We talked."

She placed her hands on her hips. "Well, something must have happened. You were gone for four days."

He cocked his head to one side as he studied her. "You noticed."

"Oh!" She stamped her foot in frustration and turned her back to him.

Neil chuckled softly, thinking that women were the noisiest of creatures. "I'll tell you what," he said, still smiling, "I will make a trade with you."

She looked at him warily. "What sort of trade?"

"I will tell you of our meeting if you will wash my back."

She considered his proposal for a moment before nodding curtly. She had hoped he would simply tell her what she wanted to know, but she couldn't see any harm in his request.

She took the soap from him and started to lather the broad expanse of his back. She waited for him to begin, and when he did not, she said tersely, "We had a bargain."

He nodded thoughtfully. Dorcas's firm but gentle touch felt good as her hands glided smoothly over his back. It made him forget everything else. "So we did," he said, trying with difficulty to put his thoughts in order. "There really is not much to tell. It took me a day and a half to get to the monastery. I spoke to Kevin, but he could shed no light on what happened to my father. He said that Cedric was lying facedown, half in and half out of the water when he found him, and that he pulled him from the river."

Neil neglected to add that he'd threatened to beat the truth out of Kevin, but that his brother-by-marriage had remained calm throughout their exchange. When Neil insisted that Kevin swear on the cross that he'd not been the one who attacked Cedric, the younger man had readily agreed to do so. Neil knew then that Kevin was indeed telling the truth, and he felt a twinge of guilt at his treatment of him.

Dorcas's hands stopped their movements, though she did not remove them from his back as she asked, "What about the other set of tracks?"

"Kevin could not be sure about that. The ground was badly torn up where my father lay. He only said that he'd seen no one else."

"I do not know who could have committed such a foul deed, but I knew that Kevin was innocent," Dorcas said happily.

Neil glanced at her sideways, slightly irritated by her smug attitude. He, too, was glad that Kevin was not responsible, but he was still no closer to knowing the truth.

He winced as she resumed her scrubbing more vigorously than she had to. "You don't have to tear my hide off," he muttered. "Why don't you get that bucket over there and rinse me off? We just might make a passable wife out of you yet."

Dorcas snatched her hands away as though she'd been stung and glared at the back of Neil's head. How dare he treat her like a lowly servant! "With pleasure," she said. Wearing a grim expression, she reached for the bucket that sat on the floor beside the tub.

Neil sputtered and choked gasping for air as the now cold water poured over his head and body. He made a grab for her, but she agilely sidestepped him and scurried out of his reach. He wiped the water from his face, opening first one eye, then the other, to peer at her stonily. "It would appear that you need extensive training," he ground out, starting to rise.

Dorcas made a dash past him for the door, but was caught when his arm snaked out to grab her about the waist. She felt herself being lifted in the air. Her toes brushed the floor as she struggled to get free, and she screamed in outrage when Neil pressed her to him. The water that clung to him soaked through the back of her gown, and she fought all the harder to get away.

"It is time you learned to show your husband some respect," he said in a low, growling tone.

"Nay! You cannot do this!"

There was a sharp rap on the door, but neither one of them heard it as each strained to overcome the other.

Erik stepped into the chamber and stopped in his tracks. His mouth dropped open at the sight of Neil trying to pull his wife, who was fully clothed, into the tub.

Dorcas spotted him first, and called out, "Erik, help me."

Too stunned to do anything else, Erik merely stood rooted to the spot. "What the . . ." he started to ask, perplexed.

"You stay out of this," Neil ordered in a menacing voice.

Erik started to back out of the room, his eyes still riveted in on the combatants. "I, uh, I've come at a bad time."

"Nay, you have not!" cried Dorcas. "Come back here!"

Erik stood uncertainly in the doorway. The grim look on Neil's face told him that all was not fun and games, or was it? He suddenly grinned. "If you are really intent upon giving your wife a bath, my friend, don't you think you should remove her clothing first? I would certainly find no reason to leave then. In truth, it might prove to be a fascinating view."

Neil threw Erik a withering glance and let Dorcas fall to the floor. She crawled away until she reached the dressing table, then stood and started to clear it of the objects on top by hurling them at Neil's head.

Neil's rage was so intense that he stepped from the tub, easily ducking the articles flying at him, and stalked toward his wife.

Dorcas's throat constricted with fear at the murderous expression on his face. A hasty retreat was called for. She ran past a laughing Erik and out the door that he quickly shut behind her.

Neil shoved Erik aside, ready to follow his wife, when his friend's calm voice penetrated his anger.

"Are you really going to go outside in your present, er, condition?"

With his hand on the door latch, Neil stopped, realizing at last that he had no clothes on. He swore soundly and whirled around. Picking up a rough cloth, he began drying himself briskly.

Still wearing a huge grin, Erik strolled over to the tray of food. He broke off a piece of cheese and popped it into his mouth, then sat down, eyeing Neil curiously. "What brought all of that on?"

"The little witch tried to drown me," Neil answered, pulling on a clean pair of breeches.

A deep chuckle rumbled from Erik's chest. "And you were going to pay her back in kind, eh? It's a good thing I walked in when I did. I would hate to see the peace that her father and yours worked so hard to establish shattered so quickly."

"Peace!" Neil spat. "I will never know a moment's peace being tied to that shewolf! I curse the day I ever came home to be faced with a life of hell."

"Neil, where is your sense of humor?" At the scathing look Neil threw him, Erik snorted in derision. "If I know you, you said something to set her off. You probably got just what you deserved."

"I did not ask to be tied to that demon in skirts!"

"Perhaps not, but now that you are, why don't you stop complaining and try to make the best of the situation?" Erik asked sharply, clearly showing his irritation. Damn! Neil could be a stubborn ass. He let out a heavy sigh and tried reasoning with his friend. "I have never known you to be so antagonistic toward the fairer sex. You have always conducted yourself in the most courtly manner, even to those women who did not deserve such treatment. Why you have elected to treat your wife with less respect than you would show the most vicious harpy, I will never understand."

"It is not for you to understand anything," Neil snarled, clenching and unclenching his fists at his side. "Respect works both ways, and I have yet to see my 'wife' show anything but a deplorable lack of that trait for me, her husband. And I will tell you now that I intend to teach her the meaning of the word, even if I have to beat it into her!"

Erik leapt from the chair to face his longtime friend. "You are a fool, Neil, if you think Dorcas will submit to your tyranny. The only reason you wish to bring her to heel is that you feel she is to blame for your present situation, when in truth she is not at fault. She is as much a victim as you are. From the moment you were married she has been frightened to death of you, and instead of trying to allay her fears, you have only added to them by your harsh demands."

"Fear! That hellion knows no fear. You do not know what you're talking about. I think you've said enough."

"Nay, not nearly enough," Erik cut in, ignoring the twitching muscle in Neil's jaw and the stance that warned him that his friend was ready to pounce on him. Neil was taller and broader, a deadly match when angry, but Erik was too enraged at what he'd seen since his arrival. It was time that Neil heard a few truths about himself. "You have been so caught up in self-pity for what you believe you have lost that you cannot see what you have gained. Dorcas is a rare and precious jewel and should be treated with the gentle care you would give a priceless gem. She should not be broken of her fine spirit. She is beautiful and courageous, a fine match for any man."

Neil's eyes burned. "I suppose you would like nothing better than to expound your feelings to my wife. I know your reputation with women, 'friend,' but it has never taken the course of starting out as their champion."

"You misunderstand me. I think too highly of our friendship to come between you and Dorcas."

"You never felt that way in the past when you decided that one of my women would suit you better."

"That was only a game, and you know it. You wooed as many women away from me as I did from you, but none of them was your wife. For all her bravado, Dorcas is still a woman with a spark of vulnerability, and if a champion is what she needs, then I will fulfill that role."

The idea that another man was so quick to come to his wife's defense enraged Neil. A picture of Dorcas with Erik invaded his mind, and unable to see anything but his closest friend's treachery, he dealt Erik a blow that sent the man sprawling.

Just then the door flew open and Dorcas entered the chamber. She took in the scene at a glance, and shouted Neil's name as he started forward to press his attack on Erik. She placed herself between the two men, shoving against Neil's chest with all her strength. "What are you trying to do?" she yelled.

Neil pushed her aside. His eyes blazed in fury as they bored into Erik. "Get up."

Dorcas stepped between them again, undaunted.

"Is it your intention to hide behind my wife's skirts?" Neil taunted as Erik got slowly to his feet.

Dorcas felt a movement behind her and knew that Erik was ready to meet Neil's challenge. "Stop it, both of you!"

Erik checked himself and straightened, glaring hotly at Neil. "I will not fight you, but only because it would distress Dorcas. You are angry, for what I said was the truth, and you know it. I can only hope that you come to your senses before it is too late."

"You have overstayed your welcome, 'friend.' I suggest you leave here at once."

"I will be only too happy to comply." Erik stalked to the door and flung it wide, but before leaving he turned to Neil and warned, "Just remember, if you hurt her again, you will answer to me, 'friend.'"

Dorcas stared at the closed door for a moment, then looked in bewilderment at Neil. She caught her breath sharply at the look of rage on her husband's face and the cold gaze he turned on her.

What had Erik meant, and what had caused two such close friends to part in such bitterness?

The gray overcast sky matched Dorcas's mood perfectly as she stood beside her mother and father in the yard outside the McNeil keep. She felt as though her heart were being ripped from her breast, and fought down the panic that held her in its iron grip. Cedric and Astrid stood beside them, and the four older people conversed quietly.

Dorcas cast suspicious glances at Neil, who stood some distance away talking to Hugh, wondering if her husband was behind her family's abrupt departure. Duncan had not mentioned leaving so soon, and Dorcas couldn't help the thoughts that flitted through her mind. Neil had ordered Erik to leave his home. The little Viking had done so immediately. Had Neil also demanded the McMahons leave? She would not put it past him.

Upon Erik's departure the previous day, Gwendolyn had sought out Dorcas to tell her the reasons behind his leaving, and to receive consolation from her sister for the loss of her own heart's desire. As the distraught Gwendolyn's story unfolded, Dorcas's eyes had widened in astonishment. She found it incredible that the Viking had so readily come to her defense. But, of course, she had not expected her husband to do so. He knew only how to bring out the worst in her. When Dorcas had scoffed at her words, Gwendolyn had quickly pointed out that Neil had struck Erik out of jealousy. Why else would he have been so ready to fight another man, even his closest friend, and one who simply wanted to embrace Dorcas in friendship?

Dorcas had laughed scornfully at her sister's romantic ideas. The only reason Neil would fight to keep her was that he looked upon her as a prize. One that had been forced upon him, but nevertheless, she was his possession, as he was always so swift to point out.

Dorcas felt as though she would choke on the fear that consumed her, and she trembled at the thought of her family leaving her in the midst of her enemies. She fought the bitter tears that threatened to fall as Heloise turned to her. She would not shame her family in front of the Vikings.

"Child, remember all that I have tried to teach you," Heloise said gently, laying a hand on her daughter's arm. "The way might be slow and frustrating, but Astrid is here to help you. She is quite fond of you, you know. And remember, I am not so far away. If you need me, I will be close by." She hugged Dorcas and kissed her cheek as Gwendolyn and Thalia come up to them.

Rory Fitzgerald trailed behind Thalia like a lost puppy and stopped a short distance from the three sisters to give them some privacy.

Dorcas glanced away from the young man and smiled tremulously at Thalia, murmuring, "Your ardent swain misses you already."

Thalia flashed Rory a brilliant smile, then blushed when

he eyed her boldly, his lips turning upward in a slow grin. She looked back at Dorcas quickly. "He will escort us home before he travels on to his own estate."

Dorcas's eyebrows arched upward. "Us?" she asked teasingly.

"Well—me." Thalia took her sister's hands in her own. "Oh, I am going to miss you."

"You mean you will miss 'borrowing' my possessions," Dorcas teased.

Thalia laughed. "Aye, that too." Her face suddenly grew serious as she searched Dorcas's pale countenance, and she threw her arms around her sister, hugging her tightly. "I do mean it. I will miss you dreadfully, you know. You will not forget about us, will you?"

"Don't be a goose," Dorcas chided, swallowing the lump that had formed in her throat. "You will not be so very far away. I will expect you to visit, and I shall come to see you."

Thalia did not trust herself to speak as she stepped away and nodded, tears brimming her eyes. She turned abruptly and hurried to where Rory waited to lift her atop her mount.

Dorcas blinked to hold back her own tears and turned to hug Gwedolyn to her. "I am going to miss you too."

"And I you. Things will not be the same."

"They will never be the same again," Dorcas said morosely.

"Nay, but they can be better," Gwedolyn whispered. "Cedric and Astrid are kind, and I think that Neil can be too—if you let him."

Dorcas gently pushed her sister away and smiled rue-fully. "I do not believe there is a chance of that happening." She glanced at the object of their conversation, only to find Neil staring at her, his face unreadable. A prickly sensation ran up and down her spine, and she wondered what fate lay in store for her now that she would be alone with him. With difficulty she dragged her gaze away to look at Gwendolyn once more. "Go now. Before I lose my courage and return home with you."

As Gwendolyn moved away, Hugh said something to Neil and approached his sister. He looked down at Dorcas sheepishly and cleared his throat before speaking. "I hope that you can forgive my teasing you these past weeks."

"I can forgive your teasing me. What I do not understand is the tie that has now bound you to my husband," she said stiffly. "You have always hated the Vikings as much as I."

"That is true. But Neil is now your husband, and my brother. Our father wants peace. I will honor his wish, until such time as it is no longer warranted." Hugh caught the resentment that flickered across Dorcas's face, and frowned. "Neil is a good man, Dorcas. I respect him, and I trust his word." He leaned down to kiss her cheek. "Try to make the peace work."

Dorcas scowled at her brother's back as he walked away. It seemed that everyone was telling her to make her marriage work for the sake of the peace between the clans. She was getting awfully tired of hearing it. After all, the McMahons were not the only ones to agree to the peace.

Her mother's worried voice penetrated her senses, and she realized Heloise was asking where Conan and Bevan were. Everyone said they hadn't seen the boys all morning, and Heloise groaned. At that moment they all heard a furious barking.

A yapping dog came tearing across the yard, a stick tied to its tail. The poor animal dragged his posterior along the ground, trying to free himself of the offending article. When it was clear he could not loosen the stick that way, he ran around and around in a circle, whining and barking, trying to grab the stick between his teeth. Conan and Bevan were clearly enjoying the scene from where they peeked around the corner of the keep.

Duncan roared at his sons to unloose the animal immediately. The boys jumped at their father's sharp command

and ran to do his bidding. The dog was so happy at being freed from the torture, he pounced on first one boy, then the other, knocking them to the ground and slobbering kisses all over them until they cried out to be rescued from his gratitude. Neil rushed to their aid and spent a few comical moments untangling dog from boys before the animal bounded away, barking wildly.

At Duncan's order to say good-bye to their sister, Conan and Bevan ran to Dorcas.

She grinned at them, shaking her head. "When will you two ever learn to give some forethought to your actions?"

The boys stared up at her and swallowed hard. "We are in trouble again, aren't we?" asked Conan.

She burst out laughing. "Aye, I believe you are."

"We did not mean any harm," Bevan pleaded.

"Do not tell me, tell Father."

Conan's eyes grew wide at the realization that his big sister would no longer be there to intervene with Duncan on their behalf. "You will no longer be around to help us, will you?" he asked in horror.

Dorcas's expression softened as she took in the two pairs of frightened eyes. She dropped to the ground and hugged the boys close to her, tears once again threatening to spill. "Nay, I will not. It is just as I've always warned you. Someday your actions would catch up to you, and now they have. Do not worry. I don't think Father is too terribly angry, but you have got to mend your ways." She squeezed them to her and kissed each one soundly, then smiled through the blur of her tears as they grimaced and wiped a grubby hand over their cheeks to rid them of the stain of her kiss. "Oh, I think I am going to miss you two and your escapades the most of all."

"Could we stay here, then?" Bevan asked hopefully. "Mayhaps Father will forget all about punishing us."

Dorcas laughed. "Nay, you may not. You will take whatever retribution comes your way like the McMahons you are. Remember to always carry your name proudly. You must never turn your back on your duty. Now scoot," she added, and watched them scamper away.

Dorcas looked up slowly to find Duncan standing over her. He helped her to her feet and drew her into his arms. Kissing the top of her head, he murmured, "I need have no fear in leaving you here, daughter. You know your duty, and you will complete it without fail."

Dorcas made no reply as he set her from him and helped his wife to mount. Then he swung into the saddle and led his family across the yard toward the gate. She felt trapped by her own words. She wanted to run after them, to yell at them that it was unfair of them to leave her behind among the enemy, but she did not. She stood with her head lifted proudly, unmindful of the tears streaming down her face, as she called out to them, "God speed." She was only vaguely aware of Neil coming to stand beside her, for her gaze was glued to her family as they disappeared one by one.

Neil was surprised at the tears that slipped down Dorcas's cheeks, and an uncomfortable feeling washed over him. He was still debating whether he should try to comfort her when she threw him a scathing look. Then she whirled and stalked into the keep.

12

The days passed in a blur for Dorcas. She braced herself for what would come now that she was alone in the enemy camp, but soon found that Astrid's friendliness and concern for her were not pretense, as she had thought, but genuine feeling. Even Cedric displayed a courteousness that amused her.

Once she realized that no one intended her harm, she began to relax. She found Cedric's tales of life among the northmen exciting, if mayhaps exaggerated, and argued good-naturedly with him that if his feats were so considerable, then he would have escaped them easily. He merely laughed, gazing at his wife, and told Dorcas that he had stayed only because he needed to win the greatest prize of all. Dorcas smiled at that, and looked up to where Neil leaned against the fireplace. He was watching his parents with such warmth, she could not pull her gaze away.

Though it should not have, the idea he cared deeply for someone other than himself surprised her. If only he would look at her as he looked at his parents, she thought, and was at once horrified by the notion. She did not want her husband. She disliked him, just as he disliked her.

As if sensing his wife's turmoil, Neil turned to her. The

warmth and tenderness in his eyes did not disappear, but subtly changed to reveal desire for her. Her stomach fluttered in excitement and her pulse started racing. A knowing smile touched his lips, making her blush and look away in confusion. There was no mockery on his face. Instead, an intimacy had passed between them at that moment, reaching into Dorcas's very soul and leaving her flustered and wary.

Thinking about the incident later, Dorcas decided she must have imagined it, for things went on as they always had, with Neil either ignoring her or making demands on her. Because of his father's illness, Neil was taking on more responsibility, making certain that the everyday running of the stronghold went smoothly. Cedric still made the final important decisions as head of the clan, and when Neil was not seeing to the execution of his father's orders, he was in Cedric's company, reporting on the happenings of the day.

He seemed content to leave Dorcas in his mother's company, and Dorcas didn't mind. The only thing she regretted was her lack of knowledge in running a large household. Her mother-by-marriage was enormously patient, worsening Dorcas's guilt at not having paid closer attention to Heloise. Astrid merely smiled and told Dorcas not to worry, that in time she would learn. And Dorcas did try, for she really liked Astrid, but she became very frustrated when things didn't go well, as when she sent the serving girls to cleaning the wrong rooms, or bought too little salt to cure the meat when the pigs were slaughtered.

As if to make amends, she would don her breeches and tunic to go hunting, bringing back some kind of game for the tables. Astrid insisted that it wasn't necessary, but only in this way did Dorcas feel she was contributing to the welfare of the household.

If Neil was aware of his wife's activities, he gave no hint of it. He remained cool and aloof toward her when others were present. It was when they were alone that his attitude changed, which only confused her. It seemed to Dorcas a night didn't go by when he didn't reach for her, setting her on fire as he took her to the heights of passion.

When he began to ignore her in their chamber, too, she made no effort to intrude upon his brooding silence. Instead, she cursed him silently for instilling within her a need for him, only to leave it unfulfilled. She would not humiliate herself by going to him. She would not!

For days she fretted about the cause of her husband's preoccuption. Her black mood matched Neil's, and like a wayward child she deliberately baited him, picking little fights, thinking that even his anger was better than his indifference. Sometimes he would explode, shouting at her as he stalked from the room; but other times he would look at her blackly and say nothing before leaving. At last she decided to ignore him in the same manner, and was oddly disturbed when he seemed not to notice.

After several weeks of his pensiveness, her curiosity was finally appeased as they dined one evening.

Cedric and Neil were quietly discussing the day's events. Dorcas listened with only half an ear until she heard Cedric ask "Have you thought more about my plan, Neil?"

Neil set his cup down and frowned. "Aye, I've thought of nothing else since you proposed it."

"You've had a considerable amount of time to make your decision, but I would like to add one more thing in favor of the proposition. Your ship sits idle in the harbor at Wexford as long as you remain here. You would be killing two birds with one stone by taking the goods that Erik has to trade to Norway, and you can inform your grandfather of your marriage."

"I, too, have though of that, but I do not understand why Erik would want me to help him. After all, we did not part under the best of circumstances."

Cedric guffawed and reached for his cup. "You have quarreled before."

"Not in that manner," Neil replied with a scowl.

"It is so unlike you to hold a petty grudge, son. And apparently Erik has forgotten all about the argument, whatever it was." He hoped Neil would confide in him, for he'd not learned what the men had argued about, but sighed resignedly at Neil's stubborn silence.

"Very well. I will go," Neil said shortly. "You are right. Gunnar should know about the marriage."

Cedric looked at Neil in surprise, then he laughed heartily and clapped his son on the back. "Good, good," he said, raising his cup in salute to Neil. "Well, daughter, what do y—"

The words died on Cedric's lips as he turned to Dorcas, only to see her striding from the hall. Puzzled, he glanced at Neil. His son's eyes were riveted on his wife as she disappeared from sight.

After Dorcas had left, Neil shrugged noncommittally at his parents' murmured questions of concern and left the hall. In his chamber he stopped just inside the doorway to study his wife as she stood at the window staring out at the night-dark garden. She did not turn when he closed the door and walked toward her.

Dorcas felt her husband's presence close behind her and tensed. Fear and anticipation mingled inside her. She could not let him touch her. If she did, she would be lost. It was as if he possessed not only her body, but her soul as well.

She was ashamed of her wanton craving for him, appalled that more than once she had considered changing her mind and making the first move toward him. Now she knew the reason for his distance. He'd been wondering how to break the news to her, his wife, that he would be traveling the seas to reach the side of his mistress. She almost laughed aloud at the ludicrous situation, and if she were not so angry, she would have. She'd begun to think over the past weeks that mayhaps they could live together peacefully. What a fool she was for so much as entertaining such a notion.

Well, damn him to the eternal fires, and damn her father and Cedric as well. She would show the Viking that she did not care. She did not have to be a witness to her own humiliation, watching his family and friends pity her as he ran off to his Anika.

"You are unhappy about the journey," he said quietly, reaching for her.

She stepped away quickly. "It is no concern of mine."

Neil frowned. What was the matter with her? "Of course it concerns you," he said, following her. He halted in his tracks when she once again moved out of his reach. His frown deepened in growing irritation.

"I do not see why," she said in a rush, "if you choose to go traipsing off to Norway, I should be concerned. However, I will not remain here among your people."

So that was it, he thought. She was afraid that she would have to stay behind. The frown left his face to be replaced by a huge grin, but that grin faded quickly at her next words.

"I will return home, to my father's house, where I will be among my own people."

"You are among your people here."

She whirled to face him and laughed harshly. "I am with my enemy, Viking!"

"Damnation, woman!" he bellowed. "The peace is in effect. We are no longer enemies!"

"Nevertheless, I shall feel more comfortable at home."

Neil closed the distance between them in two strides. He held her by the shoulders and shook her. "You will not return to your father's house, nor will you remain here to stir up trouble. You are coming with me so that I can keep an eye on you."

Oh, Lord! It was worse than she'd imagined. He was planning to humiliate her in front of his true love.

She started to protest, but before she could speak, Neil's mouth swooped down to claim hers. Her heart seemed to plummet to her stomach as his tongue invaded her mouth. She moaned as the fires only he could kindle within her flared once more. His lips pressed against her neck where her pulse beat rapidly, leaving her skin burning at his touch. His mouth moved lower to kiss the tops of her breasts through her gown, and she suddenly resented that gown.

As if reading her mind, Neil raised his head. Their eyes locked for a timeless moment while his hands slid to the neck of her gown. She gasped when he ripped the fabric to her waist, but she was not afraid. Nor did she try to fight him as he pushed the gown from her body. A raging storm was rising within her, and she gazed steadily into her husband's eyes, seeing clearly the flaming desire in them. Her breasts heaved in growing excitement as Neil let his gaze roam over her. He scooped her up in his arms and carried her to the bed. After laying her down gently, he doffed his clothes and stretched out beside her.

His hands stroked boldy over her, his mouth following their path. He left no inch of her unexplored as he stoked her passion to a mighty blaze, until she thought she would surely die for want of him. And for the first time since becoming his wife, Dorcas felt an urgent need to touch him in turn. She ran her hands slowly down his back, feeling the corded muscles tauten at her touch, marveling at his strength.

Neil groaned softly, shivering when her fingers brushed across his ribs. He covered her body with his, and winding his hands in her hair, kissed her hungrily as he slid into her.

Dorcas moaned in pleasure, arching upward to receive him, to pull him ever closer. The ecstasy of their bodies becoming one swept over her like a crashing wave. Their worlds exploded into rapturous delight, sending them spiraling upward into the heavens before, at last, they slowly returned to earth on peaceful clouds of contentment.

Dorcas stood at the railing of the Viking ship as it glided

smoothly down the fjord toward Gunnar Nordstrom's home. She shivered, and pulled her dark green woolen cloak more tightly about her. Her cheek brushed the gray fox fur that edged the garment, and she smiled as she stroked it, remembering how she'd come by it.

Upon reaching Wexford a few weeks before, Neil had deposited her at a house, leaving her in the care of his Viking friend, Selwyn. Then he'd abruptly departed, stating that he had to attend to matters of business. She was angered at having to spend her time in the company of the taciturn Viking and felt cheated because she was not allowed to explore the rapidly growing port town. Neil was adamant in his refusal to allow her to roam Wexford on her own, and claimed he was too busy to show her around. At the time she'd thought he was being his usual spiteful self, and that he was carrying his threat of "keeping an eye on her" too far. It was all right that he was gone long before the sun rose until late into the night, but she was not permitted any freedom. She'd not even seen Erik, and she wondered if that was why her husband would not let her go out—to keep her from her friend.

On the last day of their stay in Wexford, she was surprised by a number of visitors to their rented quarters—all of whom bore parcels that Selwyn accepted as though he had been expecting them. When Neil returned earlier than usual, he asked her to open them.

Perplexed, Dorcas did so, and gasped in astonishment when she untied the first bundle and revealed the new cape. Like an excited child, she tore open the others to find chemises of the finest linens and wools, gowns and shawls in vibrant colors of peacock blue, green, yellow, scarlet, and violet, and shoes of the softest calfskin. The last parcel contained an exquisite box of gold, worked in a leaf pattern and inlaid with ivory.

She held the delicate case on her lap, running her hands over it, too stunned to speak. Neil opened the lid to reveal two compartments.

She was unable to believe her eyes. One compartment held a pair of golden arm bands in the shape of coiled snakes. The deep etching in the precious metal looked like snakeskin. Each one had a carnelian eye that stared menacingly at Dorcas from its upraised head. In the other compartment lay a magnificent necklace of two tiers of silver discs, six in the top row and four underneath, each one two inches in diameter and inset with crystals.

She raised her eyes questioningly, and Neil told her they were gifts. They would be seeing his grandfather and friends in Norway. He wanted his wife to look her very best.

Remembering those words, Dorcas frowned at the high cliffs they were sailing past. She'd thought over what Neil had said quite often, and wondered if he was afraid she would shame him. Did he look upon her as most other Vikings looked upon the Irish, as uncouth barbarians? Did he really think that clothes and jewels would change her?

Her mouth set in a line of distaste. She already knew what he thought of her abilities as a warrior. Mayhaps she should wear her linen tunic and breeches for her stay in Norway. She could swap stories of her conquests in battle with the Viking warriors. She would show him! She bit her lower lip, thinking of how angry that would make Neil. Nay. She would not do it. She would not shame her husband, for to do so would be to shame herself also. Besides, she was not at all sure what Neil had meant by his words. He'd not been speaking snidely. Instead, he'd cut off her words of thank-you and immediately had made glorious love to her. They'd forgotten everything else then, wrapped up in their world of bliss.

Dorcas was startled out of her thoughts when a pair of strong arms wrapped around her middle. She tensed as she was pulled back against a hard male body, but immediately relaxed at Neil's soft voice.

" 'Tis beautiful, isn't it?"

"Aye, it is breathtaking," she said, her attention returning to her surroundings. The rugged wildness of the passing countryside was an awesome sight.

"May I add, my lady, that your presence only compliments these environs."

Dorcas turned in the circle of his arms to stare up at him searchingly, trying to decide if he was mocking her. "My, what honeyed words for one who feels the need to keep a watchful eye on me," she said.

"It is a pleasure to do so," he answered, grinning.

She took his light tone for ridicule, and her face flushed in agitation. "Are you so afraid, then, that I will shame you in front of your grandfather and your friends?"

Neil chuckled deeply and pushed back a wisp of hair that had escaped from beneath the hood of her cloak. He felt her tremble at his touch, and he grew somber as he studied the fine planes of her face, the high cheekbones stained with color, the long, straight nose that tilted up at the tip. Her deep emerald eyes gazed back at him from under finely arched eyebrows. He was tempted to carry her to the shelter that had been erected for their sleeping quarters as the warm stirrings of passion flooded through him, but he fought back the urge. There was not enough privacy for them there.

Dorcas watched the play of emotions cross his face—first amusement, then longing, then disappointment. She'd been right in her assumption. He was afraid she would humiliate him. "I will do my best not to shame you," she said stiffly.

He laughed suddenly, startling her. "The only way in which you could embarrass me would be to dismember anyone who might displease you."

She opened her mouth to protest, but quickly shut it again as she remembered her confrontation with Egan McNeil. "Is there anyone who would make me that angry?" she asked in a half whisper.

He laughed again. "I hope not! Besides, Gunnar is considered a king among his people. I am his grandson and you are my wife. No one would dare to insult you."

"Well, if it will help, I give you my solemn oath that I will try very hard to hold my temper in check."

He grinned. "I suppose that I will have to accept that as your promise to stay out of mischief."

The nagging doubts about Neil's motives for bringing her along surfaced once more. There was one other thing that she'd tried desperately to push to the darkest corner of her mind ever since she'd learned of their journey, but before she could contemplate further on it, Neil's mouth covered hers and all rational thought fled.

When he heard his name being called, Neil reluctantly raised his head. He looked with annoyance at Selwyn, then his gaze followed the direction in which the other man pointed. Smiling, he turned Dorcas around in his arms and held her in front of him. "We are here."

Dorcas was filled with trepidation as she watched the people run to the landing. Neil told her there were more men about than usual at this time of year, joining the women and children in welcoming the new arrivals, so Gunnar must not be on a raid. Spirits were high as laughter and shouts of greeting were called between those aboard the longship and those waiting eagerly onshore. One little boy, who did not wish to be left out, ran along with the others as fast as his short legs would carry him, a gander right on his heels.

Disquieting thoughts crept into Dorcas's mind once more as she wondered what she, an outsider, would be faced with here. Her gaze strayed to the women, and the one disturbing shadow that she'd tried for weeks to stifle rushed to the forefront of her imagination. She wondered which one of them was Anika.

Once ashore, Neil's face lit up with sheer pleasure at being in his second home. He laughed and joked with an abandon Dorcas had never seen, changing his otherwise austere features. She stood to one side, spellbound at the ease with which he conversed with his friends. A feeling of dejection wrapped around her at the thought that he was so happy to be in Norway again, but instead of letting her despondency show, she straightened her shoulders and raised her chin. She'd promised Neil that she would not shame him. She promised herself that she would not let his actions humiliate her.

As she gazed curiously at the people around her, she slowly realized that she was becoming the center of attention. Though she couldn't understand what they were saying, the pointed stares and whispers directed at her made their meaning clear. Feeling uneasy, she stepped closer to Neil.

At that moment a burly man with an unkempt beard and long hair grabbed her arm. He laughed harshly, speaking a few words to Neil. Neil's casual demeanor changed to one of coldness as he answered the man abruptly. The Viking's eyes flickered in surprise. Then he laughed again and crushed Dorcas in an excruciating hug. When he released her, she watched the big man warily as he beamed at her. The people around them kept chattering at Neil, but he was no longer in the mood to tarry. He took Dorcas by the arm and led her away from the dock and along a broad lane.

The moment of panic that Dorcas had felt ebbed as she accompanied him without protest. Finding her voice, she asked, "Who was that man?"

"That was Wolfram the Mighty. He is one of Gunnar's fiercest warriors. Some call him a berserker, though as far as I could see, he is no better or worse than some others."

"What is a berserker?"

"One who goes crazy during battle."

She shuddered, thinking of the wild look in the man's eyes. She could believe such a thing was true. "Why did he grab me?"

"He wanted to buy you," replied Neil tightly.

"He what!"

His hand tightened on her arm as she halted abruptly.

At the look of disbelief on her face, he suddenly saw the humor in the situation. He didn't think even Wolfram would be able to control this hellcat. The corners of his mouth quirked upward in a little smile. "Actually, you should be flattered," he said teasingly. "He offered far more than what you are worth."

Her mouth dropped open. "Why you—"

Before she could finish, Neil cut her off. "Do not worry. I told him that you are my wife and unavailable for sale."

"I am surprised you did not jump at the chance to barter me away."

"I must admit, the idea was tempting. But then, how would I ever explain your sudden 'fondness' for Norway to our fathers? Besides, I have invested a great deal in you, with all your new clothes and jewels. I am afraid that Wolfram would not have been able to meet my price."

"Oh!" sputtered Dorcas, but before she could say anything further, Neil laughed and propelled her toward an imposing stone house.

She fumed in silence as they entered the dwelling. The large hall was dominated by a huge round fireplace in its center. Tables and benches lined the walls. Doors led off the main room to what Dorcas could only assume were sleeping quarters. Along the far north wall stood a thronelike chair where a large man sat, staring hard at the couple. He seemed not to pay heed to the slaves who stopped their work to gaze curiously at the new arrivals, but then his booming voice filled the air.

"Now that you have managed to disrupt my household with your arrival, mayhaps my servants' curiosity is appeased and *they can get back to work*."

At their master's sharp words, the slaves immediately bustled about the room, seeing to their tasks.

"The difficulties in Erin must not have been too great," said the man, rising and coming forward. "You wasted no time in returning" His sparkling blue eyes belied the stern quality of his voice as he grasped Neil and embraced him warmly. His white hair stood out starkly against Neil's own dark locks.

"Welcome back, my grandson."

"It is good to see you again, grandfather."

Gunnar stepped back to eye Neil critically. The gruffness appeared once more in his voice as he asked, "What foolish chase did your father call you home on?"

Neil smiled. "No wild chase, I assure you. There was a slight, er, problem with which he needed my help."

Dorcas was standing a little behind Neil, and apprehension filled her when Gunnar glanced sharply at her before once more speaking to Neil.

"Is she the problem?"

Neil chuckled softly. "You could say that. She is my wife."

Surprise flashed across Gunnar's face. He studied Dorcas, noting her defiant stare, the proud tilt of her chin. He grunted and looked away. "Irish?" he asked shortly.

"Aye. Her family's settlement borders ours. We've always had trouble with the McMahons, and Cedric felt that an alliance between our clans would put an end to the fighting. Actually, my wife was the cause of my long exile in Norway."

Gunnar's eyebrows arched upward. He turned his attention to the young woman once more. "Come here, girl," he commanded in her tongue.

As Neil drew Dorcas to his side, she studied the old man as intently as he studied her. He reached up to push back the hood of her cloak, then paused, his hands hovering near her face as if he waited for some reaction from her. When she did nothing, he swept the hood back. He caught his breath at her beauty, and his gaze flickered across her face, then strayed to her mass of red curls. Fascinated, he touched the silky, soft hair.

"You are in accord with the union?" he asked her gruffly.

Her lips tightened. "I agreed."

Gunnar caught her sardonic tone and glanced at Neil.

His grandson was staring at his wife, his face expression-less. All was not well between the young couple, and he intended to find out what the trouble was. Above all else, he wanted to see his grandson happy.

Dorcas sat between Neil and Gunnar at the high table, trying hard not to show her boredom. She stifled a yawn, then jumped, startled, when uproarious laughter filled the room. Her attention was drawn to one of the tables, where men clapped one another on the back, howling, she as-sumed, at a joke being told. She watched them warily, con-cerned that such high spirits could turn sour at any moment, making enemies of the closest friends.

So far Gunnar had been able to stop any serious harm from befalling his guests. Though there'd been arguments from time to time, there had been only one brawl in the three days spent feasting. Gunnar had insisted on sending far and wide for his friends to welcome his grandson and his new bride, as well as to celebrate his recent victory on the coast of England.

Dorcas had had to endure, gritting her teeth and smil-ing, some of the bolder Vikings' embraces of welcome, glad that Neil was close by. And though she saw in other men's eyes that they were wont to insult her, they did not—not with Neil and Gunnar flanking her. The hostility emanating from these Vikings made her wonder what her fate would be at their hands should Gunnar and Neil not be around. Up to now the two men had shown an amazing ability for holding the ale they consumed, but she knew that sooner or later they would succumb to the effects of the potent beverage.

Her gaze strayed to one of the lower tables and came to rest on Olaf Olafson, the worst of her antagonists. Though he'd not openly shown his hostility, his eyes bespoke his hatred each time they met hers. He reminded Dorcas of another whose hatred she'd earned. She could understand Egan McNeil's animosity toward her, but she could not fathom the mindless enmity that the strange Viking held for her.

She was suddenly jolted by the nagging thought that she, too, had felt the same emmity for all Vikings. But she'd had reason, she argued silently. She forcefully pushed the disquieting thoughts from her mind, willing her attention back to the festivities, unaware of the hate-filled eyes turned her way.

Placing a hand over her mouth, she yawned again and wondered irritably if the Vikings were made of stone. She needed sleep even if they didn't.

"Why don't you retire?" Neil asked, leaning close to her.

Dorcas turned to her husband. He picked up her hand and, holding it to his lips, added, "I will be along momentarly."

Her heart skipped a beat at his penetrating gaze. Without saying anything she arose and made her way to their chamber. All traces of her fatigue had fled at the promise in his eyes.

She entered her chamber and was struggling to remove her gown when the door opened.

"You wasted no time," she said, laughing softly as she turned. Then she froze.

Olaf Olafson shut the door quietly and started forward, a wolfish grin on his face.

Dorcas backed away. "What are you doing here? What do you want?" She swallowed hard. "Neil will be here soon."

The man halted at the mention of Neil's name, then he laughed a short, ugly laugh and started toward her again. He couldn't understand anything she'd said, and obviously didn't care.

Dorcas edged closer to a table where Neil's knife lay. The man must be mad to be so bold, she thought. And she would kill him for that.

She lunged for the dagger just as Olaf leapt forward. She swung around and felt hot satisfaction as the man's flesh tore open under the knife blade. A guttural sound was ripped from his throat. He blocked a second assault from her, knocking the dagger from her hand. She made another lunge for the table, desperate for any weapon, and felt a stabbing pain in her head as her hair was grabbed from behind. She brought her heel down hard on his foot. He grunted and loosened his hold.

She wrenched herself free and heard a tearing sound as the back of her dress ripped beneath the big Viking's hands. Filled with outrage at the man's senseless assault, she grabbed Neil's sword and turned in blind fury. But Olaf wasn't there.

He was pressed against the far wall with Wolfram the Mighty's hands around his throat, choking the life from him.

Dorcas's shaking knees could no longer hold her, and she sank to the floor, the sword still grasped tightly in her hands. She felt someone's gentle touch, and looked up into the concerned face of Wolfram. Clutching the front of her gown to her, she started to rise with his aid when a low growl came from the doorway, and Neil bolted into the room.

Seeing his wife's torn dress and the mighty Viking's hands on hers, Neil didn't stop to think. He threw himself at the man, pulling him off Dorcas.

"Nay!" she cried. "Neil, stop it. He is not to blame. He saved me from rape by that one."

Her words slowly penetrated through the fog in his mind, and Neil looked to where she pointed. His eyes darkened in fury at the lifeless form of Olaf, crumpled on the floor. He let go of Wolfram's tunic front and pulled Dorcas to him.

"I am sorry, my sweet. You are safe now. I never should have let you leave by yourself," he said against her hair. He looked over her head at Wolfram. "Thank you for coming to my wife's aid."

The Viking nodded. "Your wife is most courageous, but she was no match for Olaf."

"Nay, she was not." A sudden thought occurred to Neil. "How did you know?"

Wolfram grinned hugely, remembering the pleasure he'd received just a short time before. "I was coming down the hall from Maida's room when I saw that swine"—he tossed his head in the direction of Olaf—"enter your chamber. I became curious to see what he was up to."

"It is good that you did. I cannot imagine why he would want to attack Dorcas. I never would have thought that some fool would become so befuddled with drink that he would mistake my wife for one of the serving maids."

Wolfram grunted at Neil's blindness. He had a pretty good idea why the man had attacked Dorcas. He'd made some very rude and suggestive remarks about the young woman, well away from his host and Neil, of course. Olaf Olafson was extremely bitter about the insult he felt Neil had dealt his family, for Anika Thornstein was his cousin, and a close one at that.

So far Anika had not shown up at the festivities, and for that Wolfram was grateful. He was glad Neil had not married her. He looked at Dorcas and thought once more that the young man could not have chosen better. "Dorcas the Valiant," he murmured.

Hearing her name, Dorcas glanced at Wolfram. "What did he say?" she asked Neil quietly.

"He called you Dorcas the Valiant."

She blushed under the man's scrutiny. "Will you thank him for me?"

Neil whispered the words of gratitude in her ear and she repeated them aloud, bringing a huge grin to the mighty Viking's face.

13

Dorcas opened her eyes slowly and looked about her in confusion. The events of the previous evening suddenly jolted her fully awake, and she jerked her head around to stare at the spot where Olaf had lain. She breathed a sigh of relief and lay back, remembering that Wolfram had taken the body from the chamber.

After he'd gone, Neil had held her close, murmuring soothing words to quiet her. He'd made love to her then with such a fierce possessiveness that she had been transported to the highest realms of pleasure. She had welcomed him gladly, savoring the thrill of desire that he awakened in her each time he touched her.

Thinking of the night past, she tried to sort out her feelings. She should not have fallen into her husband's arms so willingly, but she'd wanted to. Aye, she had wanted Neil last night as much as ever. She'd wanted to wipe the memory of the first time she had lain with him from her mind—a painful memory conjured up by Olaf's attack. She had needed her husband's tender caresses. Like a master craftsman, he made her want him . . . always. She was no longer ashamed to admit it. But what of Neil?

After their wedding night he never again bedded her with such bitterness and hate, but had instilled within her a sense of passion and excitement that took her breath away. Even as she reveled in his touch, she did not know his feelings toward her. She wondered if he would put her aside should his Anika come back into his life. Would he want them both?

Dorcas felt the chains of doubt and fear wrap themselves around her heart. Her pride was such that she would not share her husband. But what could she do? She tried to convince herself that it did not matter, but a little voice told her differently.

She was shaken from her musings when the door opened and Neil entered, carrying a tray. He smiled and greeted her cheerfully as he set the food on a table by the bed. Then he sat down beside her, pushing her hair back. His expression grew serious as one hand slid behind her head to bring her face to within inches of his own.

Dorcas's heart hammered at his look. Could she continue to make his eyes grow dark with passion? The answer was lost to her when his mouth hungrily devoured hers. Her arms went about his neck of their own volition, and she clung to him, as if to let him know that she was his.

He drew back to gaze at her curiously. Her eyes were a wide bright green, and he wondered if she was still frightened by the past evening's events. She'd responded to his lovemaking the night before with an eagerness that mightily pleased him, but also bewildered him. He cursed himself for letting her out of his sight.

He smiled to reassure her, and said lightly, "Eat your breakfast, Dorcas the Valiant. I have a surprise for you."

She blushed at the name Wolfram had bestowed upon her, and chided Neil for calling her that.

He laughed. "Ah, but my dear, your exploits have become known far and wide. Even now the skalds dedicate verses to your bravery."

"Oh, Neil, you jest," she said, laughing at the comic expression on his face.

"Nay, I do not. Wolfram let it be known that you defended your honor in the manner of a true warrior, and the poets have composed rhymes to your courage."

She gasped. "What does Gunnar think?"

Neil shrugged. "He was a bit perplexed at first, until I told him something of your background. Now he is *more* so." He laughed when Dorcas flashed him a wry look and slapped his arm. He kissed her quickly, then released her. "Now eat, so that I can show you the surprise I have."

"What is it?"

"You'll see," he answered cryptically, making Dorcas all the more eager to know what he planned.

She ate quickly and dressed hurriedly while Neil lounged on the bed enjoying the sight. Then he threw her cloak over her shoulders and led her outside. Heads turned to stare in wonder at the object of the poems by the skalds. Dorcas flushed at the attention, but Neil seemed not to noticed as he led her to the landing.

He helped her into a smaller version of a longship before climbing in himself. Then he started rowing down the fjord, staying close to shore.

"Where are we going?" Dorcas asked.

"I want to show you something. Besides, I think we could use a few days alone."

She stared at him in amazement. He wanted to be alone with her. Surely that was a good sign.

Neil continued rowing until they were on a huge lake. Its blue surface shimmered brightly under the sun—one of its few appearances before the onset of winter. Pine trees stood like proud soldiers at attention along the banks, and the only sound was the occasional call of a hunting bird. Dorcas gazed in wonder at the peaceful beauty surrounding her.

She listened as Neil spoke quietly, telling her of Norway and its people. He told her of their love and hate, their joys and sorrows, their pain and passion, and she was enraptured by the history of this proud people she called enemy.

At last he rowed ashore and helped her out of the boat. He breathed deeply of the clean fresh air, then took her hand and led her up a slope to higher ground. Once they reached the top of the hill, he turned Dorcas around to look below. She sucked in her breath sharply at the view of the shining lake, its crystal blue vivid against the vibrant green of the trees.

" 'Tis beautiful," she murmured in awe, her gaze sweeping the vista before her.

Neil put his arms about her middle and pulled her against him. "This is my favorite spot. I used to come up here every chance I got. I never tire of this view. In truth, I am made speechless each time I see it, for each time is more beautiful than the last."

"I can see why you would think so," she said almost reverently.

"No one knows of this place but me." He turned her around to face him. "I wanted you to see it."

"This must be the most beautiful place on earth that God ever made," she said quietly, pleased that Neil wanted to share it with her.

Without answering he took her face between his hands and kissed her with such heartrending tenderness, she felt she would cry. After a moment he released her and smiled broadly. "Come, I want to show you something else." He led her down a worn path, through the trees, and stopped before a small hut.

"I thought you said no one knew of this place?" she asked in surprise.

"To my knowledge, no one does. I built the house."

"By yourself?"

"Aye." He ran a hand proudly over the doorframe. "I would stay here for days, sometimes weeks, at a time. At first my grandfather was worried by my disappearances, but he soon learned to shrug them off, once he knew no harm had befallen me."

"Wasn't he ever curious about your absences?"

Neil laughed softly, like a small boy caught in some mischief. "Aye, but I told him that I needed time to myself. He never questioned me after that."

There was much laughter and loving in the idyllic days and nights Dorcas and Neil spent in the hills. They played in the woods like children, and fished in the lake for their meals. One evening, after much coaxing on Neil's part, they even went swimming in the icy water. Afterward, Neil warmed Dorcas by firing her passions and setting her body aflame with his touch.

They talked of their homes and families. Dorcas ached for Neil, sorry that the closeness he'd shared with the two older brothers who'd lived to manhood had been snatched from him, while Neil felt the pangs of jealousy at the intimacy that his wife shared with her twin. As though in an effort to wipe those feelings from her, he'd taken her then with a fierce need, hoping to make her forget there was anyone else in the world but the two of them.

Neil marveled at her ability to catch game, and laughed at her perplexity when it came time to cook it. His teasing about her cooking enraged her, so he patiently taught her how, and found her an apt pupil.

As each day passed, Dorcas dreaded more the time when they would have to return to the world outside their Valhalla. She liked having Neil to herself. Not once had they had a fight, and she enjoyed the feeling of peace that had settled over her. But she was no closer to knowing how her husband felt about her than she'd been before.

She was curious about the woman Neil loved, wondering what Anika Thornstein was like, but thankful she'd not had the opportunity to find out. It appeared her fears that Neil would leave her for Anika were unfounded, for the woman had not been at Gunnar's as Dorcas thought she might be. But was it only for a time? Dorcas was terribly confused. Her husband professed his love for another woman, yet he made her feel that *she* was the only woman in his life. How could he stir her passions so if he felt nothing for her? Was he only amusing himself, or was he beginning to accept the situation they'd been thrust into? Was he content with her as his wife? She tried to find answers to all the questions running through her head, but none would come. She wished fervently that they could remain as they now were, but instinct told her it was a short-lived interlude.

As they lounged beside the lake on the fourth morning, Dorcas was once again struck by the devastating handsomeness of her husband. She was sure he had known many women. His expertise at making her body come alive proved that. He claimed to love one woman, yet why hadn't he married her? Why had he waited? She was startled out of her reverie when Neil turned to her and shrugged. She realized she'd asked the question aloud.

"I always felt there was no rush," he said.

Was there a caustic tone to his reply? She couldn't be sure. She stared at his hard profile, and her heart sank at his stern expression. She had not wanted this, and neither had he.

"Instead," she said, "you find yourself forced into a situation that you never wanted."

He shrugged again and replied shortly, "Aye," making her stomach churn and her heart race.

"And now you are trapped."

"No more so than you. As I recall, you did not want our alliance any more than I. But now that we are bound, it is up to us to see that peace lasts between our clans."

Dorcas felt as though she'd been kicked squarely in the stomach. She jumped up and ran blindly through the woods. She heard Neil calling after her and ran all the harder to escape him. His words from so long ago came back to haunt her.

My father wishes peace. You will bear my heir.

Now she knew for certain that her husband held no tender feelings toward her. He felt only carnal pleasure with her—and far more important to him was his pride and loyalty to his father. His words cut like a knife into her heart. How could he arouse such soul-stirring sensations within her when she meant nothing beyond physical sensation to him? How could she have allowed herself to become trapped by her need for him? Her belief that the only bond they shared was a physical one was confirmed. She should not care, but she did. Why should Neil's feelings for her matter? She didn't know. All she knew for certain was that she could not let him see how much his words had stung.

She paid no heed to where she was going, but ran in an erratic pattern away from Neil, and the sham that was their marriage.

Her breathing became ragged and her side ached from the exertion. A small sob escaped her when she tripped and fell to her knees. She touched her face, realizing for the first time that she was crying. What was the use? She was trapped, she thought miserably, with no way out. How could her father have placed her in a loveless marriage with a hated Viking? Great racking sobs shook her. She hadn't wanted marriage, hadn't wanted it at all. She was a warrior. Yet Neil had shown her that she was also a woman with wants and needs, and it frightened her to think that she could so easily yield to him.

She was sitting on the ground, crying her heart out, when she felt something brush against her thigh. She looked down to find a tiny wolf cub scrambling onto her lap. Alarm settled in her like a dead weight, and she jerked her head up to look about warily. The mother would certainly not take kindly to the intrusion upon territory she considered hers, or the handling of her offspring. But Dorcas saw no sign of an adult wolf anywhere. Just two more cubs who stood at a distance, growling and whining, as though in disapproval of the bravery shown by their sibling. The little pup paid no heed to the calls. Instead, he rubbed his head against Dorcas's hand, willing her to show him some attention.

She smiled at the dogged boldness of the little cub, ruffling its downy, soft fur and thinking that perhaps the poor mother had been caught off guard. A frown touched Dorcas's forehead. Could it be that the cubs were orphans? If that was the case, they would never make it through the coming winter. She was tempted to try to make friends with all three of them and take them back with her. She couldn't bear the thought of the poor things having to fend for themselves.

She was trying to coax the other two cubs to come to her when Neil caught up with her.

"Dorcas, put the pup down and come over here to me, now," he said with more calm than he felt. His heart thudded painfully against his ribs at the sight of his wife unconcernedly sitting on the ground, playing with a wolf cub and trying to coax two more into her lap.

She looked over her shoulder at his concerned face and smiled. "There is nothing to fear. They must have been abandoned, or else the mother was killed."

The corners of Neil's mouth lifted wryly. "I assure you, they've not been abandoned. Didn't you see those tracks leading off into the trees?"

She slowly turned her gaze to where Neil pointed. Her mouth went dry and she wet her parched lips with the tip of her tongue. In truth, she had not seen them. She'd been too intent upon her own problems. Then when the overly friendly cub had made his presence known and she'd not been immediately attacked, she'd assumed they were alone.

"Dorcas, put down the cub and come to me," repeated Neil.

She automatically did as she was instructed. Her heart beat a staccato rhythm as she arose and backed toward

Neil. To her dismay, the cub followed on wobbly legs. She groaned inwardly. What had she done?

She was two feet away from Neil when she heard a low, warning growl coming from the trees to her right. She froze and jerked her head around. Her eyes stared straight into those of a huge angry wolf.

Fear paralyzed Dorcas. She couldn't make her limbs move as she continued to stare into the hot, glaring eyes fixed on her. The wolf's mouth pulled back in a feral snarl. The powerful muscles of her neck and shoulders were bunched, and her stance was that of one ready to spring. All Dorcas could think of was to get away before the mother wolf attacked them for messing with what was hers. She couldn't bear the thought of harming the mother and making the cubs orphans. But she could not move.

Neil grabbed her and flung her behind him.

"Run!" he commanded.

She lost her balance and fell to her hands and knees. She swung her head around in time to see the mother wolf spring through the air toward Neil. She scrambled to her feet in the same instant, crying, "Do not hurt her!"

Neil's arm came up to deflect the blow as all one hundred pounds of wolf landed on him. He staggered backward at the force of the attack but managed to remain on his feet. He felt tearing flesh as the wolf's teeth sank into his forearm, and knew from the strength of her grip that she would not easily let go. He balled his free hand into a fist and sent it crashing into the side of the animal's head. The wolf's tight hold immediately slackened, and with a little whimper she fell to the ground.

A cry of alarm escaped Dorcas upon seeing the mother wolf fall limply to the forest floor and lie still. The three little cubs ran clumsily to her and crawled all over her, whining, trying to nudge her into awareness.

"You killed her!" Dorcas screamed, running forward.

Neil grabbed her when she tried to get past him and

shook her. "She is only unconscious," she said harshly.
"We must leave here before she awakens. Now come."

Dorcas reluctantly let him lead her away, casting anxious glances behind her until she could no longer see the animals. Yanking her arm free of Neil's hold, she stalked ahead of him, throwing over her shoulder, "You did not have to be so cruel. She was only trying to protect her young."

Neil stopped in his tracks. His mouth unwittingly dropped open. He snapped it shut again and glared at his wife's back. "How thoughtful of you to be so concerned for what I suffered in trying to protect you," he said dryly.

Dorcas whirled around to face him. Her eyes widened at the sight of the blood dripping down Neil's arm. She rushed to his side and reached for his arm, only to have him jerk away from her. Sparks of fire flew from her eyes as she glared at him. He glared back and said tauntingly, "Mayhaps you would rather tend the wolf."

Undaunted, she reached for his arm once more. "How bad is it?" she asked softly.

" 'Tis only a scratch."

There was so much blood, Dorcas couldn't tell if what he said was true or not. "Come down to the water so that I can clean and bind your wound," she ordered.

She washed away the blood and found a nasty bite that would eventually heal without having to be sewn together. Tearing off a piece of her tunic, she bound the wound, all the while avoiding Neil's eyes.

He, in turn, studied Dorcas, perplexed by her sudden changing moods. He tried to recall what had made her flee as she had, and remembered that they'd been discussing the bargain between their fathers. Surely that was not what had upset her! His eyes narrowed in speculation. Nay, of course not. She'd made it very clear that she wanted nothing to do with him, and yet . . .

He closed his eyes, remembering those soft lips yielding to his, her skin, softer than the down of a baby bird, the velvety warmth of her womanhood as she responded to his touch. He never tired of Dorcas, and he wondered if he ever would. He knew only that she was his, would always remain his. He would never give her up, for without their union there would be no peace between the clans. A niggling question crept into his mind as he looked once more at Dorcas. Was the bargain for peace the only reason he wanted his wife, or was he falling in love with her? That notion horrified him! The woman sitting beside him was the last person in the world he would choose to fall in love with. She was much too wild.

He suddenly frowned. What if she was falling in love with him? He inwardly scoffed at the idea. It was too preposterous to consider. The hellcat would just as soon slit his throat if she thought she could get away with it.

Dorcas glanced up to find Neil frowning at her. "Am I hurting you?" she asked with concern.

He stared into her emerald eyes, wide with innocence, and shook his head. She looked down again and continued wrapping the bandage around his arm.

"Why did you run away?" he asked quietly.

She jumped in surprise and sent him a quick look. Blushing, she turned away quickly, unable to stand his penetrating gaze. "I did not run away," she murmured.

"You did."

She jerked her head around to glare at him. "I did not!" she cried hotly.

Perplexed blue eyes stared into furious green ones for a moment before Dorcas looked away. Neil let the matter drop. "We will have to return to Gunnar's soon," he said.

Dorcas's heart sank. The time she'd been dreading was upon them. But then, what did it matter if they went or stayed? Mayhaps with others around, she would not be so susceptible to Neil's will.

"When?" she asked quietly, tying off the bandage.

"I thought tomorrow. Rolf Thornstein should have left Gunnar's home by now."

Dorcas's eyebrows knit in a frown at the familiar name. "Who is Rolf Thornstein?"

"Olafson's cousin, and the head of his household."

"Why should you wish to avoid him?"

"Though Rolf's grandfather and Father were very close to Gunnar, I fear that he is not, and would look for any excuse to start trouble. He hates anyone who is not a Viking," he added, casting a sideways glance at Dorcas. "Seeing you, who are Irish and was involved in his cousin's death would set him off."

Dorcas flushed in anger at Neil's words. Her eyes burned brightly as understanding dawned. She jumped up and stood glaring down at him. "So you felt the need to get me out of harm's way? I am a McMahon, a warrior, and I fight my own battles."

Neil leapt to his feet. "I will not allow you to create problems for my grandfather when trouble can be avoided."

"Running away is the act of a coward," she spat. "We McMahons are not cowards."

With a low growl he grabbed her. "You are now my wife, therefore, under my protection," he said fiercely, shaking her.

She wrenched herself free, shouting, "I can protect myself!"

They stood glowering at each other for a moment, then Dorcas broke the heavy silence. "I want to leave here, now," she demanded.

Neil swore soundly, and, turning on his heel, left her standing by the water's edge. The minutes passed slowly as she stood there motionless. She wondered miserably how their happy, carefree time could have been spoiled so quickly, and decided it did not matter. No matter how much Neil looked down upon her abilities, she was who she was—a warrior, and she would not let him mold her into a helpless female. The sooner he saw that, the better off he would be. She would not change, no matter how much she liked the feel of Neil's arms around her. She did not need him. She did not.

In moments he was back with their belongings. He strode purposefully toward the boat, and she had to hurry to keep up with him. Touching her as little as possible, he helped her inside before climbing in himself.

Not one word was spoken on their return trip to Gunnar's. Both were too wrapped up in their angry thoughts.

Neil wished he'd never brought his wife along. In truth, he wished he'd never chosen her for his wife in the first place.

Dorcas's thoughts ran along the same vein, and she wished her husband would vanish into thin air.

When they reached the settlement, Neil guided the boat up to the landing. Jumping agilely ashore, he tied the boat to the dock and helped Dorcas out, but stepped away as soon as she was on land. Without a backward glance, he strode toward the house. He entered the front door and stopped dead, causing Dorcas, who was following close behind, to plow into his back with a thud.

She stepped away and eyed Neil darkly for a moment before moving to his side. Her eyes traveled curiously to where he gazed intently across the room. A tiny woman sat on a stool at Gunnar's feet, her oval faced turned upward as she listened with rapt attention to what the old man said. Her flaxen hair hung in one long braid down her back. She was dressed in a simple dark blue gown.

Dorcas felt as though a swarm of butterflies had been let loose in her stomach. The woman was petite and lovely, every inch a lady—everything she was not. She knew without having to be told that she was facing Anika. She glanced at Neil, but his gaze was riveted on the woman across the room, his eyes filled with such warmth and tenderness that Dorcas's heart sank.

"Here is Neil now," Gunnar shouted.

Anika's head jerked around. Her lips parted as her blue eyes devoured every inch of Neil. Like a cat ready to pounce on a juicy mouse, Dorcas thought disgustedly. A small smile touched Anika's lips as she arose and moved toward them. When she spoke, her voice was like the sweet chiming of a bell, unlike Dorcas's huskier voice.

"Welcome back, Neil."

"Anika," he croaked. He cleared his throat and tried again. "How are you?"

"I am well," she said quietly, searching his face.

A heavy silence hung in the air for a moment, then Anika inquired, "And you?"

Neil gestured with his hand as if to shrug off her question. "I have been well."

"Oh!" she gasped. "Your arm."

Neil, having forgotten about his injury, held his bandaged forearm out. "It is nothing. Just a scratch."

"I am glad to see that it has been tended."

"My wife . . ." Neil suddenly realized he'd not given Dorcas a thought since entering the house. He glanced at her to find her appraising Anika with cool detachment. Drawing Dorcas to his side, he said, "Anika, I would like you to meet my wife, Dorcas."

Anika's eyes flickered over Dorcas, then she dismissed the Irish woman and turned her wide-eyed gaze on Neil. "I—I'd heard of your marriage."

Dorcas noticed cynically the innocent, hurt look in Anika's eyes as she stared at Neil. In the second it had taken her to appraise and disregard her, Dorcas had caught the contempt in the other woman's eyes. She touched Neil's arm gently and murmured, "My husband, if you will allow me, I think I will retire to freshen up after our journey. I am sure you have much to discuss with your . . . friend."

Confused, Neil watched as Dorcas left the hall. The honeyed tone and soft eyes were in complete contrast to her earlier mood. Besides, she was not given to asking his permission for anything. He stared after her until she was out of sight. Only then did he allow his attention to return to the woman at his side.

* * *

Dorcas sat in a chair opposite Gunnar's, trying very hard to concentrate on mending one of his tunics, but her mind continued to betray her. No one seemed to be aware of her difficulty with the mending, nor did anyone care, she thought sullenly. How she managed to get herself in these situations she didn't know. In a burst of generosity she'd offered to do the work after Helga, the woman who normally did Gunnar's mending, was badly scalded in an accident in the kitchen.

Dorcas sighed heavily. Mayhaps she'd been wrong to volunteer her services so readily, but she'd felt at the time that it would do her good to keep busy—even at something she despised. It was not only for that reason that she'd offered her help. Anika, too, had eagerly offered her services, but the way she went about it had set Dorcas's teeth on edge. She'd poked fun at Dorcas's abilities as a warrior, saying that Dorcas could probably wield a needle about as well as she could a sword, and Dorcas had found the open challenge too good to pass up.

The tip of her tongue caught between her teeth and her brows knit in determination as she tried once more to concentrate on the job at hand. But it was so very hard to sit quietly by, knowing that another woman was captivating her husband.

Dorcas had hoped they would return to Erin before winter, but Neil had informed her they would remain in Norway until spring. She'd felt terribly sad when the first snow came, though it had quickly melted. She wished that Anika Thornstein would disappear as swiftly, but it looked as if the woman had every intention of remaining as Gunnar's guest for as long as Neil was in his home. And everywhere Neil went, Anika went.

It cost Dorcas a great deal to leave her husband in the clutches of the other woman and to hold her head high in the process, but she didn't know how to deal with her rival's unrelenting persistence. The thought that she considered Anika a rival jolted her. Neil was *her* husband, yet, if the truth be known, he preferred Anika's company. Anika was the woman he loved. The idea threw Dorcas into a greater state of sadness, and she silently chided herself. It should not matter. *But it did*, answered a tiny voice in her head. Neil was hers!

She wished she could run Anika through with a sword, or beat her over the head with a mace, but that would solve nothing. Neil would only mourn his love and hate her. She sighed again. There was nothing she could do but endure the nauseating presence of the other woman. She'd had to bite her tongue many times in the last weeks to keep from lashing out at Anika and her viperous remarks. Dorcas had given her word to Neil that she would conduct herself like a lady, and she meant to keep her promise.

"You do not have to mend my clothing if you don't want to," Gunnar said quietly.

Dorcas looked up to find the old man staring at her intently. She blushed, realizing that the tunic had lain in her lap for some time, untouched. "I do not mind, really."

"Humph, at the rate you are working, I will end up with no tunics at all," he grumbled.

"I'm sorry." The blush deepened. "I—I am not used to such work. At home my mother and sisters did women's work while I went hunting and warring with my father and brothers." At the startled look on Gunnar's face, she smiled in embarrassment and dropped her eyes. "My mother always said I would rue the day I did not pay heed to her instructions."

"One of the other women could do that."

She looked up quickly. "Nay, please. I really do not mind." She suddenly grinned, showing the dimple in her cheek. "Besides, I need the practice."

Gunnar chuckled and shook his head, and Dorcas's grin widened.

Gay laughter filled the hall, and Dorcas turned her head to find its cause. Her smile froze as she watched Neil enter, Anika clinging to his arm and laughing at something he'd said.

Gunnar's eyes trailed to where Dorcas stared, then back again to the young woman sitting beside him. His eyes narrowed as he studied her. He'd not been at all pleased upon learning that Cedric had outwitted him by providing Neil with an Irish wife. Gunnar had hoped that Viking blood would flow strong and free through his great-grandchildren's veins, but after coming to know his proud, beautiful new granddaughter, he had no fear that the children springing from Neil and Dorcas's union would be anything less than spectacular. Dorcas's attitude toward Anika baffled him. He'd seen the tender look in her eyes when she gazed at her husband, and the murderous ones she bestowed upon Anika. Why did she just sit back and let Neil go his own way?

The couple approached them, with Anika holding on to Neil's arm so possessively, Dorcas was sorely tempted to pull the woman off him and slap her silly.

"My, what a cozy picture you make," Anika purred.

Dorcas gritted her teeth at the honey dripping from her voice.

"As I recall, dear, you were working on that tunic when we left here early this morning, weren't you?"

"Aye, but only because I want it to be perfect," Dorcas answered with as much calm as she could muster.

Anika's tinkling laugh filled the air. "Well, if it takes you this long to do one tunic, soon poor Gunnar will have nothing to wear."

It took all of Dorcas's willpower to keep her temper in check at Anika's unwitting repetition of Gunnar's words.

"Mayhaps," Anika added snidely, "Gunnar would prefer someone who knows what she's doing to mend his tunics."

"I prefer my granddaughter to do them."

Dorcas turned to look at Gunnar in surprise. A smile tugged at the corners of his mouth as he eyed her in turn, then he added gruffly, "Besides, I need to get to know

Dorcas, and what better way than to keep her at my side with some small task?"

Nonplussed, Anika stared at Gunnar. She could have sworn that he loathed the Irish bitch. What had the witch done to change his mind, Anika wondered as it struck her that her ploy to reveal Dorcas to Neil and his grandfather as a crude, uncivilized barbarian had not succeeded. She'd tried to goad Dorcas into attacking her, for she'd heard of the woman's exploits as a warrior. How could she keep from hearing of them? The skalds composed the silliest poems in her honor. If Dorcas tried to do her physical harm, then Neil would see what an uncouth person she really was and divorce her. But the insults thrown at the stupid bitch seemed to go over her head. Anika was furious at this latest development, but she was careful not to let it show. Instead, she smiled tightly and said, "Of course."

Neil looked from the angry Anika to his wife, noting Dorcas's calm despite the insult shown her. Her attitude puzzled him. He'd fully expected to have to come between the two women, for he thought that with this last, his wife would have shot out of her chair, eager to do Anika bodily harm. Instead, she simply picked up the tunic to start working on it, and threw to Gunnar what looked to Neil like a conspiratorial smile.

The tense atmosphere around them eased when the front door flew open and all eyes turned to see who had caused the disturbance. A glad cry escaped Dorcas's lips. Bolting from her chair, she ran to embrace the new arrival, unmindful of how her actions would be taken.

"Erik!" she exclaimed, throwing her arms around the Viking.

Laughing, Erik embraced her in turn. "Ah, 'tis good to be greeted with such enthusiasm."

Suddenly shy, Dorcas stepped back as far as his loose hold on her would permit.

Erik eyed her appreciatively and declared, "You grow more beautiful each time I see you."

Dorcas blushed and looked away. She spied Neil striding toward them, wearing a dark scowl. Erik saw him, too, and released her with a sigh.

When Neil reached them, Erik grinned engagingly and held out his hand. "It is good to see you, my friend," he said quietly, searching Neil's face.

Neil's brows arched upward. "Is it indeed?" he asked coolly. "Or is meeting my wife the purpose of your journey here?"

Dorcas caught her breath sharply. "Neil!"

Erik straightened and dropped his extended hand. "Regardless of your presence here, you know that I have business to attend to. If you did not wish me to see Dorcas, you know that there was nothing to stop you from returning to Erin before my arrival." His icy tone matched Neil's.

Dorcas felt a wave of dejection wash over her. They could have left, but it had been Neil's decision to stay. A nagging thought crept into her mind that he'd not made the choice until after he saw Anika. She threw that woman a baleful look as a spurt of anger coursed through her. What right did he have to accuse her and Erik of any wrongdoing when he so blatantly flaunted his relationship with Anika?

"You are being ridiculous, Neil," she said through gritted teeth.

"Aye, Neil, you are," added Erik. "I should have thought that our last meeting would have convinced you of that."

"It convinced me of nothing."

"Then you are a bigger fool than I suspected."

Neil made a move toward Erik, but Dorcas quickly stepped between the two men. "Stop it, both of you! You are acting like children. I am your wife," she said to Neil, "and Erik is your friend. And, I hope, mine. That is all he is or ever will be. At least I will honor the bargain between our fathers, which is more than you can say," she added scathingly. Her eyes brimmed with tears as she fled from the room, unaware of the surprised stares of the other occupants.

Erik's gaze traveled past Neil. A look of irritation crossed his face. Anika Thornstein stood close to them, a calculating gleam in her eye.

A sharp knock on the chamber door roused Dorcas from her depressing thoughts. She preferred to be left in her misery and tried hard to ignore the insistent raps. She finally gave up and dragged herself off the bed, silently cursing the one who would disturb her. She flung the door open to find Erik standing on the threshold with a tray of food in his hands.

He eyed her sheepishly for a moment, then cleared his throat. "You did not come to the table to sup."

She turned and walked back into the room. "I was not hungry."

"I couldn't help noticing that you've lost some weight," he said, venturing into the chamber.

She sighed as she sat down on the edge of the bed, but she did not answer.

"Has it been very bad for you here?" he asked, placing the tray on a table. The only answer he got was a shrug. He fished inside his tunic and brought out a packet. "I, uh, never got a chance to give you these."

She looked up and saw the letters he held out to her.

"I stopped by your home before coming here. Gwendolyn and Thalia asked me to deliver them." He watched Dorcas's face brighten as she tore open one of the letters, and he joined her on the bed. "I also did not have a chance to tell you my good news."

She stopped reading Thalia's letter and looked up. "What good news?"

"I will become your brother-by-marriage in the fall."

"You asked for Gwendolyn in marriage?"

"Aye."

"And Father approves?"

Erik laughed. "Aye, but only after a year's betrothal. I think he is still getting used to the idea of losing two of his daughters to Vikings. Though he need not worry about Thalia." He chuckled. "Young Fitzgerald is constantly on her doorstep."

Dorcas giggled. "She will lead him a merry chase to be sure." She threw her arms around Erik and hugged him. "I am so happy for you and Gwen. Treat her kindly."

"I have every intention of doing so."

"It would appear that your intentions are quite clear," came a cold voice from the doorway. "Apparently, my accusations have not been without grounds."

Dorcas looked past Erik into the darkly furious face of her husband. She slowly released Erik and stared, dumbfounded, at Neil. Though she knew they would do no good, the words came automatically. "It is not what you think."

Neil moved into the room like a deadly cat ready to spring. His eyes were the darkest that Dorcas had ever seen as he turned them on Erik. "Get out of here," he growled.

Erik calmly arose. "I am taking Dorcas with me. In your frame of mind—"

"You will *not* take *my* wife anywhere! Now, get out of here before I lose all sense and break you in half."

Dorcas shivered at the suppressed anger in Neil's voice. "Go, Erik," she said quietly.

"But . . ."

"Go. I will be fine."

Erik cast her an anxious glance before striding from the room, forcefully slamming the door shut behind him.

Dorcas clasped her hands in front of her to keep them from shaking, and in the process crumpled Thalia's letter. She took a deep breath.

"Nothing happened between Erik and me," she stated calmly.

"Shut up! I will not hear your lies!" Neil thundered.

Fury filled her at his outburst. "Lies!" she shouted back. "I tell no lies. The biggest lie between us is our marriage. I have done nothing to dishonor our union, yet you would flaunt your whore in front of me every hour of the day!"

Neil sprang forward and grabbed her. His fingers dug into her shoulders as he shook her with such force, Dorcas was sure her head would fly from her neck.

"Do not tell me that my eyes deceived me," he ground out. "Not when I find you in another man's arms. You are my wife. No man takes what is mine." He abruptly thrust her from him, sending her reeling onto the bed.

She looked up at him with hate-filled eyes. "What's the matter, Neil, are you afraid that you are not man enough to keep me satisfied? Mayhaps I wish to indulge in another pursuit, just as you have."

He started toward her again. But before he could reach for her, her hand snaked out to grab her eating knife from the table. She swiped it at his midsection, her eyes lighting in triumph when the weapon cut through his tunic to nick him. He reared back in surprise, and his hesitation gave her enough time to scramble to a kneeling position on the bed. He brought his left hand up and watched her swing the knife in that direction. Just as quickly his right hand shot out to grab her wrist, putting an excruciating amount of pressure on it. She gasped in pain and let the knife fall to the floor.

Neil fell forward, and there was nothing Dorcas could do but tumble backward with his weight on top of her. They lay, panting heavily, their eyes shooting sparks at each other.

"You are mine, and only mine," he declared thickly. He placed one hand at her throat. The longer it hovered there, the wider her eyes grew in alarm. A slow, grin crossed his face, and she shuddered uncontrollably. With a sudden movement his hands ripped the front of her gown open.

Fear rushed over her. She struggled underneath him to get away. Dear God! She was reliving a nightmare.

Neil pressed his body onto hers to stop her struggles. When she whimpered in anguish, he caught the terror in her eyes before her lids dropped to shut out her impending rape. He lay still, watching her pale face tighten as she waited for the oncoming pain, and the anger that had consumed him slowly ebbed. He did not want to hurt Dorcas.

He shifted his weight and let his gaze travel the length of her. He shuddered inwardly at the thought of marring her silky flesh. After the fiasco that was their wedding night, he'd vowed never to take her against her will again. Yet, moments ago he'd been ready to rape her, to prove to her who her master was.

"Dorcas," he whispered huskily.

Her eyes remained tightly shut, and he saw two tears slip from beneath her closed eyelids. He lowered his tongue to first one temple, then to the other, to lick the salty wetness away. She flinched, then her eyes opened warily at his gentleness. His mouth lowered to hers and he nipped softly at her lips. His tongue ran in playful circles from one corner of her mouth to the other. At last his persistence elicited a response from her, and she tentatively opened herself to him.

He moaned in pleasure. His hands tangled in her hair, loving the feel of the silky tresses. Her hands flew to the lacings on his tunic, plucking them free. He brushed her shaking fingers away and finished the job for her, all the while placing feathery kisses on her arms, her shoulders, her breasts, anywhere his lips could taste the sweetness of her flesh.

Dorcas ran her hands boldly over Neil's body, delighting in the warm skin over hard muscles. When he released himself from his breeches, she was more than ready for him, clutching him to her. There was no tenderness in their union as a primeval, animalistic instinct took over.

An overwhelming force shot through her, and she cried out once before Neil emitted a low growl, and his mouth devoured hers.

Dorcas slowly became aware of their heavy breathing, of their hearts thudding together as one as they lay wrapped in each other.

Rolling off her, Neil pulled her to him and held her tightly. It was as if he were afraid to let her go for fear that she would vanish.

Dorcas snuggled closer and sighed contentdly. She was asleep almost immediately.

14

Neil's booted feet crunched over the hard snow, leaving his personal stamp on the perfectly smooth white blanket. It had snowed intermittently for the last two months, huge white flakes hurtling to the ground and obscuring the distinct shapes placed there by God and man, until everything became one. However, being discontented with the arrangement, gusting winds went to work, picking up the fluffy white crystals and swirling them about like small whirlpools in a whimsy all their own, and, finally satisfied, allowing them to settle.

Neil breathed deeply of the crisp clean air as he strode purposefully toward the stables to see that all was ready for the trip he and his wife and grandfather were embarking on. He was glad for the chance to escape outdoors. The atmosphere inside the house was one of enmity and bitterness. He grimaced, thinking of the cause of the hostility. Anika was no longer prudent in her verbal attacks on Dorcas. Where before, her veiled insults had sometimes passed over his head, he was now quick to catch the cunning remarks turned on his wife. Knowing the extent of Dorcas's temper, it puzzled him that she did nothing about it. And Anika's penchant for hanging on him was driving him mad. He couldn't turn around without her being right behind him. What irritated him even more was that Dorcas didn't seem to mind.

Since the night he'd almost raped her, something inside him had changed. He'd become attuned to his wife's feelings, and could sense the hurt and anger she felt at Anika's jibes, yet she said nothing, did nothing. And when Anika clung to him, Dorcas ignored them both.

Neil's brows came together in a dark frown as he stomped through the snow. He wondered how it was that he'd ever thought he loved Anika. He never realized what a cruel person she could be. He felt bad that Dorcas had to endure Anika's biting tongue, and it puzzled him that his wife did not retaliate. Instead, she remained a true lady, with a calm, quiet assurance he'd been unaware she possessed. As always, the different facets of her character befuddled him. But at least she was honest. That was more than he could say for Anika.

When he first laid eyes on the woman he thought he loved, he'd been transported back in time. Anika was so beautiful and pure, or so he'd thought. He'd stumbled over the words, trying to explain about his marriage, but they wouldn't come out right. He'd succeeded only in bringing huge tears to her eyes, and her hurt and bewilderment made him feel guilty.

At first he was glad to be in her company, happy for the chance to look upon her serene beauty. He soon learned that she was not as sweet as she appeared, however, when she started throwing subtle hints his way that he could free himself of Dorcas to marry her. As gently as he could, he told her that he could not go back on his word to his father. The peace and harmony between the two clans depended upon his marriage to Dorcas. Anika seemed to ignore his explanation.

As time passed, he noticed other small things about the woman he'd professed to love. The sharp barbs she shot at his wife with the accuracy of an archer. How she hung on him whenever Dorcas was around, but how she stepped quickly out of his reach whenever they were alone. In looking back he remembered that she had always done so. Once, he'd found that an endearing quality, thinking that she was shy. But he recalled how she never seemed to enjoy his touch, and now it only made him wonder. The few times she'd allowed him to kiss her, she'd held herself stiffly, as though his kiss were something to be endured.

He found himself comparing her to Dorcas. He'd felt honored to be the one to capture such a sweet, unde-manding woman as Anika, and had felt cheated when he found himself married to a shewolf instead. But Dorcas never shoved him away when they were through making love. She cuddled up to him, holding him in her arms. The vision of Dorcas's lithe body molded to his stirred his passions. Although she had yet to come to him, his wife was more than willing to give herself to him without any reservations whatsoever. He wondered if it would be so with Anika. Somehow, he did not think it would be. He could not imagine Anika's cool beauty yielding in desire while his wife was fierce in her passion.

His pace slowed. How could Dorcas give herself to him the way she did if she did not care about him? But if she did care, why did she continue to put up with Anika? Though he no longer cared about Anika, he allowed her attentions, hoping for some reaction from his wife. The only response he received was when they were alone, and she refused to speak to him at all. A quick grin lit his face. Her attitude did not last long, though, not when he touched her. He enjoyed wiping away her anger like that, playing with her as he would the strings on a supple harp, until she gave herself to him in abandon.

Neil shook his head, feeling in a quandary. He did not understand any of it, but he was sure of one thing. He wanted his wife. He would not give her up. He smiled at the thought of what a pleasure it was to melt her cold reserve. And he wished with all his heart to make her admit that she no longer hated him.

A frown quickly replaced the smiled. Surely she did not hate him anymore. She couldn't. Not with the way her flaming desires blazed out of control when he touched her. But then, she never gave him any encouragement either. She didn't have to. All she had to do was be in his presence and he wanted her. If he closed his eyes, he could smell the sweet, heady fragrance of wildflowers that surrounded her. He could clearly see the ripe, lush body that became like pliable clay under his fingers, waiting for him to mold the unbridled passions within. And she was his.

He knew how foolish he'd been with his accusations about Erik, once she had explained to him what had happened. All he'd been able to see at the time was another man's arms around his wife. The sight had filled him with a murderous rage. When she told him that Erik would soon become a member of her family, and that she was merely showing her happiness, a wave of relief such as he'd never before known had washed over him. He was chagrined by the treatment he'd dealt his closest friend, and felt an overwhelming need to apologize, but the only way that could be accomplished was by venturing north. Erik had already journeyed to his sister Ailsa's home.

Neil remembered how surprised and pleased Dorcas had been when he suggested the trip a few nights earlier. He was unsure of the greeting he would receive from Erik, but he knew he had to try. Not merely because it would please Dorcas, but because he had to recapture the closeness he and Erik had once shared.

After making sure that all was ready for the trip, Neil returned to the house. Some of the sparkle left his eyes when he stepped through the front door to be faced with a stilted silence from the three cloaked figures in the hall. He turned to Gunnar, a silent question written on his face.

"Anika is coming with us," his grandfather said gruffly.

Neil's brows shot upward as he stared at Anika.

She sidled up to him and placed her arm through his. Neil had all he could do to keep from letting his irritation show at her boldness.

"I thought it would be nice if we kept each other company," she said in her sweet voice, coyly lowering her eyes. Then she raised her head to stare beseechingly at him. "I have been contemplating a trip to my dear friend Ailsa. What better plan than to have you escort me? And I am sure that Sigurd would be pleased to know that you saw me safely to his doorstep."

Neil swore silently. He'd forgotten that Ailsa's husband, Sigurd, was a cousin of Anika's. He glanced quickly at Dorcas, but she had her attention fixed on the task of pulling on a wrap, and appeared to be ignoring them. He disentangled himself from Anika's hold, murmuring, "Let's go."

Neil strapped Anika's bags to the back of the horse-drawn sleigh. She was waiting impatiently for him to finish so that he could help her into the backseat, when Gunnar approached her. He took her arm and led her to the front of the sleigh.

"My dear, it would please me if you sat up here with me. I am always charmed by your presence."

With more strength than she knew he possessed, Gunnar lifted her into the front seat. As he climbed in beside her, she could do no more than watch Neil hand his wife into the back of the sleigh and sit beside her. He smiled with genuine warmth as he solicitously covered Dorcas with the fur lap robe.

The welcome they received at their journey's end was generously warm and friendly, putting Dorcas's mind at ease as to what awaited them. Ailsa had the same sparkling good humor as her brother, and quickly made them feel at home. Dorcas instinctively knew she'd found a new friend.

Neil went off in search of Erik and Sigurd when Ailsa

explained that the two men were hunting. Though Ailsa's time was not yet near, Neil realized Sigured wouldn't have gone far. He knew how much the couple had longed for a child, and was pleased the happy event was close at hand. His thoughts flitted to Dorcas, and he wondered how she would look when big with his child.

Ailsa made her guests comfortable and tried to ease the tension in the air that she'd felt upon their arrival. Though she'd been forewarned by her brother, she was still surprised to find Anika in the company of the newlyweds. She studied Dorcas overtly, pleased by what she saw. She knew something of the circumstances of Neil and Dorcas's marriage, for Erik had vented his wrath at the unjust way Neil treated his wife. Trying to be objective, Ailsa decided that either Neil was a fool, or Dorcas was, or both of them were. She viewed the match as perfect, and hoped that things would work out for the couple. She wanted everyone to be as happy as she.

When the men returned, Dorcas looked anxiously at them. She breathed a sigh of relief at the easy grin on Neil's face, and the booming laughter rumbling from Erik, thankful that all was well.

For Dorcas, the winter months spent as Ailsa and Sigurd's guest were torture. She'd never seen such an abundance of snow, or felt such harsh, unrelenting winds, and to have to spend most of her time indoors at the mercy of Anika's sly remarks was almost too much for her. She found herself constantly fighting down her quick temper, for she meant to keep her vow to Neil. She intended to show him that the word of a McMahon was worth something, even if a McNeil's was not. The only consolation she found was that Erik and Gunnar treated her with a special kindness that she found heartwarming; and Ailsa, in her quiet way, acted as a buffer against the continual tension in the air. Even Sigurd became a staunch ally of Dorcas's against his cousin, and for a time Dorcas had a respite from the woman's attacks on her character. But it was not to last. When the weather cleared, the men sought the outdoors to resume their hunting and fishing, and Dorcas was once again left at the mercy of Anika's vicious tongue.

She did her best to ignore the woman, tuning her out as she would a petulant child, for if she didn't, she knew that she would throttle her. At least she and Ailsa had become fast friends in the months spent together, both enjoying their quiet talks that often turned into giggling sessions. For the first time Dorcas realized what fun she'd been missing by not joining her sisters in their daily tasks. She especially liked helping Ailsa sew the coming babe's clothes. Surprisingly, she had become quite proficient in the art of embroidery—a pastime she had once abhorred.

One morning in late February, as Dorcas and Ailsa sat close to the fireplace, bent to their task and talking quietly, Anika joined them. Dorcas held her breath while the woman eyed her critically for a moment, waiting for the coming attack. As usual, Anika did not disappoint her.

" 'Tis a pity that you must sew all those tiny garments for another woman's child."

Dorcas looked up slowly. "If I can be of any help to Ailsa, then I am happy to do so," she replied quietly.

Anika's mouth curved in a self-satisfied smile. "I only meant that it is unfortunate you do not sew for your own child."

Surprise struck Dorcas. Though it was expected she would produce an heir, she'd not given any thought to having Neil's child. She remembered how Neil had informed her, with such sublime sureness, that she would bear his child. He'd not been too pleased at the prospect. How would he feel now? She suddenly wondered what it would be like, and was startled that she looked forward to that day.

"Of course," Anika went on, "you may find that you will always be engaged in your present activity."

A frown puckered Dorcas's brow. "I do not understand."

"Well, you and Neil have been married for some time now, and I do not see any evidence of a child on the way."

"Anika!" gasped Ailsa, shocked by the woman's boldness.

Dorcas's eyes narrowed as she answered icily, "There is a long future ahead of Neil and me."

Anika shrugged unconcernedly. "Mayhaps. Of course, there is always the possibility that you are barren. Have you ever thought about what would happen if that were the case? Neil will want children. What will you do if you are unable to provide him any? What will he do?"

"Anika, such talk is unseemly," Ailsa exclaimed.

"Why?" Anika asked, raising her eyebrows innocently. "I am merely curious. I imagine that Neil would have to divorce you. After all," she added, smiling slyly, "he is a *very* virile man. He will want many sons." With that she turned and strolled casually out of the room, leaving behind two speechless women.

Ailsa was the first to recover as she leaned over and patted Dorcas's hand. "Pay her no heed. She doesn't know what she is talking about. Sigurd and I waited two years for this child. It may be so with you and Neil."

Dorcas stared unsmilingly at her friend. She knew that she should not let Anika's words disturb her, but when the woman spoke of Neil's virility, she had smiled so . . . knowingly.

What would happen if she were unable to give Neil an heir? Their union was contracted for the peace afforded two clans, but he did expect her to bear his child. What would happen if she could not? Would he divorce her? She would then be free to go her own way. Strangely, the thought of that happening made her feel deep melancholy.

Dorcas's brows were knit in a frown as she stared down at the board. Her hand hovered over a pawn, then slowly descended toward the chess piece. But she jerked the hand back when a woman's laugh filled the air. She scowled at the four figures across the room and watched Anika place her hand on Neil's arm. The blond woman said something that made him smile.

"Are we going to finish this game today, or not?" Gunnar asked irritably.

Dorcas jumped, and guiltily returned her attention to the chess board. She moved the pawn forward a space and looked once more at the woman surrounded by three men. Anika's laughter floated to her again, and she thought sourly that the tart was lapping up the attention like a contented cat lapping up milk. Dorcas wished she'd never promised Neil that she would behave herself and act like a lady. God! What she wouldn't give for a sword in her hands. Her patience was stretched beyond endurance, especially after seeing her husband and his lover stroll casually from the stable arm in arm only that morning. It was bad enough seeing the smug smile that Anika threw her, but to be a witness to the straw sticking to the woman's hair and sleeve of her gown had made Dorcas's blood boil.

"Are you sure that's the move you want to make?"

Dorcas threw Gunnar a cursory glance before glaring at her nemesis again. "Aye," she muttered.

Gunnar sighed heavily and moved his queen into position, grumbling, "Checkmate."

Dorcas looked down at the chess board before slowly raising her eyes to meet Gunner's. She blinked in surprise and smiled ruefully. "It would appear that you have won again."

"Only because you do not concentrate. I thought you said you knew how to play this game?"

She lowered her eyes. "I do. You are right. I'm not able to keep my mind on what I'm doing."

Gunnar leaned forward and covered her hand with his own. "Why don't you go join your husband?" he asked softly.

Because he does not want me, whispered a little voice. Instead of saying anything aloud, she merely shook her head.

"Dorcas, what is wrong?"

She sighed and looked into Gunnar's kindly face. How could she complain to him about his grandson? He had eyes. He could see how Anika fawned over Neil, and how Neil let her. Dorcas tried to convince herself that it did not matter, but it did. It was humiliating to know her husband preferred another woman. She vowed she would not let her hurt show. She could not say why it hurt, but it did. If Neil did not want her, so be it. She would not let it affect her.

She shrugged. "I guess I am just restless. The sun is shining again, the snow has melted. Most of it, at any rate. I am used to being outdoors. Staying cooped up all winter has been hard."

Gunnar slapped his hand on the table, making the chess pieces fly into the air, and grinned. "How would you like to go hunting?" He watched her face brighten, the first sign of life he'd seen in her for months, and chuckled. "You go get yourself ready and I will see to the weapons. We have some serious bear stalking to do."

Dorcas needed no more prodding, and she ran to her chamber to change clothes. A short time later she was on her way outside when she heard her name being called. She stiffened and turned to find Neil hurrying to catch up with her.

When she'd passed through the hall, she'd ignored him completely.

"Dorcas, where are you going?"

"Gunnar asked me to go hunting with him."

"I see," Neil said. "If you will wait for me, I'll go with you."

"Don't bother," she snapped. "I wouldn't want to take you away from your present pursuit."

"What are you talking about?" he asked, frowning.

"I am sure that Anika would not be pleased to know that you accompanied your *wife* on a hunting trip," she answered scathingly, turning away.

"Dorcas—"

She whirled around to face him. "If you expect me to welcome your presence like a complacent wife, you are mistaken. Go back to your Anika and amuse her for the rest of the day—for the rest of your life. I do not care. Just leave me in peace." She stalked away before he could see the tears brimming her eyes.

Neil stared after her. What was the matter with her? Why would she think that he wanted Anika? He could not help it if the woman constantly threw herself at him. After all, it wasn't as if he were in a position to tell Anika to leave, even though he wished she had the sense to do so.

He'd done everything in his power to discourage her, yet she continued to hang on him at every opportunity. Why, only that morning when he'd been in the stable, she'd snuck up on him and thrown her arms about his middle, taking him completely by surprise. At first he'd thought it was Dorcas, though she had never embraced him like that. When he turned and found Anika instead, he'd accidentally knocked her down in his effort to get away. Of course, he'd been enough of a gentleman to help her to her feet, and when she claimed to have hurt her ankle, he let her lean on him on the way back to the house.

Damnation! He was tired of his wife's indifference, and he was tired of Anika's attentions. Why she insisted on being in his company as he, Erik, and Sigurd reminisced on old times was beyond him. Loki could take both Dorcas and Anika for all he cared, he thought sourly as he strode back to the house. He let loose with a few choice invectives again. By the gods, his wife would not dictate to him!

Dorcas's enthusiasm for the hunt was forced, and she prayed that Gunnar would not notice. She was fed up with

Neil's lack of concern for her. The day they left Norway to return to Erin couldn't come too soon for her.

She and Gunnar tramped through the woods for what seemed like hours until at last Gunnar spotted some tracks. Only then was Dorcas able to forget everything but the hunt. They wound their way through the trees tracking their prey. Dorcas had the strange feeling that they were not alone, and she eyed the dense forest on each side of her warily. When she heard a twig snap, she whirled around, her heart pounding. Neil strolled up to her, and she relaxed when she realized it was her husband who stalked them and not some two-hundred-pound bear.

As she watched him approach, she was acutely aware of the strength emanating from him. A fur cloak made of wolf skins covered him. One side was thrown back over his right shoulder, and she could see the taut muscles in his arm as he held a bow with the ease of a skilled warrior. A quiver of arrows was slung over his back. His sword hung from his side and a large hunting knife was strapped to his belt.

She shivered involuntarily. He looked so much a part of his surroundings. His physical strength was overpowering, and she was irritated that his very nearness still had such an effect on her. He'd made it clear enough he did not want her. As far as she was concerned, two could play that game.

"What are you doing here?" she snapped.

He stood only inches from her so that she was forced to tilt her head back in order to look up at him. "I felt the need for some fresh air and exercise," he said quietly.

"Well, go find it elsewhere. You are not welcome here."

He smiled, undaunted by his wife's sharp tone, and gestured to Sigurd, standing behind him. "Would you tell Sigurd that he is not welcome to hunt on his own land?"

Dorcas bristled at his easy confidence. "Just stay out of my way, Viking!" she hissed before whirling away.

Neil watched her retreating back for a moment, then

turned his gaze to Gunnar. His grandfather stared back disapprovingly. He shook his head in warning and started after Dorcas.

Dorcas strode on, fuming. Why did Neil always have to spoil everything? She hated that his nearness disturbed her so. Why was he not with Anika? He certainly preferred her company.

The idea of having to compete for a man's attentions was new to Dorcas, and she did not like it one bit. Especially when the man in question was *her* husband. She was shocked by that thought. She did not want her husband. Did she?

She fairly flew through the woods, making her own path in order to escape Neil. Or was it her thoughts she wanted to run from, she wondered. She heard Gunnar close behind her, calling her name, and cast a backward glance before slowing down. Neil was no longer in sight, so she waited for Gunnar to reach her.

"Dorcas, we are in pursuit of a prey that can be very dangerous. It would be wise not to become separated."

"I'm sorry," she murmured. It was not the quarry she was chasing that disturbed her. She heard a rustling noise and glanced up, thinking Neil had followed them after all. Her eyes widened. She tried to warn Gunnar, but no sound would come.

A huge white bear came loping out of the trees, straight for Gunnar.

He saw the fright on Dorcas's face and turned just as the animal raised itself up on its hind legs to tower over them. Gunnar raised his ax, ready to strike out at the bear, and stepped backward out of the bear's reach at the same time.

Dorcas was not quite sure what happened next. Whether Gunnar was struck by the beast's massive paw, or whether he slipped on the wet earth, suddenly he lay sprawled on the ground. He cried out in pain, and she heard a scream, then realized that she'd made the sound. She stared,

mesmerized by the strange creature as the animal turned
to her. He tossed his head to the side and growled, then
he started toward her.

She came out of her trancelike state and drew her
sword. She swung it, cutting the bear's arm. The enraged
animal struck the weapon from her hand and kept coming. She jumped out of its reach before it could grab hold
of her and maul her, and tripped over a log. She fell
backward, stunned, the wind knocked from her. Her eyes
never left the creature as it lumbered toward her. Frantically,
she felt the ground for a weapon, something, anything,
and her hand touched something. For all she knew it
could be a stick! Closing her eyes, she picked it up,
thinking hazily that it was a shame she and Neil had had
so little time. The weapon felt too heavy for a stick. Her
eyes flew open to find that she held Gunnar's ax. She
grabbed it tightly and flung it at the bear.

She watched, fascinated, as the animal tried to grab the
ax where it was embedded in its chest before crashing to
the ground. It took a moment for her to see the three
arrows protruding from the bear's back. Someone pulled
her roughly to her feet, and she looked up into Neil's
concerned face.

"Are you all right?" he asked hoarsely.

She nodded, unsure she could find her voice, and clung
to him. "Gunnar," she whispered.

Erik looked up from where he and Sigurd were bending
over the old man. "I fear his foot is badly injured."

Dorcas stared stupidly at Erik. "His foot. How?"

"I twisted my ankle," growled Gunnar. "Help me up."

"It is more than twisted," Sigurd said, placing a hand on
his shoulder to keep him from moving, "and it is no
wonder, with the size of the hole you stepped in. We will
have to carry you back to the house. Your foot is broken."

Dorcas opened the chamber door a crack and peeked
around it. As quietly as possible she slipped into the room
and tiptoed toward the bed.

"Stop sneaking about," grumbled the man lying there.

Dorcas jumped, and Gunnar opened his eyes to glare at her.

"You are supposed to be resting," she chided him.

"Humph, that's all I've been doing," he growled. "I need to get out of here. I am tired of not knowing what goes on around me."

Dorcas rushed over to the bed, alarm clearly showing on her face as Gunnar attempted to get up. "Here now, you cannot do that. You will undo all of Neil's work and he will have to reset the bone."

"I am tired of lying abed. There is nothing to do, and everyone is too busy to keep me company."

Her lips twitched in amusement. Gunnar sounded like a cranky child. "You know very well that you receive visits from all of us every single day," she said soothingly.

"It is mid-morning, and yours is the first face I've seen other than Ailsa's when she rushed in with my morning meal and rushed back out again," complained Gunnar. "I've not even seen Neil yet. Where is my grandson? Why hasn't he been here?"

"He had an errand to run," Dorcas answered, straightening the covers. "He was going to your home to tell them what happened, and that we would remain here for a while longer."

"When did he leave?"

"At first light."

"He should have returned by now, unless he walked," Gunnar said sourly.

Dorcas laughed and shook her head. "I will see if he has returned, and if he has not, I will ask Erik to challenge you to a game of chess."

"And mayhaps he will play fair."

Dorcas straightened and stared wide-eyed at the old man. "Whatever do you mean?"

"You cheat."

"I what? How can you say that when you have been winning?" she sputtered.

"Aye, I have been winning because for the past week you have *let* me win. That is the same as cheating," he said smugly.

Dorcas snapped her mouth shut and eyed him sternly. "Very well. When next we play, *I* will play for blood. We will see then how you like it." She yanked the covers up roughly and tucked them under his chin, almost choking him. "You stay right where you are until I see if Neil is back," she ordered. Her gaze softened as she looked down at the frowning man, and a small smile tugged at the corners of her mouth. She bent and placed a quick kiss on his forehead before turning to leave. On her way out she heard him chuckling, and she could not contain her own laughter as she walked down the hall.

Dorcas was still smiling, thinking what a lovable, cantakerous old man Gunnar was, when she spied Neil standing in front of a chamber door, a frown on his face. It was not their chamber. She was ready to call to him just as he knocked and seconds later the door flew open. The smile froze on Dorcas's lips.

Anika stared up at Neil in wide-eyed innocence.

"Neil," she laughed. "What a surprise."

"I got your message," he said shortly.

"Message."

"What do you want, Anika?"

Dorcas watched as Neil pushed the door open wider, then stepped into the chamber and shut it quietly behind him. She felt rooted to the spot as she continued to stare at the closed door. How could he!

He'd been notably attentive to Dorcas ever since the incident with the bear over a week earlier. Only that morning he'd awakened her with his gentle caresses and kisses. After loving her thoroughly, he'd smiled down at her in a way that tugged at her heart. He told her that he would go to Gunnar's home to let the people there know what had happened, but that he would return as quickly as possible. He'd kissed her fiercely, and she had giggled as he reluctantly dragged himself from the bed, mumbling unintelligibly.

How could Neil treat her with such tenderness and warmth and then go to another woman, she wondered. How could she have allowed herself to become ensnared by his seductive charm when she knew he cared nothing for her? Dorcas was devoid of all emotion save one. Hate. Hate for Neil, and hate for Anika. She whirled around and ran from the house.

She felt sick to her stomach as she fled to the stables. She gulped in huge quantities of fresh air, willing herself not to give in to her weakness. No more would she allow her husband to humiliate her. No more would she be a pawn in his game to win Anika's affections.

She was numb as she automatically saddled a horse. When she finished, she sat atop her mount uncertainly for a moment. Then she kicked the animal into motion. Horse and rider flew across the terrain like the wind.

The frown on Neil's face deepened when he looked past Anika. He pushed the door open, literally shoving the woman out of the way, and strolled into the room. He scowled at the bare-chested man sprawled unconcernedly on the bed, and cast a quizzical glance at Anika. He took note of her disheveled appearance. Her blond hair was unbound and the top of her gown was open, and he had a view of what he'd once thought of as belonging to him. He ignored her and turned back to Erik.

"What are you doing here?"

Erik grinned. "I was just about to sample what practically every man in Norway has tasted. That is, everyone but you." He picked up a cup of ale from a nearby table and lifted it in a salute to Neil before taking a sip.

Neil heard Anika draw in her breath sharply and looked at her. Mayhaps some of the rumors he'd been hearing about her were true after all, but he felt nothing. It no longer mattered.

"Why did you send for me?" he asked her.

"I sent no message. Neil, listen to me," she pleaded, but before she could say more, Erik interrupted.

"Nay, Neil, she sent no message," he said, getting up. "I did."

"Why?"

"Because I wanted you to see for yourself what this one is," Erik answered contemptuously. "I wanted you to see the perfection you would be giving up, and for what? For her?" He sneered, gesturing toward Anika. "By Thor! You are a fool, man, and someone had to show you. This one is not worth Dorcas's little finger."

"How dare you!" Anika shouted. "You tricked me."

"You tricked yourself into believing that you could have what belongs to another," Erik said scornfully. "You have used every scheme you could think of to hurt a kind, warm, beautiful woman, all because of your greed for power." He turned on Neil. "And you. You let her. You must be deaf, dumb, and blind as well as stupid, not to see this whore for what she is. I could not believe it when you told me who it was you were so enamored of! She is a deceitful, conniving bitch who cares nothing for you. She wants you only because of your wealth, and because someone else has you. Believe me when I tell you that she has found comfort in many men's arms. It matters not whose."

"You lie!" Anika shouted.

"Lie? Nay, I do not. I can give you ten names, twenty names, and they will all swear upon their swords that it is true."

"Neil, do not listen to him. It is not true. I love you, you know that. We were to be married!" Anika cried.

Neil heard the desperation in her voice, yet he could do nothing but stare bemusedly at her. At last he spoke, carefully choosing his words. "We spoke of marriage once, and only once, but you turned me down."

"I merely needed time. Just until you returned."

"I was married upon my return, Anika."

"It does not have to be so," she cried, grasping his arms. "You can get a divorce."

"I cannot do that," he answered, shaking his head.

"You could if you wished it."

"I do not wish it."

"But—you said yourself that the marriage was forced upon you."

"And did you force yourself upon all of your lovers, or they on you?" he asked coldly, prying her hands loose.

Anika knew from his tone that she'd lost. She turned and walked to the bed, where she sat without looking at either man.

"I am glad to see you have finally come to your senses," Erik said, sighing with relief. He picked up his tunic and started to slip it on over his head.

Neil laughed softly. "There really was no need for all th—" The rest of the sentence stuck in his throat as he looked up. "Erik! Look out!"

The warning came too late as Anika shoved a knife into Erik's stomach.

15

Dorcas tore across the yard and dismounted in front of the stables. The old man who took care of Gunnar's horses could not hide his surprise when she handed him the reins, but before he could speak, Dorcas stalked away. She felt a cloud of trepidation steal over her as she strode hurriedly toward the house. She'd been on the receiving end of Neil's anger too many times not to know that his fury at finding her gone would be like nothing she'd ever experienced. She had no illusions that he would want her in any other way than a master wanted a slave, to make her bend to his will.

A sudden feeling of dejection washed over her. Nay. He would not care. He would be glad that she was gone. Her pace slowed. What if he brought Anika back to Gunnar's with him? She could not stand the thought of seeing them together again. She had to get far, far away.

Aye. Mayhaps she had been foolish. *If* he sought her, Gunnar's would be the first place he looked. More than likely, that would not happen. He was just as likely to be happy that she was no longer a burden to him. She quickly discarded the idea of getting back on her horse and riding away. She could not hide from her husband among his people. He had too many friends in Norway.

She looked about her wildly and spied Selwyn on a ship at the dock. It was Neil's ship. She hurriedly climbed aboard, calling out to him.

The quiet Viking turned in surprise. "Lady Dorcas, what are you doing here?"

"I—I was out riding, and before I knew it, I wound up here."

"Neil was here earlier."

"I know. What are you doing on board?"

"Readying the ship for sailing."

Her brows rose in surprise. "But I thought Neil said he would not leave before spring."

"He won't. He just wants everything to be ready when the time comes."

"I see," she said thoughtfully. "Could you leave now if you wanted to?"

"Are you suggesting that I would take Neil's ship?" he asked, drawing himself up.

"Nay, of course not. I did not mean you, exactly. I meant, well, could anyone sail out of here at this time of year?"

"The ice is still very thick in the fjord."

"Is there no one with enough courage to challenge the ice?"

Selwyn studied the woman before him, who seemed to be throwing down a challenge of her own. He wondered why.

"Some have tried," he answered slowly, and shrugged. "Some have failed. A very few have succeeded."

"Would you not like to be known as one who succeeded?"

"I was with Neil when he did."

The idea that Neil had been able to accomplish something where other men had failed irritated Dorcas. Was there nothing he could not do? He had a presence about him that bespoke of strength and courage. She felt it keenly, and she knew that others felt it too. He was a better archer than she. He was a better horseman. And she did not even know the first thing about commanding a ship. To know that he had conquered an obstacle that other men feared rankled.

"Then you could do it," she said triumphantly.

"My lady, it matters not whether I can or cannot sail down the fjord in this weather."

"But it does matter. Selwyn, I need to leave here."

"And you will. If the weather holds, you should be leaving within the next month or two."

"Nay! You do not understand. I must leave here now," she cried desperately. "I will pay you anything you ask."

Selwyn shook his head. "I cannot."

"But you must," she said in frustration, grabbing his arm. "I want to go home. I have to go home!"

"Does Neil know that you are here?"

She thought fleetingly of lying to Selwyn, but knew she would regret it if she did. She prided herself on her honesty. "Neil does not care about me. He does not care where I go or what I do. I could fall into the fjord and drown and it would not matter to him," she said morosely.

Selwyn let out a heavy sigh and ran a huge hand through his ash-blond hair. It was just as he'd suspected. Neil and Dorcas had had another fight. He also knew that what she said was not true. He'd watched the couple closely over the past months. Though their volatile tempers matched each other, so that when they clashed it was good to be far away from them, he'd seen something else. Neil had never been so content as he was when his wife was near. He'd also noted the softness in Dorcas's face when she gazed at her husband. The only time she became truly angry was when Anika was about. Selwyn guessed that that woman was the cause of Dorcas's fury now, and he knew that if Dorcas carried out her plan, she would be sorry later. The girl could not be allowed to act rashly.

"As Neil's wife I am ordering you to take me back to Erin," Dorcas said, breaking into his thoughts.

"This is Neil's ship. He alone commands it," Selwyn said firmly, turning his back on her to help the men repair one of the sails, thinking that Dorcas only needed time to calm down.

Dorcas eye the Viking's back narrowly. Her mounting fury bubbled to the surface, overflowing like boiling water. She was tired of everyone telling her what to do. Being among the northmen the way she'd been, she'd come to realize they were not so bad after all. She no longer considered them her enemies, but she had made up her mind. She would no longer live with them and endure their indifference to her feelings.

Quick as lightning she pulled her dagger and moved behind Selwyn. Before he realized what was happening, she had one arm about his upper chest, and the dagger in her other hand pressed against his throat.

"If you value your life, Viking, you will do as I say," she told him. When the other men on the ship saw what was going on, they started to come to Selwyn's aid, but Dorcas spoke rapidly in their native tongue. "Do not move, lest you wish to see him die before your eyes." To emphasize her point, she dug the knife deeper into his skin, nicking him.

The men remained where they were when they saw blood trickle down Selwyn's neck, all the while keeping a wary eye on the woman who held their friend.

"Dorcas, what can you hope to gain by this madness?" Selwyn asked more calmly than he felt. "You cannot kill us all."

"I do not plan to kill any of you. I will need you to guide this ship home."

"But the ice in the fjord . . ."

"You said that it was not completely impassable."

"Nonetheless, it is dangerous at this time of year," Selwyn said, trying desperately to reason with her. What in Odin's name had happened to make her go crazy? He heard a low chuckle behind him.

"Where is your spirit of adventure, Viking?"

"Neil will not like this," he grumbled.

"I no longer care what Neil likes or dislikes. He does not want me. I am merely obliging him by getting out of his way."

"That is not true—" Selwyn found it impossible to continue as Dorcas pressed the knife more firmly against his throat.

"Enough prattling. Tell the men to move. Now!"

Selwyn saw that all his reasoning had fallen on deaf ears, and he did as she ordered. He cursed his luck that there was only half of a crew to work the longship, and when he suggested that he be allowed to help the men at the oars, Dorcas only laughed harshly and replied that he would remain her prisoner for the time being.

"You cannot think to hold me this way for the whole journey!" he said in astonishment.

"Who is to say I cannot?"

Selwyn wondered how she intended to accomplish that feat. She had to sleep sometime. She had to eat. He started forming a plan in his mind. Dorcas was a mere woman. Surely it would not be too difficult to overpower her at some point along the way and turn the ship around. His spirits sank as she pulled him backward. She found a length of rope, and making him sit down, tied him up. Then she sat down behind him, all the while keeping the dagger close to his throat.

Everyone on the longship held their breath as they passed through the fjord. The ice had loosened, and floated treacherously along in gigantic chunks. It would take just the smallest mistake to hit one of the hulking pieces, ripping the bottom out of the ship. Once they were on the open sea, much of the tension left the air.

A couple of the braver men tried to approach Dorcas when it looked as if she was deep in thought, or almost

asleep, and wouldn't notice them. But each time she
brought the knife up against Selwyn's neck and ordered
them to return to their positions. Selwyn did not relish
the thought of remaining tied up for the entire voyage.
His worst fear, however, was of what Neil would do when
he found his wife and his ship both gone. He shuddered at
the thought of his next meeting with his friend, and
cursed both Dorcas and Neil for his present predicament.

The farther west they traveled, the more depressed
Dorcas became. She did not fear what would happen to
her when Neil caught up with her as Selwyn did. Instead,
she brooded on the folly of her actions. She had not really
wanted to leave Neil, but to know that she did not have
her husband's love tore at her heart, for she had realized
at last that she loved him.

What she'd experienced these past months was jealousy. She knew that now, and she knew that she could not
be jealous if she did not care. Aye, she cared. She loved
her husband. How ironic, she thought, that the very man
she claimed to be her deadliest enemy should be the one
who could so easily bruise her heart. The thought of Anika
in Neil's arms threw her further into the bowels of depression. To stay with him, knowing that he could go from her
bed to his lover's, would drive her mad. Her pride was
such that she would not share him. Mayhaps she should
have tried harder to please him. Now it was too late.
She'd set her course. She would see it through.

They'd been at sea for several days with Dorcas taking
only catnaps to ease her tiredness and coming awake at
the smallest sound. The men cursed her silently for her
warrior's instincts that made her so wary. They could not
get near enough to remove the knife from her. The one
time a man succeeded in getting close, he almost lost his
arm. He was lucky that it was not his life, for if Dorcas had
not been so tired, her aim would have been more sure.
After that the men did not try to approach her. She was
obviously mad, and they were only too willing to deposit

her on solid ground as soon as possible in order to be rid
of her.

Dorcas felt bad about having hurt someone. She'd not
meant these men harm, but she was as determined as
anyone who has been hurt and humiliated beyond all
reason. She had been foolhardy in her desperation, but
she had never given in in her entire life, and she was not
about to do so now.

She had been so enrapt in her dismal thoughts, she paid
no attention to the sea and sky around them. When she
became aware of the yellow tinge to the thick gray clouds
above the ship and the fierce, howling wind, the storm
was nearly upon them. The sea grew turbulent, the waves
rearing up and threatening to deluge the wooden ship.
Dorcas's stomach churned with every pitch and roll as the
ship was tossed by the tempestuous waters, and she had
to empty her insides several times over the side. The men
struggled to haul the sails down, then desperately used the
oars to keep the craft from capsizing. Rain beat down on
them in torrents, and Dorcas alternately cursed herself for
her stupidity—and Neil for having forced her into her
dilemma—and prayed to God to see them through the
tempest.

Selwyn shouted at her to release him. They needed
every hand they could get to see them through the storm.
At first Dorcas stood adamant in her refusal to untie him.
At one point a huge wave washed over them, terrifying
her, and she was sure they were going to drown. When it
passed, and she found the ship still afloat, she relented.
She was shaking badly as she worked with the wet knots
that bound Selwyn's wrists. Her stomach rolled with every
wave. As soon as Selwyn's hands were free, he untied his
feet and made his way unsteadily to where the crew
fought a desperate battle with the elements, forgetting
about why they were there in his effort to save them all.

Dorcas felt wretched, knowing that because of her they
could all drown. She was responsible. If only she hadn't

been so foolish. She wanted to help them somehow, but didn't know what to do. At least she could apologize for causing so much trouble. She did not want their curses upon her head when they all died. She started toward Selwyn, clinging to the side of the ship lest she be knocked into the angry sea. Then blessed darkness overtook her right where she was, and she collapsed, too numb from the cold that soaked through to her bones, and too weak from the sickness that had overcome her.

When Dorcas awoke, she was aware of two things at once. The sun shone over a calm sea, and she was lying on the deck of a ship under the cozy warmth of a blanket. She turned her head and saw the oarsmen busy at their work. Propping herself up on an elbow, she started to speak. A wave of dizziness washed over her and she closed her eyes, hoping it would go away. When it did not, she groaned at her weakness and lay down again.

"At last you are awake," came a voice from somewhere far above her.

She opened her eyes to find Selwyn standing over her. Staring at him warily, she cursed herself for letting down her guard. It now seemed that their positions were reversed. He looked like a man fully in charge while she was the one at his mercy. No doubt he was gloating over the fact that she would soon be at Neil's mercy as well.

She turned away from his penetrating gaze and said bitingly, "I imagine that you and Neil will laugh heartily at my foolishness for letting you get the best of me."

Selwyn studied the woman lying on the deck with her face turned away from him. She was very beautiful despite her disheveled appearance and pale countenance. Neil was a lucky man whether he knew it or not, and Selwyn was filled with a sudden spurt of jealousy that this woman could never be his. She loved her husband with a fierce intensity that was evident in the way she talked about him.

When the tables had been turned and he was Dorcas's

prisoner, he had tried to reason with her to go back. She'd spoken of Neil with a mixture of tenderness and bitterness in her voice, but also with such hopeless despair, he had felt sorry for her. He had sensed she was near the breaking point, and had silently cursed his longtime friend and companion for letting Anika disrupt their lives. The woman was little more than a whore who enjoyed making trouble. He'd listened closely to his friends in Norway, and they had been very informative. Selwyn felt that given enough time, Neil and Dorcas would come to terms. He'd always felt a great sense of loyalty to Neil, but he could not help it if he was beginning to respect Dorcas's courage, no matter how misplaced. He felt responsible for her now that she was in his care.

He sighed and hunkered down beside her. "When Neil catches up with me, no doubt he will kill me."

She jerked her head around to stare wide-eyed at him. "Where are we?"

"Another day and we should dock at Wexford."

"Y-you did not go back," she whispered in wonder.

He shrugged. "It seemed foolish to return to Norway when we were so close to our destination. The storm lasted for days and blew us right past the British coast."

"I did not know."

A small smile touched his lips. "Nay, you did not. You have been unaware of anything since you passed out during the storm."

Dorcas gazed at him in amazement. She'd always thought Selwyn's first and foremost loyalty was to Neil. It was a heady experience to realize that he was so considerate of her feelings, and yet she was not particularly overjoyed at the prospect of seeing her home and family soon.

An arrow pierced the earth just inches from her mount's right front hoof and the horse reared in fright. Dorcas cursed as she pulled back hard on the reins to bring the strange horse under control. She was grateful to Selwyn for having the money with which to purchase horses. When faced with the problem of how to get home, she feared that she might have to sell the golden arms bands that Neil had given her. She was surprised that Selwyn was in possession of money and said so, and was even more surprised when he told her that Neil had given him his freedom long ago. He stayed with Neil because he was devoted to his friend, not because he had to.

They'd traveled hard and fast to reach the McMahon stronghold. Dorcas was near the point of exhaustion, but no amount of coaxing on Selwyn's part would slow her down enough to rest. It was as if she were obsessed by some demon that forced her on. Her only thought was of reaching her father's house, and now that they stood outside the gate, they were greeted with a flurry of arrows instead of being embraced in welcome.

Dorcas looked at the stronghold, perplexed that its gates were shut tight against the outside world. Surely her own father meant her no harm. She called out in a clear voice that rang across the high walls. "Fagan. Rory. Hugh. It is I, the lady Dorcas and her man Selwyn." She pushed back the hood of her cloak, revealing a tangled mass of bright red hair to show those manning the walls that she spoke the truth.

A head popped up over the wall. It was Fagan, a loyal warrior of her father's. He shouted at those below to open the gate. Dorcas and Selwyn rode into the yard aware that the gate lumbered slowly shut behind them, but Dorcas had her eyes on her family as they came running to greet her.

She suddenly felt drained of all energy as Selwyn helped her dismount and kept a supporting arm around her so she would not fall. She straightened when her father reached them.

"Dorcas, child, what are you doing here?" Duncan asked in a tone that showed he was both surprised and pleased.

Then he looked past his daughter, bewildered. "Where is Neil?"

"In hell, I hope."

Duncan frowned at the animosity in her voice, and cast a quizzical look at Heloise. Hearing her daughter's words and seeing the state Dorcas was in, she asked quietly, "Dorcas, what has happened?"

"I am home, mother, that is all." She turned glazed eyes on her father. "I wish to know if I am welcome."

Duncan nodded once. The only way he could find out why she was here without her husband was to agree to let her stay. But then, his children were always welcome under his roof, and Dorcas looked as if she were about to fall apart. She needed him. "Of course you are."

She looked once again at her mother. "May I have my old room?"

"It is ready for you," Heloise answered calmly. Dear Lord, what was wrong? She could feel the tension that enveloped Dorcas reach out to her across the few feet that separated them. She wanted to take her daughter in her arms and tell her that all would be well, but she was afraid touch her.

"Then if you will excuse me," Dorcas said, "I wish to retire. I have had a long and exhausting journey." She was fighting down the queasiness that seemed to overtake her at the oddest moments. She had a terrible headache and was very tired. She silently blamed Neil for all her troubles, but her pride would not allow her to lean on her family. To let them see how affected she was by her husband's betrayal was too humiliating.

She hadn't taken two steps forward when she did something that had happened to her only one other time in her whole life. She fainted. And it was only through her brother Hugh's quick reflexes that she landed in his arms and not on the ground.

Cedric jumped up quickly from the chair where he'd sat

fidgeting ever since entering the great hall and started pacing back and forth in front of the fireplace. "I do not understand," he said agitatedly, turning to Duncan. "Dorcas has been here for over a month, yet she refuses to see us. Why?"

Duncan sighed and wearily ran a hand across his forehead. "She will not see anyone."

"Has she said nothing about why she returned? Surely she has spoken to you of her reasons."

Duncan shook his head and looked up into Cedric's worried face. "Nay. She has said absolutely nothing. Not about why she returned alone. Not about—about where Neil is. Nothing. We have all tried to reach her. I even called Kevin home to talk to her. There was always a special closeness between them, and I felt that with my son's particular calling, mayhaps he would be able to succeed where the rest of us failed, but he did not." Duncan sighed heavily. "She just sits in her chamber staring out the window."

"That does not sound like the Dorcas I know," Astrid murmured, frowning.

"She is not the same, and it frightens me," Heloise said. She tried to smile when Astrid took her hand. It was a small comfort and she was grateful for the other woman's understanding. Astrid knew what it was like to lose a child, but it had been different for her. Hers had been taken swiftly, through death. She'd not had to sit by helplessly to watch one of her children die by slow degrees, retreating within herself as Dorcas was, until she ended up shutting out everyone and everything. "I take her her meals, but she barely eats anything. She sleeps very little. Oftentimes she can be heard prowling in her room late at night. She will not speak to anyone unless she is asked a direct question, and even then, sometimes she ignores us. Oh, I wish Angus were here. I know that she would respond to him. She sent Harlan to him months ago. Why has he not returned? Why has Angus not returned home?" she cried.

Astrid placed a comforting arm about her and looked up at her husband. "Whatever has happened to change Dorcas must have been terrible indeed." Her eyes flashed in anger. "Cedric, if your son has done something to that child . . ."

Cedric gaped at his wife in astonishment. "Neil! What makes you think he is at fault?" he blustered. "We do not know what has happened, because Dorcas refuses to speak of it. For all we know, she may be the cause of her own state!" He suddenly stopped and sank back into the chair. "I am sorry," he mumbled. "I did not mean that. It is just that we have had so many problems lately, and now Dorcas and Selwyn return to Erin without Neil, and Dorcas shuts herself away in her chamber refusing to talk to anyone. I would like to know where my son is."

"I take it you were as unsuccessful in obtaining any information from Selwyn as I was," Duncan said.

"Aye. He said that Neil was well when last he saw him. He told me the most preposterous story," he added in a voice tinged with disbelief, "that Dorcas was desperate to return here, and when he refused to bring her, she forced him at the point of a dagger . . ."

"Aye," Duncan said, "he told me the same story, only he did not say why Dorcas was in such a hurry, or why they left Neil behind. He is very loyal to your son."

Cedric grunted. "I have a feeling that he is protecting Dorcas as much as he is Neil."

Dorcas stood at the window in her chamber, her arms wrapped about her. Since returning to her father's house, she'd spent most of her days in the same pastime, just staring out at nothing. Every member of her family had been to see her, but she would not speak at length with any of them. She knew she was the main topic of conversation and speculation, not only among her family, but also among her father's friends and neighbors.

Upon her return she'd learned that there had been a

series of raids on Duncan's land, so he'd taken to keeping the compound closed to all outsiders. At first she thought that Cedric was behind them, that somehow he'd found out what an unacceptable wife she was for Neil and had started the feud again. However, Gwendolyn quickly dispelled that notion. Cedric's land was being raided as well, and the friendship between Duncan and Cedric remained steadfast. Someone was trying to make it appear that one or the other of them wanted the feud to start anew, but the two men would not fall for the ploy.

She knew that Cedric and Astrid had been to see her, but she couldn't face them. She was too ashamed. If she could not explain to her own family why she'd left Neil, how could she find the words to tell them that their son preferred another woman to her?

Dorcas felt like a failure. She had failed her father in his quest for peace. If Cedric hadn't been raiding them, once he learned that the bargain was broken between the clans he would surely start. She could not face the realization that because of her, her people would soon go to war. She was miserable. She'd not only failed Duncan, somehow she'd failed Neil as well.

Angus had once warned her that she would someday regret having scorned all the men who tried to woo her. She'd merely scoffed at his words, swearing she would never fall into some man's arms willingly, as other women did. She was not like other women. Her attitude had not stopped her suitors. Then Neil had come along to claim her, as if she were a prize in some contest that was his for the taking. Only she'd scorned him as well, and look what it got her. He'd proved her wrong. All her silly ideas flew right out the window when he touched her. She was like other women, but only Neil could bring out the woman she was, and he did not want her.

She shut her eyes wearily, but quickly opened them again when the image of her husband walking casually into Anika's bedchamber came to her. How could he do that to her? How could he so easily go to that woman after having been with her, his wife, so short a time before?

A surge of anger coursed through Dorcas. She would never forgive him. Never!

Her thoughts were interrupted when the door opened and Heloise entered the room. Dorcas turned and looked at her mother without saying anything, waiting for the questions she knew were coming.

Heloise gazed thoughtfully at her daughter and prayed that she was doing the right thing. Somehow, she had to bring Dorcas back to the world of the living. She clasped her hands in front of her and took a deep breath. "Dorcas, this has gone on long enough. We have allowed you the privacy you wished. However, there is nothing wrong with you. You are no longer sick as you were upon your arrival. We cannot continue to coddle you when there is so much to be done around here. From now on, if you want anything you will have to get it yourself, and if you wish to eat, you will have to join the rest of us at the table."

Every word that Heloise uttered was done so quietly, but there was no mistaking the firm tone. Without waiting for Dorcas's reaction, she just as quietly left the chamber.

Dorcas felt that she would rather die than let anyone see the hurt and humiliation she suffered. But by the following evening she'd grown ravenous and decided she would not give Neil the satisfaction of thinking he'd rid himself of her so easily while she starved to death. She joined the others in the great hall to sup, wondering if the low murmurs and whispers were comments made about her.

Once she realized no one was snickering behind her back, she grew braver in spending her time among people. By the end of the week she'd ventured outside to take walks in the sun, and soon her cheeks lost the pallor they'd acquired during her self-inflicted exile.

She watched her father's men practice on the training

field, feeling as though that part of her life was very far away. How had the girl she'd once been lose the will to fight? She was as good a warrior as any of them. In some cases, better. Would she ever pick up the sword again? What would happen when Cedric learned that she'd left Neil? Would the feud begin again? Would she be expected to fight against her father-by-marriage? If Neil returned, could she do battle against him?

Dorcas shuddered at the thought. She could not harm him. She did not want to destroy her husband. Yet he had destroyed her. It had shocked her to learn she loved Neil. But she knew now that she did, else he could not have hurt her the way he had. She felt betrayed. Somehow she had to force her heart and mind to deny him. He was far, far away, with his true love. That thought stabbed at her heart. She fought back the tears that gathered in her eyes and raised her chin defiantly. It seemed that she had never cried so much as she had since meeting him. He was the cause of all her problems. She would get over Neil McNeil, even if it took her the rest of her life.

She started toward the house, but stopped when she heard a commotion at the gate. She raised a hand to shade her eyes and watched the gate swing open laboriously. It seemed an eternity before the portals opened wide enough for whoever was on the outside to enter. She listened to the shouted commands and greetings unenthusiastically, until she caught sight of the one who'd caused such a fuss.

She started running to the man alighting from his horse. She cried his name silently as she ran, and upon reaching him at last, the word exploded into sound. "Harlan!"

The messenger she'd sent to Angus so long ago smiled tiredly at her.

"Harlan!" she cried once more, throwing her arms about the man, surprising him. "It has been so long since you left that we thought you lost to us forever. How is my brother? Where is Angus? Why did he not return with you? Where is he? Is he safe and well?"

The questions tumbled out of her one after another, leaving no room for answers.

Laughing, Duncan pushed his way through the crowd around his daughter and the man. "Dorcas, let Harlan catch his breath. He has only just arrived," he chided her softly, still smiling. "We are all eager to hear the answers to your questions, but for now why don't you go inside to see that some food is readied for our weary traveler?"

Dorcas felt a momentary irritation at her abrupt dismissal, but she obediently did as her father requested, telling herself that no good would come of an argument now.

She sat on one side of Harlan while her father sat on the man's other side, with the rest of the family gathered about them, listening to his tale. He told them of his long journey to Brittany only to find upon his arrival that Angus was not at his uncle's house. He was curtly informed of his whereabouts, and so set out for the place. Everyone listened, spellbound, as he described the huge stone fortress that was Angus's home. There, he found to his dismay that Angus was with his uncle on a campaign, but that the lady Claudia had seen to it that he was made comfortable for as long as he had to wait.

Harlan was ready to continue his story when Dorcas interrupted him. "Who is Lady Claudia?"

He turned to her. Seeing the scowl on her face, he stumbled over his answer. "L-Lord Angus's wife."

"Wife!"

"His what?" Heloise gasped

Harlan looked nervously from one face to the other. "L-Lord Angus i-is m-married."

"Married?" Heloise repeated, dumbfounded.

"Ooh, how wonderfully exciting," Thalia cried.

"Hush up!" Dorcas snapped, turning her attention back to Harlan. "Why didn't Angus send us word of his marriage? Is his wife such a toad that he could not inform his own family?"

"N-nay, my lady," Harlan replied, swallowing hard. "L-Lord Angus has been extremely busy. As I said, he was gone when I arrived, and instead of sending me off again, Lady Claudia bade me rest. She is a most beautiful and gracious lady, highly respected by her people. I—I got the feeling that they would do anything, anything at all, to protect her." He recalled how all the servants had acted as though he were from another world and they had to guard their lady from him. In truth, he'd not seen too much of the lady Claudia, for she'd seemed to avoid him. He'd wondered about her peculiar behavior at the time, but shrugged it off as having something to do with the delicate condition she was in.

Dorcas felt a wave of dejection wash over her. Was this wife of Angus's the reason her twin had not returned? Was he so wrapped up in his adventures that he no longer cared what happened to his twin? She wanted to scream, to cry, anything to vent the frustration she felt at the unfairness of all that had happened within the last several months, but she felt only a strange numbness. As one in a daze, she arose and started toward her chamber. Before she could leave the hall, Harlan caught up with her.

"Lady Dorcas, I am sorry that Lord Angus could not return with me. . . ."

"Could not, or did not want to?" she asked bitterly.

"Nay, my lady. He would have come home if he could, but it was impossible. He did, however, give me this to give to you." He reached into his tunic to retrieve a battered letter. "Mayhaps he explains everything in here," he added hopefully, handing Dorcas the letter. "He also sent a present to you. The white stallion I had with me when I arrived, and he wanted me to tell you that—that he loves you. His heart is with you. He wanted you to know that he is thinking of you."

Dorcas stared at the letter through a hazy blur of tears. *Oh, Angus,* she thought, *why couldn't I have gone with you?*

"Mayhaps he gives you a clue as to how to avoid your upcoming wedding," Harlan ventured to say.

Dorcas let out a ragged breath and swallowed hard before answering. "Nay. It is too late. I was wed shortly after you left."

Harlan watched her leave the hall in stunned silence. All his efforts had been for naught. Damnation! If only the ship that carried him home had not been blown off course three times. He hoped that all would be well for his lady.

16

Dorcas gave free rein to the horse, reveling in the stallion's swiftness. Harlan explained that Angus had obtained the horse on the last campaign he'd fought in with his uncle. It was a rare breed that came from the far-off land of Arabia, and apparently the previous owner had purchased it from a traveling band of Gypsies. It was smaller and faster than the large destriers she was used to, and she could not help but admire the sleek lines and spiritedness of the beautiful creature. How a Gypsy could have owned such a magnificent beast, or how much the man had had to pay, she didn't know. She knew only that it was her good fortune to have the animal in her possession now. It hadn't taken long for her and the horse to become fast friends, and every time she climbed on the stallion's back, she felt as if she were riding the wind.

She touched the pouch at her waist. A tiny smile played at the corners of her mouth at the thought of the letter there. Though she'd memorized the contents from her constant reading of it, it was comforting to have it with her, so she carried it always. But soon she would have her twin with her, for she had no doubt that Angus would keep his word and come to her as quickly as he could.

After reading the long, rambling missive, Dorcas had been at last able to find a release for all the pent-up frustration, anger, and pain she'd kept locked up inside. She'd cried as she had never cried in her entire life, until there were no more tears left to spill. She was jealous that every word Angus wrote about his Claudia expressed the love he felt for his wife, but her jealousy quickly turned to guilt. She could not fault her twin for finding such happiness when she was so miserable herself. His hope that her impending marriage would bring her the same contentment that his own did was meant as encouragement, she knew, but she could find no comfort in his words.

The bitter tears she had spent seemed to cleanse her soul so that she was free at last, free of the chains of anguish that had held her captive for so long. She'd cursed herself for wallowing in self-pity, and decided that it was time to get on with her life. She had started by making friends with her gift from Angus, surprising everyone with the ease with which she managed the devil horse. She enjoyed riding the stallion as much as he seemed to enjoy flying across the land at top speed, and no amount of threats or protests from her father could stop her. The men Duncan ordered to accompany her on her wild rides over the countryside all returned to the settlement grumbling that they were of no use to her, for she left them all as if they were standing still. Only Selwyn continued to follow Dorcas faithfully, even when she left him in a cloud of dust.

Mayhaps she should have felt guilty at leaving him behind, but she did not want a watchdog, and it irritated her that he followed her every move. She wrestled with her conscience on the matter. Selwyn had been kind to her when he could just as easily have turned her over to Neil. He had helped her.

Glancing around, she saw him lagging behind and shrugged. Oh, well, if he *had* to come along, he could at least ride beside her. After all, she did owe him something.

"Since you insist upon being here," she shouted, "you may as well ride with me."

The stallion was eager to be off, and Dorcas had to use all her skills to hold him in check as she waited for the Viking to catch up with her. She heard an eerie whistling sound at the same time Selwyn cried out a warning, and was to think later that it was providence that had saved her, for her mount backed up at that moment. She turned her head, and her eyes widened in surprise at the arrow sticking in the ground. Astonishment turned to anger as she leaned down and grabbed it.

"Ride, my lady!" Selwyn commanded when he reached her, already turning his own horse for home.

"Who would dare—"

"Ask your questions later," he said tersely, cutting her off and patting the stallion on the rump to make the animal move. By Thor, he thought, the woman would probably have tried to pursue their attacker, or attackers, if he'd not been along!

He was not far wrong, for Dorcas was so angry at the audacity of anyone who would assault her or try to harm the beautiful, sleek stallion, she was ready to ride into the hills to confront them. It was probably just a poacher with very bad aim, and she was sorely tempted to teach whoever it was a lesson. Her horse had other ideas, however. He seemed to know just where home was, and he had no intention of stopping until he reached the safety of the settlement.

Dorcas chewed her lower lip, anxiously watching Duncan's reactions as Selwyn told him what had happened.

"Damnation, woman!" he exploded when the Viking had finished speaking. "Did I not tell you *not* to leave here without a guard in attendance! For the two of you to have gone off like that—you could have been killed!"

Dorcas raised her head proudly and stared steadily at

her father. "But we were not," she stated. The calmness in her voice surprised even her. She arose and moved over to Duncan, placing a hand on his arm. She smiled at him much as one would to a child who doesn't understand. "Father, we are safe. The incident is best forgotten. It was probably some poor soul who was trying to put food on the table for his family. Whoever it was was no doubt more frightened by his act than I."

"You surely do not believe that any more than Duncan or I. Especially not with all the trouble we've had."

Dorcas stiffened at the sound of the voice behind her. She had been trying so hard to avoid him. She looked into Duncan's eyes and found no help for her there, so she turned slowly to face Cedric standing in the doorway.

"Selwyn had the good sense to send a messenger to me," he said, moving forward. He turned to Duncan. "He said that Dorcas retrieved the arrow. May I see it?"

Duncan handed it over without a word. He'd recognized it immediately when Dorcas showed it to him, and was surprised that his daughter had not. It was unusual in the double-edged tip that was the mark of the clan McNeil.

Cedric looked up from his inspection of the arrow with anguished eyes. "Who is doing this to us?" he asked in a rasping voice.

Dorcas looked from the arrow to Cedric's face. When her sister had assured her that her father-by-marriage had nothing to do with the raids, Dorcas had believed her, and she'd been so angered by the near hit she'd suffered that she'd not been able to see clearly. The way in which Cedric clutched the arrow, the look on his face, told her much. The need to release her anger made her words tumble out before she thought.

"Mayhaps you would like for us to believe in your innocence when in actuality you have been responsible for the raids all along."

"Dorcas!" Duncan shouted.

She rushed on, unmindful of the hurt look on Cedric's face and the shocked expression on her father's. "Neil and I were forced into an unwanted marriage, and until your son returned to Norway, he did not realize what a mistake it was. Mayhaps you are the instrument which he is using to rid himself of a cumbersome burden."

Cedric shook his head in disbelief. He had so hoped that his son and Dorcas would come to an amiable understanding. It appeared that she still very much resented her circumstances. "Nay, Dorcas, Neil wants peace as much as I—"

"Is that why he cast me aside? Is that why my people have been plagued with attacks on them?"

"I have not been immune from those attacks!" Cedric replied heatedly.

"How convenient."

"What do you mean when you say that my son cast you aside?" Cedric asked suddenly, changing the subject.

Dorcas felt the heat rise to her face. She'd not meant to let her humiliation be known. "I am sure you already know all about that," she said scathingly, then ran from the hall before she could be questioned further, tears brimming in her eyes. Damnation and hell! She'd thought she was over the crying, but all it took for her to start was Neil's name being mentioned.

She lay across her bed, sobbing, when she felt comforting hands reach out to her. Turning in her mother's arms, she clung to Heloise, seeking the solace that was offered. After crying her heart out, Dorcas sat up and smiled tremulously while her mother wiped the tears from her face with the edge of her headrail.

"Sometimes it helps to talk of your troubles," she said in her quiet manner.

"I hate him!" Dorcas cried.

Heloise continued to gaze at her daughter, her face an expressionless mask.

Dorcas grew uncomfortable under her mother's scrutiny and lowered her eyes. "I love him," she whispered. She suddenly looked up again, her eyes full of pain. "I hate him. Oh, mother, how can I be so torn? If only he had remained cruel and unfeeling. I hated him so much on our wedding night. He—he hurt me," she said in a low voice, looking away quickly from Heloise's penetrating gaze that seemed to see so much.

"He did not mean to. He was sorry for it afterward."

She stared wide-eyed at her mother. "You knew."

"Aye. Neil told me what he'd done."

"He told you!" shrieked Dorcas, her face reddening with shame.

"Yea, he did," Heloise replied calmly. She took Dorcas's hands in hers. "Neil is not a bad man, my love. You pushed him too far."

"Why is everything my fault? It was my fault that I did not wish to wed. It was my fault that he raped me. Is it also my fault that he loves another?" she cried.

"Are you certain he does?"

"Yea. You should have seen them. The way she fawned over him. The way he allowed her attentions. He is a heartless beast. If only he'd not awakened a need in me that he alone can fulfill. But to have done so and then cast me aside—I cannot bear it. There was a time when I thought that we might have a chance," she said in a far-off voice, remembering the days they'd spent alone in the hills of Norway. "I was a fool to believe such a thing. Where once I felt complete, now I feel—betrayed, and empty." She sighed and got up to walk to the window. "Will I never get over him? The very thought of him brings tears to my eyes. I have never cried so much or felt so depressed."

A smile touched Heloise's lips. "It is natural to feel as you do. I did when I carried you and Angus, and for you to be going through such a trying time with your husband has certainly not helped your condition."

Dorcas's face drained of all color, and her lips moved silently. "What are you saying?" she managed to say at last.

"You are with child, sweeting. All the signs are there."

"Nay! Oh, nay, I cannot—I had thought to be rid of him when I left," she said bitterly. "To have his child . . . It is not fair!"

"Dorcas, that child was conceived out of your love for Neil. It is not to blame for anything that has happened," Heloise said sharply. "I am sure that if Neil knew of the babe, he would be here with you."

"He does not want me," Dorcas answered, shaking her head.

"Well, we will just have to see about that when he returns, won't we?"

Heloise slipped from the room to leave Dorcas with her confused thoughts. "If he returns," she muttered in the silence of the chamber. A babe. Neil's child, and he did not even know, or care.

Heloise stood outside the chamber door in indecision for a moment before going in search of the Viking who'd accompanied Dorcas to Erin. Selwyn knew more than he was saying, and she intended to find out the facts behind her daughter's sudden appearance on their doorstep. She knew Dorcas well and could not help the nagging suspicion that the child had once again acted without thinking.

Spring finally budded over the land, then burst forth into flowering summer that cast brilliant hues of color across the earth. It was Dorcas's favorite time of the year, awakening all her senses to the things that were fresh and clean and new.

For the most part she was content with herself, at least as long as she did not dwell on thoughts of Neil. Heloise's revelation had been like a lightning bolt shooting through her, but when she considered her actions and her feelings since returning home, she knew her mother was right. She'd assumed that the strange bouts of sickness she'd experienced had been in reaction to all that had happened to her since discovering her husband's perfidy. But upon further consideration, she realized she'd also been ill in Norway just before she left. There had been her battles with dizziness, and the queasiness that hit her in the early mornings, that she'd managed with difficulty to keep under control. At the time she'd shrugged it off, putting it down to her mental anguish over Neil's knavery.

Once she became accustomed to the idea of carrying the child, a sereneness settled over her. Her mother was right, of course. The babe was not to blame for anything that had happened to her. It was her child as well, and she quickly decided that it would have her love. It did not matter if it was a boy or a girl, she would teach it to be strong and independent, to rely solely upon itself, for only in that way would the child be impregnable to pain.

She had hoped to keep her condition from Cedric, afraid that he would summon Neil home, but that proved impossible. With the beginning of summer the raids on them ceased, as if whoever had been behind them had tired of playing his little game of trying to pit the two clans against each other.

Now Cedric and Astrid came often to visit the McMahons.

The only way in which Dorcas could avoid them was by shutting herself away in her chamber, but since she never knew when they would appear, it wasn't long before they became aware of her state. Cedric fussed and fumed, insisting that Dorcas return with them to the McNeil stronghold, saying that the child should be born in the place of its inheritance. Dorcas was thrown into a state of panic by his words, and, surprisingly, was supported in her desire to remain where she was by none other than Astrid. Her mother-by-marriage staunchly vetoed her husband's demands, telling him it would not be a good idea to uproot Dorcas from the surroundings where she felt the most secure. Besides, upsetting her could only bring harm to the babe.

Once it was known by so many that she carried Neil's child, Dorcas held her breath, waiting for him to magically appear, but her stomach grew rounder and the summer longer, and he did not come. She did not know whether to feel relieved or angry. Again, as on her arrival, everyone coddled her and she found to her irritation that her activities were curtailed for her.

Duncan put his foot down and forbade her to ride her beautiful stallion. Her mother, sisters, and Astrid were having such an enjoyable time preparing the coming babe's wardrobe, she felt like an intruder when she tried to help, with everyone reminding her how much she hated that particular pursuit. She recalled how she'd had so much fun helping Ailsa, Erik's sister, prepare the tiny garments for her coming child, and felt cheated that she was not allowed to do as much for her own babe. She was either told to rest or to get some exercise.

Her idleness merely increased her restlessness. She'd rested until she thought she would scream, and her only exercise consisted of taking walks about the village, until she was bored to tears. It seemed that even in that tame pursuit she could not resist getting into trouble.

One day as she watched Duncan's men practice on the training field, she noticed a young man struggling with the rigors of the strenuous drills. She watched him in amusement. Had she ever been so clumsy? She winced, feeling the boy's pain when his opponent caught him squarely along the side of the head with the flat of a sword, sending him reeling backward. She could almost feel the ringing in his ears. Struck by sympathy for the hapless youth, she stepped forward, calling out to Fagan, who was pressing his attack relentlessly. The two young men turned to her as she approached.

Dorcas smiled brightly. "Fagan, who, prey tell, is this young man you find such pleasure in beating so inexorably?"

"My lady, Robert Devlin," Fagan said, indicating the red-faced boy.

"Ah, Robert Devlin," Dorcas murmured. "I remember your father." She watched the boy straighten, pride clearly showing on his face. "You are new among my father's ranks, are you not?"

"Yea, my lady," the youth said, blushing.

"I, too, fought at my father's side. As a matter of fact, your father and I went on many raids together before he was killed. I remember my own training well," she mused, thinking back to those early days. "Would you mind if I made a few suggestions?"

"I would welcome them, my lady."

Dorcas proceeded to give the youth some sound advice, but even as she spoke she knew that actual experience would teach him more than words. She ended her lecture, wondering how much Robert had absorbed. "Above all else, you must not allow your close association with your friends and relatives to hold you back from fighting with the fierceness of the warrior that you are. Someday their lives may depend upon your skills." A thought suddenly occurred to her. "Uh, Fagan, loan me your sword and shield."

"My lady," Fagan exclaimed, backing away, "I cannot."

Dorcas shot him a look of surprise. "And why not?"

"I dare not. You—your—condition," he finished lamely, finding himself blushing as furiously as Robert had only moments before.

"Oh, do not be ridiculous," Dorcas said exasperatedly, grabbing the weapon and shield out of Fagan's hands. "I only wish to show him a stance that Angus taught me."

Wearing a dubious expression, Fagan glanced at Robert and shrugged.

"Now, stand thusly," Dorcas instructed. Out of the corner of her eye she could see that the young man's attention had wandered to Fagan, and said sharply, "Pay attention, Robert. This might serve as a lesson for you as well, Fagan. Keep your shield close to your body at all times, except when using it as a weapon in itself, or to parry your opponent's sword. Remember to keep your back straight. It also helps your balance to keep your knees bent slightly." She watched Robert follow her instructions to the letter, murmuring, "Good, good."

Suddenly she swung around to face the youth. "Now attack me," she ordered.

Unable to conceal his shock, Robert dropped both arms to his sides. "My lady, I—I cannot."

Dorcas raised her shield and sword and said determinedly, "You most certainly can. That is, if you do not wish to be cut to ribbons," she added with a wicked grin. She lunged forward, forcing the startled Robert to bring his sword up to parry her attack. Dorcas swung her weapon again and again, all the while voicing her encouragement to the young man to strike back.

Others had stopped to watch in stunned disbelief as Dorcas continued to attack the youth unmercilessly while Robert retreated. Suddenly Dorcas's name rang out from across the compound. She lowered the sword and turned to see Duncan and Cedric bearing down on her. Both men wore furious expressions.

"What in blazes do you think you're doing?" Duncan thundered upon reaching her.

"I was only trying to help Robert improve his form," she answered innocently.

"In your condition?" Cedric sputtered. "This is just the very thing that I was talking about preventing from happening by having you return to my hall with us. You must be careful. . . ."

"My condition be hanged! Everyone treats me as if I were an invalid. I am not allowed to do anything, and my idleness is driving me mad. I am not ill. I am just going to have a child," she shouted.

"My son's child!" Cedric shouted in turn.

"My child," she shot back.

Duncan released a heavy sigh. "Nevertheless, my dear, you must be careful. None of us wants to see harm befall you or the babe. We are only trying to see to it that your time is made easier."

"That's just it," Dorcas cried, stamping her foot in frustration. "I am sick of all the pampering." She thrust Fagan's sword and shield at him and ran to the keep.

Dorcas noticed a definite change in the days that followed, and she wasn't at all sure she liked it. Her family no longer treated her as if she were breakable, but instead, included her in their everyday activities. Her mother and sisters constantly asked her advice about the kind of stitches she preferred to see embroidered on the babe's clothes, or sought her approval on the handiwork that had been completed thus far. Conan and Bevan came to her, regaling her with tales of their adventures, or seeking her help in getting them out of trouble. In the evenings Duncan and Hugh often invited her to sit with them as they discussed the day's events.

She knew perfectly well what everyone was trying to do, and knew she should appreciate their efforts, but she was still bound by a restlessness she could not explain. Every day she took a stroll around the village, hoping the exertion would help her to fall asleep at night without tossing and turning, only to find herself lying awake until the wee hours of the morning with thoughts of Neil haunting her.

Heloise grew concerned about Dorcas's listlessness and lack of attention to the happenings around her. This was not the same girl whose inattentiveness was due to her wanting to be on the training field, or on a raid with the men. She plainly did not care what went on around her.

Heloise watched Dorcas surreptitiously while her daughter sat holding the nightshirt she'd been embroidering. Gwendolyn and Thalia talked quietly together, every so often breaking into giggles. Dorcas ignored them. It was as if she were in her own little world, and Heloise was becoming quite worried. She was reminded of Dorcas's arrival, and how she'd shut herself away then. Heloise sighed, wishing something would happen to bring her daughter back to life. If only Neil would come home.

As though in answer to her wish, Hugh ran into the hall at that moment shouting for the women. "Mother! Dorcas! Come quickly. Come, girls, you will never believe who is here."

Heloise eyed her firstborn with amusement. Hugh was so like his father. "Who has created such excitement, my son?"

Hugh was already pulling Dorcas to her feet. He grabbed the small nightshirt out of her hands and threw it on the chair. "Angus is home, Dorcas," he said quietly. He watched as the blank expression she wore turned to one of incredulousness, and she mouthed her twin's name before the impact of Hugh's words hit her.

Dorcas ran outside, where her sisters, father, and little brothers were congregated around a laughing Angus as he tried to embrace them all and answer the multitude of questions hurled at him. He disengaged himself from Thalia's embrace when he saw Dorcas. Their eyes locked and held, silently communicating in an affinity known only between the two of them. She took in his hulking frame for a moment, satisfying herself that he was well and was finally home, before propelling herself into his waiting arms. She embraced him fiercely, then stepped back. As though still not believing he was real, she ran her hands across his shoulders and down his arms.

"You are safe and whole," she said.

"Aye," he replied, chuckling. The grin left his face, replaced by a slight frown when he saw the look in her eyes. "You have had some bad dreams again." It was more a statement than a question.

She could only nod her head. "I am so glad that you are here."

"As you can see, I am in one piece." He laughed and held her away from him. "You, too, look fit, though I see that I did not arrive in time to prevent your marriage."

"Oh, Angus."

The smile left his face altogether at the flash of pain he saw in his sister's eyes. "All is not well with you."

"Nay. Yea. Oh, it is so complicated."

Afraid that Dorcas would dampen her brother's homecoming before he even had a chance to get inside the keep, Heloise stepped forward. "Am I not entitled to a proper greeting from my own son?"

"Mother." Angus encircled Heloise in his arms and kissed her warmly. He hugged Dorcas once more, as if to reassure her, then, grinning like a little boy about to do mischief, his gaze swept over his family. "I have a surprise for you." He walked over to where a beautiful young woman sat atop a palfrey. Taking the babe she held, he cradled the child in one arm and helped her to dismount. She tilted her head up to look adoringly at Angus, and the hood of her cloak fell back to reveal a shining mass of red-gold hair. He waited impatiently for the young boy with them to climb down from his mount and help an older woman to the ground. With a possessive hand on the young woman's back, Angus led them forward.

"I would like you to meet my wife, Claudia. This is her brother," he added, indicating the youth, "Lord Vail Edward Justin Cherveny, and that is Marian, my lady's maid."

Angus watched proudly as everyone greeted his wife and brother-by-marriage, warmly embracing them, making them a part of the large, loving family that was his. His mouth twitched in amusement when he spied Conan and Bevan off to one side eyeing Vail curiously. He noticed that Vail stared back shyly.

As Dorcas touched her cheek to her new sister's, she said, "You have made Angus very happy."

"No more so than he has me."

Dorcas studied Claudia for a moment, and seeing the contentment in the woman's shining face, smiled. Because of the closeness Angus shared with his wife, she was prepared to love the woman who held her twin's heart. She caught the tender look that passed between the two of them, and could not help feeling she was missing something in her own life. It saddened her to know she would never find such happiness.

"And this," Angus said, holding up the sleeping child for their inspection, "is my son, Robert."

A cry of joy escaped Heloise as she reached out to take the babe from Angus. "My first grandchild!" She led the way inside the keep with Duncan peeking over her shoulder at the strapping infant. The others followed, all talking at once. With an arm around both Dorcas and Claudia, Angus tagged behind everyone else.

"From the look of you, you have been married for some time," he stated.

"As far as I am concerned, it has been too long."

He glanced sideways at his sister and noted the proud tilt of her chin, the glint of steel in her eyes. "Where is your husband?"

"In Norway," she answered shortly.

Angus frowned. It appeared that Harlan, the messenger that his twin had sent to him in Brittany, had been right after all. He'd told Angus that the Viking would do his duty, then return to Norway. It was obvious that Dorcas was desperately unhappy. He found it inconceivable that the man was not even interested in the birth of his own child. How could he simply run off to Norway so soon after the marriage and leave Dorcas to fend for herself? This McNeil was a cruel, unfeeling barbarian, and if he were here now, Angus would enjoy tearing him apart with his bare hands.

"He should be here with you," he grumbled.

"He is not interested in me, nor—nor I in him," Dorcas replied firmly.

Angus stopped and stared at his twin. She glared back at him, as if daring him to repudiate her words. "Has the man no conscience? You are about to have his child. He should be here."

Dorcas opened her mouth to reply, but before she could say anything, Claudia placed a hand on Angus's arm. "Angus, please do not upset your sister. We have only just arrived and do not know the circumstances of why her husband is not here. Remember, my love, you were not with me during my time either."

"That was different," Angus replied through gritted teeth.

Dorcas watched as Claudia merely smiled and touched his cheek lovingly. She was amazed by the serenity emanating from her new sister. Most people would have cowered away from the dark scowl marking Angus's features.

"Mayhaps then again . . ." Claudia let the sentence trail off.

Angus grasped her hand and pressed it to his lips. He shuddered inwardly, thinking of how close he had come to losing his beautiful wife. She was right. He'd not been there, and when he did return home, he'd been so tired from having waged a long battle that he'd felt was a wasted effort, and so angered by her accusations that he did not understand, he'd lost his accursed temper. It was rare when he did. Dorcas was the more volatile of the two. But when he did become angry, God help the one on whom that fury was unleashed. If it had not been for his overhasty tongue, Claudia would not have run from their chamber, nor would she have fallen halfway down the stairs in her attempt to escape him. It was because of that that she had gone into labor too soon. He thanked God every day of his life that his son and wife were both all right.

Nay. He did not know what problems plagued his twin's marriage, but he silently vowed to find out. If McNeil thought he could get away with mistreating Dorcas, he could just think again. The Viking had yet to deal with him.

"Angus, Claudia is right," Dorcas said. "I do not wish to speak of Neil. What's done is done. But you—you have been gone for such a long time, you must have all kinds of adventures to relate to us. Come, sit by the fire and tell us all that has happened."

He smiled. "Very well. But first . . ." He turned to the old woman who'd arrived with them. "Marian, if you like, I will have someone show you to your quarters so that you can rest. Some food can be brought to you there."

At his words the woman straightened from her tired slouch and took on an affronted air. "Humph, and how do you expect me to rest in the midst of this heathen land? I came along to make sure that no harm befalls my little pigeon. You drag us out of our nice, safe home on such a long journey, hardly giving any of us a chance to catch our breath along the way before we start out again. Why, if I hadn't been along to take care of my little ones, you would not have stopped to rest at all. Just because you can go for days without sleep does not mean the rest of us can, and now that we are here does not mean that my work is finished. Rest indeed! When I have my charges to look after. I can rest only when I know for certain that they are all being well taken care of and only then." She glanced over her shoulder several times as she walked away grumbling.

Dorcas stared in astonishment after the woman. In practically one breath she'd insulted her home and her twin. She turned in surprise to look at Angus when he merely laughed and walked over to where his family was gathered around Heloise and the babe. She looked at Claudia to find her sister-by-marriage also smiling. "You allow a servant to speak that way?"

"Marian is more than a servant. She is part of our family." She leaned forward and murmured in a low voice, "Besides, she likes to grumble and growl, so we indulge her. Look." She nodded to where Angus sat by the fire.

Dorcas's gaze followed Claudia's. The old woman yanked

a tray of food out of a young serving girl's hands, inspected its contents, and threw the girl a disgusted look. She marched to the cooking pot and ladled some more stew in the bowl. Tossing both the cook and the young girl a smug look, she tramped over to Angus and set the food down on a table in front of him, admonishing him to eat.

"When Marian speaks of her charges," Claudia said, "Angus is at the top of her list. Though it was not always so, she fusses over him just as much as she does Robert. Come, let us join them."

Dorcas stared after her sister-by-marriage as Claudia strolled over to her husband. Clearly bemused, she followed.

As Angus ate, he brought his family up-to-date on his adventures. He told them of the battles fought, of how his uncle Felix had persuaded him to marry the beautiful prisoner, Claudia Cherveny. He admitted to being shocked by Felix's attitude to Claudia, but stated firmly that he had never looked upon his wife as a captive. A secretive look passed between them, and Dorcas was once again struck by pangs of loneliness and jealousy. She was truly happy for her twin, but his contentment only pointed out her own failings.

Angus told them in a quiet voice tinged with sadness of Felix's treachery and madness. His uncle had tried to kill him for something that had happened long ago, and had nothing to do with him at all. He watched his mother's face as he related the things her brother had said, and what he'd learned from Eudora, Felix's wife.

Heloise was stunned as Angus told his story, and when he finished she let out a ragged sigh. "I thought that when he came here seeking our help that he had at last forgiven me," she said quietly. "I am sorry that you had to go through so much simply because Felix wanted revenge. You see, he had planned that I should marry Theo Archibald so that Theo's estate would be joined to ours, but I knew that Theo loved Eudora and she loved him. When your father came along and we fell in love, my parents saw that it would not do to thrust me into a marriage where I would be so unhappy. They gave their consent when Duncan asked for my hand. My brother was livid with rage. He swore that he would have his vengeance on me and told me that as far as he was concerned, I was dead.

"When he was here I recalled how enraged he had been all those long years ago. That is why I sent Owen with you, to look after you. It is such a pity that Felix's hatred and bitterness reached out its ugly hand to touch so many." Tears shone in Heloise's eyes as she looked at Claudia. "I am sorry about your parents and brother. I knew Robert and Jeanette. Two kinder, loving souls there were not."

"I will always miss them, but the strength of Angus's love sustains me," replied Claudia.

"I don't believe that anyone regrets what happened more than I," said Angus, taking Claudia's hand in his. "Felix's perfidy has been a lesson well learned."

"Why didn't Owen return with you?" Dorcas asked suddenly, realizing that her father's dearest friend was not with Angus.

Angus grinned, showing the dimple in his cheek that matched hers. "He remained at Orguielleux to look after things. He had his hands full, as he is not only in charge of my home, but he is helping Aunt Eudora look after Talus as well."

"More than likely he is arguing with her on every point of running the estates," Claudia added, giggling. At the look of amazement on Duncan's face she said hastily, "But do not worry. Their little spats are not to be taken seriously. In truth, I think they rather enjoy baiting each other. Mayhaps in the time they are alone together, they will come to realize what everyone else has seen—just how much they really mean to each other."

If Duncan appeared speechless, it was only because he could not conceive of Owen ever speaking at length with anyone, let alone argue. Especially with someone of the female gender.

Everyone listened in awe as Angus described the stone fortress that was his home, marveling at how the feat of building such an impregnable structure had been accomplished. Lord Robert Cherveny, Claudia's father, began the construction of the keep, and after his death, Angus finished it. Even Hugh Capet, the king of France, had visited them, and decreed that more fortresses like it should be built to stave off attacks from their enemies.

Dorcas felt a deep sense of pride in her twin brother and all that he'd accomplished. She wondered how different her life would have been had her father allowed her to go with Angus, instead of insisting that she remain at home. At least she would not have been forced into a loveless marriage to a man who cared nothing about her or the babe she carried. She was sure that by now Neil would have heard the news of her condition from someone. He plainly did not care about her, or else he would have come home.

In the days that followed, Angus was able to extract Dorcas's story from her. He was alternately outraged and pensive as she unburdened herself. She was glad to be able to tell someone the whole tale at last, but became angry when her brother chastised her for stealing her husband's ship. She felt as if Angus were taking Neil's side against her. They had a terrible row over it that could be heard throughout the settlement, until Dorcas locked herself in her chamber and refused to see anyone.

After she'd cooled down, she went in search of Angus so that she could make her peace with him. She did not want to fight with him, for he was the only one who truly understood her. She knocked on her twin's chamber door and heard Claudia call for her to enter. She took a deep breath and stepped into the room to find Claudia alone, dressing her son.

"Dorcas!" she exclaimed, smiling over her shoulder. "Please, come in!"

"I was looking for Angus."

"Oh, dear, he and Hugh rode over to the monastery to see Kevin."

"Oh."

Claudia watched Dorcas's face fall and added, "They will be back in a few days, hopefully with Kevin, for I've not yet met him. But I would love some company while I dress this little rascal," she added as Dorcas started to leave.

Dorcas stood in indecision for a moment, then she shut the door. She walked over to the bed and lay down beside the babe. Robert turned his head to stare inquisitively at her for a moment before he smiled, waving his little hands and kicking his chubby legs excitedly. His reaction to her brought a smile to Dorcas's lips, and she leaned over to kiss his forehead.

"May I ask you something without making you angry?" Claudia ventured.

Dorcas glanced sideways at her sister-by-marriage as she held out a finger for the babe to grasp. "Aye."

"Do you and Angus always show your tempers the way you did yesterday?"

Dorcas's mouth curved in a little smile. "Nay. We've fought often, and only with words, but it has never been quite that loud. I'm sorry if we frightened you."

"It is not so much that you frightened me, as . . . Well, I do not wish to see the closeness you share destroyed. Angus loves you. He wants only to see you happy."

Dorcas stared intently at Claudia for a long moment. "You love Angus very much, don't you?"

"Yea, I do." Claudia chuckled suddenly. "But I will let you in on a little secret. It was not always so." Her face sobered. "In the beginning I hated him so much that I wished his death. In fact, on our wedding night I—I tried to kill him." She watched Dorcas's eyes widen and laughed. "It is true. Ask him. I am so thankful that my dagger missed its mark. I could not bear it if anything happened to Angus."

"But Angus loves you," Dorcas whispered, "and you love him."

"Now we do. But not at first. Our love grew stronger with each passing day. I really think that that is the only kind of love worth having. I thank God that I finally realized how much I needed your brother."

Dorcas impulsively embraced Claudia. "I am truly happy for you, really I am."

"Someday I hope to say the same thing to you."

"I am afraid that will never happen," Dorcas said quietly, shaking her head.

17

Dorcas sat before the fireplace in the great hall, polishing her sword. The weapon had lain neglected in her chamber since her return, and on impulse, with nothing better to do, she'd decided to give some decent care to the blade. Besides, she felt guilty for not having done so sooner. She was a warrior. Simply because she was big with child was no reason to be remiss in her duties.

She listened with half an ear to the boys at her feet as they related their latest adventure—a preposterous tale of being chased by a one-armed robber, with wild black hair down to his knees. And only one eye, Vail, who had become Conan and Bevan's co-conspirator in their daring escapades, added. With the brave conviction of one who is safe from harm, he stated firmly that he would have liked to turn and fight the assailant, but since none of the boys had a weapon, they hastened for home, and soon lost sight of the man.

Dorcas struggled to hide her smile. A one-armed robber indeed! More likely the overactive imaginations of three little boys. She tuned them out and strained to catch the other conversation going on near her.

Duncan was fascinated by his son's description of the

stone fortress called Orgueilleux in Brittany that was now his home, and at every opportunity had Angus tell him about it once more. It now appeared Duncan had a definite purpose in mind, for Angus was not only telling his father about the keep, he was drawing a detailed plan of it for him.

The quiet afternoon was interrupted when Hugh burst into the room. He was not alone. A distraught Cedric followed him, but instead of going to Duncan, he approached Dorcas. He stopped in front of her and asked, "Daughter, are you well?"

Though his eyes softened as he gazed at her, Dorcas could sense that something was terribly wrong. She inclined her head. "Aye, I am, and so is your grandchild."

"Good, good," Cedric said distractedly.

At Dorcas's words, Angus was on his feet and by her side in a flash. He forgot that the man was his twin's father-by-marriage. In the instant the McNeil entered the room, all he remembered was the years of fighting between the two clans.

Cedric looked up to find Angus scowling at him. "Ah, I see that your twin has finally arrived," he said, taking in Angus's fiery good looks that were so like his sister's.

"Not in time to prevent the marriage," Angus said coldly, "but I can assure you that I will prevent any hurt from befalling my sister."

Duncan had joined them, concerned at his son's black look and tense stance. "Angus, Cedric is welcome here."

"Angus, please," Dorcas whispered, not taking her eyes off her father-by-marriage. "Something is wrong."

Unable to say anything, Cedric merely nodded.

"Is it Neil?" she cried, jumping to her feet and surprising everyone by the concern in her voice.

"Nay, child. I did not mean to frighten you. Neil is fine."

"You've heard from him? Is he here?" Her mind whirled frantically. Why hadn't he come to *her*?

"He sent a message to us. Gunnar is extremely ill. Naturally, Astrid wants to go to him."

"Of course," Dorcas murmured. Gunnar. How could Gunnar be sick? He was fit enough when she last saw him. *He is an old man*, whispered a little voice in her head. A message. From Neil. But he'd sent it to his father, not to her. "D-did Neil mention me, or say when he would be home?" she asked, trying to still the pounding of her heart.

Cedric gazed steadily at her for what seemed an interminable amount of time, and Dorcas knew what his answer was.

"He did not," she said in a low voice.

Pain seared through Cedric at the look of hurt in her eyes. By all the gods! When he caught up to his son, he was going to beat him to a pulp! "I am sorry," he said uncomfortably. "This could not have happened at a worse time. Astrid has been back to Norway only once in all the years we've been married. Gunnar—Gunnar may be dying."

Dorcas's head jerked up. Her eyes were like two emerald pools as she stared at Cedric. "Then, of course, she must go to him at once. If you like, I can accompany you. I—I grew fond of Gunnar when I was in Norway." She blushed at her confession that she actually liked a Viking.

"You'll do no such thing," Cedric said sternly. "You are in no condition to travel. I will not allow you to place yourself or the babe in danger. In truth, I—I came here to ask a favor of you."

"I will do anything I can to help."

"It may not be easy, but I thought, well, your father and brothers will be close by if you need them."

"What is it that you want?" Dorcas asked warily.

"I want you to stay at McNeil Hall while we're gone."

"You are determined to see that my child is born there, aren't you?"

"In truth, that idea never crossed my mind." He suddenly grinned. "There is a chance of that happening, however, if you agree. Dorcas, I cannot afford to leave knowing that my home would not be properly protected. My land is being raided again, and no matter how many traps I set, I cannot catch the villains.

"I found two cows killed and left to rot in the sun on the way over here today," he said angrily, "and if that is not enough, on top of everything else I've received word from Nissa that she is married. Married," he fairly shouted, "to none other than my cousin, Egan McNeil!" He spat the name as if it were the most vile curse. "I cannot leave knowing that Egan may try to move into my home in my absence. I must be assured that things will be looked after by someone I know and trust."

Dorcas's mind whirled with Cedric's words. Nissa married to Egan McNeil? She had never met her sister-by-marriage, for the girl had shunned her brother's wedding, sending a curt message that she would be unable to attend. A tremor shook Dorcas as she thought of the poor girl married to Egan McNeil. Mayhaps Neil had been right in counting his sister as one of those belonging in the class of mindless females.

"Will you agree?" Cedric asked, breaking into her thoughts.

"McNeil," Angus said, "my sister hesitates because she would be among her enemies."

"We are not enemies, son, but family," Cedric said quietly. "If Neil were here, he would be in charge. Since he is not, the task falls to Dorcas, for as his wife only she can hold what rightfully belongs to him, and to her son."

"They are all strangers," Dorcas whispered. She was terrified of not being able to handle Cedric's people. She tried to recall if she'd had any trouble with them when she was there before, but could not think of a time when they hadn't shown her proper respect. But then, she'd felt more like a guest than one of them.

"Selwyn will remain here to assist you, should the need arise."

"Dorcas, would you feel more comfortable if Claudia and I came with you?" Angus asked. He sensed his twin's anxiety at the huge responsibility looming before her. Here in their father's stronghold she would have no problem coping, but to be thrust among the McNeils all alone . . . He gave no thought as to what Cedric might say about his offer. As far as he was concerned, his sister needed him. He would not fail her this time.

Her face brightened as she turned to her brother. "Would you come?"

"That is an excellent idea," Cedric said, smiling broadly and surprising Angus. "You can bring the whole family if you like, just say that you will do it so I don't have to worry."

Duncan laughed and clapped Cedric on the back. "I don't think that will be necessary, but I do believe that having Angus and Claudia along would put Dorcas's mind at ease. And, as you say, Hugh and I are close by should they need us."

Dorcas was relieved that the move to Cedric's home went smoothly. Claudia, Angus, and the babe rode with her to the settlement, where they were met by a grateful Cedric and Astrid. Selwyn was already there to greet them. Of course, Marian could not be left behind, nor Vail. The one felt duty-bound to look after her charges, balking at the idea of staying amid strangers, and the other would not hear of letting Angus go off without him. And where Vail went, Conan and Bevan had to go. The three boys sulked and moped around until Dorcas threw up her hands and allowed them to stay together. After all, things would not be the same without the three mischief-makers. Besides, Dorcas felt the respite of having the boys underfoot all the time would do her mother some good.

Cedric made it clear to his people that Dorcas held the final authority, and they should go to her if the need arose. Her word was the last one.

She watched for signs of discontentment, but found none. Everyone smiled in greeting and welcomed her warmly. All in all, the transition from just Neil's wife and Cedric's daughter-by-marriage to the one in command went very well.

She thought that she'd have a reprieve from the pampering she'd undergone at her mother's hands, but to her dismay she found herself waited upon hand and foot. She could only grit her teeth and smile politely at the fuss made over her, knowing it was Astrid's doing. She secretly admitted that some days it felt good to let others do for her. If she'd calculated correctly, she was almost seven months pregnant, but she was so ungainly that she wished the babe would take it into its head to pop out anytime. Her moods shifted from quiet tranquility to unrestrained rampages that made everyone within close proximity scatter.

She'd been at McNeil Hall for only a few weeks, but found herself worrying about Cedric's promise to send her word as soon as he and Astrid reached Norway. She knew it would be months before such a message arrived, and fervently prayed for their safety and Gunnar's recovery. She worked endlessly, trying to still her anxieties, and fell into bed in exhaustion each night, hoping the child would let her get a much-needed rest.

She awakened one night to a strange discomfort and lay quietly for a moment, irritated that the babe picked the most inopportune times to stir. She rolled onto her back, and placing a hand on her abdomen, released a heavy sigh. A slight frown puckered her brow when she felt another stirring. The sensation was not quite the same as those she'd experienced before—and she needed to relieve herself.

She threw back the covers and got out of bed slowly. As she made her way to the chamber pot in the corner, she tried not to awaken Rowena, her maid. Claudia had insisted that the girl sleep in Dorcas's room to be near in case she needed someone in a hurry. She was not so fortunate, however, when Rowena spoke softly in the darkened chamber. "M'lady, is everything all right?"

A startled Dorcas gasped. "Don't ever sneak up on me like that," she snapped.

"I'm sorry, m'lady, but you did not light a candle. Are you all right?" she repeated.

Dorcas's legs were shaking badly as she stood. All she wanted was to return to the comfort of her bed. She strained to see Rowena in the dark. "I think it is time," she said.

Rowena helped her mistress back to bed and calmly set about the task that she'd been instructed to see to. She awakened Claudia and Marian, and among the three of them they brought the new life that was within Dorcas into the world.

Duncan stared down at the sleeping babe, its tiny hands curled in balls at the sides of its head. Long eyelashes swept downward over the chubby pink cheeks. A shock of dark red hair covered its head. Then Duncan looked in the other cradle and found the child's exact image.

He glanced up to find Dorcas watching him with amusement, and grinned. "It is impossible to tell which one is which when they are so small."

"It is difficult only if you are not their mother," Heloise said. She stood by his side, admiring her grandchildren while holding Robert, who was staring with fascination at his new little cousins. "The one to your right is Celia and the one on your left is Kenneth," she said smugly.

"Hmph, how would you know? You are just their grandmother," Duncan said.

Dorcas laughed softly. The only reason Heloise knew which was which was because she'd helped to dress the twins that morning, but she would not give her mother away. "She is right, father."

Duncan cast his wife a speculative look. Mayhaps women were instilled with some secret knowledge, or mayhaps it was because she'd had twins of her own. "Well, I will be glad when they are older and you start dressing them differently," he said gruffly, ignoring the fact that they now wore different colored nightshirts. "I never could tell Dorcas and Angus apart at this age either."

Dorcas laughed again. "Never fear, father, the time will pass swiftly and soon you will have no trouble in telling your grandchildren apart."

Thalia stared at her sister, a mixture of awe and envy showing on her face. Dorcas seemed like a different person since the birth of the twins. She'd always been so sure of herself, but now she seemed calmer, more relaxed. "I only hope that I will have an easy time such as you when I have my first child," she said admiringly.

Duncan frowned in her direction. "To speak of such things when you are still a maid is unseemly," he grumbled.

Angus laughed heartily. "I see that my little sister still says whatever pops into her mind."

"Well, I think it is disgusting that everything comes so easily to Dorcas," replied Thalia. The teasing quality of her tone belied her words.

Angus grinned fondly at his younger sister. She was right. Instead of the long, grueling hours that his own Claudia had endured in giving birth to Robert, Dorcas was in labor only four hours when the first of the twins appeared. He knew how much Thalia looked up to and admired Dorcas, and knew that she'd meant no harm. She was just being her usual honest self.

"Besides, father," Thalia said, blushing, "I will not be a maid much longer." Her marriage to Rory Fitzgerald, the brother of a distant cousin-by-marriage, would take place in three months.

Her sister, Gwendolyn, smiled sadly at her. "It appears as though you and Rory will have your own wedding after all," she said quietly. She and Thalia had planned to be married together, but since Erik had gone off to Norway the fall before, she'd not heard from him.

"If Erik is so inconsiderate of your feelings, then it is best to find out now," Duncan said gruffly. "I was not too happy with your choice anyway. With Dorcas it was a different matter, for her union would afford a much-needed peace. Now—now I am sorry that I ever forced her into marriage with Neil. It seems that the Vikings go off to their homeland, never to be heard from again."

Dorcas looked at Gwendolyn's bowed head in the stilted silence. She felt sorry for her sister. Surely Erik was not like Neil. He had seemed so happy at winning Gwendolyn's heart, and truly looked forward to making her his wife. He was not like her husband. A surge of anger coursed through her. If she never laid eyes on Neil McNeil again it would be too soon! A lot of good her father's regret did now!

Her gaze softened when she looked at the twins. Two good things had come out of her marriage, and for that she was grateful. It still surprised her that she could feel such a fierce love for the babes. But she did, and that alone helped to ease some of her pain.

Dorcas strode angrily back and forth in front of the huge fireplace as she listened to Selwyn's report. Curse it all anyway! Up to now the raids on Cedric's land had been confined to killing the animals. It was bad enough that his livestock was being slaughtered and left where they were. Such a deplorable waste! But the burning of one of the outlying homes was intolerable. Thank heavens no one was injured.

Angus lounged in a chair, his long legs outstretched, watching his twin's irritation grow. He knew how frustrated she was by the blatant attacks. "What we need to do is figure out who Cedric's enemy is that wishes to see him destroyed. If we could narrow that down to a few, then we would be able to set a trap."

Selwyn grunted. "That's the problem. There are many who would wish to see his ruin. It has not been easy for him since he returned to Erin with a Viking bride and so many of her people. Even some of his own family wish to see his downfall."

Angus eyed the huge Viking. He'd come to respect Selwyn as a warrior and as a man, and knew that he felt a strong loyalty equally to Neil McNeil and to Dorcas. Like Neil Selwyn was of mixed blood, the offspring of an Irish mother and a Viking father. Angus wondered if he found that a curse, for he was not fully accepted by many himself.

Calling himself back to the problem at hand, Angus turned to Dorcas. "Would you feel better if you saw the situation for yourself?"

Dorcas's face showed her relief. Her twin always seemed to know how to calm her. "Aye, I would."

Angus arose, stretching his tall frame. "Let's go."

Seeing the wanton destruction did not alleviate Dorcas's fury, but fed it. The family who'd been the victim of the attack had crept back from the hills, but wished that they'd remained there awhile longer as the redheaded woman vented her rage. She swore that they would have a new home again in no time in the same breath that she swore vengeance upon the one who wreaked such havoc. True to her word, Dorcas ordered a number of Cedric's men to rebuild the house immediately, and commanded that troops patrol the land day and night. He who perpetrated such acts of violence would not go unpunished, for he was a coward, always staying well away from the settlement in his little forays.

Dorcas's fury grew whenever someone reported another cow or sheep slain. Even with the steps she'd taken, the attacks continued. There simply were not enough men to safeguard the enormous spread of McNeil lands.

One afternoon she and Selwyn sat in the hall discussing the possibility of asking for Duncan's help. Mayhaps her father would loan her enough men to discourage their enemy. For some unfathomable reason, when the attacks began again they were directed only at Cedric, but Dorcas was afraid that if her father sent some of his warriors to her, it would leave him vulnerable. The decision was hers alone to make, for Angus had taken a group of men out that morning on patrol.

Her father could help, and if he became the unknown assailant's target, then she would go to his aid. She opened her mouth to tell Selwyn to go to Duncan when Angus noisily entered the hall. The words died on her lips. She was vaguely aware that Selwyn had jumped to his feet, but she had eyes for only one person in the room.

Neil stared back at her, his face dark with fury.

Angus shoved Neil ahead of him and Dorcas noticed Neil's hands tied with a rope in front of him. His left cheek was puffed and bruised. There was a nasty gash along his right temple where blood had dried.

"I caught this one sneaking about Leander's home," Angus said. "Mayhaps he was considering burning it to the ground again."

"Nay, he would not harm his own people," Dorcas said in a barely audible voice. She continued to stare at Neil, her eyes wide with wonder. "Did you not tell my brother who you were?"

"He never gave me a chance," Neil replied through gritted teeth.

"Then it is time you met my twin. Angus, you have just captured my husband."

"I might have known that he was your twin brother," Neil spat. "He looks enough like you. Not only that, he is just as stubborn."

Angus shifted uncomfortably at the scathing tone of Neil's voice. "You should have told me who you were," he mumbled in way of apology. He took his knife and cut the bindings on Neil's wrists.

"How could I after you'd knocked me over the head?" Neil retorted. He didn't hesitate a moment once he was free, but sent a fist crashing into Angus's midsection. His brother-by-marriage doubled over in pain, trying to regain his breath. "That is for jumping me and not letting me explain who I was," Neil said in a low, menacing tone. Then he whirled and charged Selwyn, catching his friend with a right to the jaw that sent the man sprawling. As he bent down to haul Selwyn to his feet, bringing his arm back for another blow, Dorcas leapt to her feet.

"Neil! Stop it!" she cried.

He ignored her and smashed his fist into Selwyn's face once more. "That is for stealing my ship."

He went to hit Selwyn again, but Dorcas rushed to him and grabbed his arm. "Selwyn did not steal your ship!" she shouted. "I did."

He turned to stare at her in astonishment, his eyes blazing in anger.

"I forced him to bring me home," she stated more quietly.

"So," he said. It was all she could do to hold her ground in the face of his fury. "You found marriage to me so intolerable that you had to run away. I could divorce you for that."

"I am surprised that you have not done so already," she retorted scathingly. "If that is what you want, then do it. I no longer care."

He emitted a low growl and took a step toward her, but halted in his tracks when Angus called out to him. "Do not even think about harming my sister. If you do, you will answer to me," he said, drawing his sword.

Neil was aware that Selwyn had gotten slowly to his feet and edged closer to Dorcas as well. His eyes shone like twin flames from hell as he turned to stare once more at his wife. "Since you find my presence so distasteful, I would suggest you leave my sight before I lose what little control I have left and strangle you with my bare hands."

Dorcas stared back at him, numb with disbelief. She was heartsick that he did not want her. He'd not even asked about his children. Surely Cedric and Astrid had told him that he was to become a father. It was obvious he was not interested in her or the babes.

"Go! Get out of here!" he shouted. "When I return I want you gone."

Dorcas needed no more urging as she turned and fled.

Sometime later Angus found her pacing her chamber, her eyes red from weeping. He hugged her comfortingly and smiled down at her. "We are all ready to go. Shall I take your bags out to the wagon?"

"I—I've not packed," she said, moving away nervously.

"Surely you are not considering staying," he said.

"I am Neil's wife."

Angus let out a heavy sigh. "Frankly, my sweet, I do not trust him to be alone with you."

The vision of Neil's murderous rage came to Dorcas. Mayhaps this was not the time to be stubborn. Yet they'd accomplished nothing by shouting at each other. Her shoulders slumped in defeat. Where had Neil gone? Mayhaps he'd gone to fetch Anika and wanted her out of the way when he returned. She was so confused. She'd been totally unprepared for her husband's return. He had looked so handsome, and she had been assailed by memories she'd tried so hard to stifle. What she'd really wanted was to run into his arms, to feel his mouth pressed to hers. But things had not happened that way. She recalled the coldness in his voice, the hard set of his mouth, the hate in his eyes, and shivered. Nay. Neil did not want her.

With Rowena's tearful help, Dorcas was finally packed and seated atop her mount, holding Celia in her arms. Marian refused to climb on a horse and sat in the wagon beside Vail, holding Kenneth, while Claudia held Robert atop her palfrey. Dorcas hardly spoke as the little group left for her father's house once more. Even the boys were subdued, sensing her unhappy mood.

Duncan was surprised at the arrival of his children and became outraged at Angus's explanation of why they were there. Only through Heloise's intervention did he remain where he was instead of going to thrash his daughter's husband. Once she related to her husband and sons some of the things she'd learned, they calmed down enough to think clearly, and agreed that Dorcas and Neil would have to settle their own problems.

Neil strode through the hall none the worse for wear. The black scowl he wore made those within distance scurry out of his way. His ribs hurt. His left eye had swelled considerably, and dried blood from a nosebleed spattered the front of his tunic.

He'd been incensed by his wife's confession that she had taken his ship. He'd not believed his father when Cedric told him that tale! In truth, he had been so enraged that he did not trust himself around her, so he had ridden out of the stronghold in order to cool down.

He was devastated to learn that Dorcas would go to such lengths to escape him. How she must hate him.

When Neil had learned she had left Sigurd's, he'd ridden after her, only to find upon reaching Gunnar's home that his wife, his ship, and his good friend were all gone. He'd felt a terrible emptiness, and numbly had returned to Sigurd's home. For days he was like a sleepwalker, unable to come to grips with the painful void in his life. Gunnar said nothing, but Neil could sense the old man's condemnation, and knew that his grandfather blamed him for Dorcas leaving them. Erik could not condemn him, for a fever had flooded his body, making him unaware of anything.

Once Erik was out of danger, instead of belittling Neil, he listened as Neil, in turn, ranted and raved about his faithless wife, or spoke of the love he felt for her but had never had the courage to tell her of. Together, the two men spent many a drunken hour, berating the falseheartedness of women in general, until one day Neil awoke and decided it was no longer worth it. He was filled with pain and emptiness, and from that day forward he refused to speak of his wife, and refused to remain in the presence of anyone who did. Only he knew of the vision imprinted in his memory of the long-legged, red-haired temptress who would not leave him alone.

When Cedric and Astrid had arrived and told him of the state Dorcas had been in upon her return to Erin, he'd had trouble believing them. Dorcas weak and heartsick? That didn't sound like the shewolf he'd married. When he found out that he was about to become a father, his plan to forget about his wife suddenly changed. He was going to win Dorcas back to him. This time he would woo her slowly. But things could not have gone more wrong upon their meeting again.

He'd not planned to get taken by surprise and knocked senseless by his wife's twin. The idea that he would be mistaken as the one raiding his own land was ludicrous in itself, but when he was bound and gagged without even the chance to explain who, he was outraged. Then, when he found Selwyn and Dorcas sitting so cozily before the fire, he'd lost what little sense he had left. He'd not meant to become violent, nor had he meant to say the things he had. They had just slipped out. Damnation! It was all Dorcas's fault. If she'd not stood there looking at him in such wide-eyed innocence, mayhaps his thoughts would not have been so jumbled.

All he'd really wanted to do was grab her and kiss her soft mouth until her eyes turned that fathomless green that he could lose himself in. He wanted to feel her flesh next to his, burning in the heat of passion until she cried out her need for him. How could everything have gone so awry? He'd not even found out whether he had a son or a daughter.

He threw open the door to his chamber only to find it empty. He whirled and stalked down the hall, flinging open every door in his path. All the rooms were unoccupied. He almost ran back into the hall, panic seizing him. Surely Dorcas had not taken him at his word.

Selwyn ambled into the hall just then, looking in no better shape than Neil. One eye was puffed and already darkening. He'd followed his friend when Neil left and had had a heart-to-heart talk with him. He stopped short at the look on Neil's face.

Neil grabbed a maid as she made to pass him. "Where is Lady Dorcas?" he demanded.

"G-gone," the girl stuttered, frightened by the look of dark rage on his face.

Neil noticed that her eyes were red from weeping. He dropped his hands and turned dazed eyes on Selwyn.

"What did you expect?" the Viking asked disgustedly. "You are the one who told her to leave."

Vail scuffed his toe in the dirt, kicking up a dust cloud, and sighed heavily. Since returning to the McMahons, the boys' activities had been curtailed sharply. As long as Dorcas had been in charge of them they'd been left pretty much to their own devices, but now that they were back in Heloise's domain, things had changed drastically. All three of them were overcome by a sense of boredom, and now Bevan was downcast as well. He'd overhead Dorcas and Angus arguing about Neil again when he passed her chamber. Then Angus had stormed out and Bevan could hear his sister crying.

Vail sighed once more, then raised his head and squinted in the bright sunlight. "I wish there was some way to help your sister," he said wistfully.

"I do not see how," Bevan said. "Everyone insists that she should talk to Neil, but whenever his name is mentioned she flies into a rage."

"Is there no way either of you can think of to get them together?" Vail asked hopefully.

"Nay, I overheard Angus telling her that if she loved him, she should go to him, but she became furious and started shouting at him. Then he shouted at her. That's when she—she started to cry."

"But there must be something we can do."

"I tell you there is not!" Bevan said heatedly. He started to walk away.

Vail's face lit up and he called out, "Oh, yea, there is."

Bevan turned around curiously.

"If we caught the one who is raiding Cedric's land and brought him here, then Neil would be sent for, would he not?"

Bevan and Conan nodded in unison, and Vail continued. "When he comes, Dorcas will have to speak to him."

"Our father will speak to him," Conan replied, rolling his eyes heavenward.

"But we could see to it that your sister is present when he does. Once they are together, they will have to talk," Vail said, warming to his subject.

"Just how do you propose that the three of us catch this raider without a weapon?" Bevan asked.

Vail pulled the dagger at his waist. "I have this. Angus gave it to me, and he showed me how to use it." He saw the light of admiration and envy in the other boys' eyes and pressed on. "We could get a sword also. The three of us against one cannot fail."

Conan laughed nervously. "It might work," he said, trying to sound sure of himself, when in actuality he was full of doubts.

18

———

Dorcas sat on a bench in the garden putting the finishing touches on a nightshirt for Kenneth. The twins were on a blanket at her feet, fast asleep in the shade. She wondered why she'd not seen her little brothers. They usually made an appearance early in the morning to check on the twins. Contrary to their denials, Dorcas knew they enjoyed the little ones' antics, and looked forward each day to playing with the babes. Bevan actually strutted like a peacock at the idea of being an uncle at the tender age of nine.

She smiled, thinking of the little pranksters, and recalled soothing Claudia at her distress over her missing brother, for Vail could not be found either. The three of them were probably up to mischief once more, and Dorcas's smile grew when she thought of all that her poor mother had to put up with. She hoped that her own children would not give her so much trouble.

A shadow fell across her and she looked up, startled to find a strange little man in little more than filthy rags standing before her. He seemed quite nervous. His left eye was covered with a dark patch. He had a bulbous nose and a long thatch of dirty black hair that hung down past his shoulders, that more than likely was crawling with lice.

Dorcas had all she could do to keep from showing the revulsion she felt as he leered at her. His gaze shifted to the twins.

"Them yours?" he asked in a hoarse whisper.

She could only nod in answer. People were always coming up to her to remark on the babes. She just hoped this dirty creature would not try to touch them.

"You the lady Dorcas?" he asked shortly, looking at her once again.

"I am." She wondered why the man spoke in such a gravelly whisper.

He tossed a folded piece of parchment on her lap. "This be for you."

Dorcas picked it up and turned it over. The plain sealing wax on it gave no indication who had sent it. Her heart started beating fast. Mayhaps Neil— She looked up to find the man staring at the twins again.

"I s'pose if you don't come, it won't matter much. You got others to take their places," he said cryptically.

A feeling of unease washed over her as she watched the man walk away. She tore open the letter and scanned the contents quickly, then read the note more slowly a second time. She sat for a moment, stunned, then a burning rage built within her. Her first impulse was to show the missive to her father and brothers, but she quickly squelched that idea. The note said to come alone, or she would never see her brothers again.

She quickly gathered the twins to her. Kenneth merely stretched without opening his eyes before relaxing in her arms. Celia snuggled closer, secure in the knowledge that her mother would take care of her. Dorcas took the babes to her chamber with strict instructions to Enid, her maid, that she was not to let them out of her sight. Then she hurriedly donned her linen tunic and breeches, and her sandals. As she strapped on her sword, she told a wide-eyed Enid that she had an urgent errand to run and didn't know when she would return.

Dorcas rode west across the countryside to Egan McNeil's home, all manner of questions running through her head. Why had the man taken her little brothers and Vail? What could he hope to gain by such an act? She knew Egan for a cruel, self-serving bastard, but not one who had ever resorted to harming children. A cold shiver of fear ran up her spine when she thought of the day she'd sliced off his hand. She also knew McNeil for a vengeful man and was sure that he'd never forgiven her.

She clearly remembered the day she last saw him—the unadulterated hate that burned in his eyes. That had been the day she was promised to Neil. If it had not been for Egan, she would never have found herself married to Neil. She would never have fallen in love with her husband only to be spurned by him.

Mayhaps if they had not gone to Norway, things might have been different. If only Anika had not come into their lives.

Dorcas mentally shook herself. It did no good to think of all the "if onlys." They would not change what had happened. The one truth she must learn to face was that Neil did not want her.

She tried to force the image of her husband from her mind, but it was too clear. Would Neil always haunt her so? She could vividly see him, sitting proud and imposing upon his great black destrier.

Dorcas pulled up hard on her reins, making the white stallion rear up. She was not imagining Neil. He was there, thundering down on her in all his magnificent glory. Her heart fluttered erratically at the sight of him. He looked more invincible than ever. A thrill of excitement shot through her as he stopped before her.

"I thought I made myself clear at our last meeting," he said roughly.

Her heart sank at his fierce words. She opened her mouth to speak, but no sound could get past the lump in her throat.

"What are you doing on McNeil land?" he asked sharply.

Her idea that he would help her get the boys back once she explained everything quickly vanished. He was not at all interested in her or her problems.

"I—I . . ."

"You what? Came to do a little raiding? Are some of your men just over the rise, waiting to pounce on me?"

Anger flushed her face. "How dare you accuse me of such a thing! Are you forgetting that it was I who tried to catch the ones who raided your land?"

He laughed harshly. "How very convenient for you to have my father place you in that position. Tell me, how many men are with you?"

"I have no men!"

He cocked an eyebrow in feigned surprise. "Nay? There is one way to find out." He edged his horse closer. Suddenly Dorcas found herself lifted from the stallion's back. She struggled frantically against Neil's tight hold, but he just laughed at her efforts and pulled her to him. His mouth took hers with sweet savagery, rousing the long-submerged passions within her to a shocking violence. His tongue found its way past her teeth, plundering, searching, tasting, and at that moment Dorcas wanted to stay in his arms forever. It was where she belonged. There were only the two of them. The world had ceased to exist, for they were the world—life and breath and love.

But then the image of Anika invaded her mind. Anika laughing up at Neil. Anika possessively clutching Neil's arm. Anika beckoning Neil into her chamber.

Dorcas whimpered like a small, hurt animal and pushed against him with all her strength. He moved back to look at her. The harsh lines on his face had disappeared to be replaced by puzzlement.

"Why are you doing this to me!" she cried. She took a ragged breath. "You have made it quite clear that you do not want me. Just go away and leave me alone. Get your divorce if that is what you want. Let Duncan and Cedric work out a peace that does not include us if they so wish. We should never have allowed them to force us to do their bidding to begin with. It was wrong. All wrong. Please, go away and leave me in peace. You never wanted me. Never. And—and I do not want you." She knew she was babbling nonsensically, but she couldn't help herself. Was that really her voice that was shouting hysterically?

Through the blur of her tears she could see the tightening of Neil's jaw, the hard set of his mouth. His eyes turned such a dark blue, they looked almost black.

Without a word he deposited her roughly atop her mount, then turned the destrier about and galloped off. Tears streamed down her face as she watched him ride away. Dear Lord, what had she done? She'd not meant to say any of that. Why did Neil's nearness always confuse her and put her in such turmoil? She'd felt so safe in his arms and had wanted to stay there for an eternity. But that was impossible and she knew it. She was torn between letting him go and calling out to him until, finally, it was too late.

Dorcas sat for a long time staring at the empty rise over which Neil had disappeared. At last she collected her wits about her and, remembering the task that lay ahead, started out for her destination.

Egan McNeil's home was not as large as either the McMahon or the McNeil strongholds, but upon seeing it, Dorcas remembered bits and pieces of various conversations she'd overhead years before. It was a well-defended fortress. The master was a skilled warrior.

Dorcas surveyed the structure from a distance, wondering why everything was so quiet. There were no sentries that she could see, and the gate stood wide open. Those were hardly the signs of one who held hostages. Had she misread the note? She walked her horse down the rise. The closer she'd come to the stronghold, the more she'd chastised herself for coming alone. Now that she was here, she berated herself for her wild imaginings.

She remembered how Egan McNeil had bragged about his plentiful harvests, his fat livestock, and how he used the whip to make his people obey his every command. He had railed at her father and others like him for being too lenient with the peasants. Dorcas had always thought of Egan McNeil as a strutting peacock for his fastidious manner and dress. He was always preening about in the finest woolens and silks. Now, as she rode toward the gate, she was appalled by the flagrant neglect of the land, and when she passed into the courtyard, the stench and filth almost made her sick. The place seemed deserted.

She dismounted and looked around warily. Where was everyone?

Drawing her sword, she moved to the main door of the keep and pushed it open. She stood there waiting for her eyes to adjust to the dimness of the hall. At last she saw the lone figure of a man sitting in a chair before the unlit fireplace. He appeared to be sleeping.

"McNeil!" she called to him, and took pleasure in watching him wake with a start.

Egan McNeil squinted at the doorway, trying to discern who his visitor was. All he could make out was a profusion of flaming red hair. He grunted in satisfaction. "I see you wasted no time in getting here."

Dorcas gritted her teeth at the sureness in his voice and strode into the room. "Where are my little brothers?" she asked.

Egan chuckled wickedly. "It is good that you obeyed me so swiftly. I am glad to see that even the imperious Dorcas McMahon, or should I say McNeil, is willing to do the bidding of those more forceful," he said, still grinning.

Ignoring his confident tone, Dorcas stopped in front of him and pressed the tip of her sword against his chest. "I do not like the brand of force that exacts its price from nine- and ten-year-olds, McNeil. I want to see them."

"All in good time, my dear. However, I must warn you that if any harm comes to me, you will never see those boys again," Egan said smoothly. He felt the pressure from the sword ease and gestured toward the weapon. "Now, why don't you put that thing away before someone gets hurt, umm?"

She sheathed the blade and glared at the man sitting so unconcernedly in front of her. "If you have a bone to pick with me, then do so, McNeil, but leave my family out of it. What is between you and me is personal and has nothing to do with my little brothers or with Vail."

"Ah, yea. I do have a bone to pick with you. However, I do not agree that it is merely a personal matter between the two of us. My hatred of all the McMahons runs deep." His voice was suddenly harsh. "And if I could annihilate the lot of you, I would!"

Dorcas almost flinched at the hate that spewed forth from Egan, not only from his words, but from the face contorted in rage. "If revenge is what you want, then exact it from me, for I am here now. But I beg of you to let my brothers and Vail go free. They are not responsible for my actions."

Egan leapt from his chair. "Beg! Beg! It is good to hear you say that." He suddenly threw back his head and laughed. "The haughty Lady Dorcas begs." The grin suddenly left his face as he caught her staring at him unflinchingly. "Your eyes do not beg," he murmured. He lifted his right arm and gently stroked her cheek with the blunt stub where his hand used to be. When she flinched at the contact, he chuckled softly. "That's right. I forgot. You do not like me to touch you," he said in a half whisper. He suddenly thrust the useless stump in her face and shouted, "Not even with this!"

Dorcas had to use every ounce of willpower she possessed in order to remain where she was. She stared expressionlessly at the evidence of Egan's hate, afraid to show any emotion lest it be wrong. She was at the mercy of a madman!

"Are you not in the least bit contrite for your actions?" he spat out.

"You were warned to keep your hands off me," she said calmly.

"That does not hold true for all McNeils, though, does it? What matters if it is I or my cousin's son who touches you?" He grinned. "It is all in the family, is it not?"

"You are not my husband. I told you what would happen if you pushed me too far. I am a woman of my word."

His grin left as quickly as it had appeared. "And I am a man of my word," he snapped.

"I wish to see the boys," she said quietly. Her stomach tied in knots, she watched Egan's face turn a mottled red in anger.

"Quinn!"

Egan's companion appeared from nowhere, and McNeil waved his left hand in dismissal before turning his back on Dorcas.

She followed Quinn from the hall, realizing for the first time that her heart was beating erratically. At last. She'd worn McNeil down. She didn't know what fate lay ahead for her, but at the moment she didn't care. All she cared about was seeing that Conan and Bevan and Vail were released, even if it meant placing herself in their stead.

Quinn stopped before a door, and lifting the heavy bar, opened it. He grabbed Dorcas's arm, taking her by surprise, and pushed her into the chamber.

Dorcas eyed her surroundings hastily and turned in protest, but the door had already banged shut and she could hear the bar falling into place. She stared at the closed portal disbelievingly. He'd lied to her! She whirled and scanned the empty room once more before sitting down dejectedly on the cot.

The longer Dorcas had to think about her situation, the angrier she got. She cursed herself as a fool for having trusted Egan McNeil, wishing that she had told her father and brothers about the note. She'd had the chance to tell Neil where she was going. Instead, she'd lost herself in his arms. Her thoughts had been so muddled when he kissed her, and he'd made her so angry with the things he'd said, her tongue had gotten the better of her—once again. She'd not meant what she had said in turn. Now she would never have the opportunity to tell him so.

Oh, yea, she would, she thought determinedly. She still had her sword. If she could somehow work it between the crack in the door to push on the bar, she could free herself.

She scratched endlessly at the door with her weapon, in hopes of whittling away enough of the wood to use the blade as a lever, then she heard the bar being lifted from the other side. She stepped back, keeping her sword pointed at whoever was in the hall. If it was Egan or Quinn, she was ready for them.

She started to charge the door as it opened slowly, but halted in her tracks when a woman let out a scream.

Dorcas eyed the girl darkly. She couldn't be much more than Gwendolyn's age, and so petite that Dorcas felt like an amazon next to her.

The flaxen-haired beauty stared back in wide-eyed astonishment.

"Who are you and what are you doing skulking about in the hall?" Dorcas demanded brusquely.

The girl blinked in amazement. Her deep-set blue eyes turned a darker hue as she drew herself up. "I am Lady McNeil, and I was not skulking. I heard a noise as I passed this chamber and I came to investigate," she answered haughtily. "If anyone has a right to ask questions, it is I. This chamber is never used. Just who are you and what are you doing here?"

"You—you are Neil's sister," Dorcas blurted out in surprise. Why had she not seen the resemblance to Astrid before? And those eyes. She'd thought there was only one pair in all the world like them.

"What are you? A soothsayer?" Nissa asked tartly.

Dorcas laughed suddenly and sheathed her sword. Still

grinning, she stood with arms akimbo. "Neil said you had the tongue of a viper."

Nissa frowned. "How is it that you know my brother?"

"He is my husband."

The cold expression on Nissa's face did not leave, and when she spoke, her tone matched her look. "So. You are the lady Dorcas. I certainly would not have expected you to turn up here of all places."

"Ahh, well, I had no choice under the circumstances," Dorcas replied dryly.

"What circumstances?"

"It appears that I am your husband's prisoner."

"Well, what do you expect after what you did?"

Dorcas shrugged. "He brought his afflictions upon himself."

Nissa gasped, horrified by Dorcas's nonchalance. The woman had not had to deal with a hysterical, useless Cora when Egan arrived minus a hand. In truth, most everyone in Egan's home turned out to be useless. It had been she who'd nursed him back to health, through the terrifying fever that had held him in an iron grip for days, and after. "You almost killed him," she yelled.

" 'Tis a pity I did not! He was warned what would happen if he persisted in laying his hands on me." Despite the puzzled hurt in Nissa's eyes, she rushed on. "As a warrior I can understand his thirst for revenge. I can even admire it. What I cannot stomach is his means of attaining his goal."

"What are you talking about?"

"His device of using my little brothers to get at me. He is holding them as hostages, along with my twin's brother-by-marriage. They are only children."

"Egan would not do such a thing!" Nissa cried hotly.

"Nay? Then why did I recieve a message from him warning me that if I did not come here he would kill them?"

"You lie!"

"I do not lie," Dorcas said firmly but quietly. "I only pray that they are alive even now."

"But, I tell you, there are no children here. No one is here except Egan and myself, and Quinn."

A shadow of doubt crossed Dorcas's face for a moment. The boys were missing. At least, no one had seen them since breakfast early that morn, for she'd made inquiries after she'd received the missive. Were they indeed just hiding, or out somewhere getting into mischief with one of their wild schemes? Why had Egan sent such a message to her if, in truth, he was not holding them? She had to know, and only Nissa could help her.

"Do you really know your husband so well?" she asked the girl.

Nissa's hands were clenched tightly into fists at her sides. "Egan does not harm children!" She grew uncomfortable at the steady look Dorcas gave her. "I will prove it to you," she cried, whirling about. Before Dorcas could move, she ran into the hall and slammed the door shut. Throwing the bar into place, she stood panting heavily. The witch lied! Hadn't she?

Egan *had* changed drastically since his return home that fateful day. He'd become bitter and hateful, with an underlying cruelty that would come to the fore at the least provocation. Nissa shuddered, thinking of the smoldering rage that always seemed to be just beneath the surface.

She held her rough-worn hands out in front of her and studied them dispassionately. She was little more than a servant in her own home. She'd tried to keep things from slipping from bad to worse, but had had to stand by helplessly and watch as Egan let his home deteriorate into a wasteland.

Cora had been no help. Her friend had turned out to be totally useless in dealing with her brother. Nissa had finally gotten sick of listening to her whining and had sent her packing. She'd heard that Cora was making the rounds of those relatives who would have her. Cora's departure had incensed Egan so, that upon learning of it, he'd beaten Nissa unmercifully.

After that Nissa had decided that if she and Egan got married, things would change. She would show him through her patience and devotion how much she loved him. He'd not had an easy life, for too much responsibility had been thrust on him at too tender an age. She'd loved Egan for as long as she could remember. The obstacles he'd had to overcome to get the respect he deserved as master in his own home only made her admire him more, and when he'd become a feared warrior, she was so proud. He was such a handsome man, and whenever he smiled at her, her heart fluttered in her chest. But he did not smile anymore. Things did not get better as she'd hoped they might. Instead, they'd worsened. It was all Dorcas's fault. That witch had robbed them of the happiness they could have had.

Dorcas paced the little room endlessly. It seemed like hours had passed since Nissa had left her. What was happening? If only she could escape her prison to find the boys.

She whirled at the sound of the bar being lifted.

Egan stood in the doorway, an evil grin on his face. He chuckled at the surprised look on Dorcas's face and stepped into the chamber. "I find such pleasure in having you at my mercy at last," he purred.

She stared coldly at him. "Where are the boys?"

His grin faded quickly at the calmness she displayed. It irritated him that she was no longer begging him. But she would. She would. "You really should not have sent Nissa snooping, you know. I had to chastise her severely for meddling in matters that did not concern her."

Dorcas's eyes flickered in alarm before she masked her inner thoughts and stared at him blankly. The bastard! Only a coward would harm women and children. "I'll make a bargain with you, McNeil. If you allow me to see the boys, to make certain that they're all right, and then set them free, you can do whatever you like with me."

Egan laughed shortly. "You are hardly in a position to bargain. You forget that you are my prisoner."

"Nevertheless, if you have hurt those children, I will kill you, and if I do not, my father and brothers will," she said coldly.

Egan was unperturbed. "My, what brave words." He studied her for a moment before adding, "However, I am feeling magnanimous. I will grant your wish to see your brothers and their little friend. Come." As Dorcas started past him, he said, "I'll have your weapon."

Dorcas's eyes flashed as she removed her sword and placed it in his outstretched left hand, her hopes that he'd forgotten about it dashed.

She was surprised when Egan stopped at a door next to the chamber she'd been in. He opened it, motioning with the point of her sword to enter. She stepped into the chamber and cried out in relief. Conan and Bevan rushed to her, and she swept them up into her arms. Vail was kneeling beside the cot where Nissa lay, battered and bruised, her eyes closed. Dorcas held out her arm to him and he, too, rushed to her. Their adventure had soon turned into a nightmare, and he was glad for the comfort now offered.

Dorcas gasped when she caught sight of Nissa, so pale and still. Her right cheek was turning purple, and even in the dim light of the room Dorcas could see that her right eye was swollen badly. She glared at Egan as he lit a torch on the wall. "What a courageous man you are to pick on those who cannot fight back," she spat out.

His gaze went slowly to the bed, and he frowned slightly. "She merely got what she deserved for interfering. I will not allow anyone to stand in the way of justice."

"Why don't you call it what it really is, McNeil? Revenge."

He shrugged unconcernedly. "Revenge, then. But I will

have it, and I intend to make certain that you see it all."
He lit another torch, then turned to stare at her. She
shrank back from the glazed madness in his eyes. "You
will all pay. Every one of you."

She shoved the boys protectively behind her as Egan
moved in front of her. "You did this to me!" he shouted,
thrusting his handless arm in front of her face. "You
ruined me. I am no longer able to wield a sword because
of you. I could no longer protect my people, so they all
ran off. I am laughed at and scorned, and it is your doing.
I have waited long enough to see you destroyed. You have
escaped my retribution in the past, but no more."

"What do you mean?" she asked in a barely audible
whisper.

"You should have been dead long ago," he snarled. "I
was extremely disappointed that you escaped the rock
slide, nor was I too happy to learn that Quinn's arrow
missed you, so I devised another plan. First I raided both
your father's land and Cedric's, hoping they would fight
each other. 'Tis a pity they did not. But then, when I
learned that you were in command of McNeil Hall during
Cedric's absence, I confined the raids to there. I enjoyed
watching your fumbling attempts to try to stop me." He
chuckled, but then his evil smile quickly disappeared.
"You stripped me of everything. Now you will pay. You
and that pompous, superior husband of yours.

"Even now Quinn is delivering a message to him. Your
husband will come riding in here to rescue you, but you
will not be alive to see it." He started laughing, caught up
in his own fantasy. "And he will die a quick death."

Fear gripped Dorcas in an iron fist. She had to force
herself to remain calm. "Let the boys go first. They have
done you no harm."

Egan looked at her as if seeing her for the first time,
and frowned. "Nay," he answered flatly. "They are
McMahons and as much to blame for what happened as
you."

Her heart thudded painfully. Dear Lord! He intended to kill them all. "What about your wife? Nissa will not countenance such action. Once she finds out about the murders you plan, her love will turn to hate."

"Love," Egan scoffed. "I never wanted her love. I loathe the sight of the little termagant. I hate her as much as I hate her brother." He frowned once more, looking at the inert form on the cot. " 'Tis a pity I cannot get rid of her as well," he mused. "Unfortunately, I need her. For once Neil is dead, she will be next in line to inherit all that is Cedric's."

"But it will be Nissa's, not yours," Dorcas pointed out.

"My wife knows her place. As her husband, she will need my guidance. It took me long enough to gain what I wanted. After my attack on Cedric failed, I did not think I would ever be able to attain my goal."

Dorcas gasped. "It was you who tried to drown Cedric."

"Aye. I knew he would never accept the joining of his precious daughter to me, so I devised a plan to eliminate him and then stake my claim on Nissa. It is time that I reap some of the rewards from that branch of the McNeils. I figured that in her bereaved state, she would welcome me with open arms and be glad to accept my offer. After all," he sneered, "no one else would have the harpy. She should feel flattered. 'Tis a shame that your brother came to Cedric's rescue. He spoiled all of my carefully laid plans. But then, things worked out well, for the little fool took pity on me and saved me after you'd disfigured me. But I don't want her pity," he spat out. "I will show her how strong I truly am. I will show you all. You tried to take away my courage, but you did not succeed."

Dorcas stared at him, transfixed by the mad light in his eyes.

"Now," he purred, "I think it would be appropriate if I started with the youngest one here first, don't you?"

A moan came from Nissa across the room, drawing Egan's attention.

Dorcas didn't hesitate a moment. She grabbed one of the torches off the wall and thrust it at him. He stumbled backward and clumsily swiped at it with the sword, knocking it from her hand. The filthy, molding rushes covering the floor caught fire instantly. No one paid any attention. The boys were too scared, staring at Dorcas and Egan. Dorcas leapt back out of Egan's reach again and again as he swung the weapon at her. She shouted at the boys to help Nissa, and they instantly obeyed, helping the woman to her feet.

Egan ignored the youngsters as he lashed out wildly at Dorcas, only to have her jump away. His fury grew every time she outmaneuvered him, and she used it to her advantage. He was no longer the practiced warrior she knew, but an ineffectual amateur.

She edged closer to the door and grabbed another torch. Just as she turned, Egan lunged for her. She swiftly side-stepped the intended blow and saw the sword imbedded in the door where she'd stood only seconds before. In the same instant she flung the torch at him. He screamed as it hit him, setting his tunic on fire. She watched, horrified, as he continued to struggle to pull the weapon free instead of trying to save himself. She turned away quickly, unable to bear the sight.

Smoke roiled upward, stinging her eyes. She looked around swiftly and saw the three boys trying to shepherd Nissa out of the chamber, avoiding the burning rushes. Running to them, she threw Nissa's arm about her shoulder and half dragged the girl out of the inferno, ignoring her groan of pain.

The boys raced ahead, and the five of them reached the courtyard gasping for breath, coughing the smoke from their lungs. Dorcas sank to the ground, easing Nissa down with her. She looked at the girl and saw tears streaming down her face.

"You heard," she said.

Nissa nodded, unable to find her voice.

Dorcas reached out a comforting hand, but her sister-by-marriage shrank back and turned her head away.

"Look!" Conan cried, pointing toward the gate.

Dorcas's gaze followed his. Duncan, accompanied by Hugh, Angus, and Neil, came riding furiously into the courtyard. The boys jumped up and down gleefully at the sight, but she could only stare dully at their rescuers.

All of the men leapt from their horses.

"Where is he?" Duncan thundered.

She merely pointed to the keep, smoke already pouring from the door and uncovered windows. She watched as her father and Hugh rushed inside with swords drawn, wanting to call them back lest they be lost in the blaze, but unable to speak. She heard Neil gasp and felt his presence close at hand. It was not concern for her, she realized when he called his sister's name softly. She turned her head and saw Nissa pressed against him, crying her sorrow.

Angus knelt beside her and took her in his arms. "Are you all right?" he asked quietly.

Dorcas felt tears well up in her eyes. She couldn't get the words past the lump in her throat, so she simply nodded. She wanted Neil's arms around her. She'd wanted him to ask after her welfare. Instead, in the brief glance he'd bestowed on her, she was faced with burning eyes filled with anger.

Duncan and Hugh rejoined them and at the questioning look on the other men's faces, Duncan shook his head. "Egan is dead. There is no sense in remaining here. The fire is spreading quickly." He was already mounting up as he spoke, seating Conan in back of him. "We will all have to ride double," he said, surveying the number of people and the number of animals.

Dorcas gasped as Angus helped her to her feet. "My horse!" She started for the stables but felt a hand clamp down firmly on her arm. She turned her head to find Neil's stony gaze on her.

"I will fetch it. You stay here."

She watched him stride away, wondering why he was so angry.

Once everyone was settled, they started for home. Vail rode behind Angus and Bevan behind Hugh, while Neil carried his sister. When Dorcas warned him to be careful of Nissa's injuries, he turned and glared at her, making her wince. She could finally endure his silence no longer and asked him why he was so angry with her.

He pulled up on the reins. "Because of your foolishness," he said harshly. "Why didn't you have sense enough to tell me where you were going this morning?"

She bristled at his tone. "His message said to come alone."

"And what did you think that would accomplish?" he asked. "You could have been killed, and so could the boys, and possibly Nissa. Lord knows, she's in a hurtful condition as it is. Nor do I appreciate the idea of you leaving my children motherless! If you could not trust me to help you, you could at least have asked your father and brothers to do so. I am sick of your lack of faith in me. As far as I am concerned, there is no longer any bargain between us. If you want your freedom so badly, you can have it."

Dorcas watched him ride off, too stunned to say a word. Why did he always turn everything around? It was not she who wanted her freedom. It was he. Well, if he did, she thought angrily, he would have to be the one to get it. She knew why he wanted to be rid of her, but she would not make it easy for him.

19

Dorcas lay on her belly, as flat to the earth as she could make herself, her head barely over the rise, eyeing the cows that grazed peacefully in the meadow below her.

Fagan, lying beside her, shifted uncomfortably, moving his sword out of the way so it would stop jabbing him in the leg. He shooed a fly from his forehead and scratched his nose where the pesky thing had brushed against him. Then he let out a heavy sight of sheer boredom. He scanned the field beyond, wondering what Dorcas had seen that had made her dismount in such a hurry and tell her men to do likewise. Now, here they were, all stretched out on the wet ground. He didn't know how the other five men viewed their position. For himself, he thought it foolish to risk life and limb to aid a man who'd turned his back on his own wife and children. In Fagan's estimation, Neil McNeil could fend for himself without their help.

He strained to see what it was his mistress saw, but the only thing in sight were cows. Fagan sighed again and glanced at the woman by his side. "Lady Dorcas, why are we here?" He suddenly realized he'd whispered the question and felt silly that he'd done so.

Dorcas turned her head to look at him blankly. Without giving him an answer, she returned her gaze to the cows.

Why indeed! she thought.

She'd been home for a month now, and not one word had she heard from Neil. He'd not petitioned for a divorce. He'd not asked to see the twins. Nothing. It was as if he'd vanished from the face of the earth. Yet she knew he was running the McNeil estate until Cedric and Astrid returned from Norway. Nissa had told her.

To everyone's surprise, her sister-by-marriage had ridden over one day asking to see Dorcas. She'd looked much better than when Dorcas had last seen her. Her physical scars were healing well enough, and Dorcas hoped that the invisible hurt she suffered would disappear in time too.

The two women had a long private conversation, in which Nissa had expressed her concern for her brother. He'd always been a hard worker, but now he drove himself beyond all reason, and he expected others to do the same. He was moody and remote so much of the time that it scared her, and when she prodded him for answers to her questions, he grew terribly angry.

"I am at a loss as to what to do," Nissa said, anxiously twisting her hands in her lap. "I—I thought that you would know of some way to bring him out of his depression."

"Why don't you ask Anika to help you?" Dorcas said scathingly.

Nissa frowned in bewilderment. "Who?"

"I-Isn't there a woman with Neil?"

"Nay, there is no one." She sighed heavily. "I believe that you are the crux of his problem."

Dorcas's eyes widened in astonishment. "Me!" She grew uncomfortable under Nissa's steady gaze, and at last sat down beside her sister-by-marriage. Haltingly, she began to relate the story of how she and Neil had married, of their time in Norway, of how she'd returned to Erin, alone and hurt.

When she finished, Nissa nodded. "Now I understand much of what Neil has ranted about in his fits of temper." She looked askance at Dorcas. "But what I do not understand is why, if you love him, you have not gone to him."

"He does not want me. You heard him that day." She glanced at Nissa. She did not want to hurt the girl by dredging up bad memories. "He wants nothing further to do with me."

"I do not think that is the case," Nissa said musingly. "But I will tell you this. Neil will not come to you. His pride will not let him. So, you must make the first move."

Dorcas had doubted the girl's words. Nissa had tried to give her some hope, but she was afraid. Afraid that Neil would turn his back on her once again. She knew that she could not bear it if he did.

Nissa had returned a few times since that first visit. Each time she related—with relish, now that Dorcas thought about it—how Neil seemed to be sinking deeper into depression, and tried to press Dorcas into some sort of action. But Dorcas did nothing.

"My lady," Fagan asked in a low voice, breaking into her thoughts, "what do you find so interesting down there?"

She turned to him and grinned. "We are going raiding."

The man's eyes almost bulged out of his head. "Lady Dorcas! You cannot!"

"I can, and I will!" she snapped.

The atmosphere at the table as the McMahons supped was one of joviality. The beef that Dorcas had supplied was indeed succulent. Heloise had outdone herself in the dishes that accompanied the meat, thankful she'd had the foresight to tell her daughter to slaughter one of the cows for a feast that night. Dorcas had no sooner left when Gwendolyn received a message from Erik, saying he was back in Erin and would join them for dinner. Just as the glorious fare was being spread on the table, Erik had ridden in, sweeping Gwendolyn into his arms, unmindful of Duncan's glare.

As they ate he related stories of Norway to them, painting a picture of brilliant splendor.

"I am surprised you could tear yourself away from such magnificence to devote time to your betrothed," Duncan said.

"Father," Gwendolyn gasped.

Duncan set his cup down forcefully. "Well! Where has he been? He has been gone for almost a year. It is nearly time for you to be wed, and he just barely arrives to participate in the ceremony. This is hardly what I meant when I said that you should have some time to become acquainted."

"I fell ill," Erik said quietly.

"Oh, Erik!" Gwendolyn cried.

He smiled and squeezed her hand. "I am fine now, and nothing and no one is going to tear us apart again," he vowed.

Duncan caught the underlying strength in Erik's voice and sat back to study the Viking. Mayhaps he had been a little hasty in his judgment. He said no more, and the meal continued in a lighter mood.

Dorcas glanced up at one point, and the smile she wore froze on her lips. Neil stood across from her, staring at her with a strange expression.

"Neil!" Duncan cried. "I did not hear you come in. What a pleasant surprise. Come, join us."

Neil tore his eyes from Dorcas to look at her father, then he scanned the table loaded with food. "That is quite a feast," he said quietly. Staring at the platter of meat in its honored place at the head of the table, he asked, "Beef, is it not?"

"Aye." A frown creased Duncan's forehead when he saw how intently Neil was staring at the meat. "You act as if you have never seen the stuff before," he laughed.

"Oh, I have. Unfortunately, one of my herd is missing.

I came to see if you have been having trouble again, or if you've seen any strangers about."

Duncan dropped his meat into his trencher in shock, as did everyone else at the table. Everyone except Dorcas and Erik. Duncan stared disbelievingly at his daughter, but she sat eating her beef, her gaze fixed intently on her food.

Erik's eyes darted back and forth between Neil and Dorcas in amusement. He had to keep stuffing his mouth, for if he didn't, he would burst out laughing. He'd been with Neil when one of his men had come in to tell his master a cow was missing. Neil had been infuriated, of course. Now everything was clear. Well, not exactly. But Erik knew what he was eating. And it was delicious! He wondered what Neil had done this time to precipitate such an action, and he wondered also what recourse his friend would take.

"Dorcas!" Duncan bellowed.

Heloise gasped. "Dorcas! You didn't!"

For all her parents' outrage, it was the one quiet word that her husband spoke that got her attention.

"Why?" Neil asked, bewildered.

She raised her chin defiantly and stared at him without answering.

He sighed. "If you wanted the cow, Dorcas, you did not have to resort to stealing it. You are my wife. What is mine is yours."

She was taken aback by the quiet resignation of his voice. She had expected his rage. His capitulation took her by surprise.

"I did not come here to fight with you," he went on. "I would like to talk to you privately."

Her guard went up once more, but she arose and preceded him from the hall.

Once inside her chamber, she turned to face him. "This is the most private place I know," she said coolly.

Neil walked to the window and stared out, seeing nothing. "I have had news from Norway." He turned back to her, his eyes showing much pain. "Gunnar is dead."

Shock struck her dumb. She shook her head numbly as if to deny what she'd heard. "Nay, it cannot be."

"Erik brought me the news."

"Why didn't he tell me? Why—it is not true!"

In two strides Neil was in front of her. He gripped her shoulders, then pulled her to him to give comfort as much as to seek it.

"How? When?" she asked in a ragged whisper.

"He was old and tired. One night he just slipped away."

"He would not have liked that," she murmured, thinking of the fierce Viking Gunnar had been. He would have found it shameful not to die in battle.

"Nay," Neil replied quietly. He held Dorcas away from him and was touched by the tears on her cheeks. His grandfather had been fond of her and she of him. That much was true. "I came here to tell you that my parents are going to remain in Norway a while longer, until my uncle Harold returns. All that was Gunnar's is his now. I—I want you to come home with me," he suddenly blurted out.

Stunned, Dorcas backed up to gape at him for a moment until she recovered herself and dashed away her tears. "How can you ask such a thing? You do not want me. You've told me often enough!"

"As you have me!" he said hotly. He started to say something else, but quickly shut his mouth.

Things were not going as he'd planned, he thought with frustration. He could no longer bear being apart from this woman. Nissa had nagged him unmercifully about going to his wife to make peace with her, but he would not budge. He had waited for Dorcas to come to him, but when she did not, he'd fluctuated between anger and self-pity, until he thought he would go mad.

He took a deep breath to calm himself. "Dorcas, I want

you to come home with me. It is where you belong. It is where the twins belong."

Her head shot up. "That is what you want, isn't it? Your children. I do not see why, when you have shown no interest in them before. You were not even around when they were born!"

"I did not know about them!" he hollered in exasperation.

"That is a lie. It must be. Surely Astrid or Cedric told you of my condition. You had plenty of time to get here."

"I had my hands rather full what with Erik being so ill, and then Gunnar falling sick."

"Oh! And I suppose you nursed them both with your own two hands."

His mouth twitched with amusement at the picture she created. "Nay. But I did feel a certain duty to stay by Erik's side when it was because of me he was wounded."

"Wounded!" she cried in surprise.

"Anika stuck a knife in him because she did not like the truth about herself."

"Anika!"

"It does not matter. All that matters is that you are my wife, and as such I demand that you return home with me."

"How dare you demand," she sputtered. "I hate you as much as—" She found that she couldn't finish as Neil grabbed her and pressed her to him. His mouth swooped down to claim hers hungrily, igniting the all-too-familiar fires within her soul. His hands roamed possessively over her body, bringing her long-restrained passions roaring to the surface.

Neil raised his head to look at her. His eyes were a smoky blue with desire. "That kind of hate?" he asked huskily.

"Yea," she breathed. Suddenly she pushed against him. Caught by surprise, he let her go and she stumbled backward. "Nay! Oh, you confuse me. Do not touch me," she cried, holding him off when he made a move toward her. "Neither one of us wanted marriage. All we do is fight."

"Damnation! We were not fighting just now." He growled deep in his throat and lunged for her.

She let out her breath with a great swoosh as he threw her over his shoulder like a sack of meal. She struggled to get free, but he swatted her backside and flung open the chamber door.

"I have had enough from you, woman! I asked nicely, but I see that I am going to have to do this the hard way."

Heads turned in surprise as Neil stomped into the hall with his burden screaming at him in three languages. For a moment no one moved. Then Angus regained his senses and leapt to his feet.

Neil glowered at him and casually withdrew his sword. He stood where he was and pointed the weapon at Dorcas's twin. "I am taking my wife home, where she belongs," he said fiercely, "and no one is going to stop me from having what is mine!"

Angus's mouth dropped open and he immediately sat down again. His eyes changed from the murky green of anger to a lighter color, and his mouth curved in amusement as he waved a hand in dismissal.

Dorcas shrieked her brother's name, but Neil was already outside. He threw his wife unceremoniously over his horse and mounted, then he galloped through the gate.

When Dorcas realized that her screaming was having no effect on Neil, she gritted her teeth and asked in as near normal a voice as possible, "Will you kindly let me up! I am not a piece of baggage to be tossed about."

He stopped and hauled her up in front of him. "Are you going to behave yourself?" he asked gruffly.

She just glared at him.

He put an arm around her and crushed her to him, making it hard for her to breathe. His mouth brushed hers caressingly. She shivered in response and he chuckled.

His supreme confidence infuriated her. "You are without a doubt the most arrogant, overbearing, domineering tyrant I have ever known."

He cocked his head to one side and grunted. "You left out high-handed and bold-faced."

"That too!"

"And I am your husband. And you belong to me."

"I am not your possession!" she hollered.

Neil's eyes flashed dangerously. "Tell me that when we are in bed!" he shot back.

She drew in her breath sharply. "That is all we have," she said quietly.

"That is not all we have, my sweet. We already have two children whom, I might add, I have not yet met."

"That is not my fault," she cried. Her eyes filled with pain. "Oh, don't you see that it won't work. When we are not in bed, we are fighting."

"Then I guess I will just have to keep you in bed."

"It is no joking matter." She suddenly burst into tears. Why was he doing this to her? She meant no more to him than his land or his ship, to be owned like a piece of property.

Neil pulled up on the reins once more. "Stop your sniveling," he growled.

Dorcas cried that much harder.

Neil sighed heavily. His wife had always professed her hate for him. He needed her as surely as he needed air to breathe, but he'd always been afraid to bare his heart to her, fearful she would laugh at him. If she did, he knew he would never recover from it. He'd not realized himself how deeply he felt about her until after she was gone. "Dorcas, sweet, please stop crying," he said gently. "Don't you know that I cannot bear another moment away from you. I need you by my side always. I—" he took a deep breath and said in a rush, "I love you."

The tears quickly stopped and Dorcas stared at him. Her eyes were large and luminous and beautiful. "What?"

Neil frowned. Hadn't she been paying attention? "I said I need you—"

"Nay, not that. The thing after that. What you just said."

"I love you," he said warily.

Her face split into a huge grin. "Oh, Neil. I love you too."

He stared at her unbelievingly. "You do?"

Still smiling, Dorcas nodded happily.

Neil studied her glowing face for a moment before murmuring in awe, "I do believe we have a lot of wasted time to make up for."

Dorcas muttered in agreement and snuggled closer to him. Then she pushed herself upright and looked earnestly at him. "You know, of course, that we will still fight, don't you?"

Laughing, he brought her head down to rest against his chest and kneed the destrier into motion. "No doubt we will," he answered. "No doubt we will."

THE DELANEY DYNASTY

Men and women whose loves and passions are so glorious it takes many great romance novels by three bestselling authors to tell their tempestuous stories.

THE SHAMROCK TRINITY

☐ 21975	RAFE, THE MAVERICK *by Kay Hooper*	$2.95
☐ 21976	YORK, THE RENEGADE *by Iris Johansen*	$2.95
☐ 21977	BURKE, THE KINGPIN *by Fayrene Preston*	$2.95

THE DELANEYS OF KILLAROO

☐ 21872	ADELAIDE, THE ENCHANTRESS *by Kay Hooper*	$2.75
☐ 21873	MATILDA, THE ADVENTURESS *by Iris Johansen*	$2.75
☐ 21874	SYDNEY, THE TEMPTRESS *by Fayrene Preston*	$2.75

☐ 26991	THIS FIERCE SPLENDOR *by Iris Johansen*	$3.95

THE DELANEYS: *The Untamed Years*

☐ 21899	GOLDEN FLAMES *by Kay Hooper*	$3.50
☐ 21898	WILD SILVER *by Iris Johansen*	$3.50
☐ 21897	COPPER FIRE *by Fayrene Preston*	$3.50

Buy these books at your local bookstore or use this page to order.

Prices and availability subject to change without notice.

- -

Bantam Books, Dept. SW7, 414 East Golf Road, Des Plaines, IL 60016

Please send me the books I have checked above. I am enclosing $_____ (please add $2.00 to cover postage and handling). Send check or money order—no cash or C.O.D.s please.

Mr/Ms _____

Address _____

City/State _____ Zip _____

SW7—9/89

Please allow four to six weeks for delivery.

FIVE UNFORGETTABLE NOVELS
by
CELESTE DE BLASIS

☐ **THE NIGHT CHILD** (27744, $3.95)
The story of a proud, passionate woman and two very special
kinds of love.

☐ **THE PROUD BREED** (27196, $4.95)
THE PROUD BREED vividly recreates California's exciting
past, from the wild country to the pirated coast, from gambling
dens to lavish ballrooms. Here is Celeste De Blasis' beloved
bestselling novel: a world you will not want to leave, and will
never forget.

☐ **WILD SWAN** (27260, $4.95)
Sweeping from England's West Country in the years of the
Napoleonic wars, to the beauty of Maryland horse country,
here is a novel richly spun of authentically detailed history
and sumptuous romance.

☐ **SWAN'S CHANCE** (25692, $4.50)
SWAN'S CHANCE continues the magnificent saga begun in
WILD SWAN: an unforgettable chronicle of a great dynasty.

☐ **SUFFER A SEA CHANGE** (27750, $3.95)
Her love, world and very future change under the light of an
island sun as Jessica Banbridge comes to grips with the past
and opens herself up to life.

Available wherever Bantam Books are sold or use this page
to order.

- -

Bantam Books, Dept. CB6, 414 East Golf Road, Des Plaines, IL 60016

Please send me the books I have checked above. I am enclosing
$_____. (Please add $2.00 to cover postage and handling.) Send
check or money order—no cash or C.O.D.s please.

Mr/Ms _____

Address _____

City/State _____ Zip _____

CB6—9/89

Please allow four to six weeks for delivery.
Prices and availability subject to change without notice.

60 Minutes to a Better, More Beautiful You!

Now it's easier than ever to awaken your sensuality, stay slim forever—even make yourself irresistible. With Bantam's bestselling subliminal audio tapes, you're only 60 minutes away from a better, more beautiful you!

__ 45004-2	**Slim Forever**	$8.95
__ 45112-X	**Awaken Your Sensuality**	$7.95
__ 45081-6	**You're Irresistible**	$7.95
__ 45035-2	**Stop Smoking Forever**	$8.95
__ 45130-8	**Develop Your Intuition**	$7.95
__ 45022-0	**Positively Change Your Life**	$8.95
__ 45154-5	**Get What You Want**	$7.95
__ 45041-7	**Stress Free Forever**	$7.95
__ 45106-5	**Get a Good Night's Sleep**	$7.95
__ 45094-8	**Improve Your Concentration**	$7.95
__ 45172-3	**Develop A Perfect Memory**	$8.95

Bantam Books, Dept. LT, 414 East Golf Road, Des Plaines, IL 60016

Please send me the items I have checked above. I am enclosing $_____ (please add $2.00 to cover postage and handling). Send check or money order, no cash or C.O.D.s please. (Tape offer good in USA only.)

Mr/Ms _____

Address _____

City/State _____ Zip _____

LT-8/89

Please allow four to six weeks for delivery. This offer expires 2/90. Prices and availability subject to change without notice.